ANY HUMAN HEART

"Crammed with incident and adventure and sex and travel. . . . Mountstuart's life may be too extraordinary to belong to any old human heart, but heart is something this superb book is full of."
—*LA Weekly*

"Boyd's writing here is flawlessly journal-like, fluent; calculatingly ragged and unflashy; shaded by grief, weariness, failure, wistfulness, gusto."
—*The Miami Herald*

"Witty and well-crafted."
—*Rocky Mountain News*

"A madcap wonder of a tale . . . Boyd's previous fiction has been brilliantly inventive. This may be his most cunning yet."
—*Book Magazine*

"Such an antic plot should not succeed, and yet disbelief remains suspended, thanks to Boyd's skill in producing a novel that successfully mimics a diary in all its human pettiness. He allows Mountstuart's voice to age like port."
—*The New Yorker*

"Boyd does such a nimble job of ventriloquism . . . that we find ourselves forgetting that Mountstuart is a fictional character."
—*The New York Times*

"Some people get their Brit fix from Harry Potter. They will get that, and much more, from William Boyd's brilliant, beautiful, and exceptionally British *Any Human Heart*. . . . Carr[ies] the full, devastating force of a lifetime of intermingled joy and pain."
—*Time*

"A sweeping, romantic novel . . . beautifully written and heavy in emotional content, with deftly drawn portraits worthy of an Old Master."
—*The Star-Ledger* (Newark, NJ)

"Tautly intricate. . . . Boyd endows his narrator with no special quality of perception or sensibility. . . . What he does give him is integrity of voice if not of spirit, the lightest mockery of his own inconsequentiality and a gracefully chiseled play of sentence and phrase."
                                        —*The New York Times Book Review*

"Boyd took on the twentieth century once before, with his brilliant novel *The New Confessions*, but this is no repeat performance. On the contrary: He's outdone himself."   —*Bookforum*

"Boyd has long been known as an inventive writer. Mountstuart is arguably his most compelling and unarguably his most credible invention to date."   —*Richmond Times-Dispatch*

"Picaresque. . . . Boyd's world is not an orderly or reasonable place, but it proves to be the best venue we have in which to celebrate the resilience of the human heart."   —*The Dallas Morning News*

"A glorious, sweeping saga. . . . Flows with energy, wit, honesty and humor. Its plot lines of love and lust, of loss and intrigue, pull the reader along as quickly as any thriller. Boyd manages to create characters you come to love, hate and miss when they are gone."
                                                    —*The Plain Dealer*

"Compelling . . . a fin de siècle novel, a moving distillation of one man's experience of the last century."   —*The Oregonian*

"Strangely powerful. . . . The exquisite lyricism of [Boyd's] prose left me in tears or nearly so, and sometimes the underwritten pathos left me astonished at its quiet resignation."
                                        —Logan Browning, *Houston Chronicle*

"Boyd punctuates [his novel] . . . with an addictive intimacy, the tangible impress of life lived."   —*The Village Voice*

"Brilliant. . . . *Any Human Heart* gives us a chance to witness [Kierkegaard's] paradox . . . [that] 'Life can only be understood backwards; but it must be lived forward.'"   —*St. Petersburg Times*

William Boyd

ANY HUMAN HEART

William Boyd was born in Accra, Ghana, and attended university in Nice, Glasgow, and Oxford. He is the author of seven novels and eleven screenplays, and has been the recipient of several awards, including the Whitbread Award for best first novel, the John Llewellyn Rhys Prize, the James Tait Black Memorial Prize and the *Los Angeles Times* Book Prize for fiction. Boyd lives with his wife in London and southwest France.

INTERNATIONAL

ANY HUMAN HEART

ANY HUMAN HEART

A NOVEL BY

William Boyd

Vintage International
VINTAGE BOOKS
A DIVISION OF RANDOM HOUSE, INC.
NEW YORK

FIRST VINTAGE INTERNATIONAL EDITION, JANUARY 2004

Copyright © 2002 by William Boyd

All rights reserved under International and Pan-American Copyright
Conventions. Published in the United States by Vintage Books, a division
of Random House, Inc., New York. Originally published in Great Britain by
Hamish Hamilton, London, in 2002, and subsequently in hardcover
in the United States by Alfred A. Knopf, a division of
Random House, Inc., New York, in 2003.

Vintage is a registered trademark and Vintage International and
colophon are trademarks of Random House, Inc.

The Library of Congress Cataloging-in-Publication Data is on file.

Vintage ISBN: 1-4000-3100-1

www.vintagebooks.com

Printed in the United States of America
20 19 18 17 16 15 14 13 12 11

For Susan

Never say you know the last word about any human heart.

—Henry James

Contents

Any Human Heart

THE INTIMATE JOURNALS
OF LOGAN MOUNTSTUART

PREAMBLE TO THESE JOURNALS

"Yo, Logan," I wrote. *"Yo, Logan Mountstuart, vivo en la Villa Flores, Avenida de Brasil, Montevideo, Uruguay, America del Sur, El Mundo, El Sistema Solar, El Universo."* These were the first words I wrote—or to be more precise, this is the earliest record of my writing and the beginning of my writing life—words that were inscribed on the flyleaf of an indigo pocket diary for the year 1912 (which I still possess and whose pages are otherwise void). I was six years old. It intrigues me now* to reflect that my first written words were in a language not my own. My lost fluency in Spanish is probably my greatest regret about my otherwise perfectly happy childhood. The serviceable, error-dotted, grammatically unsophisticated Spanish that I speak today is the poorest of poor cousins to that instinctive colloquial jabber that spilled out of me for the first nine years of my life. Curious how these early linguistic abilities are so fragile, how unthinkingly and easily the brain lets them go. I was a bilingual child in the true sense, namely that the Spanish I spoke was indistinguishable from that of a Uruguayan.

Uruguay, my native land, is held as fleetingly in my head as the demotic Spanish I once unconsciously spoke. I retain an image of a wide brown river with trees clustered on the far bank as dense as broccoli florets. On this river, there is a narrow boat with a single person sitting in the stern. A small outboard motor scratches a dwindling,

*This preamble was probably written in 1987 (see p. 458).

creamy wake on the turbid surface of the river as the boat moves down-stream, the ripples of its progress causing the reeds at the water's edge to sway and nod and then grow still again as the boat passes on. Am I the person in the boat or am I the observer on the bank? Is this the view of a stretch of the Río Negro where I used to fish as a child? Or is it a vision of the individual soul's journey through time, a passage as transient as a boat's wake on flowing water? I can't claim it as my first reliable, datable memory, alas. That award goes to the sight of my tutor Roderick Poole's short and stubby circumcised penis, observed by my covertly curious eyes as he emerged naked from the Atlantic surf at Punta del Este, where we two had gone for a summer picnic one June day in 1914. I was eight years old and Roderick Poole had come to Montevideo from England to prepare me for St. Alfred's, my English prep school. Always swim naked when you can, Logan, was the advice he gave to me that day, and I have tried to adhere to it ever since. Anyway, Roderick was circumcised and I was not—which explains why I was paying such close attention, I suppose, but doesn't account for that particular day of all others being the one that sticks in my mind. Up until that precise moment the distant past of my earlier years is all vague swirling images, unfixed by time and place. I wish I could offer up something more telling, more poetic, something more thematically pertinent to the life that was to follow, but I can't—and I must be honest, here of all places.

The first pages of the lifelong, though intermittent, journal that I began to keep from the age of fifteen are missing. No great loss and, doubtless, like the avowals that begin almost all intimate journals, mine too would have commenced with the familiar determination to be wholly and unshakeably truthful. I would have sworn an oath to absolute candour and asserted my refusal to feel shame over any revelations which that candour would have encouraged. Why do we urge ourselves on in this way, us journal-keepers? Do we fear the constant threat of backslide in us, the urge to tinker and cover up? Are there aspects of our lives—things we do, feel and think—that we daren't confess, even to ourselves, even in the absolute privacy of our private record? Anyway, I'm sure I vowed to tell the truth, the whole truth, etc., etc., and I think these pages will bear me out in that endeavour. I have sometimes behaved well and I have sometimes behaved less than well–but I have resisted all attempts to present myself in a better light. There are no excisions designed to conceal errors of judgement ("The Japanese would never dare to attack the USA unprovoked"); no additions aimed at conferring an unearned sagacity ("I don't like the cut of that Herr Hitler's jib"); and no sly insertions to indicate canny prescience ("If only there were some way to harness safely the power in the atom")–for that is not the purpose of keeping a journal. We keep a journal to entrap that collection of selves that forms us, the individual human being. Think of our progress through time as one of those handy images that illustrate the Ascent of Man. You know the type: diagrams that begin with the shaggy ape and his ground-grazing knuckles, moving on through slowly straightening and depilating hominids, until we reach the clean-shaven Caucasian nudist proudly clutching the haft of his stone axe or spear. All the intervening orders assume a form of inevitable progression towards this brawny ideal. But our human lives aren't like that, and a true journal presents us with the more riotous and disorganized reality. The various stages of development are there, but they are jumbled up, counterposed and repeated randomly. The selves jostle for prominence in these pages: the mono-browed Neanderthal shoulders aside axe-wielding *Homo sapiens;* the neurasthenic intellectual trips up the bedaubed aborigine. It doesn't make sense; the logical, perceived progression never takes place. The true *journal intime* understands this fact and doesn't try to posit any order or hierarchy, doesn't try to judge or analyze: I am all these different people–all these different people are me.

Every life is both ordinary and extraordinary–it is the respective proportions of those two categories that make that life appear interesting or humdrum. I was born on the 27th February 1906 in Montevideo, Uruguay, the sea-girt city on its bay in that small country wedged between beefy Argentina and broiling Brazil. The "Switzerland of South America" it is sometimes dubbed and the land-locked associations of that comparison are apt, for, despite their country's long coastline–the republic is surrounded on three sides by water: the Atlantic, the vast estuary of the Río Plata and the broad Río Uruguay–the Uruguayans themselves are defiantly non-seafaring, a fact that has always warmed my heart, divided as it is between seadog Briton and landlubberly Uruguayan. My nature, true to its genetic heritage, is resolutely divided: I love the sea, but I love it viewed from a beach—my feet must always be planted on the strand.

My father's name was Francis Mountstuart (b. 1871). My mother's was Mercedes de Solís. She claimed to be descended from the first European, Juan Díaz de Solís, who set his foot on Uruguayan soil early in the sixteenth century. An unfortunate move on his part as he and most of his band of explorers were swiftly killed by Charrua Indians. No matter: my mother's preposterous boast is unverifiable.

My parents met because my mother, who spoke good English, became my father's secretary. My father was the general manager of Foley & Cardogin's Fresh Meat Company's processing plant in Uruguay. Foley's Finest Corned Beef is their most famous brand ("Foley's Finest": we have all, we British, eaten Foley's corned beef at some stage in our lives), but the bulk of their business was in the exporting of frozen beef carcasses to Europe from their huge *frigorífico*— a slaughterhouse and massive freezing unit combined—on the coast a few miles west of Montevideo. Foley's was not the biggest *frigorífico* in Uruguay at the turn of the twentieth century (that honour went to Lemco's at Fray Bentos), but it was very profitable—thanks to the diligence and perseverance of Francis Mountstuart. My father was thirty-three years old when he married my mother in 1904 (she was ten years younger than he) in Montevideo's pretty cathedral. Two years later I was born, their only child, named Logan Gonzago after my respective grandfathers (neither of whom was alive to meet his grandson).

I stir the memory soup in my head, hoping gobbets of Uruguay will float to the surface. I can see the *frigorífico*—a vast white factory with its stone jetty and towering chimney stack. I can hear the lowing of a thousand cattle waiting to be slaughtered, butchered, cleaned and frozen. But I didn't like the *frigorífico* and its chill aura of mass-produced death*—it made me frightened—I preferred our house and its dense and leafy grounds, a big villa on the chic and swanky Avenida de Brasil in Montevideo's new town. I remember a lemon tree in our garden and lobes of lemon-coloured light on a stone terrace. And there was a lead fountain set in a brick wall, with water spouting from a putto's mouth.

*Eighty thousand cattle a year were slaughtered at the Foley *frigorífico* and numberless sheep.

A putto who looked, I now remember, just like the daughter of Jacob Pauser, the manager of the Foley *estancia,* 30,000 acres of the Banda Oriental, the purple-flowered flatlands where the beef herds roamed. What was this girl's name? Let's call her Esmerelda. Little Esmerelda Pauser—you can be my first love.

We spoke English in the house and from the age of six I went to a church school run by monoglot nuns on the Playa Treinta y Tres. I could read English but barely write by the time Roderick Poole arrived in 1913 (fresh from Oxford with a pass degree in Greats) to take my slipshod education by the scruff of its neck and make me fit for St. Alfred's School, Warwick, Warwickshire, England. I had no real concept of what England was like, my whole world was Montevideo and Uruguay. Lincoln, Shropshire, Hampshire, Romney Marsh and Southdown—breeds of sheep routinely slaughtered in my father's *frigorífico* were what my country meant to me. One more memory. After my lessons with Roderick we would go sea-bathing at Pocitos (where Roderick had to keep his bathing suit on) and would take the number 15 or 22 tram to reach the resort. Our treat was to order sorbets and have them served to us in the gardens of the Grand Hotel—gardens full of flowers: stock, lilac, orange, myrtle and mimosa—and then rattle home in the tender dusk to find my mother in the kitchen shouting at the cook, my father on the terrace smoking his quotidian cigar.

The Mountstuart family home was in Birmingham, where my father had been born and raised and where the head office of Foley & Cardogin's Fresh Meat Co. was to be found. In 1914 Foley's decided to concentrate on its meat-processing factories in Australia, New Zealand and Rhodesia, and the Uruguayan business was sold to an Argentine firm, the Compañía Sansinena de Carnes Congeladas. My father was promoted to managing director and summoned home to Birmingham. We sailed for Liverpool on the SS *Zenobia* in the company of 2,000 frozen carcasses of Pollen Angus. The First World War began a week after we made landfall.

Did I weep when I looked back at my beautiful city beneath its small, fort-topped, conic hill and we left the yellow waters of the Río Plata behind? Probably not: I was sharing a cabin with Roderick Poole and he was teaching me to play gin rummy.

The city of Birmingham became my new home. I swapped the

eucalyptus groves of Colón, the grass seas of the campo and the endless yellow waters of the Río Plata for a handsome, Victorian, redbrick villa in Edgbaston. My mother was delighted to be in Europe and revelled in her new role as the managing director's wife. I was sent as a boarder to St. Alfred's (where I briefly acquired the nickname "Dago"– I was a dark, dark-eyed boy) and at the age of thirteen I moved on to Abbeyhurst College (usually known as Abbey)–an eminent boys' boarding school, though not quite of the first rank–to complete my secondary education. It is here in 1923, when I was seventeen years old, that the first of my journals, and the story of my life, begins.

THE SCHOOL JOURNAL

1923

10 DECEMBER 1923

We—the five Roman Catholics—were walking back from the bus stop up the drive to school, fresh from Mass, when Barrowsmith and four or five of his Neanderthals started chanting "Papist dogs" and "Fenian traitors" at us. Two of the junior sprats began weeping, so I stood up to Barrowsmith and said: "So tell us what religion you are, Barrowboy." "Church of England, of course, you dunce," he said. "Then count yourself very fortunate," said I, "that one religion at least will accept someone as physically repulsive as you are." Everyone laughed, even Barrowsmith's simian crew, and I shepherded my little flock together and we regained the purlieus of school without further incident.

Scabius and Leeping* declared I had done work of sub-magnificent standard and that the encounter and exchange were droll enough to deserve entry in our *Livre d'Or*. I argued that I should have a starred sub-magnificent because of the potential risk of physical injury from Barrowsmith and his lackeys, but Scabius and Leeping both voted

*Peter Scabius, LMS's closest friend from his schooldays, along with Benjamin Leeping.

against. The swine! Little Montague, one of the blubbers, was the witness, and Scabius and Leeping both handed over the honorarium (two cigarettes each for a sub-magnificent) with goodly cheer.

When we brewed up after second prep I hatched a plan for the Martinmas term. It was no good, I said, just waiting for the various categories of magnificents to happen—we had to initiate them ourselves. I proposed that we should each be presented with a challenge: that two of us, in turn, should think up a task for the third and that the endeavour would be documented (and witnessed as far as possible) in the *Livre d'Or*. Only in this way, I averred, could the ghastly rigours of next term be survived, and, after that, we were on the home stretch: summer term was always more agreeable and could take care of itself. There were the School Certificate and scholarship exams and then we'd be free—and of course we hoped Oxford would be waiting (for me and Scabius, at least—Leeping said he had no intention of wasting three years—of what was bound to be a short life—at university). Scabius suggested the raising of a fund to privately print and publish a deluxe limited edition of the *Livre d'Or* if only to preserve the iniquities of Abbey for all time. "Or as a terrible warning for our offspring," added Leeping. This was unanimously agreed and we each deposited one penny into the new "publishing fund," Leeping already pondering weight and weave of paper types, embossed leather binding and the like.*

In the dormitory that night I pleasured myself with delectable visions of Lucy. No. 127 of the term.

12 DECEMBER [1923]

To my intense and gratifying embarrassment Mr. Holden-Dawes commended my essay on Dryden to the English upper sixth as a model of the form. "I'm sure that if any of you seek enlightenment Mountstuart will allow a private reading for a modest fee," he said. (Unkindly, I thought: H-D has a malicious streak. But perhaps he was simply sensing the blooming of my overweening pride?)

---

*As far as is known, the *Livre d'Or* was never printed. No trace of the manuscript survives.

His benign streak was more evident at the end of the day, however, when he came up beside me in the cloisters and we walked to chapel together. "Have we managed to convert you yet?" he asked at the door. I said I didn't understand. "All this Anglicanism hasn't undermined your faith?" It was an odd question and I vaguely muttered something about not having given the matter much attention. "Not like you, Mountstuart," he said and wandered off. At supper I asked Leeping what he considered H-D was up to. "He wants you to be a fanatical atheist like him," Leeping said. We talked on about faith in an interesting and not too pretentious vein, I thought. Leeping has a good mind, I suspect, if only he could get over his amazing complacency. I asked him why, if he was a Jew, he didn't go to the synagogue in the same way as we RCs went to Mass. I may be Jewish, he said, but I'm a third-generation, Church-of-England Jew. It was all a bit obscure to me and now I understand why I don't give religion much thought. The awful boredom of uncritical faith. All great artists are doubters. Perhaps I might work this idea into my next essay for H-D. It would please him. Leeping confessed, as we filed out of the dining hall, that he has developed a bit of a passion for little Montague. I said little Montague was a corrupt brute in the making—a brutette. Leeping laughed loud. That's why I like him.

18 DECEMBER [1923]

Writing this on the train to Birmingham, a feeling of sour and persistent depression coursing through me. It was galling to see Scabius and Leeping and what looked like 90 per cent of the school boarding the train for London and the south. After the locals dispersed, about twenty of us were left standing around the station waiting for the various trains to our distant and unsavoury provincial towns (Norwich Station, it strikes me, represents the epitome of the dullness at the soul of provincial life). Eventually my train arrived and I managed to find myself a solitary compartment at the rear. I have picked up a few companions as we've travelled, however, but I sit here crouched over my notebook writing, and covertly watching, my heart growing ever more leaden as the miles between me and "home" diminish. The burly sailor and his painted doxy, the commercial traveller with his cardboard suit-case, the fat woman eating sweets, taking two for every one she feeds her tiny, bright-eyed, quiescent child. Rather a good sentence.

Later. Mother's interior decoration has continued apace in my absence. She has papered my room—without permission—in a dark caramel brown with a motif of blurry silvery grey shields or crests. Perfectly vile. The dining room has been converted into her "sewing room," so we are now obliged to eat in the conservatory, which, it being the mid-dle of winter, is infernally cold. My father appears to accept these and other transformations without complaint. Mother's hair is as dark as a raven's wing and I'm afraid she is beginning to look absurd. And we have a new car, an Armstrong-Siddeley, which sits resplendently undriven in the garage under a tarpaulin. Father prefers to take a tram to work.

Went for a walk through Edgbaston, already consumed with bore-dom, and looked in vain at the big houses and villas for any sign of individual spirit. The Christmas tree must surely be the saddest and most vulgar object invented by mankind. Needless to say we have a giant one in the conservatory, its tip bent over by the glass ceiling. Popped into a cinema and saw thirty minutes of *Bride Fever*. Left over-whelmed with lust for Rosemary Chance. Thank God Lucy arrives the day after tomorrow. I shall kiss her this holiday or else become a monk.

24 DECEMBER 1923

Xmas eve. Lucy says she wants to go to Edinburgh University to read archaeology. I asked, are there any women archaeologists? And she said, well, at least there'll be one. She is beautiful—to my eyes, any-way—tall and strong, and I love her accent.* Though I do miss her long

*Lucy Sansom, LMS's first cousin, was one year older than he. Her mother, Jennifer Mountstuart, had married Horace Sansom, an engineer from Perth, Scotland. Horace Sansom was currently working for the Bengal Railway Ser-vices, hence Lucy's presence at her uncle and aunt's at Christmas 1923.

hair. My mother said, contrariwise, that she thought Lucy's bob was "très mignonne."

Wrote to Scabius and Leeping suggesting possible challenges. I also declared that we should call each other by our Christian names next term and make a point, publicly, of doing so. I signed off "Logan," with a small thrill of revolutionary pleasure: who can know where these gestures of independent spirit may lead? I'm sure they'll both agree. Mother has just put her head around the door (without knocking) to remind me that father's colleagues are due shortly for the ritual Xmas eve cocktail party: tense, ill-at-ease managers and under-managers who possess a sole topic of conversation, namely, the canning and conservation of beef products. And so the long hell of Christ's Mass begins. Thank God for Lucy, once again. Delectable, adorable, difficult Lucy.

1924

1 JANUARY 1924

It is 2:30 a.m. and I am tight. As a tick, as a lord, as a newt. Must write this down before the sublime memories fade and blur.

We went to the golf club for the New Year's Eve dance. Mother, Father, Lucy and me. A bad meal (lamb) followed by dancing to a surprisingly good band. I drank copious amounts of wine and fruit cup. Lucy and I danced a kind of quick-step (all those embarrassing and costly lessons from Leeping paid off: I was fine). I had forgotten how tall she was in her high heels—our eyes were level. We left when the band struck up a tango and my mother led my father to the floor to general applause.

Outside on the terrace overlooking the first tee and the eighteenth green we each smoked a cigarette, commented briefly on the drabness of the venue, the gratifying expertise of the band, the unseasonal warmth of the night. Then Lucy tossed her cigarette into the dark and turned to face me. Our conversation went something like this, as far as I can remember:

LUCY: I suppose you'll be wanting to kiss me now.
ME: Ah . . . Yes. Please.
LUCY: I'll kiss you but I won't marry you.
ME: Lucy, I'm not even eighteen yet.
LUCY: That doesn't matter. I know that's what you're thinking. But I just want to let you know that I'm never going to marry anyone. Never. Not you, not anyone.

I said nothing, wondering how she knew my most secret fantasies, most private dreams. And so I kissed her, Lucy Sansom, the first girl I've ever kissed. Her lips were soft, my lips were soft, the sensation was . . . a kind of fleshy softness, not at all unlike the practice kisses I have bestowed on the inner portion of my upper arm or the crook of my elbow. It was pleasant—and the sense of otherness was nice, that there were two people involved in this process, that we were each giving something to the other (this is a bad sentence and is not making much sense, I'm afraid).

And then she stuck her tongue in my mouth and I thought I would explode. Our tongues touching, my tongue on her teeth. Suddenly I understood what all the fuss over kissing a girl was about.

After about five minutes of more or less uninterrupted kissing Lucy said we should stop and we went back in, separately, Lucy first, then me after a gap long enough to take a few puffs at a nervous, exulting, trembling cigarette. The golf club crowd were gathered round the bandstand, as there were three or four minutes left until midnight. I was in a kind of daze and couldn't see Lucy anywhere. My mother beckoned me over (actually, Mother was looking her best, I now think, the red dress suited her new, lustrous hair). As I reached her, she took my hand, drawing me to her and whispering in my ear, "*Querido,* have you been making love to your cousin?" How does she know these things? How can women tell?

And now to bed and the first pleasuring of 1924—and dreams of sweet Lucy.

3 JANUARY [1924]

Curiously, annoyingly, Lucy has not let me kiss her again. I asked her why and she said, "Too much, too soon." Mystifying. Leeping and Scabius have replied to my letters and the respective spring term challenges begin to take shape. Scabius wrote that he and Leeping had come up with a "particularly taxing" challenge for me and I should "prepare for an interesting and strenuous term."

This afternoon I played golf with Father, reluctantly, but he was unusually insistent that we go out and get some fresh air. The day was cold and blustery and we were practically alone on the second course. The greens were mossy and hairy—"The particular stringencies of winter greens," Father said, as I missed a 15-inch putt—and we were obliged to place all fairway balls. I hacked around erratically while Father played his usual cautious and precise game, "playing for par," and won comfortably, eight up and six to play. We walked in the last six holes, chatting inconsequentially—about the weather, about the possibility of a return trip to Uruguay, what colleges at Oxford I was thinking of applying for and so on. As we strolled up the side of the eighteenth fairway towards the clubhouse (I could see the small terrace on which Lucy and I had kissed), he stopped and touched my arm.

"Logan," he said, "there's something you must know."

I said nothing but I thought at once, for some reason, of financial ruin. I could see Oxford evanesce and melt as if it had been an ice sculpture left outside in the blazing sun. But my father made no move to continue the conversation, merely stroked his moustache and looked solemn, and I realized he was waiting for the symbolic and rhetorical reply.

So I dutifully said, "What is it, Father?"

"I'm not well," he said. "It seems . . . It seems I may not live very long."

I was useless. What is one to say in these circumstances? I muttered something vaguely negative: surely not; how can you be; there must be some other—but I felt more shocked by my absence of shock: it was as if he had said we must get someone in to help with the gardening. As I think about it now I still can't really believe it: that stark announcement of a future fact has a tenuous hold on the present moment—its potential reality seems virtually ungraspable. It's as if someone had said to me, equally soberly, your hair will fall out before you're thirty, or, you'll never earn more than a thousand pounds a year. However alarming these prognostications are, they have no real impact as you stand there hearing them, they remain forever, ineffably hypothetical. And this is how I felt, how I feel, about Father's announcement of his impending death: it has no meaning. It has no meaning for me at all despite the fact that he went on at some length about his will, his small fortune, how Mother and I would be well provided for, all necessary provisions made. And, moreover, now I should be a support and a calming presence for my mother. I hung my head and nodded, but it was more dutiful than sincere. When he finished speaking, he offered his hand and I shook it. His hand was dry and smooth, his grip surprisingly strong. We walked back to the clubhouse in silence.

This evening before dinner I kissed Lucy on the landing outside the airing cupboard. She did not resist. We used tongues and this time I put my arms around her and held her body against mine in a hug. She's a big, solid girl. When I tried to touch her breasts she pushed me away easily, but I saw she was flushed and excited and her chest moved with the intensity of her breathing. I told her I was in love with her and she laughed. We're first cousins, she said, it's illegal, we're committing incest. She goes back up north tomorrow—how will I live without her?

At dinner tonight I looked across the table at my father as he sawed lumps of mutton off the slices of joint on his plate and popped them in his mouth, chewing vigorously—at least there seemed nothing wrong with his appetite. Perhaps it is too gloomy a prognosis? He's a sober and cautious man, Father, and it would be entirely in his nature to read too much into a doctor's professional circumlocutions. My mother, I noticed, seemed oblivious, chatting away to Lucy, showing her some new nacreous paint with which she had decorated her fingernails. But perhaps she didn't know? But if she was meant to be in the dark, wouldn't Father have said something to me about keeping the matter between ourselves?

After dinner Lucy and I played Splash while Mother and Father listened to music on the gramophone and Father smoked his quotidian cigar. When Mother left the room I followed her and asked her if Father was all right.

"Of course he is. As fit as ten fiddles. Why you asking, Logan, *querido*?"

"I thought he seemed a bit tired at golf today."

"Listen, he's no more such a young man. Did you beat him?"

"No, actually, he won easily."

"The day he lose to you at golf, my darling, is the day I start to worrying."

So that was that, and now I sit in my hideous brown and silver bedroom reassured by the famous "golf test" for determining your state of health. Down the corridor Lucy lies in her bed—is she thinking of me, I wonder, as I think of her? I think I truly love her, not for her beauty so much as for her honesty, her strength of character, so much stronger than mine. Perhaps that's why I'm drawn to her so: I sense my own flaws and failings so acutely and I feel I need Lucy's strength to compensate—to help me thrive and flourish, to achieve everything I know I am capable of achieving.

[LATE JANUARY 1924]

Filthy school and filthy weather. I have consulted separately with Scabius and Leeping—sorry, Peter and Ben—and we will announce the challenges to each other at brew after second prep.

Holden-Dawes summoned me to him at the end of History this afternoon and asked what colleges I was thinking of applying to at Oxford. I told him it was a toss-up between Balliol and Christ Church and he gave me one of his sardonic smiles and counselled against both. But Scabius is trying for a Balliol scholarship, I reminded him. And you are, of course, the chummiest of chums, H-D said, adding that this was not a tactically sound reason for applying for an Oxford scholarship. He looked at me silently for a while and then prodded his pen in my direction several times as if he'd come to an earth-shattering decision.

"I see you in the Turl," he said, "not the Broad or the High."

"And where are these places situated, sir?" I queried.

"They are streets in Oxford, Mountstuart. Yes, I see you nicely ensconced in one of those charming smaller colleges on the Turl— Exeter or Lincoln. No, even Jesus. I've an old acquaintance at Jesus who could be helpful—yes, one of those will be ideal. Not Balliol or the House for you, Mountstuart, no, no, no. Trust me."

He went on in this annoying, slightly patronizing vein for a while, saying he would have a word with the Lizard* about it, adding that there were some very "gettable" scholarships and exhibitions at Lincoln, Exeter and Jesus that he thought were well within my capabilities. I had no idea what he was talking about, unable to identify any Oxford colleges apart from the famous ones, as I'd only been to Oxford once when I was about twelve. However, I'm now not sure whether to be pleased or irritated by H-D's interest in me—it's most unusual that he concerns himself with any individual's future. Have I, perhaps, become a favourite?

Later. The challenges. They are cads and villains, Scabius and Leeping— they do not deserve the intimacies of a Christian name after what they have done to me. Mind you, we were all pretty taken aback at what we'd thought up for each other. The term will certainly be an interesting one and not without humour. And one more thing is clear—we know each other very well. So, the challenges—I'll save mine till the end. First Ben Leeping. Scabius had this idea that I endorsed enthusiastically and immediately. Leeping—the Jew—has to become a Roman

---

*Henry Soutar, LMS's housemaster, a sexagenarian, not much liked by LMS and his set and dubbed "the Lizard" because of his exceptionally seamed and wattled face.

Catholic but, better still, has to be considered as fit for the priesthood. Leeping was, to put it mildly, somewhat shocked when we told him. "Bastards," he said several times, "absolute bastards."

As for Scabius's challenge, this was my idea, not Leeping's, though Leeping was quick to see its merits. Near the school is the Home Farm, a place we often walk by and occasionally visit (it forms part of our curricular activities, particularly biology). The farm manager's name is Clough and he has a daughter (as well as a couple of strapping sons). We had spotted this girl a few times working around the farm buildings—carrying pails, driving cattle—and established her as the child of the Cloughs. She looks to be about nineteen or twenty, a sturdy small girl with a mass of crinkly brown hair that she tries vainly to keep hidden under a succession of head scarves. Our challenge to Scabius—lanky, shy, introverted Peter Scabius—is to seduce her: a witnessed kiss will be the ultimate test. Peter laughed out loud when we told him actually, his laugh sounded like a terrified neigh, like a donkey being tortured—and he refused to accept the challenge on the grounds that it was a sick joke, impossible, dangerous, potentially illegal. But we were implacable and, reluctantly, he agreed.

And then they told me what my challenge was, and I felt the same cry of "No!" "Impossible!" "Unfair!" rising up within me. My task was to win my school colours for rugby before the term had ended. I not only had to become a member of the First XV, I also had to flourish and shine within it.

The point is, and this is where I feel I have been hard done by, that we in our set have a loathing for organized school sports—it is one of the key factors that binds and draws us together. For Scabius sport presents no problems as he is wholly and utterly unsuited to it—he is uncoordinated, weak, inept—he could not kick a ball against a barn, let alone a barn door. Both Leeping and I have avoided the worst of this sports-mad school by carefully nurturing feigned illnesses: Leeping has migraines, I have a bad back. In this way, as far as rugby is concerned, the most and the worst I have to do is turn out once a week for the House XV in the school leagues. I play on the right wing: if I'm lucky an entire game can go by without my touching a ball or dirtying my knees.

But as I sit here now—and I imagine Peter and Ben contemplating their own tasks—a small, acute thrill of excitement runs through me. This is, in effect, exactly what the challenges were designed to do: we had to manipulate our penultimate, dreariest term of our school life into something more exciting and edifying. And who knows what gems we will provide for our *Livre d'Or*?

WEDNESDAY [23 JANUARY 1924]

The Lizard summoned me into his study tonight. He was drinking sherry from a tumbler and spent about ten minutes trying to light one of his biggest pipes—he must have had a couple of fistfuls of tobacco crammed into that bowl. Once he'd got the thing going (the air blue with smoke, sparks rising as he tamped down, with some sort of penknife device, his fuming shag), he said that H-D had spoken to him about Oxford and he—the Lizard—thought it an excellent idea that I try for the Griffud Rhys Bowen history scholarship at Jesus College, to which end he asked me if I had any Welsh blood in my veins. I said not as far as I knew, but there was Scottish family on my father's side. "Ah, well," he said, "you Celts seem to stick together. You'll probably be fine." He really is a loathsome old bigot.

25 JANUARY [1924]

Preliminary moves. The three of us went down to the Home Farm at afternoon break. Boys were encouraged to visit and "lend a hand," as and when Clough (a solemn, dour man with half a mouthful of brown teeth) deemed it necessary. He met us in the farmyard and said bluntly that there wasn't much call for help in January but, now we were asking, we could muck out the stables of his plough horses, seeing as his Tess was at the dentist in Norwich.

Tess! We could hardly keep our faces straight when, armed with shovels and pitchforks, we were led round to the stables, where half a dozen massive shire-horses stamped and chewed and swished their tails. As soon as Clough left so did Ben and I, leaving lovelorn Peter to await the return of the beautiful and mysterious Tess.

28 JANUARY [1924]

After Greek this morning I approached Younger, who is in the First XV, and, as casually as I could manage, asked him how the school team was doing and what its weaknesses were. He was a little surprised at this line of questioning coming from a notorious Bolshevik like me but was forthright enough in his replies. "Our pack's the problem," he said gloomily. "Our scrum's not what it was, particularly the front row. All last year's men have gone, you see." I nodded sympathetically. What about the backs, I asked? "Oh, spoilt for choice," he said. "Oozing with talent."

It seems to me almost impossible, this challenge. In order to win my colours I must get a place in the First XV, which means, logically, I have first to find a place in the Second XV, from where I might have a chance, all being well, of being selected. Yet currently I am a reluctant wing three-quarter in the Soutar House XV, which resides third from bottom in the inter-house league table. It is clear I shall have to resort to nefarious ruses in order to succeed.

The same conclusion had obviously struck Leeping because—as we were enjoying a calming cigarette before the misery of Corps—he began to moan about his challenge and said I had to give him a helping hand. I agreed, but in return said I would need some favours from him, so we shook on it. We both considered that Scabius had far the easiest road. He was already established ("Thanks to us," Leeping wisely observed) as an eager mucker-out at the Home Farm, and although he had yet to meet the delectable Tess (he'd had to leave before she returned from the dentist), it was inevitable that the encounter would occur—and then it was up to him.

29 JANUARY 1924

I had a double free period before tea and asked the Lizard if I could take a bus to Glympton* to see Father Doig about a "religious matter." The Lizard agreed instantly, the old toad. While I was waiting at the bus stop at the school gates—a vile, freezing day with an angled, sleety rain coming in off the sea—H-D pulled up in his motor, asked me where I was going and offered me a lift. He lives in Glympton, as it turns out, and he dropped me at the church door. He pointed out his house to me on the main street and invited me for tea after my "church business" was over.

Father Doig's glee was almost disgusting when I told him I had a friend of "the Jewish persuasion" who wanted to convert to Catholicism. I said it had to be done with the utmost discretion because if this boy's parents ever found out . . . etc., etc. Doig could hardly contain himself and said to tell this boy to telephone and he would arrange private instruction, absolutely no problem, not so much a pleasure as a duty and the rest. Doig is really rather a slovenly fellow—he always looks in need of a good shave and his fingernails on his smoking hand are an unpleasant yellow colour from the nicotine.

H-D, by contrast, is the quintessence of spic-and-span. He has a small, narrow, neat cottage giving on to a long, thin, neat garden at the rear. The front room was lined with bookshelves, the spines of the books all aligned like soldiers on parade, flush and precise. Everything on his writing desk was squared off: blotter, paper knife, pen rack. A good fire was burning efficiently in the grate, and H-D had changed into a cardigan and was wearing no tie. This was the first time I had ever seen him tieless.

He served me tea and fruit scones and hot buttered toast with a choice of three jams. I admired his pictures—mainly watercolours and drypoint etchings—looked at some of his prize books and talked about my latest essay (on *King Lear*), which I was rather pleased with but

---

*The village where St. James's Roman Catholic church was located and where Abbeyhurst sent its Catholic boys for Mass. About three miles away from the school.

which he had pedantically ranked alpha-beta plus query plus. Then I noticed on his chimney piece a brass artillery shell casing, which was intricately worked with a complex embossed pattern. I asked him where he had bought it and he said it was a gift from a wounded French soldier he had befriended at a base hospital near Honfleur. As he talked it became clear from the context that he had also been convalescing at the same time from some wound or injury.

"Oh, so you were in the war, sir," I said—a bit breezily, I admit.

"Yes. I was."

"Whereabouts? What regiment?"

"I prefer not to talk about it, if you don't mind, Mountstuart."

And that was that—said very abruptly, too—and it rather took the edge off our cosy tea. With the mood now formal and somewhat chill I said I thought I had better catch the 4:30 to Abbeyhurst and he showed me to the door. You could see the spire of St. James's from his small patch of front garden.

"Odd day to go to church," he said.

"I had to see Father Doig on a personal matter."

He looked at me fiercely and I wondered what I had said wrong this time.

"You're a very intelligent boy, Mountstuart."

"Thank you, sir."

"Do you believe in your god?"

"I suppose I do, sir."

"I've never understood how a person of real intelligence can believe in a god. Or gods. It's all balls, you know—complete balls. You must enlighten me one day. Ah, there's your bus."

Strange man, I thought on the way back. Not sexless, because he was leanly handsome enough, H-D, and sure of himself too. Very sure. Too uncompromising, really—perhaps that was it. Because it seems to me that to be human you have to be able to compromise. And sometimes there appears something inhuman about Mr. Holden-Dawes.

Good news on my return. A letter from Lucy, and Leeping told me he'd spoken to Beauchamp—who runs our house team—and I am to play in the scrum for our next match. As hooker. So it begins.

2 FEBRUARY [1924]

Scabius has finally met the elusive and ineffable Tess. They worked on some giant of a shire-horse preparing it for a show—grooming it, varnishing its hoofs, plaiting its mane and tail with ribbons and the rest, spending a whole afternoon together. So, what was she like, we asked? Really quite shy, Peter said. We reminded him we were indifferent to her personality; it was her physical charms that intrigued us. "Well, she's quite small," he said. "I tower over her. And she has this terrible frizzy corkscrew hair she's ashamed of, always hiding it under hats and scarves. Quite well endowed in the bosom department, as far as I can tell. And she bites her nails, down to the quick." They seem to have liked each other well enough, however, and she had invited him back to the farmhouse for tea.

Ben, in his turn, telephoned Father Doig and was told that, in the interests of absolute discretion, he should not come to the church at Glympton but rather meet in the house of one of his parishioners—a Mrs. Catesby, who happened to live in Abbeyhurst itself—at times convenient to Ben. Thus Ben's first encounter with Father Doig and the Roman Catholic Church is arranged for next Saturday afternoon in Mrs. Catesby's back parlour—a week from today.

In the meantime, I have played my first rugby match as hooker.

It was a wet, drizzly, cold afternoon as Soutar's XV turned out on the south-east playing fields against Giffords' XV. As both sides reluctantly stripped off and vaguely warmed up for the kick-off, it was apparent to me that we were the usual mix of lazy misfits, inept hearties and hopeless inadequates. Somewhere at the other end of the expanse of playing fields another match was going on and the routine shouts of encouragement and despair carried faintly to us over the sodden grass. We had one spectator, Mr. Whitt, our assistant housemaster and theoretical coach of the house side, who, after we kicked off, bellowed and screamed on the touchline as if he were at a cup final. The teams were equally matched in terms of their deficiencies: balls were dropped, tackles fluffed, penalties missed. At half-time the score was 3–0 to Giffords'.

I was slowly accustomizing myself to life in the scrum, which

seemed mainly to involve galloping about the field chasing the ball
(which I didn't touch once in the first half). This herd-like meandering
was interrupted by whistle blasts, when we would line up for a throw-
in or a scrum down. The two packs would face each other and then
interlock. We then became a 32-legged human beetle trying to evacuate
an oval leather ball. I knew the two props on either side of me: improb-
ably named Brown and Smith (Smith minor, in fact, Smith senior was
head boy). Brown was a muddy enthusiast, tireless and full of get-up-
and-go; Smith minor—who has truly distressing acne—is a miscreant
poseur like me. It was strange to be in the curious dark cave of the
scrum: so many heads and faces so close to each other, strange smells
and exhalations, strange cheeks rubbing against yours, arms gripping
your thighs, and the mixed shovings and heavings against your buttocks, aimless exhortations ringing in your ears, the scrumhalf with the
ball screaming instructions (at, I suppose, me): "Ready, Soutar! Wheel
right! Wheel right! Hold it! Coming, one, two, three!" And there was
the sodden dirty ball at my feet and I would hack away trying to heel it
out and back, sometimes succeeding, sometimes not, as everyone
around me grunted and heaved and swore. This is not sport, I was
thinking: give me my lonely, chilly isolation out on the left wing—at
least there I could look at the landscape and the sky.

And then the ball would be out of the scrum. The shouts and
instructions would become more distant and we would break out of
our crab-like clinch, look around to see where the game was and lum-
ber off in pursuit. I have to confess I was in a state of some despair as
we neared the end of the match: I was filthy, covered in mud, exhausted
and I had no real idea how the score had reached 9–all.

Then something happened in our half—a three-quarter kicked ahead
and there was a fumble by the opposing fullback. Confusion, the ball
over the line, fallen upon by one of the defending side. A tweet on the
whistle and a drop-out on the twenty-five was ordered. Now I knew,
from my perusal of the rule book, that it was one of the hooker's duties
to confront the kicker of the 25-yard drop-out, to face him down and
distract him as best he could. So I jogged up to the opponents' 25-yard
line, my boots as heavy as a deep-sea diver's, my breath coming in
great hoarse pants and with steam rising, it appeared, from every part
of my body, from my shoulders and my bare knees. I still don't know

what made me do it, but, as I saw their fly-half stepping up to take the drop-kick, I simultaneously flung myself up and forward, arms raised in a vain attempt, at the very least, to put him off his stride. It worked: he kicked badly, low and hard, not high and hanging, and the ball blasted into the side of my face with such velocity that it rebounded a good twenty yards, close enough to the enemy line for one of our nippier three-quarters to dart in, snatch the ball up and score under the posts. Try converted—five points—victory to Soutar's, 14–9.

The side of my face was on fire. I remember that once my mother slapped me on the cheek for some misdemeanour and the same pulsing, peppery, eye-watering heat was the result. The scarred wet leather of the ball left a smarting red weal across my left cheek and on my forehead above the left eye: my face felt molten, my flesh prickly and seared.

People—teammates—were slapping me on the shoulders and on the back. Smith minor was shouting in my ear, "You mad bastard, you mad bastard!" We had won and my inadvertent block had brought the win about: and somehow the pain I was in diminished, magically. Even Whitt, pipe jutting, thin hair strands blowing wildly, called out, "Damned good effort, Mountstuart!"

Later, after I had showered and changed and the redness had faded to a blushing, warm pink, I was heading for our set when I encountered little Montague. "Well done, Mountstuart," he said. "Well done for what, you filthy harlot," I replied (uncharitably, I confess). "Well," he said, "your charge-down. Everyone's talking about it."

My "charge-down" . . . So, this is how myths and legends are born. I realize now, with a small sense of absolute revelation, what the way ahead involves. The only possible route to the First XV and my colours is now revealed to me: I have to play with reckless, careless stupidity, the grossest foolhardiness. The more senseless I am, the more I risk life and limb, the more I will be recognized—and hailed. All I have to do is play rugby like a suicidal maniac.

5 FEBRUARY 1924

Letter from Mother announcing that the Mountstuart family will be going to Austria for Easter, to Bad Riegerbach, to be precise, where Father is to take the waters. "He has a sort of anaemia," Mother writes, which is making him lose weight and become easily tired. So he is now officially ill, it is no longer just a confidential matter between him and me—but what, pray, is a "sort of anaemia"?

Ben has had his first session with Fr. Doig, which he described as "eerie." Ben's account sounded very Doig, to me, the man full of ill-concealed self-satisfaction at this potential scalp rather than displaying any concern to explore young Leeping's religious doubts. They are to meet at least once a week at Mrs. Catesby's. Ben said that Doig could not conceal his huge disappointment that he was a lapsed Jew. An Anglican was small beer. At least, he'd said to Ben, you *look* Jewish. I think he was expecting some sort of bearded rabbinical figure with long curls dangling around his ears. Ben thinks his challenge will now be a walkover, Doig is so desperate. We both agree I have the most onerous task of the three of us.

Wrote a Spenserian ode on loss of faith. Not very good. I quite liked the line: "When faith has died *we* must paint the colours on the sky."

11 FEBRUARY 1924

Scabius, me, Lacey, Ridout, Sandal and Tothill all travelled to Oxford by train for our scholarship examinations. Eleven others went to Cambridge—Abbey boys have always been favoured by Cambridge colleges; but we are more of an unknown quantity in the City of Dreaming Spires. Peter and I deliberately lingered in the train until the last moment, so as to separate ourselves from the others, and then hired a pony and trap (more like a horse and cart) to take us and our luggage to our respective colleges. We were deposited on Broad Street—the Broad, as I must learn to call it—and Peter went to Balliol while I wandered up Turl Street with my suitcase looking for Jesus. As it happened I chose the wrong one (why do these colleges not post their names outside the main door?) and the porter at Lincoln, a surly brute, pointed me in the right direction.

Jesus was neither inspiring nor disappointing: two rather elegant small quadrangles and a perfectly acceptable chapel. But no college, however grand, could have looked its best on a damp and drizzly February afternoon—the sooty façades of the quads rendered almost black by the rain and the lawns tufty and unmown. I was shown to my rooms and I dined in hall. There seemed to be a lot of bearded, moustachioed, older undergraduates and I was told they were war veterans taking up their places at the university after their time in the army. I slipped out of college and went to Balliol to meet Peter but found the place firmly locked up. It's a bad start for Oxford, in my opinion: it seems a gloomy, dirty, closed place. I feel I could find more kindred spirits at Abbey, it pains me to say. And Jesus, with all these mature men—like uncles, with their pipes and tweeds and facial hair—does not inspire. Perhaps Leeping is right: why do we want to waste three precious years of our life in these institutions?

12 FEBRUARY [1924]

A morning and afternoon spent taking the History papers, which seemed to pass off well enough. I answered questions on Palmerston's second government, the French Revolution and Walpole's financial reforms (dull stuff but full of arcane facts) and I think I gave a fair account of myself. After the afternoon paper I was summoned to meet the History fellow, Le Mayne—P. L. LE MAYNE, it said on his door. This was the "friend" H-D had talked about. He was a pugnacious, stocky, bearded man, and he looked me over with what can only be described as a mixture of distaste and mild curiosity.

"Holden-Dawes says we should take you come what may," he said. "Why?"

"Why what?"

"Why should we take you, Abbey boy?"

I muttered a few platitudes—Oxford, distinguished college, huge privilege, the honour—but he cut me short.

"You're losing it," he said.

"Losing what?"

"What vestiges of good opinion I had of you—stimulated by James. Why do you want to read History at Oxford? Convince me."

I don't know what came over me—perhaps it was the sense that all was lost already, perhaps it was Le Mayne's abrasive indifference, not to say his overt dislike of me, so I said, regardless: "I don't give two farthings for history. The only reason I want to come to this depressing place is that it will give me time—time to write."

Le Mayne groaned, threw his head back and stroked his beard.

"Heaven preserve me," he said, "another bloody writer."

I thought about walking out but decided to play this one through.

"I'm afraid so," I said suddenly, freshly audacious. "Please don't expect an apology."

He was unperturbed and said nothing, glancing tiredly at me, and then shuffled through my examination papers.

"Oh, all right," he said wearily. "You can go."

Later. Scabius told me that he had met three fellows and had even shaken the hand of the Dean of Balliol, Urquhart, himself. I had been in Le Mayne's room about five minutes, if that. It seems to me that my Oxford career isn't even going to get to the starting line. Before I came here Father wrote to say that there was always a job in junior management at Foley's. I think I would rather slash my wrists.

13 FEBRUARY [1924]

Peter and I found a public house down by the canal where we drank beer and ate bread and cheese before catching our train back to Norwich. Peter's tutor had shaken his hand at the end of the interview and said he looked forward to seeing him in September. I saw Le Mayne cross the quad in the morning and he had looked right through me with no sign of recognition at all.

Writing this on the train back, fighting against a mounting sense of depression. Ridout and Tothill are playing gin rummy. Peter is asleep, confidently asleep. If I don't get into Oxford, what will I do? Go to

Paris with Ben? Join Father's firm? It's all too damnably frustrating. Thank God we had the foresight to set ourselves these challenges this term: it is almost shaming to say this, but, currently, the one thing in my life that I anticipate with some excitement is the prospect of the match tomorrow against O'Connor's. Younger said he might come and watch. Could this be the first step?

14 FEBRUARY [1924]

Scabius and the lubricious Tess held hands for a few minutes as they walked along some path somewhere after lunch. Peter says she took his hand but he didn't dare do anything else, then she had to release it when they reached a stile and that was that. I said it was an excellent sign and in future he should take more advantage of such opportunities.

Leeping meanwhile had a second meeting with Doig while we were away in Oxford (he says Mrs. Catesby is really quite charming) that did not go so smoothly: he says he thinks Doig is becoming suspicious of him already. "Why on earth?" I said. "He couldn't wait to convert you." "I think the problem is because I have no doubts," Ben said. So I told him all he had to do was develop some doubts and Bob's your uncle. But he couldn't think of any convincing doubts, he said; he had no idea what a potential convert to Roman Catholicism would be doubtful about and so has asked me to suggest some. I think Transubstantiation is too obvious, safer to go with Purgatory and Hell, perhaps. Hell is always a bit of a poser. I'll come up with something, something doctrinally meaty to soothe Doig, keep him happy.

My own progress continues with some genuine triumph. This afternoon's house league match between Soutar's and O'Connor's was watched by both Younger and Brodrick (who's also in the First XV). Towards the middle of the second half of an unexceptional game (we were leading 11–3) in which I'd done nothing of any real note, I was suddenly passed the ball and as I received it was upended in a tackle and dumped on my head. I must have been knocked out briefly because everything went black and, when I came to, play had moved on to the other end of the field on the O'Connor line.

I rose to my feet feeling suddenly nauseous and groggy, and, just as I did so, there was a break-out counter-attack from the O'Connor line in the shape of a fly-hack ahead. A whole group of forwards came pounding towards me, booting and dribbling the ball onwards as they went. Our fullback (a weedy fellow called Gilbert) tried to pounce on the ball and, naturally, missed, leaving me as the last line of defence.

I think I must have still been slightly stunned because, to my perception, everything appeared to be happening with precise and logical slowness. I could see the mass of O'Connor forwards thundering on and was aware of our team scampering back trying to make up lost ground. There was a big black-haired brute of a man leading the O'Connor charge who kicked the ball too eagerly in front of him and I saw, with absolute clarity, what I had to do. Somehow I urged my legs into action, ran forward and, just as he was about to kick the ball again, fell upon it and gathered it into my arms.

I heard the crack but felt no pain. I hugged the ball to my chest as bodies thudded heavily on top of me. The whistle blew. The big O'Connor forward (Hopkins? Pugh? Lewkovitch?—I can't remember his name) was sobbing and moaning—he had broken his leg, badly: the normally straight line of his right shin below his sock now had a distorted kink in it. And blood, I quickly realized, was also streaming down my face. I managed to clamber to my feet and the referee tried to staunch the flow with his handkerchief as urgent calls were made for a stretcher to carry the injured man off. The game was abandoned.

At dinner this evening an ironic cheer went up from the house when I came in, my head bandaged (four stitches). It was not my own injury that drew the admiration of my fellows so much as the damage I had inadvertently done to my opponent. "He broke the other man's leg, clean through" was the real symbol of my temporary renown rather than "He received a nasty gash above the eye." Once again there was much gleeful banter about my alleged insanity, my death wish, my suicidal desire to die on the rugby field.

After dinner, Younger approached: I am to turn up for Second XV training as soon as the wound is healed. I can hardly believe that two matches were all it took to advance this far up the rugby ladder, but there you are—perhaps the school team needs an insane hooker. However, a vague worry has started up alongside my self-satisfaction: I have established, with amazing rapidity, a reputation for maniacal, self-destructive courage, and so far my single badge of honour is a really rather nasty cut, but I'm a little perturbed at the thought of future injuries I might incur in the line of this particular duty—I can hardly go all coy and sensible, now. Leeping joyfully predicts all manner of horrible fates—a broken spine, a coma, an ear ripped off. But, while I'm concerned, I know I have to go on. I am going to emerge victorious: I am going to win this challenge.

21 FEBRUARY 1924

Lucy's letters to me seem either strangely abstract or maddeningly matter of fact. I write to her and talk about what happened between us at Xmas and the night in the golf club and she replies with a lengthy account of an evening of Gregorian chant she attended at St. Giles's Cathedral. I write—poignantly, in the most heartfelt way—about how I miss her and how I detest my life in this school and she responds with detailed plans for her future life as an archaeologist or philosopher or—new, this—a veterinary surgeon.

Ben L. says his new-found doubts about Purgatory have worked wonders with Doig. They spent a whole afternoon debating over just how long he—Ben—would have to linger there after a lifetime of run-of-the-mill, suburban sinfulness. He says he finds my religion "positively bizarre" and is amazed at how seemingly well balanced I appear with all this mumbo-jumbo in my background. Yes, I said, it's all balls, isn't it. H-D would be proud of me.

It's my birthday in a week—I'll be eighteen. My only thoughts are of leaving school and beginning my life afresh at Oxford. I feel I cannot make any plans until I leave this place; it's as if the years here have been some sort of tiresome, ultimately useless apprenticeship for the real thing that lies ahead. Indeed, these challenges prove the depths of my—our—boredom. This system has to be the most iniquitous and crippling way of educating the intelligent young (it may be wonderful for the stupid and backward young, for all I know)—four-fifths of the things I'm obliged to do here strike me as an utter waste of time. Without the company of my few friends, English Literature, History and the rare engagement with some higher mind (H-D) this school—and the expense it entails my parents—strikes me as a national scandal.

Parcel from Mother—the books I ordered: Baudelaire, De Quincey, Michael Arlen—and chocolate and a two-foot-long chorizo sausage. Do not forget, Logan Gonzago Mountstuart, your unique heritage. The sausage is delicious: hot, shouting with pepper and garlic—and irresistible. I was nibbling slices in chapel and I had this horrible feeling that a miasma of garlic was spreading along the pew. My cut is healing fast: I shall be back on the rugby field very soon. It has the makings of a rather interesting scar.

After morning chapel Peter and I had a couple of free periods so we went into Abbeyhurst and took tea and crumpets at Ma Hingley's. Hot crumpets with butter and jam—what could be more ambrosial? The day I can't enjoy these pleasures will signal some kind of death of the soul. The place was empty apart from a couple of local crones gossiping about their bunions and arthritis. Peter told me he thought he was falling in love with the delectable Tess. I refused to humour him: this is a test, a challenge, I said, something coldly objective—we have to keep feelings completely out of it. But Peter went mooning on about her sweet nature, her innate sensuality, her firm, full figure and how he feels this strange union with her when they work in silence on the horses. I probed a bit further. She prefers men's clothes, it turns out, for stable work: cavalry twill trousers with elastic-sided ankle boots, and, beneath her jacket, wears braces. As he talked on I could see that it was this image of a girl turned stable lad that was stimulating him, it was the very absence of sexual allure that was arousing. I told him so and he seemed nonplussed. "You are two manual workers," I said, "she sees you as some sort of farmhand, a fellow groom and equal. How can you ever become lovers if you allow this to go on?"

Then he confessed, or rather he blushed, and sipped his tea noisily. "She lets me kiss her," he said, "when we finish. In fact it was Tess who made the first move. She lets me touch her breasts—but only when we finish with the horses."

"Please don't lie to me, Peter," I said. "It's too shaming." But he protested and I could sense, from something in his demeanour, that he wasn't lying. He swore to me that everything he said was true and this was why he had fallen in love with her. "She's a bold, rare spirit," he said, and I felt the sour, bilious grip of envy around my heart. Well, you've won the challenge, I told him, congratulations. All you have to do now is find a way of letting Ben and myself witness your lovemaking. He nodded seriously: he seemed truly relieved to have told me all this. In fact he seemed all at sea, lost in this strange romance with the farmer's daughter. Ben and I had a good, sophisticated laugh about it all later, but I was aware that Ben was as surprised—and vaguely irritated—as I was. This sort of thing, this fantastic good luck, was not meant to happen to Peter—it was meant to happen to us. But we agreed we felt sorry for him: poor old Peter Scabius suddenly face to face with sex. Perhaps we have done him a favour.

25 FEBRUARY 1924

Second XV match against Uppingham. Freezing, icy day with a strong east wind. I was extra man and ran the touchline and brought on the quartered oranges at half-time. I suppose what I have achieved in these few short weeks is extraordinary enough (even the Lizard congratulated me for my "unforeseen sporting zeal"), but, as ever, my predominant emotion is one of disappointment. The Second XV hooker is a blond oafish fellow called fforde who, I'm sure, in the fullness of time, I could supplant: he doesn't have anything like my dash, my insane audacity. But beyond him lies the First XV, whose hooker is a man called Vanderpoel—small, wiry, sporty—who is also captain of the squash team. The term has a few weeks to run and I wonder if I can possibly advance beyond the position I have reached now, if I could supplant a real athlete—I wonder if it is even worth trying . . . A horrible thought: could this be the pattern of my life ahead? Every ambition thwarted, every dream stillborn? But a second's reflection tells me that what I'm currently experiencing is shared by all sentient, suffering human beings, except for the very, very few: the genuinely talented—the odd, rare genius—and, of course, the exceptionally lucky swine.

Peter Scabius, at the time of writing, seems extremely well placed in the second category. He has gone as far as to specify a location for the "witnessed kiss." This will take place, according to him, the day after tomorrow on a bridle path in a wood near the farm—he will tell us exactly where to position ourselves. Ben, meanwhile, is as frustrated as I am: Doig has turned hostile again and has insisted that the meetings be moved from Mrs. Catesby's to the rectory at St. James's. Ben is convinced that this is merely a form of test, Doig's thinking (transparent, according to Ben) working along the lines that if Ben is truly sincere then the effort of making his way to the rectory will not be an impediment.

H-D told me this afternoon that Le Mayne had found me "diffident, but with underlying charm and intelligence." Stark nonsense: I cannot think of a more inaccurate description of my personality.

26 FEBRUARY 1924

Ben and I met after second tea and hurried off to observe the famous "witnessed kiss." Peter had been very precise in his directions and we found the sunken lane—not too far from the Home Farm—and then the blasted oak and the small grassy hollow to its left-hand side. Ben and I hid some fifty yards off, higher up and well screened by dense leafless bushes with nasty thorns. We huddled in our overcoats and shared a cigarette, wondering how Peter might initiate the erotic moment. Ben, typically, had brought some opera glasses so we would have an excellent view. We talked also about our respective challenges and their respective disappointments but both agreed that they had been worthwhile exercises and had at least livened up, somewhat, the dullest, deadest term of the year. Mrs. Catesby, it transpired, has invited Ben for "tea and cake"—*sans* Doig, interestingly.

After a wait of about half an hour we saw Peter and Tess emerge from the direction of the lane. Peter spread his overcoat on the grass and they sat down with their backs to the blasted oak. Tess produced a packet of cigarettes and they both lit up—we could catch unintelligible snatches of their conversation and Tess's rather deep (rather attractive) throaty laugh. A pale sun suddenly shone and the wintry scene took on the aspect of a modest bucolic idyll. They continued talking for a while—though the mood seemed to have gone more earnest, all laughter ceasing—and then Tess shrugged off her own coat and reached into Peter's pocket for something.

It was his handkerchief, as it turned out, and then Ben—who was peering through the opera glasses—whispered, "I don't believe it. She's unbuttoning his flies."

We watched in snatched five-second glimpses, Ben and I, as the solicitous Tess dug her hand into Peter's open fly and fetched out his flaccid white penis. She then wrapped the handkerchief around it and proceeded to toss him off—which process seemed to last no more than thirty seconds (Peter with his head back, eyes screwed tight shut). When it was over Peter's face registered more astonishment than rapture and when—the deed done—Tess handed him back his handkerchief, neatly folded into a thick two-inch square, he simply put it back in his coat pocket without a thought or a glance. Then they kissed for a while, lying back on the coat for about ten minutes or so, but Ben and I could no longer be bothered to watch: we were so astonished and both, we later concurred, so angry. Angry that we had dreamed up this challenge for Scabius (when we could have appropriated it for ourselves) and angry that he seemed to have carried it off so effortlessly—and with the bonus we had just witnessed being thrown in as the cherry on the sundae.

We left before they did, pushing our way through the snaggy undergrowth, as they rolled around on Peter's coat petting each other, kissing and caressing. We both agreed that Scabius was the luckiest bastard in the school, not to say the British Isles.

Later. Peter could not keep the imbecilic smile off his face all through dinner. He kept leaning over and saying to us, "She touched it, actually touched it, took it in her hand." We both paid him the pound that the winner was due—which leaves me seriously short of funds this term (I shall have to borrow off Ben). But both Ben and I agreed that we would persevere with our challenges, if only to preserve our integrity rather than out of any enthusiasm. This wasn't just a bet—there is a more philosophical urgency and import to the whole enterprise. As we filed out of hall, Peter said that he was now "definitely in love" with Tess. I find the idea utterly disgusting.

29 FEBRUARY 1924

Ben arrived back early from his meeting with Doig in Glympton, say-ing that Doig had thrown him out. I reminded him that we had both made a pact to continue our challenges. "But Peter's already won," he said with some weariness. "I just couldn't see the point of sitting there in front of that reprobate talking about angels and the Virgin Birth."

Hard to disagree, I suppose. It turned out that Ben kept bringing the discussion back round to the priest's vow of celibacy and the diffi-culties involved in maintaining it. Doig eventually lost his patience and told him to leave forthwith—Ben protesting all the time that if he felt a genuine calling for the priesthood then he had every right to examine all the pros and cons. He said Doig got in a fearful bate and practically hurled him out of the door.

Anyway, I told him I was going to persevere, come what may, and, now that he wasn't doing anything perhaps he might be able to help me out: we only had a few weeks left of term and I still had to reach the First XV, let alone play well enough to earn my colours. He said he thought I was a mad fool, but if I wanted to continue I could count on his full and unswerving support.

SUNDAY [2 MARCH 1924]

After Mass, just as I was trying to slip away from the church unnoticed, Doig confronted me and drew me back into the shelter of the porch.

"What's going on, Mountstuart," he said, plainly furious, "with you and your Jewboy friend?"

"That's not very charitable, Father," I said.

"What's your game, boy?"

"There's no game."

"Lying little gobshite."

"Leeping was perfectly sincere in his desire to convert," said I. "In fact I think he found *you* the disappointment. I'm thinking of writing to the bishop about your feeble proselytizing—"

Well, he really blew up at that and threatened to report me to the

Lizard. I kept a straight and pious face throughout. When I told them about it, Ben and Peter awarded me another sub-magnificent. We all agreed it had been extremely droll.

After the row, while we were waiting at the bus stop for the bus back to Abbey, Holden-Dawes walked by with a young woman on his arm—quite a pretty young woman. I said "good morning" and he gave me his usual sardonic look, without, however, introducing me to his paramour. I watched them continue on their Sunday stroll, thinking it odd to see H-D with a female; I had always thought him quite sexless, somehow.

4TH MARCH [1924]

Ben said he had been making discreet inquiries about Vanderpoel, seeing if there were any possibilities for blackmail, but as far as he could tell the man was sinless and had no obvious passions for any of the sprats. I wondered if we could get little Montague to whore for us, but Ben wisely counselled caution—corruption of minors and the rest. Then I had my grand idea—not blackmail but bribery. I would bribe Vanderpoel to feign injury, thus opening up a gap in the first team for me. But how much money would we need to seduce the sinless Vanderpoel? Ben was commissioned to be my go-between.

Letter from Mother bringing pleasing news: Lucy is to join us on our Austrian jaunt. Mother suggests we can amuse ourselves "hiking up mountains." What can she be talking about?

7TH MARCH [1924]

At last. I am selected as Second XV hooker for tomorrow's match against Walcott Hall (fforde has fflu). Ben has been sounding out Vanderpoel and has discovered that he is not rich (his father is a barrister's clerk, it turns out) but for all that thinks only the most munificent of bribes will tempt him. How munificent, I ask? Five guineas, Ben reckons. Disaster: even between us we can't muster a third of that. I will write to Father and ask if I can borrow the money—if I can think of some convincing and worthy cause. On second thought I will write to Mother.

8TH MARCH [1924]

Somehow we beat Walcott Hall 64–0, some sort of school record. It appears their ranks were depleted by a chicken-pox epidemic and they had to fill places with the unfit and infirm. It was a joyous rout, actually, and I nearly scored myself, hauled down by three or four men just short of the line. The Second XV preen and strut about the school. fforde claims he will be fit and well by next Saturday but only a fool would change this winning team.

Lucy writes to say that she will come to Austria on the condition that our "romance fantasy" is understood to have terminated. I will write back reluctantly, with pleasing melancholy, to agree. Once I have her there all will be different. Scabius's maddening success with the farmer's daughter has emboldened and encouraged me. Lucy shall be mine.

To my vague surprise I find my thoughts turn more and more to next Saturday and I realize I am looking forward to the match—Harrow at home. I mustn't lose any more of my Bolshevik spirit.

11TH MARCH [1924]

Ben and I cashed Mother's postal order for five guineas (bless her: I said I wanted to buy Lucy a really special birthday present) and we treated ourselves to tea and anchovy toast at Ma Hingley's. Ben said that Vanderpoel was willing to drop out for one match only but that he wanted to meet the person who was prepared to pay such a high price. "He suspects it's you, of course. Or he might just think it's that ass fforde, I suppose—you'll have to do it." He's right, I have to admit. By the way, we drew 9–9 with Harrow; while our first team were thrashed 3–27—I sense my star is in the ascendant.

Ben told me he was going straight to Paris after school—it seems he's been offered a job in an art gallery, and he wants to be a dealer. I felt a throb of jealousy: maybe Ben is right? Maybe we are fools to postpone our adult, proper lives by three years at varsity? Three years that, as far as I can see, might be just as frustrating as life at school . . .

The really pleasing news is that Clough has become suspicious of Peter and Tess's closeness and has contrived to keep them apart. On his last three visits to the farm Peter has been occupied shredding mangel-wurzels—or some such menial task (his hands are fearfully blistered)—with no sight of the delicious Tess to distract him or compensate. Ben and I privately rejoice—though I admit such an attitude reflects badly on us both.

Later. Went over to Foster's after second prep to seek out Vanderpoel. He's a pale-faced fellow with an unpleasant bulbous nose. We haggled a bit over the price and I was able to knock him down to £5.

"One game, mind you, that's all," he kept repeating, pocketing his fiver. Then he looked suspiciously at me: "Why's it so important for you?"

"My father's dying," I said spontaneously. "He played rugby for . . . Scotland. It was his dearest wish to see me in the First XV. Following in his footsteps and all that. Before he went."

Vanderpoel was so touched that he insisted I have my £5 back—which I naturally accepted (I will not tell Ben this, however). Vanderpoel assured me that he would "twist" his ankle or something during the Friday training session before the game. The match is against Oundle, he said—very rough bunch. "I'll even suggest you replace me—not that peasant fforde. Don't worry, Mountstuart, your old man will be proud of you."

Why am I lying so much? To Mother, to Lucy, to Vanderpoel, to Ben . . . Is this normal, I wonder? Does everybody do it as much as me? Are our lives just the aggregate of the lies we've told? ("Lives"—the "v" is silent.) Is it possible to live reasonably without lying? Do lies form the natural foundation of all human relationships, the thread that stitches our individual selves together? I shall go and smoke a cigarette behind the squash courts and think more great thoughts.

13TH MARCH [1924]

Snow—a good six inches—and all sports are cancelled. Yet the newspapers say London is clear—it seems only to have snowed in wretched East Anglia. Why do I feel so frustrated by the thought of the Oundle match being postponed? Longing to get on the field—I must be turning into a true hearty. Vanderpoel sidled up to me in the cloisters and asked me how my father was. I was about to tell him to mind his own business when I remembered.

"Will he make it?" Vanderpoel asked.

"Make what?"

"Make it through to next weekend—or whenever the Oundle match is played?"

"I hope so. My mother says he's clinging on."

I did feel some real guilt about this—especially given that Father is actually ill. I worried that by placing him on death's door like this I was imposing some sort of malign curse upon him. But then I say to myself: they're only words I've uttered. Mere words are not going to accelerate or retard the course of an illness. Yet at house prayers this evening I prayed for him, the hypocrite that I am. How H-D would mock me: having my cake and eating it—like all lazy believers—routinely going through the motions of piety when it suits. Perhaps I should insist Vanderpoel take back the £5.

FRIDAY [22 MARCH 1924]

Worked like the proverbial charm. There we are training when Younger and, to my surprise, Barrowsmith trot over from the First XV pitch. "Mountstuart!" comes the cry. I jog over innocently. Vanderpoel's lame, twisted his knee—are you up for the match tomorrow? "I'll do my best," I say modestly. "Good man!" says Barrowsmith, clapping me on the shoulder. Vague alarm at earning the Barrowboy's approval. I had forgotten he was in the First XV—no Fenian bastard now.

Ben and Peter seem genuinely delighted for me—and not a little admiring, I think, at my dogged perseverance—and Ben vows he will break the habit of a lifetime and voluntarily watch a game of competitive sport. Peter told me he had had a clandestine meeting with Tess: her father has banned all contact between them (he, Peter, was close to tears as he told me this). He thinks Clough saw them holding hands. He talked wildly of staying in a boarding house in Norwich during the Easter vac in the hope they can surreptitiously meet. We urged him not to be such a fool.

Ben, on his part, said that Mrs. Catesby had written to him offering to give him private instruction in place of Doig. "I think she plans to seduce me," Ben said. "What an odd lot you RCs are." What's she like, your Mrs. Catesby? I asked. "Sort of plump and powdery and pink," he said, shuddering. "I'd rather sodomize little Montague." Do you know, I think he would. We talked filth for a pleasant half hour.

EASTER SUNDAY [20 APRIL 1924]

BAD RIEGERBACH

I told Mother my arm was hurting and so have been excused from Easter service. She, Father and Lucy have taken the funicular down to the old town, where the church awaits their pieties. Immediately after they left I ordered a bottle of hock from Frau Dielendorfer and am already feeling better—nothing nicer than being pleasantly tight on a Sunday morning at 10:30—so I thought I would take up the journal again.

The portents for the match against Oundle could not have been better: a clear, sunny, sharp-shadowed day, a thin frost, which had melted by lunch time. In the changing room I could hardly hear the captain's pep talk: I felt light-headed, as if there were too much oxygen fizzing around my blood vessels. I rubbed horse liniment on to my knees and thighs, stamped my boots upon the tiled floor and grinned at my teammates like an idiot. And when we ran out—and it seemed as if the entire school was on the touchline cheering—I thought (and I must be honest, here of all places) that my heart would burst it was beating so strongly.

The referee tossed a coin for the captains: we lost and prepared to face the kick-off. I jogged across the pitch to join my fellow forwards. From the touchline I heard Ben and Peter screaming my name and I gave them a quick, confident wave.

The whistle blew, the ball was kicked and lofted high in the air before falling directly towards me. I sensed, rather than saw, the charge of the opposing forwards and I caught the ball a second before the first three or four hit me. I had just enough time to tuck the ball under my right armpit and stick out my left arm to ward off the big second-row man who was now, suddenly, on top of me. He fell and then I ducked my head before the whole wave of Oundle forwards crashed against me.

I never felt a thing. The referee's whistle blew and I found myself buried under a pile of bodies. Slowly they peeled off me, regaining their feet one by one. "Scrum down, knock on," the referee said, and I realized I no longer had the ball. I felt winded, a little dazed by the series of collisions. Soon I was left lying on the ground alone and looked up, aware of Barrowsmith and some others looking down at me with concern. Then Younger (I think) said, "I say, Mountstuart, is your arm all right?" I looked: it definitely was not—my left forearm had a distinct hump in it, as if there was a golf ball under the skin, and it already looked oddly discoloured. I was helped to my feet, my right hand cupping my left elbow as if my arm were made of the most fragile and translucent porcelain. Then the pain began to surge and pulse and I felt myself stagger as yellow and green lights started to flash before my eyes. Shouts for a stretcher. All my sentient being seemed to contract and focus on that fracture in my shattered and agonized radius. I knew, even through my pain, that my rugby days were gone for ever.

WEDNESDAY, 23 APRIL

Lucy and I went to Innsbruck yesterday, largely at Mother's behest, to which end she provided us with generous funds. It rained. We sat in a damp and dripping park, umbrellas open above our heads and listened to a military band play Strauss without much enthusiasm. I long to go to Vienna but Mother says it's too far for a day trip. I long to hear Wagner at the opera house, see the Votive Church and stroll up the Korso. Innsbruck seemed very quiet with hardly any motors, just the clip-clop of horse carriages and the patter of the rain. Lucy was in a taciturn and uncommunicative mood so I asked her what was wrong. She said there was no fun to be had wandering around a new and strange town with a companion who had his arm in a sling. I protested: it was hardly my fault, I said, it was not as if I was trying to start a new fashion trend, for silk waistcoats or multi-coloured berets, or such like. "People will think I'm your nurse," she said. Preposterous. What a wayward and difficult girl she can be.

Eventually we decided to go to a café for shelter and found one with a glass veranda where we drank interminable cups of coffee. Lucy wrote postcards while I struggled with my Rilke. I would like to speak German but it seems so fearfully complicated: if only there were a way of arriving at moderate fluency (it's all I ask) with minimum effort. Perhaps I'm not a linguist . . . I developed a sudden longing for English food: veal and ham pie, shoulder of mutton with onions, jam pudding. We ate a cake and decided to go back early.

At the pension there was no sign of Mother. So Lucy and I walked over to the sanatorium to greet Father after his day of baths and scrubs and saltwater showers. When he emerges from these sessions he gives off the illusion of good health for a short while, almost glowing, red spots on his cheeks, his eyes bright. But I have to say he has become noticeably thinner since last vac and in the morning he looks gaunt and tired. He finds it almost impossible to sleep, he says, from the strange pressures in his lungs. He still has a healthy appetite, though, tucking into Frau Dielendorfer's slabs of cheese, ham, and rye bread with what seems desperate hunger.

Then we saw a curious sight. As we approached the main portico of the sanatorium (it looks like the entrance to a provincial art gallery) we saw that Mother was there, waiting, but on the steps beside her stood a tall man, in a macintosh and a Homburg, and they were talking to each other with some urgency. He left as we drew near. Mother was obviously very surprised to see us back so early from Innsbruck. She cannot feign unconcern, Mother—anger, yes, indifference, no.

"What're you doing here?" she said, cross, despite her best efforts. "You go to Innsbruck for two hours? What a wasting."

"Who was that man?" I asked, somewhat audaciously, I admit. "A doctor?"

"No. Yes. Of a sort, yes. A, ah, physician. Yes. I was asking him some advice. Very helpful."

Her lying was so inept it was all we could do not to laugh. Later, comparing suspicions and intuitions, Lucy and I both agreed he was an admirer. Lucy's mood, I'm glad to report, improved at the discovery of this subterfuge. We played dominoes in the lounge and she let me kiss her (cheek only) when she said goodnight.

FRIDAY, 25 APRIL

Spent the morning effortfully pushing Father in his bath chair through the streets of Bad Riegerbach. A bath chair can be an unconscionably difficult thing to steer if you only have one hand to provide the power. Father worked the wheels as best he could but I asked him to stop, as all his energies being expended in this way rather defeated the purpose of having him in the chair in the first place. So I parked him in the small square by the post office and I read him articles out of last Wednesday's *Times*. He was well wrapped up and the day was not cold, but every time I glanced up at him he looked pinched and uncomfortable.

I asked him from time to time how he was feeling and his replies never varied: "Absolutely tip-top," "Right as rain." My mood kept surging from ineffable sadness to huge irritation. Sad that his son was obliged to push him about in a *fauteuil roulant*, irritated that I should be spending my precious time thus engaged. And yet I can't remain angry with him for long. I was furious with him when we arrived for presenting Frau Dielendorfer with a gift package of Foley's potted meats, corned beef, hams in aspic and such like. I said to him, Father, we are not travelling salesmen, there is no need to disperse Foley's products around Europe. Don't be so pretentious, Logan, was all he replied and I felt very ashamed. I apologized to him later—he has this effect on me.

Mother had told me to take Father out for a "good three hours," but when we returned to the pension, Mother was away. "She's been

out all morning," Lucy said, "left immediately after you did." Father
was served some soup and then hauled himself up the stairs for a nap.
For the first time an awful foreboding strikes me that he may never be
fully well again and I feel angry at myself for my chronic inability to
think more often of others and how they may be feeling.

I am writing this in the pension's drawing room, alone, listening to
Brahms's first piano concerto on the gramophone. The adagio is reli-
ably calming and contemplating its serene beauty I find myself wondering why Lucy has turned not cold, exactly, but lukewarm towards
me. I tried to take her hand in the train back from Innsbruck but she
snatched it away. And yet five minutes later she was chatting away
(about her father's new hobby: lepidoptery) as if we were the best and
oldest of friends. But I don't want to be her "friend": I want to be her
lover.

SATURDAY, 26 APRIL

Father back to the sanatorium routine for baths of boiling mud and
gallons of sulphurous water and God knows what else. Lucy came to
my room after breakfast and said to my surprise that she had formu-
lated a plan—which we duly carried out. We told Mother we were going
to take the train to Lans, where there was a local festival (a festival of
what, we did not specify: it could have been a festival of lederhosen for
all Mother cared)—Mother thought it an excellent idea. So we had
Franz, the head waiter and general factotum, drive us down to the station in the pony and trap, whereupon, as soon as he had left us, we
took the funicular back up to the old town.

We waited in a souvenir shop with a view of the pension, pretending to choose postcards for a good half hour before Mother emerged,
splendidly got up in her sable coat ("See!" hissed Lucy) and wearing a
hat with a veil. She hurried past the sanatorium and went into the
Goldener Hirsch Hotel. Lucy and I gave her five minutes before we
wandered casually into the lobby. We spotted her almost immediately
in the residents' lounge, at the far end, half obscured by a potted palm.
She was leaning forward in her armchair talking to the tall, lanky man
we'd seen outside the sanatorium.

Lucy called a bellboy over and discreetly indicated the man. "Would you tell Mr. Johnson that I'm here to see him," she said. The bellboy immediately corrected her: that's not Mr. Johnson, he said. That's Mr. Prendergast. From America. Lucy apologized for her error and we left.

I have to say I feel strangely neutral about Mother's behaviour—I was more impressed by the guileful way Lucy discovered Prendergast's name. But I have to accept the fact—Lucy refuses to admit any other interpretation—that in the midst of my father's illness his wife seems to have taken up with an admirer.

TUESDAY, 29 APRIL

Sitting at lunch today I watched my father slowly masticating a chunk of Frau Dielendorfer's roast veal. He caught me looking at him and automatically gave his faint apologetic smile, as if he'd been doing something wrong. I felt a spasm of hurt on his behalf and also felt tears warm my eyes. Mother was in rampant, unstoppable form, in loud debate with Lucy. They were arguing about polka-dots for some reason, Mother claiming that no one over the age of ten should be allowed to wear them. "Otherwise for servants or dancers," she said. This was harsh, as Lucy was actually wearing a yellow polka-dotted blouse (in which she looked very fetching, I thought). Mother declaimed on, allowing that polka-dots were suitable for circus clowns as well. Father looked over at me again and winked. Suddenly, I knew he was going to die soon.

FRIDAY, 16 MAY

ABBEY

I thought H-D was more than usually patronizing today when he complimented me on my history exhibition to Jesus College. You would have thought from his self-congratulatory attitude that he'd purchased the place for me himself as one used to purchase a commission in the army. I told you Jesus was the college for you, didn't I? And so on, as if he'd done me some great seigneurial favour. I said, without the slightest hint of a smile, "I couldn't have done it without you, sir. Thank you so much, sir." I think he got the message. By way of apologizing he invited me for tea at his cottage Sunday, promising to tell me more of Le Mayne.

Peter has his place at Balliol confirmed so at least there will be one fellow spirit at Oxford. We went into the woods during sports for a calming cigarette. We both think it strange and something of a shame that Ben is so dead set against varsity. Mind you, I said, given the choice between Paris and Oxford I don't think I'd hesitate long. We decided that Ben must have some form of private income, though we couldn't calculate how much. Clearly it wasn't a fortune or he wouldn't need to get a job. "Just enough not to worry," Peter said ruefully. The thought of having to earn a living one day does seem somewhat alien just now, but we both agreed we couldn't wait to leave Abbey. I said I'll probably end up a schoolteacher and asked Peter what he dreamed of becoming. "A famous novelist," he said. "Like Michael Arlen or Arnold Bennett with his yacht." This took me back somewhat. Peter a writer? The mind does boggle.

The summer term seems to stretch ahead interminably. I realize, with hindsight, how invigorating the "challenges" had been, how they had transformed the boredom and banality of our life at school. H-D lent me a poem called *The Waste Land* by Eliot, advising me to read it. There were some rather beautiful lines but the rest was incomprehensible. If I want music in verse I'll stick to Verlaine, thank you very much.

SATURDAY, 17 MAY

At Corps Sergeant Tozer was in a fearful bate. He looked like he was about to explode as he shouted and screamed at us on the parade ground. We are intrigued by Tozer—we find him droll—so we take every opportunity to ask him about the war and how many Germans he had killed. He's always very vague about the exact figure but gives the impression it was many dozen. Obviously he was nowhere near the front line. Today I told him I'd been in Austria for the vac and that Karl, the major-domo at the pension, had been in the war too—"opposite British troops."

"What's that got to do with the price of beer, Mountstuart?"

"I mean it's funny to think you might have faced each other, sir, across no-man's-land."

"Funny?"

"You could have been shooting at him and he at you."

"Or," Ben chipped in, "when you attacked the German lines you might have come face to face."

"I'd have given him short shrift, I tell you. Bloody Huns."

"You'd have had his guts for garters, wouldn't you, sir?"

"Damn right."

"You'd have had your bayonet in his tripes soon as look at him, eh, sir?"

"I'd do whatever I had to do, Leeping."

"Kill or be killed, sir."

We can and do keep this sort of banter going for ages and as a result Tozer likes us and gives us soft jobs. But he was in a state today because the night exercise was looming and he saw what a feckless bunch we were (Abbey is taking on St. Edmund's). Ben says ragging is not enough: we have to come up with a memorable act of sabotage.

MONDAY, 19 MAY

I cycled out to Glympton. Still hot—a summery heat but with, some-where, a layer of spring freshness lingering. We sat in deckchairs in the sun in Holden-Dawes's back garden and ate sponge cake and drank tea. I complimented H-D on the cake and asked him where he'd bought it. He said he'd baked it himself and somehow I don't think he was lying. He asked me what I thought of *The Waste Land* poem and I said I thought it was somewhat pretentious. He found that very amus-ing. When he asked me what poetry I preferred I told him I'd been reading Rilke—in German. "And you think that's not pretentious?" he said—then he apologized. "I look forward to reading your own work," he said. I asked him how he knew I wanted to write and he said that it was just a wise guess—and then admitted that Le Mayne had told him what I'd said at my interview.

"Show anything you do to Le Mayne," he said. "He'll be honest with you. And that's what you need when you're beginning more than anything—honesty."

"What about you, sir?" I said suddenly, spontaneously. "Could I show you something?"

"Oh, I'm just a humble schoolmaster," he said. "Once you go up to Oxford you'll forget all about us."

"You're probably right," I said. I didn't mean this but H-D brings this sort of thing out in me. He leads you on and then abruptly rebuffs you; seems to admit you into the circle of his affections and then slams the door in your face. It's happened too many times to me now and I see it coming—so I say something hard and callous just to let him know. All it did was make him laugh again.

Then the doorbell rang and he came back out into the garden with the woman I'd seen him with before, last term, at the bus stop. She was pretty and dark with very arched, pronounced eyebrows. He introduced her as Cynthia Goldberg.

"And this is Logan Mountstuart," he said. "We expect great things of him."

She looked at me keenly and then turned to H-D.

"James! What a terrible burden to place on anyone," she said. "I shall be scanning the newspapers for the rest of my life."

"Mountstuart needs burdens," H-D said.

"He said, as the camel's back snapped," I added.

They both laughed at this and for an instant I felt ridiculously pleased and sophisticated, making these adults laugh, as if I were an equal with them, and I sensed a sudden warmth for H-D and his ironic, distanced interest in me. Maybe he was right: this was the only way a master could develop a relationship with one of his charges—goading, provocative, testing, but genuine for all that.

And I was impressed with Cynthia Goldberg, my God. H-D went to fetch some sherry and she offered me a cigarette. I almost dared to accept it but declined, explaining the school rule.

"Don't you let your boys smoke?" she asked when H-D reappeared. "Poor Logan says he's not allowed."

"Poor Logan smokes enough, as it is. Here–" He handed me a glass of pale sherry. He raised his own in congratulation and explained about my exhibition to Jesus. We clinked glasses. Cynthia said, eyes mockingly narrow, "And clever with it, I see."

It was a rather magical time that afternoon. H-D lit a pipe, Cynthia smoked her cigarette and I drank three glasses of sherry as we talked about this and that. The late sun lit the new leaves on the apple trees from behind, turning them a glowing lime green, and the swifts began to swoop and swerve above our heads. Cynthia Goldberg is a concert pianist—"a poor and striving one," she said. I find her profoundly, stirringly beautiful—intelligent, worldly, gifted. Oh for a world that contains Cynthia Goldbergs! I feel a growing jealousy for H-D—that he knows her, that she's a part of his life (Are they lovers? Can they be?). And what will she remember of our encounter? Nothing, probably. Who? Mount-what? Oh, the *schoolboy*. A schoolboy. Jesus Christ, I have to start my real life soon, before I die of boredom and frustration.

FRIDAY, 23 MAY

Peter, who has not seen the toothsome Tess for weeks, has finally managed to construct a means of communication. They leave notes for each other behind a loose brick of an old gatepost. He is trying to arrange a rendezvous as far away from Abbey as possible and together we have come up with the idea that it might be best achieved during the night exercise which, according to Tozer, is due to take place in the woodland around Ringford. Ben quizzed a school gardener who lived in Heringham and he said there was a nice pub in Ringford called the Lamb and Flag. Peter left a note in the gatepost urging Tess to meet him in the Lamb and Flag at 9:30 p.m. on the 5th of June. Peter invited us along as well—which I thought was unduly civil of him, but there you go.

The school play was last night, I forgot to mention. *Volpone*—wretchedly bad. Cassell says he has a place at Christ Church—perhaps Oxford won't be so grim after all.

THURSDAY, 29 MAY

Sergeant Tozer, bless him, has given us a wonderfully idle role in the night exercise: six of us are to guard a signal box on the branch line to Ringford, somewhere on the left flank of the Abbey defence. The section is under the command of a man called Crowhurst-Joyce (a corporal) and the other two are a couple of fifth formers from Swinton's—all malleable, Ben thinks, though I'm a little worried about Crowhurst-Joyce—he has a little too much military zeal and I don't think he'll be easily suborned. It might not be quite so easy to slip away.

At Corps today Tozer was all fire and brimstone. Abbey was meant to be defending a notional ammunition dump that St. Edmund's would try to capture. Tozer was disappointed to have been cast in a defensive role, but, as he kept repeating as though he'd forged the axiom himself, "The best means of defence is attack." Aggressive patrolling would be Abbey's secret weapon, he insisted; in this way we'd stop them as far off as possible, never let them get close.

"How 'aggressive' is aggressive, sir?" Ben asked, with due eagerness.

"Use your initiative, Leeping."

"What—even up to a mile in front of our positions?"

"The aim, boy, is to sow confusion in the enemy ranks."

"So the sooner our aggressive patrols make contact the better."

"Catch on fast, Scabius."

We carried on for another minute or two—as much for Crowhurst-Joyce's benefit as anyone else's—ensuring that the idea of aggressive patrolling was firmly established in everyone's mind.

THURSDAY, 5TH JUNE

Well it all worked like a charm—at first. We were paraded after luncheon and issued with our rifles and ten rounds each of blank ammunition. Then Mr. Gregory, who looked a sad sight in his uniform (How did he ever become a captain?), lectured us on the importance of what we were about to do. "This is not a game," he kept repeating. "You boys may be called upon one day to fight for your country. What you learn here will stand you in excellent stead." Then we were all bussed out to Ringford Woods—which turned out to be a mixture of patches of oak and elm coppices, scrubby heath land and some newish plantations of conifers.

The signal-box section were dropped off at the branch line. The box itself stood high on an embankment from where we were afforded a good view of the countryside to the south—whence the St. Edmund's forces would be advancing. Our brief was that, if we saw any St. Edmund's activity, we were to send a runner back to base and an aggressive patrol would be dispatched to intercept. Crowhurst-Joyce had been issued with a pair of binoculars.

It was a coolish overcast afternoon and evening. We lay about the embankment (under the amused and curious eye of the signalman—who obligingly brewed us up some tea) with someone always scrutinizing the woods and fields beyond. Studying the map we had been issued with, we reckoned we were about a half-hour walk from Ringford and the Lamb and Flag.

At about 7:30—the first hint of dusk coming upon us—Ben, who had the binoculars, said he had spotted some movement at the fringe of a stand of elms. Crowhurst-Joyce scampered over and peered through the lenses. "Can't see anything," he said.

"No, there was about a dozen or so," Ben insisted. "I just got a glimpse of them."

"I volunteer to go and check," I said.

"You can't go alone," Peter said. "I'll come with you."

"We'll all go," Ben said. "I'll show you exactly where they were."

"Hang on—" Crowhurst-Joyce said, sensing his authority being threatened.

"We won't engage," Ben said. "We'll scout, then report back. Then you can send one of these sprogs back to Gregory."

"But I'm in charge of this section," Crowhurst-Joyce whined.

"You're still in charge, Crowhurst," I said. "But remember Tozer said we should use our initiative."

"You'll get the credit," Ben said. "Don't worry."

So we picked up our rifles, crossed the tracks and slithered down the other side of the embankment and headed into the woods. As soon as we were lost to sight we circled round and rejoined the branch line—a quarter of a mile or so down from the signal box—and tramped on down it until we could see the church spire of Ringford in the distance. Our plan—to explain our non-appearance in the night exercise, or if we were discovered—was to say we had got lost in the woods and had decided to rejoin the main unit, only to become further lost as night closed in. We hid our rifles in a bramble bush and unwound our puttees. We had our own shirts on under our tunics and our own ties in our kitbags. We looked a little odd, I had to admit: not quite soldiers but not quite bona fide civilians either. But Ben said no publican was going to query our outfits: we certainly didn't look like schoolboys, and we were hardly deserters. We made Peter discard his tunic just to differentiate ourselves somewhat, then pushed on through a hedge and on to a lane that led into Ringford. We were ensconced at a table in the Lamb and Flag by 8:20.

It was quite a nice pub, the Lamb and Flag, not too busy, and we had pickled eggs and sardine sandwiches with our pints of bitter. We did attract a few strange glances from some of the regulars as one or other of us went to the bar for replenishments—our khaki trousers and hobnail boots did rather signal "military," I thought—but nobody queried our presence. The landlord asked us if we were anything to do with the archaeological dig at Little Bradgate and Ben said, very smartly, that we were on our way there to lend a hand, so that seemed to settle the question of our identity.

Tess arrived early, just before 9:00, and asked for a port and lemon. Ben and I both went to the bar to fetch the drinks to allow the lovebirds a moment alone. When we returned they were sitting squeezed up against each other, holding hands.

This was as close as we had ever been to Tess and, given we had witnessed her tender ministrations, both Ben and I could hardly conceal our curiosity. She was a quiet plumpish girl with a pale square face and the slightest hint of dark downy hair on her upper lip and a slightly more luxuriant silkiness upon what we could see of her forearms. When Peter introduced us she said, in a quiet voice, "How do?" to each of us, her eyes lowered demurely.

She and Peter talked to each other in hurried, almost inaudible voices. I could tell from the pitch and timbre of her words that she was tense—a crisis brewing at the Home Farm—and that whatever they were planning clearly was of some urgency. Ben and I went back to the bar for our third pint. By now I was feeling a little tight.

"Look at them," I said. "I can't believe it. It's like a dream."

"A bad dream," Ben said. "How did Peter end up with this wench? What've we done for him, Logan? What did we think we were playing at?"

We talked on resentfully, glancing round from time to time, not bothering to conceal our jealousy from each other. I looked at Peter, almost with hatred, as he sat there holding hands with his sturdy country girl.

"I can't take much more of this," I said.

Ben looked at his watch. "Ten to ten," he said. "Better telephone school and tell them we're lost."

Then the door of the pub swung open and Captain Gregory and Sergeant Tozer walked in.

FRIDAY, 6 JUNE

In half an hour I'm up before the Lizard. We have been separated, like prisoners, and have each been moved into new studies. I feel curiously indifferent about my fate—in fact I think I'd rather like to be expelled. Ben feels the same: the sooner he goes to Paris the better, he said, and invited me to join him. Only Peter is in a state of shock, terrified as to what his father might do if he were sacked.

The only bit of luck we had was that Tess was not discovered. Peter had leapt away from her the minute he spotted Tozer and Gregory (who were making for us at the bar) and, besides, they would never have dreamed there could have been a girl with us. They were in a filthy mood: St. Edmund's had captured the Abbey ammunition dump with conspicuous ease.

Things became worse when we couldn't find the bramble bush beneath which we'd hidden our rifles and Tozer swore vilely at us until Gregory asked him to stop.

Parker has just poked his snouty face round the door and has said that the Lizard will see me now.

*   *   *

Later. I am going to be controlled about this. I am going to set down the facts and record the sequence of events as they unfolded while they are fresh in my mind. I must never forget this, I must never forget what happened.

I knocked and was summoned in. The Lizard was standing looking mournfully out of the window, his pipe going hard. He puffed steadily as I stood there and I could hear his lips making unpleasant little popping sounds like a gas mantle not firing properly.

"I've bad news for you, Mountstuart," he said, still looking out of the window. "But I'm not going to sack you—nor Leeping and Scabius. I would have to sack all three of you. I can't sack two and not the third."

"Yes, sir." I wanted to say something audacious, something devil-may-care, something haughtily indifferent—but I couldn't think of anything.

"The bad news I have to tell you prevents me from sacking you, you see."

I knew before he uttered the words.

He turned. "I'm sorry to say that your father died this morning."

And then the stinking FUCKING bastard flogged me. Twelve strokes of the cane. He told me I was gated for the rest of the term and I would be charged with the cost of replacing the missing rifle. Then he opened the door of his study and showed me out. He never uttered one further word of sympathy. I hope he dies in pain and rots in hell.

THE OXFORD JOURNAL

Logan Mountstuart went up to Jesus College, Oxford, in the Michaelmas term of 1924. The journal commences in the following term, 24 February 1925. In the meantime, following the death of Francis Mountstuart, his wife, Mercedes, had sold the house in Birmingham and moved to London, to South Kensington, where she bought a five-storey, white-stucco terraced house in Sumner Place and fitted it out in some style. Peter Scabius was also up at Oxford, at Balliol College, and Ben Leeping, as he had always promised he would, was established in Paris working for an art gallery and learning his trade as a dealer.

1925

TUESDAY, 24 FEBRUARY

To Balliol for lunch with Peter. Balliol's commons are so much better than Jesus's: three types of cheese, bread and oatmeal biscuits and a jug of beer. I felt strangely depressed, for some reason. I think it's because Peter so unreservedly and uncritically loves Oxford and all it holds for him and I find the place stifling and disappointing. He had also received a letter from Ben—and I thought, jealously, why is Ben writing to Peter and not to me?

I went on to King's lecture on Constitutional Reform—inaudible and therefore a waste of time. On the way out of Balliol I met Quennell,* who told me he was writing a book on Blake. I did not tell him about mine on Shelley. Why? Was I afraid it would make me look presumptuous or pretentious? Just because Quennell has already published a book of poems doesn't make his ambitions superior to mine. I really must make more effort to—at least—*appear* confident: all this hiding my light under a bushel is pathetic.

THURSDAY, 26 FEBRUARY

Le Mayne was very complimentary about my essay on Cavour and the Risorgimento and has invited me to one of his celebrated lunches on Saturday. Stevens† kindly reminded me that I needed to go to roll-call tomorrow or risk a gating. This place is so like school: a school where one can smoke and drink, but an extension of school none the less.

FRIDAY, 27 FEBRUARY

Les Invalides‡ was quiet for a Friday night and Mrs. Anderson was not yet drunk and consequently recognized me. She made me a plate of foie gras sandwiches and I drank a bottle of claret as I read the newspaper. Cassell came in with a couple of friends and asked me to make up a four at bridge, but, as they were already half stewed, I decided it would be better to make my excuses—they play for too high stakes, especially when drink has been taken.

Went to the cinema (the Super) and saw Diana Vale in *Sunset Melody* for the third time. She is currently my ideal of feminine beauty.

*Peter Quennell (1906–88), writer and historian.
†Stevens, LMS's college servant, known as his "scout."
‡A drinking and dining club, formerly a debating society founded in 1914.

Popped into Wadham on my way home and drank whisky with Dick Hodge*—the more I come to know him the more I grow to like his generous soul.

SATURDAY, 28 FEBRUARY

I quite enjoyed Le Mayne's "do," to my vague surprise. Some younger dons, a journalist from London (didn't catch his name) and about a dozen hand-picked undergraduates. Le Mayne's house is off the Banbury Road. We gathered in the drawing room (no sign of the mysterious Mrs. Le Mayne) and from there could wander through to a large library overlooking a rear lawn that sloped down to the Cherwell. In the library the food was set out: cold cuts and pies with potato salad, beetroot and such like. Cheese and apple pie and cream to follow. A couple of kitchen maids circulated with bottles of hock and claret. We filled our plates and ate standing up or perched on armchairs or seated at small round tables—very informal. It was a bit like being at a small wedding with Le Mayne as a busy and practised host, circulating, moving people about, introducing them or prompting conversation with an apt remark or observation—"Ah yes, Toby, you've spent time in Rome" or "Logan has a very controversial view about the new building at Oriel." It was a little stiff and self-conscious to begin with, but it was far better than being at a formal dinner (like Bowra's salon†) and, as the wine flowed, and Le Mayne did his work, you realized that pretty soon you had met and talked to just about everyone.

And there were females! A woman don from Somerville and two undergraduettes. Le Mayne introduced me to one but I couldn't make out her Christian name: something Fothergill. I asked her to repeat it.

"Land," she said.

"Land? Is that short for something?"

"No. Just Land."

So: Land Fothergill. She said she was reading "Modern Greats,"

*Richard Hodge, a new Oxford friend of LMS.
†Maurice Bowra (1898–1971), scholar and critic. His hospitality at Wadham College (where he was later warden) was legendary.

which turned out to be Philosophy, Politics and Economics. She is petite with a severe short fringe that doesn't really suit her broad forehead. She has curious olive-green eyes and smokes with aggressive ostentation.

"What are you doing?" she asked.

"Dying of boredom."

"I won't take up any more of your time, then."

"No," I said hastily. I was already quite taken with her. "I mean here in Oxford: I can't stand the place. I'm reading History."

"Oh, one of Le Mayne's young stars. Well, if it's any comfort, I don't like Oxford either."

She said she felt that she was living in a kind of women's prison or barracks. She mentioned that her father was a painter (clearly I was meant to have heard of him) and that they lived in Hampstead. I told her I was writing a book about Shelley. We exchanged cards.

"Jesus College," she read.

"Perhaps we could meet for a coffee, one day."

"If I can escape my chaperone."

Thinking about her now, I do find her rather attractive. Those strange eyes could certainly haunt one.

[NOTE IN RETROSPECT. Why Shelley? I can't really remember now. I had read the lyric poems at school and, like most adolescents, thought I understood them. I remember reading a quotation from Teresa Guiccioli, Byron's mistress. She came to know Shelley in Pisa not long before he died and described him as being very tall, with a slight stoop and reddish hair. He had very bad skin, she observed, but absolutely impeccable manners. I think it was this brief portrait—which presented me with a Shelley that I did not recognize—that stimulated me. Shelley was suddenly real—not the fey, blond genius of popular iconography—and I wanted to know more about him, and, as I did learn more about him, I wanted to present *my* Shelley to the world as the accurate, veridical one. Whatever the defects of the book I subsequently wrote, no one could claim it idealized or sentimentalized its subject. Also Shelley died young—aged twenty-nine—and premature deaths of the greatly gifted always fascinate young writers.]

TUESDAY, 3 MARCH

Peter called this morning, obviously in something of a state. He wouldn't give a reason but asked me to cycle with him to Islip. I put my essay on Chartism aside and went to find my bicycle.

When we reached Islip (within an hour—we cycled hard) we went straight to the pub. Peter sat staring fixedly at the foam on his half-pint of beer as if he had just learned he was suffering from a terminal illness.

"Is it bad news?" I said finally.

"Tess is here."

"Tess? Here? Where?" (This is how you speak when you are astonished.)

"Here in Islip. She's renting a cottage and working at a nursery in Waterperry. She's run away from home."

"Jesus Christ."

"What am I going to do? She says she loves me."

"Of course she *says* that. You must understand, Peter, women—"

"And I love her too, Logan. At least I think I do. I want to marry her, at any rate."

There was no answer to that. We left the pub and walked down a lane towards a row of modest thatched cottages. Peter knocked on the door of one and Tess opened it. Tess Clough, last seen in the Lamb and Flag in Ringford, an aeon ago. Inside, the place was clean and meagrely furnished: there was a fire going in the grate and a couple of chairs and an oak table. Tess seemed pleased to see me and shook my hand vigorously.

"So glad to see you, Mr. Mountstuart. Oxford doesn't seem so strange knowing you and Peter are here too, just down the road."

I insisted she call me Logan. She went off to make some tea in a little kitchen scullery.

"What's that noise?" I said. Rustling, scratchings everywhere.

"The place is infested with mice."

Peter said she had arrived last week, settled in, bought the few sticks of furniture (I assumed there was a bed upstairs) and had left him a note in the porter's lodge at Balliol. "She's told the landlord I'm her brother," he said.

"Oh, very convincing," I said. "You know what'll happen if the college hears about it. The proctors will have a field day."

"She only had money for a week's rent after she bought her bits and pieces. So I've paid three months in advance."

"You're worse than Alfred Duggan,"* I said. "They'll think you're keeping a mistress: 'Have you heard about Scabius? The Balliol man who kept his mistress in Islip.'"

Then Tess came back in with the tea and we talked aimlessly about this and that. It turned out that Tess was now referring to herself in the village as Tess Scabius. The whole pretence is bound to be exposed within days. The rent, however, is only a pound a week and Peter can afford that. It turns out also that Tess is older than us—she's twenty-two. She looked rather pretty sitting by the fire in her blue print dress. Peter says he only has to wait until he's twenty-one and then his father "can go hang himself." Brave words. It's all gone to his head rather: this seems too rich and romantic a thing to happen to Peter. I stayed up late and wrote a long letter to Ben telling him of our exciting new developments.

WEDNESDAY, 18 MARCH

Coffee with Land Fothergill at the Cadena. She was wearing a velvet coat that matched her eyes. We talked a little stiffly about Mussolini and Italy and I was embarrassed to note how better informed she was than I—her opinions were strong and full of idiosyncratic detail; mine seemed straight from the editorials of the *Daily Mail*—at least those that I've bothered to read. I excuse myself by remembering that she is actually studying politics but the fact remains that my brain is rotting here in Oxford, dulled and numbed by the constant clamorous bells. I owe Blackwell's £18 for books, Halls £73 for assorted tailoring; college bat-

---

*Alfred Duggan, stepson of Lord Curzon, a contemporary at Balliol 1923–6, notorious for driving up to London most nights during term time to "have a woman."

tels are another tenner and God knows what the wine merchant will dun me. Dick Hodge has asked me to go with him to Spain at Easter and I'm tempted. He says £10 is all we'll need, everything is so cheap, especially if you travel third class. Perhaps I'll wait until summer. I rather relish the thought of London—still virtually unknown to me, after all.

FRIDAY, 10 APRIL

SUMNER PLACE, SOUTH KENSINGTON

Mother has transformed the house. Outside the fresh white stucco gleams. Inside it is all lacquered walls, curtains and materials of such richness and vibrancy as to make the eyes water. She has fitted out the top floor for me: my bedroom and dressing room are a dark burnt orange with emerald-green curtains and I have a small sitting room where the colours are reversed. We have a butler called Henry, a chauffeur (and a new motor) called Baker, a cook called Mrs. Heseltine and two (elderly) housemaids called Cecily and Margaret. Mother has her own maid also—Encarnación. They talk sharply and loudly to each other in Spanish to the visible consternation of the other servants. Clearly we are rich: Father wasn't wrong when he said we would be well provided for.

And for the first time I really miss his gentle unobtrusive presence in my life. It is Easter Friday and Mother asked me if I wanted to go to Mass at the Brompton Oratory but I declined. The day Father was buried my faith, such as it was, went with him into his grave. Shelley was so right: atheism is an absolute necessity in this world of ours. If we are to survive as individuals we can rely only on those resources provided by our human spirit—appeals to a deity or deities are only a form of pretence. We might as well howl at the moon.

Tonight at dinner Mother announced she was going to Paris on Monday for a week, or maybe ten days. I said she deserved a holiday after all her interior decorating.

"I'll be meeting a friend," she said, with truly horrible coyness. "An American gentleman of my acquaintance—Mr. Prendergast."

Ah, the famous Mr. Prendergast, I thought, but feigned ignorance.

"Who is this Mr. Prendergast?"

"I hope you'll become friends."

"I can't stop you hoping, Mother."

"Don't be difficult, Logan. He is very nice man—*muy simpático*. He give me very good advice about my investments."

I said I'd look forward to meeting him. Perhaps all these servants, all this ostentatious display is the result of Prendergast's financial acumen. I asked her if I might invite Dick Hodge to stay while she was away. She made no objection.

SATURDAY, 18 APRIL

Mother is still away and Dick Hodge is still here, though today he and I are both very sick. Last evening we went to the Café Royal and drank champagne. Then to the Alhambra for the show. Afterwards, at the 50-50 Club we drank some more—brandies this time—and spoke to two tarts. Dick is very forthright with them—it was highly comical.

DICK: How much?

FIRST TART: Depends what we get up to, don't it?

DICK: I want to know your rates.

SECOND TART: What d'you think we are? Piece-workers?

DICK: I wouldn't sit down in a restaurant without knowing what I'd be charged for the meal, would I?

They soon got tired of us and wandered away. Dick told me he'd been to a brothel in Madrid and the resulting experience was "nothing to write home about." We came home and I found some port and we sat up late drinking. I smoked half a cigar which, I think, is why I feel so decidedly rum this morning. Dick asked me if I'd ever kissed a boy. I confessed I had no passion for boys. He said he'd kissed dozens at school (Harrow), but then, he added, there was no alternative and everyone had someone they lusted after. I told him about Lucy and he seemed quite impressed. "I don't want sex without love," was the last thing I remember him saying.

MONDAY, 20 APRIL

Dick left for Galashiels this morning. I had Baker drive us to King's Cross and I felt a great wellspring of affection for him (Dick, not Baker). I think it's good for me to have another close friend apart from Ben and Peter—someone who did not know me at school and takes me as I am today. But when he went through the barrier to board his train he didn't even shake my hand: he gave a wave of his hat, said "back to the farm" and was gone without another rearward look.

He does baffle me, Dick. He has a profound and searching intelligence—he claims to detest Shakespeare, for example—but this intelligence seems to be in constant battle with his uncompromising bluntness. God knows what he would say to Mother. It's that absolute candour in him that attracts me, and, knowing myself, it's easy to understand why I would be attracted to such a trait. But what does Dick Hodge see in Logan Mountstuart? If the manner of his parting is any indication the answer must be very little.

Mother has telegraphed that she returns from Paris tomorrow. Mr. Prendergast is travelling with her but will be staying at the Hyde Park Hotel.

FRIDAY, 22 MAY

Peter and I biked out to Islip to have tea with Tess. Amazingly, the ménage continues undiscovered by everyone: Peter's parents, the university authorities and the good burghers of Islip. Part of this is due to the fact that Tess's nursery is sufficiently far away from the village to prevent any gossip spreading. At the nursery she's just a nice girl living in Islip who's good with plants. And what little the Islip folk see of her when she's not at work arouses no suspicion. She pays her bills and, by all accounts, is liked by her neighbours. Occasional visits from her "brother" in Oxford excite no comment. Peter told me he'd spent a long weekend with her during the vacation. They lived as man and wife, he said (he didn't need to go into details). His love for her is boundless.

The cottage looked pretty, spic and span, with all manner of flowers blooming in the garden (I must get to know the names of flowers—it annoys me, this ignorance. If I can name a dozen trees, flowers shouldn't be beyond me). The floorboards are newly varnished, with small rugs upon them, bright curtains hang at the windows and there are a couple of armchairs before the fire and a small dresser. Peter, however, does admit to finding Tess and the cottage a strain on his finances and has borrowed £10 off me to tide him over.

We drank tea and ate piles of anchovy toast—Tess very sweet and, in her outdoorsy way, lovelier than ever, I thought. When Peter went out to buy cigarettes she told me that she didn't know if it was possible to be more happy. She asked nothing more from life than what she possessed now: her work at the nursery, her cottage and Peter. How enviable! Maybe this is the answer—maybe this is how to find true contentment—to live your life within confined horizons. To set modest goals, achievable ambitions. Not all of us can manage it, alas.

WEDNESDAY, 3 JUNE

Le Mayne gave a dinner last night in a private room at the Mitre for Esmé Clay* and her husband. It was a rather grand affair and must have set Le Mayne back a fair amount. I think Le Mayne's ambition is to have his circle seen as more worldly and sophisticated than Bowra's or Urquhart's, that its reach extends beyond Oxford and academe and need not be composed either of bitchy homosexuals or teetotal intellectuals. Other friends of his had driven down from London and I suppose I should feel flattered to have been asked. Esmé Clay is in rehearsals for *Antony and Cleopatra* at the Palace ("God, how I detest that play," Dick said when I told him about the invitation).

Land Fothergill was there too—wearing sheer black, flashing with diamanté and some sort of little feathered headdress in her hair. She looked entirely different with her make-up on. She introduced me to Esmé Clay herself (she's a friend of the family) and I had a longish chat

---

*Esmé Clay (1898–1947), actress. Drowned in a boating accident off Minehead, Dorset. Her days of greatest fame were the 1920s.

with her. I was trembling like a child, I was so excited to be talking to
this beautiful and famous actress—it was despicable. I wore my new
dinner jacket and the white double-breasted waistcoat and felt both
very smart and very hot. I hardly noticed what we ate—I couldn't take
my eyes off Land—who was sitting beside Le Mayne, I noticed darkly.

Later over coffee I asked her if she wanted to come on with me to
Les Invalides for cocktails or champagne but she reminded me she was
obliged to be back in college.

"We girls mustn't be corrupted by Oxford—unlike you boys," she
said, looking at me directly. "Nothing untoward is ever going to happen to us in Oxford." She plumed her cigarette smoke at the ceiling.
"It's all right for you," she went on, "but they watch us like hawks." I
said something feeble like, what a shame, or how absurd. Then she
said, "So why don't you come and see me in London?" She gave me
her parents' address in Hampstead.

She's a strange young woman, Land, but I feel a powerful sexual
urge towards her—and I think she knows it.

THURSDAY, 4 JUNE

My life of Shelley goes well—over a hundred pages written now—but I
have rather been neglecting my history. Le Mayne said my last essay
was inadequate and sub-average and reminded me that the college had
awarded me an exhibition for a purpose, not as a gift of money. I think
I'll call my book *The Mind's Imaginings*.* Quennell told me he'd abandoned his life of Blake.

Mother writes to say that she's going to New York—with Mr. Prendergast—to "consolidate her US holdings," whatever that may mean.

> *I slept . . .*
> *Within dim bowers of green and purple moss,*

*From Shelley's poem "Mont Blanc": "And what were thou, and earth and
stars and sea,/If to the human mind's imaginings/Silence and solitude were
vacancy?"

Our young Ione's soft and milky arms
Locked then, as now, behind my dark, moist hair . . .
                    [Shelley, *Prometheus Unbound*]

I can only think of Land, these lines reverberating in my head. "Soft and milky arms . . ." Madness of sexual longing, dark fantasies about her naked body. All thoughts of cousin Lucy just ancient history now.

FRIDAY, 19 JUNE

Bacchanalian night at Les Invalides. Dick and I had dined at the Spread Eagle in Thame—an end-of-term celebration and farewell. On the way back we stopped the taxi on the Iffley Road and went into Les Invalides for a nightcap. As I signed Dick in, I could hear a tremendous row of piano music and laughter and shouting. I asked Mrs. Anderson what was going on. She was completely soused, the strap of her dress slipping off her shoulders, showing some terrible undergarment.

"Some young gentlemen dressed as ladies," she said.

In fact there were only two "ladies" we saw as we went up and I recognized one of them as Udo von Schiller, a German friend of Cassell. Cassell was there too, dressed as a Master of Foxhounds, and explained that they'd been at a fancy-dress ball at a place near Burford but had been thrown out for decadence by their host's father. He asked Dick and me to join their party and for some reason we did. Dick took over the piano playing (he's remarkably good), more drink was ordered and things went from bad to worse.

Udo—who looked remarkably pretty in his wig and cocktail dress, I have to say—led me into the library, where there was a game of strip-poker under way. I didn't linger. There was a naked man walking around with an erect cock replenishing drinks. As I turned to go back to the sing-song round the piano a small blond man, completely drunk, grabbed my arm and said, "Give me a kiss: you remind me of a friend of mine who's gone away." So I kissed him and he stuck his tongue in my mouth, like Lucy had, and grabbed my tool. I pushed him away quite hard and he banged up against the panelling, looking a bit stunned and sickly. "You've had your kiss," I said. "And that's your lot." Udo had witnessed all this and started to applaud as I left.

[NOTE IN RETROSPECT. 1966. More and more I'm convinced that this blond young man was in fact Evelyn Waugh.*]

TUESDAY, 21 JULY

Up to Hampstead today to meet Land and her family. I feel a little apprehensive, never having met a famous painter before (her father is Vernon Fothergill RA, celebrated for his vivid English landscapes painted in the style of Les Fauves). I'm also worried about what to wear. Mother suggested my "beautiful tweed," but it's too hot for tweeds. I wish I had a cotton drill suit—but I can't possibly go out and buy one now. Could I send Baker out to Harrods or the Army & Navy and see what he could pick up? Ridiculous. I bought so many clothes last year surely I can find something suitable.

Later. As it turned out I wore a blazer with some fawn bags, a striped shirt and a bow tie (Abbey, First XV). Land opened the door and laughed: she said I looked like a travelling salesman on his day off. Very comical, I said, managing a sardonic chuckle, but I did feel over-dressed. She was wearing a smock-blouse thing and knickerbockers. Her feet were bare. She led me through the house to the rear terrace with a big fig tree that overlooked sloping lawns, the heath and, beyond, the vast and blurry city, hazed by the noon light. A table was set under the fig and the whole scene looked entrancing. Three or four dogs of indeterminate breed lolled about.

Her father was in his studio with a friend, she said, as she poured me a cider cup. Her mother and her brother, Hugh, would be joining us, and possibly some others. "It's always open house at luncheon

*This seems unlikely. Waugh's diaries do not cover the exact date in question but he was occasionally in Oxford during this year.

here," she said, as if this were the most natural thing in the world. The house was large and rambling, not very old, Arts and Crafts, I would say, with faux Tudor affectations—tall spiralled brick chimneys, leaded lights, and inside exposed beams and a minstrel's gallery in the big drawing room. The place was full of pictures and odd pieces of well-worn furniture. Very lived-in. I loved it, of course. The antithesis of Sumner Place.

Hugh Fothergill, brother, arrived wearing a brilliant scarlet shirt and no tie. He's rangy, thin, with wild hair and a jutting jaw. He's just finished medical school so must be twenty-five or twenty-six. Within minutes of our being introduced he told me he was a socialist. Mrs. Fothergill ("Call me Ursula") was also tall—and faintly aloof, as if lost in her thoughts, only giving the present company 75 per cent of her attention. Then old Vernon appeared—stout and florid—looking more like a publican than a painter. With him was the friend called Henry Lamb,* I think, a fellow artist. At lunch Lamb asked me if I knew Lady Ottoline Morrell and whether I'd been out to Garsington.† Land said, "I don't think Logan would approve of Garsington." I couldn't think why she made this judgement and remained silent. Lamb looked at me a bit askance after that, as if I were some sort of stuffed-shirt. She can be infuriating, Land. We ate cold roast beef, horseradish, salads, with a choice of wine or beer. To show how unstuffed-shirt I was, I drank beer.

After lunch Land and I took two of the dogs and went for a walk on the heath. We sat on the grass in the shade of a tree and smoked a cigarette. At one stage she lay back and spread her arms and I think she was expecting me to kiss her—but somehow I had lost my nerve. The day had proved too overwhelming; I was too disconcerted by her family.

So I said, "Why wouldn't I like Garsington? I should think I'd love it."

"Oh no you wouldn't. Whatever else you may be, Logan, you're not a snob."

"How do you know I'm not a snob?"

*Henry Lamb (1883–1960), artist.
†Lady Ottoline Morrell (1873–1938), hostess and patron of the arts. Her country house was at Garsington, a village not far from Oxford, where she entertained writers and artists.

She looked at me in her familiar fixed way. "I can tell. I abominate snobbery. I would never have asked you to lunch if I'd suspected for one second."

"I think I might be an intellectual snob," I said.

"Well, that's forgivable. That's about brains, not class. It's social snobbery that corrupts this country. That's what Hugh says, anyway."

We wandered back home for tea. We agreed we'd go to the cinema together. Perhaps I'll kiss her there, now I think about it, in the dark of the theatre, when I won't be able to see that look in her eyes.

FRIDAY, 24 JULY

Mr. Prendergast to dinner. I'm growing to like him—a lean, sober, ruminative man. He is incredibly polite to me, weighing every remark I make as if it were some profound philosophical aphorism. "Yes, it most definitely is unseasonably cool, Logan," "Indeed, why *do* the English alone serve mint sauce with lamb?" It is impossible to take offence, but for the life of me I cannot understand what he sees in Mother and vice versa.

A surprise telegraph and then a phone call from Roderick Poole. We are to lunch next week. It must be ten years since I last saw him—in Montevideo, my lost home, my native land. And then a postcard from Land in Cornwall. What's she doing there? Why didn't she tell me? What about our cinema-going? And I'll be off to Spain with Dick before she gets back. How tiresome.

WEDNESDAY, 29 JULY

Roderick has become sleek. He's plumper, his hair is thinning but he still sees the world filtered through his lazy air of cynicism. We went to the Étoile in Charlotte Street—very nice too. He works as an editor for a publishing firm called Sprymont & Drew, with school textbooks and children's books as his special responsibility. "The egomania of the children's book writer has to be experienced to be believed," he said.

He had a good look at me, making me turn around on the pavement outside the restaurant before we went in. "Well, you've certainly improved," he said, "and very well turned out, to boot."

We started with oysters. "How's your book going?" he asked.

"What book?"

"You must be writing a book, surely?"

"I am, as it happens. How'd you guess?"

"Because you told me when you were ten you wanted to be a writer."

"Did I?"

This knowledge made me obscurely pleased: as if something about my destiny had been confirmed. Or am I just being a young sentimental fool? Roderick was on good form. He said I had to submit *The Mind's Imaginings* to Sprymont & Drew or he'd never speak to me again.

MONDAY, 3 AUGUST

The alloyed bliss of Paris in August: tourists and heat on the boulevards but the restaurant Ben and I dined in was virtually empty. Afterwards we walked along the *quais* of the Seine in a sultry, embracing night-warmth. Ben already seems about ten years older than I, but he appeared genuinely keen to hear about Oxford and the Peter/Tess imbroglio.

He is working for a small but rather grand gallery, Auguste Dard, whose line is very modern: Gris, Léger, Pinsent, Brancusi, Dax, etc.– and of course any Picasso or Braque they can lay their hands on. He thought I was mad to go to Spain in August and was unconvinced by the argument (Dick's, admittedly) that foreign countries could only be fully known and experienced under the extremes of their weather conditions–the blazing heat of summer or the iron grip of winter.

TUESDAY, 4 AUGUST

On the train from Paris to Biarritz. Before I left, Ben insisted that I buy a small unframed oil sketch by Derain. He advanced the £7 required and said he would have it packed and sent to Sumner Place (I telegraphed Mother and asked her to refund Ben the money). I said I couldn't really afford it, what with all my debts in Oxford, but he insisted. Trust me, was all he kept saying, you'll never regret it. This is our big chance, he said, to be here now in Paris with these artists and even modest access to money. Something about the way he spoke convinced me that Ben was going to make his fortune. I noticed on his business card he calls himself "Benedict" Leeping—Benjamin no more, then. When he asked why I was so impoverished I explained that it was deliberate. I was travelling with only £10—another of Dick's strictures. Too much money, Dick feels, cuts you off from the country you are visiting. A little hardship, the need to economize, even a little suffering, brings you closer to it and its people's soul. "I hope you're not in thrall to this Dick Hodge," Ben said. No fear of that, I reassured him. Dick has been with his family at Ostend—I wonder why he wanted us to meet in Biarritz?

WEDNESDAY, 5 AUGUST

Biarritz. Dick arrives later tonight. In the meantime I stroll around this delightful *station balnéaire* buying a few last-minute provisions. We are travelling very light—one rucksack each, which contains reading matter, a large bottle of eau de Cologne (we will not have much chance to bathe, Dick said, and we don't want to smell like tinkers), brilliantine for our hair (for the same reason), two extra shirts, a couple of ties, a pair of ordinary shoes, extra socks and underwear, and, carefully folded, the linen trousers that will match the linen jackets that we will wear. I have a Panama hat against the sun, Dick prefers a beret. By day we travel in shorts and walking shoes but can transform ourselves into relatively well-dressed young gentlemen in the evenings.

The plan is to walk through the Pyrenees through one of the passes and either walk or bus on to Segovia. From there we will take the train to Madrid and then on south, stopping off where we want, to the Mediterranean. I bought a wineskin and some tough fatty sausage that, I'm assured, will keep for days. From the window of our hotel, through a gap in the roofscape, I can see the creamy breakers rolling in on to the *grande plage*. This is the liberation of travel—the sense of cleansing, of purification, of sloughing off. Oxford is a distant memory, London almost forgotten. And Land—who is this Land Fothergill mouldering somewhere in banal Cornwall?

THURSDAY, 13 AUGUST

I'm exhausted, a husk. I must have lost half a stone and am burnt to teak by the sun. Segovia—Madrid—Seville—now Algeciras. I shall have to reflect on this trip in tranquillity and solitude. Christ knows where Dick is.

It all started happily. I met him at the station in Biarritz, we dined at a bistro by the *vieux port,* then wandered round the casino, not daring to gamble. Very early the next morning we caught a bus up into the foothills of the Pyrenees and commenced our walk through the pass. At midday we paused to eat our bread and cheese and were chatting about this and that, exhilarated to be up in the mountains, and I said, apropos of nothing in particular—no, actually, we were talking about Johnson's *Lives of the Poets* (which Dick had brought with him)—and I said, "Did you know Dr. Johnson's cat was called 'Hodge'?"

He looked at me most oddly. "What're you trying to say? Go on, spit it out."

I laughed. "Just idle conversation, for heaven's sake."

He looked around, then swatted a fly on his forearm and held it out for me to see.

"And that fly's name is Logan."

"Grow up," I said.

"If I look like a cat then you look like a squashed fly."

"I didn't say you looked like a cat, you pathetic child."

"Right!" he bellowed. Standing up. He was completely enraged. "See you in Avignon on the 28th."

And with that he strode off up the hill. I waited for half an hour, convinced he'd come to his senses, but there was no sign of him, he seemed well and truly gone. There was no question of my setting off after him—he was the one who knew the route—so I retraced my steps and caught a bus back to Biarritz.

Since then I've travelled by train—third class, Dick would approve—following the vague route we had planned across Spain to the south. I've looked around me, visited churches and mosques, palaces and art galleries, always half expecting to see him, his big grinning face under its beret, but no sign. And I've travelled more as an automaton than a curious tourist—this is not the spirit in which this journey was meant to take place and I feel the whole experience is spoiled somehow. But I will be in Avignon on the 28th, at the Hôtel de Londres, come what may. Tomorrow I leave for Barcelona and then on to Perpignan, Narbonne, Arles and finally Avignon. I find my thoughts focusing pleasurably on France. Spain was Dick's idea. I'll come back here again, when I wish it, when it suits me. Ben was right—I was too much in thrall to Dick's eccentric demands and itinerary. From now on I travel only at my own instigation.

FRIDAY, 28 AUGUST

Avignon. I lunched in the square opposite the Palais des Papes, then wandered down a little canal to the hotel. And there was Dick, signing in at the reception desk. He looked like he'd been in an accident: his face was livid red, all blisters and peeling skin. He greeted me with a firm handshake and a wide smile and made no reference to our row. He told me that three days ago, one afternoon, he'd dozed off on a beach in what he thought was a deep patch of shade. And of course he slept longer than he had planned, the sun moved round and slowly the shade was dragged off him. His face and knees took the brunt but, he said, the pain was beginning to subside. We head for home tomorrow. I forgive him his childish outburst—he has been punished enough.

TUESDAY, 8 SEPTEMBER

SUMNER PLACE

I kissed Land today in a cinema (the film was called *The Merry-Go-Round*). Our lips touched for a second before she immediately pushed me away and hissed, "Never do that again!" At Kettners we ate our first course in almost total silence. Eventually, I said, "Look, I'm sorry. It's just that I like you and I thought you liked me."

"I did," she said, "I do. But . . ."

"There's somebody else." I felt suddenly very mature, as if we were in a Noel Coward play.

"Who told you?"

"I guessed. Who is it? Someone you met in Cornwall?"

"Yes. It's very irritating, you leading the conversation in this way."

So I let her tell me the story, and as it unfolded, and as I began to feel more and more depressed, so I began to find her more and more beautiful. Why does life have to be so predictable? The man's name is Bobbie (how revolting). Bobbie Jarrett. His father is Sir Lucas Jarrett, MP.

"Sir? I suppose he's a baronet," I said wearily.

"Yes."

"Now I understand: 'Lady Land Jarrett.' Yes, it has a certain ring. And is he handsome?"

"I think you could say that."

"As handsome as Croesus?"

For a moment I thought she was going to throw the remains of her egg mayonnaise at me but, instead, she began to chuckle. I smiled back and the old affectionate mood was restored between us, but I felt sick: most girls would have walked out or sworn at me or created some kind of scene. But Land found it funny—and that is why I love her, I suppose. There—it is written. And I never thought I would write this either: I can't wait to go back up to Oxford.

SUNDAY, 11 OCTOBER

JESUS COLLEGE

I actually went down to the Catholic chaplaincy today to go to Mass and take confession but the mournful tolling of the bells on every side (why are there so many bloody bells in Oxford?) and the scrofulous blackness of the damp buildings (it was raining hard) drove me away. In fact I am content to remain unshriven, my sins all mine and mine alone.

I have, secretly, joined the college Golf Society and this afternoon I went out with a dull man called Parry-Jones and played nine holes at Kidlington. The rain had stopped and I beat Parry-Jones easily, three and two. He said he thought I could get into the university team. I might even get a blue—or is it a half-blue? It might be worth it, just to be able to announce the fact to Le Mayne.

Ben has invited me to Paris in January. Shelley and golf will help me to survive until then. To Balliol tonight to dine with Peter—he will be twenty-one in four months.

1926

TUESDAY, 26 JANUARY

I keep thinking about Paris, wondering if, in fact, my future lies there. My visit was sublime, the weather cold and rainy and all the better for it. I slept on a sofa in Ben's apartment on the rue de Grenelle—no more than a large room, really, with a stove in the corner for heat and a disgusting lavatory on the landing outside, shared by the other lodgers. He spends all his money on paintings, and the walls of his room are stacked four or five deep with canvases. Most of them are mediocre, he admits, but, as he says, you have to start somewhere. I'm afraid abstraction leaves me cold—there has to be something with a human connection in a painting, otherwise all we are talking about is form, pattern and tone—and it's simply not enough for a work of art. I bought a tiny pencil sketch of a coffee pot by Marie Laurencin for 30s. to prove my point. I said I wouldn't swap all his stacked canvases for this scrap of paper. Ben was amused. "You wait and see," he said.

James Joyce is living just off the rue de Grenelle and Ben vaguely knows him, they pass often in the street. One night in a local restaurant Ben pointed him out to me. He was wearing an eye patch and looked tired and strained—but very dapper. He has a very small head, I noticed, smaller than his wife's, who was with him. The next day we went to Shakespeare & Co. and I bought a copy of *Ulysses*. It begins well but I have to confess I've become a little bogged down and have only read about a third.

WEDNESDAY, 27 JANUARY

I suppose I should record this. We were leaving a restaurant in Saint-Germain—Chez Loick—when Joyce came in with three friends, one of whom knew Ben. We paused to chat and I was introduced. Ben, who was speaking French, described me as "Mon ami, Logan, un scribouillard"—to Joyce's puzzlement—he clearly didn't know the French word. "A what?" he said. I stepped forward: "A scrivener," I said. "A scribbler?" he replied, turning his half-blind eyes upon me. "Sort of," I said, "let's say a scribivelard." Joyce gave me a rare smile. "I like that," he said, "and I warn you that I might steal it." The smile transformed his pale thin-lipped face—and I was suddenly conscious of his Irish accent. "Moight," he said; "I moight steal it."

THURSDAY, 28 JANUARY

Jesus College. Bitter cold. When I went to the lavatories this morning I put on a hat, my coat and a scarf to cross the quad and then I had to break the ice in the pan. These buildings are medieval.

Peter's debts mount alarmingly. Tess had bronchitis over Xmas, it turns out, and was unable to go to work for three weeks—and of course she wasn't paid. He asked his father for a loan but his father has refused and is in fact demanding an audit of Peter's personal account. I lent him another fiver (so far Tess and Peter's love nest has cost me £25).

I went down with my clubs to Port Meadow and I hit a few dozen old golf balls out towards Osney. The water meadows are all frozen and as the balls landed I could hear ice shatter. My drive still has a tendency to draw but my long irons are incredibly reliable. I was alone—a few shivering ponies aside—and at first the nutty crack of my stroke and the distant smash and tinkle of ice as the ball landed were wonderfully exhilarating. But golf always reminds me of Father and I found myself thinking about his last few months and how the Lizard flogged me the day he died and I grew more and more depressed. So what was meant to be an afternoon's distraction turned into a mood of sour gloom. I sit here drinking whisky wondering whether to go round to Dick, just a few hundred yards away in Wadham. He always cheers me up, Dick, but our disastrous summer has caused a certain coolness between us and he seems to spend most of his time these days with a group of Harrovians in New College.

SATURDAY, 30 JANUARY

Mr. Scabius has come to Oxford to see the Master and the Dean of Balliol. Peter is beside himself because Tess is ill again with flu and he dare not go near the cottage. He's asked me to go up to the village and explain what's going on and to say that he doesn't know when he will be able to see her again. He's right: the college authorities will be watching him very closely after his father's visit. I told him I'd pack up a few treats and cycle out tomorrow.

SUNDAY, 31 JANUARY

This is not easy to write but it must be done. My hand is shaking.

It was a slog up to Islip, cold and in the teeth of a brisk wind and the rain came on just about a mile short of the village. Tess didn't seem that ill at all—thought she had a cold coming, she said—and the cottage was snug and warm enough with the fire banked up and the curtains drawn. She busied about: taking my damp coat and spreading it over a chair, brewing up a fresh pot of tea, offering me biscuits from a tin. It was strange being alone with her for the first time, and having her fussing over me was pleasing, as if I were being offered a tiny glimpse of what it might be like to have a wife—someone to come home to, someone who took your coat off your back and spread it on a chair before a fire and who offered you tea. This fantasy grew more exciting—sexually exciting, I mean—as we talked on in complete honesty about Peter and his father and his father's suspicions. Tess was very grateful to me, she said, for being so frank and so helpful—she knew all about my financial contributions to their ménage. She said I was everything a "true friend" should be.

She was untypically talkative, glad of the company and of the chance to unburden herself. She completely dropped that tone of polite guardedness that usually coloured her discourse with me. At one moment she leant forward to refill my teacup and her shawl ends fell apart and I found myself eyeing her figure, the fullness of her curves—for God's sake, why am I writing like some romantic novelist? This journal is for ultimate frankness, total honesty. I stared covertly at her breasts and her haunches and tried to imagine her naked. She was a "nice" girl, Tess, well spoken and demure. But she didn't know that I had seen the other side of her with Peter, seen her unbutton his trousers and take his cock in her hand. There was another Tess that I was more interested in.

Then she asked me when Peter was coming up next and I said I didn't know, perhaps in a couple of weeks, maybe longer—a month?—just to let everyone's suspicions ease off. This took her aback and she turned away to face the fire and began to weep gently, saying, "A month? A whole month?" I felt truly sorry for her. She was alone, without friends or family, she was the one who had run away, after all, had made the sacrifice, who lived with the daily pressures of maintaining the pretence of being "Miss Scabius" with her "brother" at Oxford.

I knelt beside her and put an arm around her—at which point her quiet weeping degenerated into great heaving sobs and she hugged me to her, burying her head in the angle of my neck and shoulder.

I'm sorry, but I have to say that for me the contact with her body was powerfully stimulating. This warm, bonny, sobbing girl in my arms—and I couldn't help myself. I held her to me and my lips were on her neck, and before I could think or act further we were kissing with an abandon that was almost animal.

Thinking about it now (I've just poured myself another whisky) I feel sure that what I was expressing with Tess was all my frustrations with Land—and I think she was giving vent to all her frustrations with Peter. There we were, close, intimate, sharers of a secret . . . We had to have some sort of physical correlation for our respective moods. Need and opportunity—the ingredients of all betrayals.

God knows how far it might have gone but I came to my senses and gently broke it off. I stood up, and at once abandon was replaced by awkwardness and embarrassment. We were both out of breath. She pulled her shawl about her and smoothed the rumpled bodice of her dress beneath it. But for one brief second, before she turned her head away, I saw the other Tess. She looked at me, I would say, with a pure and stirring carnality.

I apologized. She apologized. I said we'd both become upset, become a bit carried away. She agreed. I said I'd better be going and pulled on my warm, damp coat.

"Will you come again, Logan?" she asked. "I mean, now that Peter's—"

"I can pop up from time to time," I said carefully. "But only if you'd like me to."

"I get back from work after six," she said, "but I always have Sundays off."

"Well, Sunday's a possibility. Look I can't tell you how sorry I am."

"Don't give it a thought," she said. "It's something just between the two of us. No one else need know."

"I'll come up next Sunday, then," I said, my voice suddenly mysteriously dry and husky.

I cycled back to college in a dream of lust.

Of course now, as I write, the doubts have set in—and the shame. How would I know what a look of pure carnality is? And what am I doing, thinking these hot and feverish thoughts about the young woman my oldest friend Peter is in love with? For all I know everything I read as enticing might have been no more than sympathy and concern.

TUESDAY, 2 FEBRUARY

Le Mayne was very hostile about my last essay on Pitt the Younger. "Beta-gamma, gamma-double-plus," he said. "Most unimpressive. What do you mean he died of gout? You don't die of gout and, anyway, what's that got to do with his career? Keep this up and I can guarantee you a third. What's going on?"

I muttered something false about family problems. He knew I was lying.

"But you're not making the least effort," Le Mayne said. "I can see that a mile off. You can be wrong—or wrongheaded—that's allowable. But I refuse to tolerate anyone who won't even try."

I made the usual abashed promises. He both frightens and irritates me, does Le Mayne: I find myself simultaneously wanting to please him and wanting to tell him I don't give two figs for his approval. Is this the definition of a good teacher? Reminds me of H-D.

I had tea with Peter in Balliol and gave him an edited version of my visit to Tess. His father thought he was in some gambling syndicate, he said, or was a hopeless drunk: not for a second did he suspect there was a whole other side to his life. But he would have to go very, very carefully. I volunteered to keep the lines of communication open between him and Tess. We were interrupted by a man called Powell,* another historian, as it turned out, whom I vaguely knew. His tutor was Kenneth Bell. Peter seems to be very thick with the Etonians at Balliol—there seem to be dozens of them. I started moaning about Le Mayne and the stultifying dullness of the History course and Powell suggested I change to English Literature. He said he had a friend reading English who raves about a young don called Coghill at Exeter.† "Just across the road from you," he said. He invited me for drinks: his friend could fill me in.

It's not a bad idea, this possible move. I long to junk History, though I'd lose my exhibition, I suppose. Wonder if it's too late?

WEDNESDAY, 3 FEBRUARY

Postcard from Tess: "Dear Logan, please try to come before lunch on Sunday. I shall be busy in the afternoon. Yours sincerely, Tess Scabius."

*Anthony Powell (1905–2000), novelist. His friend was Henry Yorke, better known as the novelist Henry Green (1905–1973).
†Nevill Coghill (1899–1980), influential young English don at Exeter College. Amongst his other protégés was W. H. Auden.

She doesn't want me there as the light begins to fade. I can read the signs. So much for the "pure carnality" of her look.

Drinks with Powell and his friend Henry Yorke at their lodgings in King Edward Street. Powell is affable; Yorke has that slightly clipped reserve you often find in Etonians. I can never tell whether it's as a result of chronic shyness or majestic self-assurance. Yorke said he was writing a novel–"Like the rest of Oxford," I said–which brought a glare from him. He thought Coghill was wonderful. I think I'd better sound out Le Mayne about changing before I meet this Coghill fellow.

THURSDAY, 4 FEBRUARY

A day in the Bodleian writing my essay on Henry VIII for Le Mayne– going for alpha. I want him to understand that this move to English Literature is not because I can't do History. I met up with Dick in the King's Head–the old friendship re-established. He had a plaster cast on his foot and needed a walking stick to get about. He said he'd broken two toes in his foot. When I asked him how he said "fishing."

SUNDAY, 7 FEBRUARY

I cycled up to Islip. I had with me presents from Peter–one hundred cigarettes, a bottle of gin, five tins of stew, a jar of plum jam and a five-pound note. Tess asked me if I could split some logs for the fire, so I spent an hour in the back garden chopping a load of greenish oak logs that a neighbour had given her. Another neighbour stuck his head over the garden wall and asked if I was Mr. Scabius.

"I'm a friend of Mr. Scabius. Mr. Scabius is indisposed."

"Sorry to hear that," he said, then dropping his voice, added, "Miss Scabius is a charming young lady. We're all very fond of her in the lane. Terrible shock to lose your parents that way–so young too."

I agreed, mystified, and went back to my log-splitting.

When my back and shoulders were sore and I could feel incipient blisters swelling on my palms I decided to stop.

As I was washing my hands in the little scullery-kitchen, I shouted over my shoulder, "I'd bring those logs in if I were you, Tess, they'll need some drying before they burn well."

I heard Tess's voice in my ear, very close. "No need to shout, Logan. I'm right behind you." And I felt the soft weight of her body press against my back and her arms come round to embrace me. I turned the tap off—the noise of the running water had covered the sound of her approach. I felt her lips touch my neck. "Come to bed, Logan," she whispered.

The first time was terrible. We slid naked into bed and took each other in our arms and I squirted all over the sheets almost immediately. Then she went and got Peter's gin and we had a glass and smoked a cigarette. I could only marvel at her nudity. It seems to me that first time of mutual nakedness is almost a more lasting memory than the sexual act. To have Tess's ripe warm soft body pressed against mine—her breasts, her thighs, her belly—is the sensuous imprint that I take away from our encounter. The second time was better: fast (I seemed only to be inside her for seconds and couldn't hold myself back) but it was achieved; it was genuine. "I get so lonely," was all she said by way of explanation. I asked no questions at all: I had switched off the rationalizing, analytical, moralizing side of my brain. We rolled around under the blankets and the quilt as we kissed and nuzzled and I explored the tactile possibilities of her body. Then she pushed me out of bed with little ceremony: "Can't spend all day in here," she said. We heated up a tin of stew, she buttered some thick slices of bread and we drank neat gin. The most delicious Sunday lunch of my life. I was drunk as I cycled back to Oxford, in every sense of the word, but I remember thinking: clever girl—the chopping of logs, a Sunday lunch, an early afternoon departure—no neighbour would question her unsullied reputation.

So I sit in my room and I hear the clatter of boots on my staircase and all the bells of Oxford seem to be tolling this winter evening. I say to myself: Logan Mountstuart, you are no longer a virgin. I feel the ache in my balls—my "eggs," as Dick Hodge calls them—and I try to ignore the nagging, irritating voice in my ear that is saying, she is the girl your oldest friend loves, the girl he says he wants to marry . . . And I say in return, it won't happen again, it was one of those insane moments between two people that will remain entirely private and we'll both go back to our previous selves, unaffected. Perhaps if I repeat it often enough I might end up believing it. 7 February 1926. The date is burned, carved, stamped on the story of my life.

SUNDAY, 14 FEBRUARY

To Islip. Tess again. Two times. We never mention Peter. When we talk it is about things of no consequence: the woman who runs the post office, the people at the nursery.

Last week Le Mayne described my essay as "a return to form."

SUNDAY, 21 MARCH

The "Tess Sundays" are over: my sex-Sundays consigned to the memory-store. Peter has gone up there today. He feels enough time has elapsed. I had five Sundays with Tess . . . Christ, I almost feel like weeping. But I knew it would end: I don't love Tess and she doesn't love me. But, bizarrely, I find I resent the fact that Peter is there, in my place. Will he be eating stew and drinking gin? It had become a ritual with us: first fucking, then gin, then lunch. I always left between 2:00 and 3:00 in the afternoon. My God, Tess—with your square impassive face, your thick brown hair, your callused gardener's hands with the bitten nails, the clumsy way you smoked your cigarettes. You liked to masturbate me, almost as if you were conducting some fascinating new experiment with my cock, always giving a little yell of pleasure when my sperm shot out—"Here it comes," you would say, "I know it's coming, any moment now!" What am I going to do without you?

WEDNESDAY, 14 APRIL

It felt like the first day of spring today and Dick and I walked out to Wytham for tea. The roads were dry and the verges full of dandelions, the white thorn all spumy billows. On the way I told him about Tess and our Sunday encounters. Then he asked me who she was and, for some reason, I told him the whole story.

"Does Peter have any idea?" he asked.

"God, no—at least I hope not."

"Well, all I can say," Dick paused to kick at a pebble on the road, "is that it's a pretty repulsive way to carry on."

"You don't understand, she's not that kind of a girl—"

"Not her, old chap. You. I think your behaviour is utterly contemptible." He looked at me. "You go way down in my estimation, way down. You must admit, it's damned low stuff."

And I did feel ashamed, for a while, for the first time. And Dick, having expressed his honest opinion, left it at that and we talked about the coming strike and whether the government would really let it happen.

Came back to college and read *North by Night* by Butler Hughes instead of writing my essay. Flashy but intriguing novel.

TUESDAY, 4 MAY

SUMNER PLACE

The strike is on—the *Daily Mail* wasn't printed today. The Old Brompton Road very quiet with no buses and no building work going on. The big hole in the road at the corner of Bute Street—where they're repairing the sewers or something—was empty of workmen, only a couple of abandoned pickaxes and a spade lying around symbolically at its foot.

I went down to Chelsea Town Hall and volunteered as a special constable. I was sworn in and given a wrist band, a steel helmet and a truncheon and ordered to report to the police station. There I was assigned to a proper policeman, Constable Darker. Darker is a handsome man in a brutal kind of way, with a broad cleft chin and dense silky eyebrows. For four hours we walked the streets of Knightsbridge but saw no sign of riot or mayhem. The only anxious moment came when Darker went to explore up an alleyway beside a public house, leaving me standing outside it. Four men who were going into the pub—working-class men, I would say—stopped and stared at me. One of them said, "Look at that, will you? A special cuntstable." And they all laughed. I wandered off a few yards, swinging my truncheon on its thong, trying to look at ease, praying for Darker's return, but they went into the pub without more ado. Presently, Darker came back, took a look at me and said, "You all right, Mr. Mountstuart? Look like you've seen a ghost." I didn't tell him about my encounter with the men. Strange and somewhat worrying to think how obviously my fear and concern were written on my face. I asked Darker, in the interests of solidarity, to call me Logan. He told me, a little uncomfortably, that his Christian name was Joseph. I think he would prefer me to call him Constable, or Darker.

Telephone call from Dick Hodge: he says he's learning to drive trains in Edinburgh. Some trams have been wrecked by strikers in Hammersmith, apparently, and there are rumours that a special constable was kicked to death by a mob in Leeds.

SATURDAY, 8 MAY

Darker and I spent the morning directing traffic at the junction of the King's Road and Sydney Street—which was hardly taxing, as the roads are still very quiet. Anyway, Darker said he was going to pop off for a cup of tea and a smoke and asked if I could handle the junction on my own for ten minutes. Absolutely, I assured him.

All was going well until I waved a small motor through to turn left on the King's Road. It immediately stopped outside the Palace Theatre and the driver got out—it was Hugh Fothergill. The conversation went something like this:

ME: Hello, Hugh. How's Land? Haven't seen her for—
HUGH: What the hell do you think you're doing?
ME: I'm a special—
HUGH: You're a scab. D'you think this strike's some kind of game?
ME: (alarmed) I just happen to think that when the country's in crisis you have to pull together—

At which point he spat in my face, pointed at me and yelled in his loudest voice—THIS MAN'S A DIRTY, STINKING SCAB! A few passers-by stopped and looked round. A man in a bowler hat shouted: Let him do his duty! There was another shout of Scab! Hugh glared at me, climbed back into his car and drove off and the King's Road returned to normal. I wiped away Hugh's spittle and a minute later Constable Darker strolled up. "How's it going, Logan?" he asked. "Nip off and have a fag if you fancy. There's a coffee stall down by Shawfield Street." Every time Darker abandons me something unpleasant seems to happen. Maybe I'll cry off with flu tomorrow . . . When I stood at the stall, later, smoking, holding my mug of coffee, both my hands started to shake, quite visibly. Delayed shock, I suppose. Something tells me I'm not cut out for politics.

WEDNESDAY, 12 MAY

The strike is over. All a bit of an anti-climax, finally. I had just turned up at the police station (there were two armoured cars parked outside, soldiers standing around them with rifles slung) when Darker told me it was all over—"Government in talks with the TUC," had just been announced on the wireless (we really must get one: I think Mother would be mad for it). I handed in my helmet and truncheon but kept my striped wristband as a souvenir.

So the great strike is over and what do I have to say about it—this significant moment in our modern history in which I played a tiny part? I have no informed comment: my feelings during the nine days were ones of tedium interspersed with two moments of fear and shame. Why did I become a special constable? I did it unthinkingly, because everyone else at Oxford was determined to "do something." Am I so frightened of the working classes? Is it the shadow of the Russian Revolution that makes Oxford's young men volunteer to serve? Ironically, the lasting benefit to have come out of the whole affair will be a friendship of sorts with a working man—Joseph Darker. He's invited me to tea on Sunday to meet his wife.

A letter from Dick. A train he was driving was derailed near Carlisle and two passengers were killed. Very "Dick," somehow.

MONDAY, 28 JUNE

JESUS COLLEGE

Staying on in college to confirm next year's lodgings. I liked the look of a place in Walton Street, not far from the canal, so I should be able to sort everything out with the bursar by Wednesday. I long to move out but Le Mayne counselled against it: "Not conducive to hard work," he said, adding ominously that in his experience undergraduates who moved out of college in their final year seldom achieved the degree they deserved. I tried to reassure him, said I was moving out because I wanted to work harder and that I found that the life around me in college was the distraction.

Yesterday, Land and I met up in Headington and cycled out along country lanes heading in the general direction of Stadhampton. She had a note for me from Hugh, apologizing for his behaviour (I suppose it's not often you spit in the face of your sister's friend) but still disapproving of my strike-breaking. We sat on the green at Great Milton and ate our sandwiches. It was clear from the way she talked that she's still very set on Bobbie Jarrett. So I let her know, in a roundabout way, that I'd had a "love affair" myself—but it was now over. "A real affair?" she asked. "As real as it gets," I said, in my best man-of-the-world manner.

Actually, Tess has saved me from Land (and from Lucy, come to that). Now that I have had a true and mature sexual encounter with another woman I can look at Land with new objectivity—without any danger of rosy mists of schoolboy passion rising to obscure the view. In this spirit I can tell that I am still attracted to her—I admit it freely—but if she prefers the Hon. Bobbie Jarrett to me then so be it.

We were free-wheeling down the hill by Garsington when there came a shout from a man standing on the verge. We stopped: it was someone Land knew, whose name, as far as I could make out was Siggy (Sigismund?) Clay.* He was carrying a sketchbook and watercolours and was wearing a rough tweed suit that looked about three sizes too big for him and was staying, it transpired, at the Manor. He was pre-

*Siegfried Clay (1895–1946), painter. Briefly married to the actress Pamela Lawrence. Died in Tangier after a short illness.

maturely bald but had a wide upswept corsair's moustache in compensation. He invited us back to tea—he would not take no for an answer (what they call a forceful personality). We wheeled our bicycles back up the hill and parked them at the front door of the house in the lee of one of the biggest yew hedges I had ever seen. He led us round to a rather beautiful stone terrace at the side with an arcade. From here we could see all the way to Didcot and below us were the gardens, sloping away to a reflecting pool, dotted with statuary and shaded by ancient holm oaks. Sigismund rang a bell and ordered tea from a housemaid, who told him tea had been served already and cleared away. "I demand tea," Sigismund said and it duly appeared with some sandwiches and half a fruit cake. While we consumed it, Sigismund pointed out the other guests to us as they strolled around the ornamental lake: Virginia and Leonard Woolf,* Aldous Huxley and someone called Miss Spender-Clay (no relation to Sigismund, he insisted, saying that he wanted to marry her as she was one of the richest women in England). Then Ottoline Morrell came out onto the terrace and berated Siggy-dear for ordering a second tea. "As meagre a second tea as you'll ever encounter," he complained in turn (she seemed to enjoy his brusque remonstrations). I was introduced—she knew Land: whom does Land not know? Lady Ottoline wore a purple dress with a Paisley shawl and had vivid red hair. She was quite charming to me at first, said I must come again to Garsington, and asked me what my college was. When I said Jesus College she went blank for a second, as if I'd said Timbuktu or John O'Groats, then she recovered herself. "Jesus?" she said, "I don't know anyone at Jesus."

"Perhaps you know my tutor, Philip Le Mayne."

"Oh, him. I should change your tutor if I were you, Mr. Stuarton."

The other guests were straggling up from the lake by now and as they appeared I was introduced (by Siggy, who remembered my name) and so I shook the hands of the Woolfs, Huxley and one of the richest women in England.

"This young man is tutored by Philip Le Mayne," Lady Ottoline said to Virginia Woolf meaningfully.

"Ah, the sanctimonious spider," she said, and everyone chuckled

*See *The Diary of Virginia Woolf. Volume III: 1925–30.*

except me. Mrs. Woolf looked me up and down. "I've upset you, I can see. You probably revere him."

"Not at all." But before I could say any more Lady Ottoline said they must all go up and change. And so Land and I slipped away.

THURSDAY, 30 SEPTEMBER

Movements: July–Deauville (with Mother and Mr. Prendergast). Agreeable house, vile weather. Then London for a while–where we sweltered. August: to Dick's place at Galashiels. Shot at many birds– hit none, I'm glad to say. Set off on my travels, Aug. 20th. Three days in Paris with Ben, then Vichy–Lyon–Grenoble–Geneva. Then to Hyères to stay with Mr. and Mrs. Holden-Dawes at a villa they had taken in the new town. Hyères was very pretty with its castle and its palm trees but there were too many English. There is even an English vice-consul (an old army friend of H-D), an English church and an English physician. James, as I must now learn to call H-D, was his old wry self and imposed a ban on conversations about Abbey. Cynthia is entirely delightful: as a couple they seem very happy and their happiness was contagious–I don't think I've spent a more relaxed ten days anywhere in my entire life. Cynthia practised at the piano in the mornings and I usually took myself off to bathe at Costabelle. They had a very good cook and we dined at home most evenings, talking, drinking, listening to music on the gramophone (very varied: Massenet, Gluck, Vivaldi, Brahms, Bruch). James says he will visit me in Oxford before I leave: I can hardly come to terms with the fact that my final year is about to begin.

Anyway the lodgings here are fine. I have a bedroom and share a sitting room and bathroom with a man called Ash who is reading Life Sciences. Consequently we have little or nothing to talk about and when he's not in his room he is usually down the road at the Victoria Arms or off in a chemistry laboratory near Keble. Our landlord and his wife live on the ground floor below us–Arthur and Cecily Brewer. Mrs. Brewer provides breakfast and the evening meal, luncheon has to be ordered twenty-four hours in advance and costs a 1/6 supplement. I shall not be happy here but I will be content.

In August Peter asked me to go to Ireland with him and Tess on a motoring holiday. I haven't seen Tess since our last Sunday together and the thought of playing gooseberry to "Mr. & Mrs. Scabius" was insupportable. I made an excuse but I think Peter is becoming a little suspicious. He asked me if Tess and I had fallen out in some way—"Every time I mention your name she changes the subject." I said, absolutely not, thought she was a super girl. I think about her now as I write and her generous, uncomplicated sexual nature. She has set something loose in me and even now it strikes me that the nature of your first, all-consuming sexual experience might determine your needs and appetite for the rest of your life. Will I spend years looking for another Tess? Will bitten-down fingernails always be a sign for me, a form of sexual bookmark?

FRIDAY, 12 NOVEMBER

Dinner at the George with Le Mayne and James Holden-Dawes. Cynthia was giving a recital in Antwerp, of all places, so the company was exclusively masculine. We were a bit guarded at first, I thought, and I felt there was a competitive, proprietorial mood in the air generated by the two others—who knew me best, to which did I owe the most, whence the greatest and most lasting influence?—but we were drinking steadily and after the soup and fish we began to relax. Le Mayne and H-D began to swap stories about mutual friends—this one an MP, that one an under-secretary of state, another gone "to the bad." I said I was very impressed by the network of connections, the spymaster in Oxford with his myriad spies abroad, and H-D said, "Oh yes, the web Philip has carefully spun is much larger than most people realize." Then I remembered Virginia Woolf's slight and related the encounter, telling Le Mayne about the hostility his name had provoked at Garsington. He was delighted to hear this—genuinely pleased—and he told us how the resentment had come about.

He had been invited up to Garsington on two occasions: the first time had been unexceptionable ("I had been tested and I had passed," he said) but the second time—in 1924—had been very awkward.

"We were standing around waiting to go into dinner," Le Mayne said, "when from a group behind me I heard a woman say in a loudish voice: 'No, I can put a pretty precise date to it: in December 1910 human character changed.'"

Le Mayne then turned to whoever was beside him and said, without thinking, "If you want a one-sentence example of fatuous stupidity you'll not find a better one than that." And thought no more about it. Then he added, "No. I think, perhaps, I was somewhat more emphatic." Anyway, what happened was that these remarks were reported to Ottoline Morrell who, immediately—a true friend—relayed them to the woman with the loudish voice—Virginia Woolf.

"She'd just given some lecture at Cambridge and was rather pleased with herself and was bandying this notion around to all and sundry. But suddenly I was persona non grata. At the end of the meal Keynes came up to me and asked me what I'd done to Virginia. Ottoline refused to shake hands when I left."

I wondered why, as an eminent novelist, she reacted so badly to criticism.

"Apparently she's incredibly, neurotically sensitive," Le Mayne said.

"It's the kind of mind she has," H-D said. "The fundamental insecurity of the autodidact." He smiled at Le Mayne. "She probably thinks you're too clever by half."

"The ultimate English put-down," Le Mayne said. "I plead guilty."

So we went on to talk about intelligence and its multifarious blessings (Mrs. Woolf taking a few more knocks on the way).

But you can be too intelligent, I said. Sometimes it's not an asset, it's a curse.

"Think your way out of the problem," Le Mayne said. I didn't agree but he wouldn't let me off. "Don't denigrate your brain-power, Logan. You're lucky—you just don't know how lucky you are: ignorance is not bliss."

Then H-D turned the conversation to my future, a little too neatly, I thought, realizing there was some plotting going on. I said I wanted to finish my book on Shelley.

"Do that in your spare time," Le Mayne said. "What about All Souls? You could try for a fellowship."

I laughed that idea away and the meal became too bibulous for serious conversation. But as we were putting our coats on (Le Mayne was still in the dining room talking to someone he knew), H-D said, "Think about it, Logan. Philip rarely offers such encouragement."

"You mean the spider wants one of his men in All Souls."

"Well, there is that, but it's an idea all the same. He obviously thinks you're capable. You don't want to end up a sad old schoolmaster like me."

"But you're happy," I blurted out, thinking of Hyères and his life with Cynthia.

He couldn't help smiling. "Yes," he said. "I suppose I am."

SATURDAY, 13 NOVEMBER

Ash knocked on my door this evening and offered me a bottle of stout. So we drank beer and talked. He was a surprisingly agreeable chap: it turns out he's a golfer and also, incredibly, from Birmingham. He detests Oxford. His father is a circuit judge who insisted he follow in his footsteps. We talked for a good while, mainly about the Birmingham we both knew. Now he's left, I feel unaccountably sad and can't think why. But then I realize that all this talk of golf and Birmingham has made me think, unconsciously, once again, of my father.

1927

MONDAY, 7 FEBRUARY

I'm beginning to wonder if I'm ill. I find it almost impossible to concentrate. I can manage one day of sustained work—which is when I produce my weekly essay for Le Mayne. I cut all lectures and spend most of my time at the cinema. It's as if it's a drug—am I having some kind of nervous collapse? The rot set in at the end of last year and I wonder if I have some sort of lassitude disease. I feel not so much fatigued—I don't fall asleep in the cinema—as deeply unenthusiastic and apathetic. Yet I look well and my appetite is healthy. Thanks to Ash's example I've developed a taste for beer and I can often be found, most evenings, in the Victoria Arms supping ale. I prefer the frowsty anonymity of the public house to the seedy cauldron of Les Invalides and have let my membership there lapse.

Ash thinks it's an intellectual malaise: I should never have read History, he says. True learning only occurs when you love the subject you are studying and then the acquiring of knowledge is effortless because it is also a pleasure. He talks a lot of sense, does Preston Ash. Le Mayne suspects nothing: the competent alpha standard essays roll off the production-line, but since I told him I wasn't interested in All Souls I suspect he's rather given up on me. Ash thinks my desire to please Le Mayne is also symptomatic. He's probably right: why should I care about Le Mayne and his good opinion? To be honest, it's because I have always rather feared Le Mayne.

FRIDAY, 4 MARCH

I calculated that this last week I've been to the cinema twenty-two times. I've seen Diana de Vere in *Fatal Autumn* three times—she has supplanted Laurette Taylor in my Pantheon. Of all the Oxford cinemas I like the Electra best but this week I cycled up to the New in Headington. Ash told me buses will drop you at the door so I can add it into my circuit. On Wednesday I sat through two shows of *Fatal Autumn* at the Electra, cycled up to the New to see *It's All Over* and was back in time to catch *Secrets* at the Super.

TUESDAY, 8 MARCH

I was waiting in the queue after lunch at the George Street Cinema when I felt a tap on my shoulder. It was Tess—I almost keeled over in shock. She looked smart in a black suit and a hat. She said she was a buyer for the nursery now and travelled all over southern England. She held out her hands. "No dirt under my nails," she said, "look." I did, her nails were manicured and polished. Despite the change I felt exactly the same about her—I wanted to be in bed in Islip, drinking gin and fucking. I asked her, trying to seem calm, if she wanted to come for a coffee but she said she had to get back to Waterperry.

"Why don't you come and see us, Logan?" she said. "Peter doesn't know what happened—he'll never know. There's no reason we can't see each other."

"I couldn't see you," I said. "It would drive me mad, being there, not being able to touch you, to hold you."

My words made tears brim in her eyes. Clearly I've seen *Fatal Autumn* far too many times. So we said goodbye and I rejoined the queue. Throughout the film I felt a pure ache of longing for her, like an agonizing stitch in my side.

WEDNESDAY, 27 APRIL

Preston has a motor in a garage at Osney Meade—he never ceases to surprise me. We drove out to Buckingham and played eighteen holes. Preston is an ambitious and reckless golfer: every brilliant stroke exacts a price of three or four duff ones. I took our five bob bet off him easily.

It was a fresh, breezy day, the sycamores and chestnuts almost fully out, the sense of greenness everywhere almost obscenely lush. Amidst all this abundance and new growth I was struck by a sense of waste, a profound feeling that I'd squandered my time at Oxford in some fundamental way. When I think of the final year at Abbey and how we—how I—dreamed of coming here . . . We stopped at a pub in Wendlebury and drank beer and ate pies. I saw a signpost to Islip and almost broke down. Preston, by contrast, and thanks to my company, is enjoying Oxford for the first time in three years.

FRIDAY, 10 JUNE

Well, it's done. Exams are over, there's no going back. I think I acquitted myself well: I'm pleased with most of the papers—no shocking surprises, no panic attacks, all questions were answered. English Political History to 1485—particularly good—as was Charters and Early Constitutional. Economic History—fair. French Translation—surprisingly easy, I thought. Later Constitutional—very good. Political Science was the last exam this morning—I wrote good, concise, fact-heavy answers.

I walked out of Schools with—if not a spring in my step—a feeling of joyful relief. Perhaps I should have worked harder these last months but I felt all the old confidence in my natural ability return after the first couple of papers. Le Mayne asked me how I thought everything had gone and I said, "As well as could be expected." He just smiled and said, "And we both expect great things." He shook my hand. I intend to get riotously drunk tonight.

THE FIRST LONDON
JOURNAL

Logan Mountstuart went down from Oxford University with a third-class degree in History. He was unable to explain how he had performed so badly, and how misconceived his confidence in the result had been. He consoled himself by saying that at least he would have no use for a degree in History for his future life, therefore the result was an irrelevance. He moved back to London, to his mother's house in Sumner Place, where, thanks to the allowance he received from her, he was free to continue with work on his biography of Shelley. However, he began to travel abroad more frequently, spending more and more time with Ben Leeping in Paris. Unlike the first two journals, the First London Journal is extremely cavalier with its dating. All dates within square brackets are educated guesses. The journal begins again some time towards the end of 1928.

1928

[OCTOBER]

SUMNER PLACE

London rain pecking against the window provokes dreams of Paris. I lie here on a sofa, imagining that Ben's new apartment is mine and how I would redecorate it.

Favourite colour: taupe/green.
Favourite piece of furniture: a Louis XIV escritoire.
Favourite painting: Ben's Vlaminck.
Favourite time: cocktails at dusk.

> *Je chante l'Europe, ses chemins de fer et ses théâtres*
> *Et ses constellations de cités . . .*
>
>   [Valéry Larbaud]

Mother is driving me mad, fussing about my meals and what I eat. "I've been away for six weeks," I say, "you have no idea what I eat." *"Exactamente,"* she says. "I don't care: in my house you eat like a proper person." This morning at breakfast she makes Henry serve me a huge plate of bacon, eggs and mushrooms. I'm entirely nauseated. I tell her a coffee and a cigarette is as much as I can manage before luncheon.

Anna.* Anna-mania setting in well and truly and I've only been back a day. The last time was so good and so sad. *Liebesträume*–dreams of love? Love-dreams? Love-dreams of Anna. When she was washing herself in the bidet, I went and stood by the window to look down on the street and there was the Colonel, standing patiently waiting: the little orange glow of his cigarette flaring as he inhaled.

[NOTE IN RETROSPECT. 1955. Anna worked in a high-class *maison de tolérance* called Chez Chantal on the rue d'Assas off the boulevard Montparnasse. It was a clean and well-run house with usually half a dozen girls available. Anna worked Fridays, Saturdays and Mondays. She must have been in her late thirties when I first started going there in the summer of '28. I remember very fine brown hair, which I always asked her to loosen, and which she did, reluctantly. Her skin was very white and beginning to lose its firmness and elas-

---

*Anna Nickolaevna Brogusova: the prostitute LMS regularly frequented in Paris, 1928–9.

ticity. She was unnecessarily bashful about her small plump tummy. She had a high forehead and a long thin nose. She spoke good French and passable English. Her husband, the Colonel, would turn up at the end of her shift and wait for her on the street regardless of the weather. They had lost everything in the Russian Revolution and the civil war. When she emerged he would offer her his arm and the two would wander off towards the Métro station at Montparnasse, a middle-aged bourgeois couple out for a stroll. I often wonder whether these early sexual experiences with Tess and Anna warped me irrevocably.]

[NOVEMBER]

When I give Roderick the typescript of *The Mind's Imaginings* he riffles through it as one would a telephone directory and reads out phrases at random. "I've a feeling this is going to make my name," he says. I say: "Isn't it *my* name you should be concerned about?" He laughs, a little edgily, and apologizes that his ambition should be so transparent. We talk a little about Maurois,* whether it would be a problem. Roderick thinks Maurois has done us a favour—prepared the way, the ideal pathfinder.

I walk home after our lunch (the Ivy) feeling both exalted and strangely bereft. I am twenty-two years old and I have just delivered my first book to my publisher. But I wonder vaguely what I will do with the rest of my life. Write another, of course, you fool.

Once when I came into Anna's room I found a comb left behind on the side of the basin. She was all untypical consternation, blushing like an ingénue and at the same time angry and unsettled. She threw it away in the waste-paper basket. It disturbed her far more than it did me, this evidence of her preceding client. Another day I asked her how

*André Maurois (1885–1967), French writer, had published, in 1923, his own romantic biography of Shelley, entitled *Ariel*.

old she was and she said with a laugh, "Oh, très, très vieille." I wondered what she and the Colonel had lived through since 1917. "Are you
old enough to be my mother?" I asked. She gave it a moment's serious
thought, frowning. "Yes," she said, "if I'd been a very bad girl." She
refuses to meet me outside Chez Chantal, saying it would not be fair
to the Colonel. What she does at Chantal's is closed off, discreet,
extending as far as the front door. Chez Chantal merely represents a
source of funds for her life with her husband, however modest that
may be (why doesn't the Colonel work, I wonder? Or maybe he does,
for all I know). I am a true regular—I don't want any of the other girls—
and when I visit I will wait in the salon until Anna's available. I pay
Madame Chantal 50 francs, which at the current rate of exchange is less
than £2. I give Anna 20 francs extra. She folds the note away carefully
and slips it in a little leather purse she has with one of those zippers. I
like to think I am doing something for their life together. I feel I care
for them both, Anna and her melancholy Colonel.

TUESDAY, 25 DECEMBER

As my Christmas present Mother has increased my allowance to £500
a year. I think we must be very rich: Mr. Prendergast has certainly
worked his magic in the United States. I can live in Paris (visits to Anna
excepted) on a pound a day. Still waiting for news from Roderick.

WEDNESDAY, 26 DECEMBER

Write to Ben asking if I can come and stay in the New Year. Thinking
about starting a novel inspired by what I know of Anna's life. Caution
dictates that I should wait to hear the fate of *TMI* [*The Mind's Imaginings*] first.

1929

[TUESDAY, 1 JANUARY]

LMS resolves:
To leave home, find his own flat, preferably in Paris.
To see more of Land.
To be more ruthless, less compliant.
To work, to write, to live.

THURSDAY, 24 JANUARY

Meet Land for cocktails in the Café Royal. I'm early but I'm happy to sit with my drink and my book covertly watching the show. I feel my time in Paris has given me a wonderful distance on what passes for intellectual circles here in London. It seems to me we have a choice between beery, Little-England journalists (Bennett, Wells) or snobbish aesthetes in their charmed circle (Bloomsbury). I watch the *scribouillards* circle and move from table to table: they take no notice of the slim young man in the corner with his copy of Proust.

Land comes in and as usual is greeted by every third person she passes. She looks tired and tells me almost immediately that she has broken with Bobbie Jarrett. I commiserate—genuinely. She touches my hand and says: you are sweet, Logan. I suggest to her that her job (working as unpaid secretary to a Labour MP)* might have posed something of a problem to Bobbie, son of a baronet and a Tory grandee. She admits I may have a point but she thought that Bobbie was "bigger than that." Nothing disappoints like a lover's failings, I remind her, thinking that the observation would sound better in French. I also said that wasn't it a bit of a waste of her degree (she got a first, of course) sticking stamps on circulars or typing letters? On the

*Oliver Lee, MP for Stockwell South, 1927–55.

contrary: she predicts a Labour government at the next election. I see her on to her underground train for Hampstead and when we kiss goodbye I give her a little hug.

Later. Mother and Mr. Prendergast are having a small dinner party and I can hear laughter from below. Any minute now Mother will be putting some rumba music on the gramophone—yes, there it is. Seeing Land again took me back to Oxford and the still fretful business of my bad degree. I can't explain how I managed to misinterpret my performance so. It really seemed to me that I had done good work; and I insisted as much to Le Mayne when I was summoned to see him—he was wholly unable to keep the disappointment off his face. H-D wrote me a sweet letter saying that anyone's degree result was only an important factor in their life for a maximum of two weeks: thereafter, as was true of all aspects of the human condition, it was up to the individual. Dick Hodge took a second, so did Peter. Cassell didn't even sit the papers. Preston took a first and has decided to stay on at Oxford and do a doctorate. Mother has never once asked me what degree I got: I wonder what she thinks I was doing at Oxford all those three years?

Anna-mania, interestingly enough, has retreated since seeing Land. Suddenly I'm content to stay in London a while longer.

FRIDAY, 15 FEBRUARY

Met up with Dick at Norwich Station (what a rush of memories!) and we travelled on together to Swaffham. Heavy frost on the fields but the low sun was shining strongly, so strongly we pulled down the blinds in the compartment. Angus [Cassell] was at the station to meet us in a rather smart Darracq. Dick had refused to lend me his second gun ("Why not?"–"Get your own.") and so I was obliged to ask Angus for the loan of one (I said mine was being repaired). Angus said the house was full of guns—there would be no problem.

The house is ugly with a vast stable block. It was built in the middle of the last century by his grandfather (the first Earl of Edgefield) but the park is nicely mature, the groupings of trees (rather too many conifers for my taste), the rides and the vistas exactly as they were designed to be seen. The great advantage about a new house is that everything functions properly: hot water, central heating, electric light. I had a bath, changed and went down. The Earl seems harmless enough—hugely bellied, jolly, always humming and wheezing away to himself. He told me to call him Aelthred; something that's beyond me, I'm afraid, though I noticed Dick was very free with the invitation. The Countess, Lady Enid, looks like she's swallowed poison: thin, sour, seamed face, black dyed hair. There were a dozen of us in the party, the young—Angus, his sister, me and Dick—and various elderly locals. At dinner I was placed between Lady Enid and Angus's sister, Lady Laeticia ("Lottie, please"). Lottie is petite, dressed in the latest London styles, but there's something about the set of her features—a broadness of the nose, a thinness of the lips (inherited from her mother), the too wide gap between her eyes—that conspires to keep her the plain side of fairly pretty. She was chatty and vivacious, however, and couldn't hear enough about Paris. "Did you go to a *bal nègre*? Did you meet any lesbians? Are the women too, too beautiful?" Lady Enid, by contrast, interrogated me like an immigration official. Where were you born? Montevideo. Where's that? Uruguay. Still blank. South America. Oh? What were your people doing out there? My father was in business (somehow I did not want to utter the words "corned beef" in this company). Where is your mother from? Montevideo. I could hear her brain working. She's Uruguayan, I said. How wonderfully exotic for you, she said, and turned to the person on her right.

After dinner, Angus apologized, said his mother quizzed everyone like a prosecuting lawyer. I said I thought she was a little disconcerted to find herself sitting beside a half-breed. Angus found this very comical. "Well, if it's any consolation," he said, "Lottie thought you were the bee's knees."

The next day—bone-achingly cold—we shot at birds driven through woods by beaters. Then we had a picnic lunch in a wooden hut and shot some more. I couldn't hit a thing but blasted away energetically to keep up appearances. Dick is a crackshot—birds falling out of the sky. On Sunday I cried off, saying I thought I had a cold coming on, and stayed in the library all morning playing sevens with Lottie (who, I have to say, grows prettier with more acquaintance—she looks better without heavy make-up). But, O!—the brain-numbing tedium of country life. Every now and then Lady Enid would wander in to make sure I wasn't ravishing her daughter on the Chesterfield. Just before lunch the butler announced that there was a telephone call for Mr. Mountstuart. It was Mother: Roderick Poole had rung. "He tell me to say you he like you book."

I could survive anything after that telephone call—the worst that the English pseudo-gentry could hurl at me. I felt I had risen above this bunch of stupid, charmless people (friends excepted, it goes without saying) with their talk about their dogs and their hunting and their boring families. At dinner I sat between a doctor's wife and some cousin of Lady Enid and chatted away to them like an old friend (I have no recollection of a word I said). All I was thinking of was my book. MY BOOK! I was going to have my book published and these stupid people sat around me ignorant of this fact: they could stew in their Philistine juices for millennia as far as I was concerned.

In the morning when we were about to leave Lady Enid drew me aside. She actually smiled at me: she said her cousin had found me charming company, and she added that they were giving a dance for Lottie in the spring—in London—and she would count it a special, personal favour if I would consent to be Lottie's escort for the evening. What could I say? But I made a silent vow to stop accepting these invitations, these importunings: these are not my people, this is not a world I want to inhabit. It's fine for Dick: this is home from home for him—an Anglo version of his Caledonian social whirl—but not for me. Angus is agreeable enough but why should I list him among my true friends just because we were at Abbey together? These are sad English compromises: Paris has made my eyes keener. It will all be behind me soon.

[FEBRUARY]

Sprymont & Drew will pay me a fifty-guinea advance against a 15 per cent royalty. I asked Roderick if this was standard for a first author (to be honest, I didn't really care, all you want at times like these is for the finished book to be in your hand). He recommended that I acquire a literary agent and he suggested a man called Wallace Douglas who had just started up his own firm after some years at Curtis Brown. Roderick and I went to his club (the Savile) to drink champagne. They will publish in the autumn. The Savile is very civilized; I wonder if I should get Roderick to put me up for membership?

Wallace Douglas is a beefy young man (thirty-two? thirty-three?) who speaks slowly with a strong Scottish burr. "Logan Mountstuart?" he said, curious. "Any Scottish blood?" Some generations back on my father's side, I said. Scots are very keen to establish this fact from the outset, I've noticed. He dresses like a banker: three-piece suit, white shirt, institutional tie, his hair oiled and neatly parted. He looks like a burly T. S. Eliot. He agreed to take me on as a client and relieved me of five of my fifty-guinea advance.

"So," he said, "what next?"

"I'm going to Paris for a while."

"Well, what about a few articles? The *Mail*? The *Chronicle*? American magazines want anything on Paris. Shall I try for you?"

I felt a sudden welling-up of warmth for this confident, overweight pragmatist. I have a feeling we will become firm friends.

"Yes, please," I said. "I'll do anything."

I sense my life as a writer—my writer's life, my real life—has truly begun.

MONDAY, II MARCH

I ring Land and suggest lunch. We meet at the Napoletana in Soho and eat meatballs and spaghetti and drink a bottle of Chianti. I tell her my news and the expression of pleasure on her face is one of authentic joy. She is so genuinely pleased for me. I wonder if I could have been quite so generous if the positions had been reversed? . . . We order another bottle of Chianti and—the wine going to my head—I start talking about

Paris and how she should come over when I'm established in my apartment and that my literary agent—how I love to say that: my literary agent—is going to find me work in newspapers and American magazines, and then when my book is published . . . I pause to draw breath and she smiles at me. All I want to do is kiss her.

[MARCH]

Wallace—I call him Wallace, now—has contracted me to write three articles for *Time & Tide* and also, remarkably, for the *Herald Tribune* (on the "Parisian Literary Scene"); £30 for the first and £15 for the second. He says that if these are well received there should be plenty more. I can't wait, and yet I find I am making excuses for putting off my trip. The Land-issue's not resolved: I cannot go to Paris without something being understood, something established between us.

TUESDAY, 2 APRIL

It is late, 11:00 p.m., and I am sitting alone in an empty compartment sipping whisky from my flask as the boat train rumbles out of Waterloo through London's grimy ill-lit suburbs towards Tilbury. I will be in Paris by dawn.

Land and I dined at Previtali's and then she came to the station to see me off. I kept trying to make her fix a date for her visit but all she would talk about was the election, Ramsay MacDonald, Oliver Lee, the constituency and so on. The train was about to leave when I drew her behind a trolley piled with mailbags and said, "Land, for Christ's sake, I love you," and I kissed her. Well, she kissed me back all right: we only stopped when a couple of porters whistled at us. "Come to Paris," I said. "I'll send for you as soon as I'm set up." "Logan, I've got a job." "Come for a weekend." "Let's see," she said. "Write to me." Then she took my face between her hands and kissed the tip of my nose. "Logan," she said, "we have all the time in the world." *Nunc scio quid sit Amor* [Now I know what love is].

[APRIL]

I went to Anna last night at Chez Chantal but somehow it wasn't the
same and she sensed it. "Is everything all right?" she asked. "Tout va
bien?" I assured her it was and pulled her close to me as if to prove it
but it was obvious nothing more was going to happen. I left the bed
and paced about the room. Then I poured myself a glass of wine. Anna
sat up in the bed, her breasts exposed, looking at me patiently.

"Is there somebody else you like?" she asked. "Here in Paris?"

"No. There's a girl in London . . ." I decided to tell her everything.
"I've known her for ages. We were at university together. She's not particularly beautiful. She's intelligent—of course. Her family is fascinating. I can't seem to get her out of my mind."

"Come and tell me all about her."

So I sat on the bed, we drank some wine, smoked a cigarette and I
talked about Land for half an hour. My time was up and when I kissed
her goodbye and pressed myself up against her I knew that my sexual
energies had returned and regretted that I hadn't made the most of my
two hours with her. I said I would see her again in a couple of days (she
was working a five-day week now). But the Land-spell had been broken.

[APRIL]

Move into the Hôtel Rembrandt on the rue des Beaux-Arts. For 50
francs a day I get a small bedroom and a sitting room under the eaves
and I can have a tin bath of hot water whenever I want for an extra 5
francs. It's almost as good as an apartment of my own. Ben has quit his
place on the rue de Grenelle and now lives in a single room above his
new gallery—there is simply no space for me. The gallery is on the rue
Jacob and he's called it "Leeping Frères"—he claims the "Frères" con-
veys a sense of longevity, the notion of a family business. He does have
a brother—Maurice—considerably older than him, a lawyer or an
accountant in London, I believe. Wallace has managed to get me a
monthly piece in the *Mercury* at ten guineas a time. Not wild about the

Mercury—the scent of pipe smoke, beer and wet tweed lingers about it—but beggars mustn't be choosers.

WEDNESDAY, 8 MAY

The Leeping Frères vernissage. I go at 7:00 p.m.—no one there. Ben is very nervous, worried about the quality of the show. He has a Derain, a couple of small Légers, a lot of lurid Russian stuff and a small Modigliani drawing. During the next couple of hours perhaps a dozen people wander in and out but nothing is sold. I buy the Modigliani for £5 and refuse to take a reduction. Ben is cast down and I mutter the usual platitudes, Rome not having been built in a day, and so on.

Anyway, I take him to the Flore for some champagne.

"Look what you've achieved, Ben."

"Look what you've achieved: you've written a book."

"You've got your own gallery in Paris, for Christ's sake. And we're only babies."

"I need cash," he says darkly. "I have to buy now. Now."

"Patience, patience." I sound like a maiden aunt.

A couple—who know Ben—stop by our table and are introduced as Tim and Alice Farino, Americans both. He is tanned and handsome, losing his hair fast. She is small and pretty with a frowning intense face, as if running on too much energy.

"You didn't come to my opening," Ben complains—he obviously knows them well.

"God, I thought it was next week," Farino says, lying easily.

"We forgot," Alice says. "We had a fight. A bad one—we had to make up. You wouldn't have wanted us in your nice new gallery."

Farino reddens immediately, clearly not as languid as he affects to be. We all laugh, the moment defused.

They are here to meet some other Americans and we are asked to join their group at the rear of the café. In the confusion of arrival and because I've drunk too much I don't catch any of the dozen names that are thrown at me. I sit beside a burly square-faced fellow with a moustache. He's very drunk and keeps shouting down the table at a smaller pointy-faced man, "You are full of shit! You are so full of shit!" It seems some sort of infantile joke between them: they both guffaw helplessly. Ben leaves because he sees a girl he knows sitting alone. I drink on in silence, quite happily, nobody taking much notice of me, fresh bottles of wine arriving by magic at the table. Then Alice Farino slides in beside me and asks me how I know Ben and what I'm doing here in Paris. When I tell her I'm waiting for my book to be published she reaches over me and tugs at the sleeve of the square-faced fellow and introduces us. Logan Mountstuart—Ernest Hemingway. I know who he is but I keep it to myself. He can hardly string two words together by this stage and becomes offensively mock English, all "old chap," "old bean," "old sport." Alice says: "Don't be a fucking bore, Hem. You're giving us a bad name." I decide I quite like Alice Farino. I slip away to join Ben, who's with a pale long-faced young French woman with a demure and serious air called Sandrine—I don't catch her last name. I suspect—with the clarity of vision that heavy drinking sometimes produces in me—that Ben has a serious interest in her. He confirms this as I steer him back to rue Jacob. He is infatuated with her, he says, and it's causing him anguish because her father has absolutely no money and she is divorced with a young child, a boy. "I can't marry for love," he says. "It's not part of the plan."

He goes to the lavatory to be sick and I prowl around inspecting the stacked canvasses. This room is even smaller than the one at rue Grenelle—a bed, a desk and chair and a filing cabinet. As I mooch about I spot on the desktop an envelope with familiar handwriting.

"You had a letter from Peter?" I ask when Ben comes back in.

Ben looks vaguely shifty beneath his pallor. "Yes, I was going to tell you—but what with one thing and another . . . He's married Tess."

He hands me the letter. It's true: they are married and living in Reading, where Peter is working as a sub-editor on the *Reading Evening News*. Tess is unreconciled with her parents and Peter has been cut off by his father. He says he has never been happier in his life.

I feel a green stain of envy seep through me, followed by a twinge of worry. Why did Peter write to Ben and not me? Has Tess confessed all?

"There's probably a letter waiting for you in London," Ben says, bless him.

"Probably," I say.

THURSDAY, 9 MAY

I am coming out of my bank (with the money for the Modigliani) when I bump into Hemingway. "Paris is a village," he says, then apologizes for his behaviour, explaining how the presence of a particular friend* always makes him "roaring and meanly drunk." We wander along the boulevard Saint-Germain, enjoying the spring sunshine, and he asks me how I know the Farinos. I explain. "Tim is the laziest man in Europe," Hemingway says. "But she's real cute." We exchange addresses (he's married, it turns out) and agree to meet again. We both have books appearing in the autumn†–he seems quite amiable after all.

FRIDAY, 7 JUNE

Summer has arrived in Paris. I went to Anna's but her room was stifling hot so we made sure our business was over with quickly. I ordered a bottle of Chablis and an ice bucket and we lounged on the bed, chatting and drinking. I told her I was returning to London in the next few days and she said, almost automatically, that she would miss me and she hoped I would be back in Paris soon.

"We are friends, aren't we, Anna?" I said.

"Of course. Special friends. You come here, *on fait l'amour*. We're like real lovers, except you pay."

"No, I mean, it's more than that, different. You know all about my life. I know about you and the Colonel."

"Of course, Logan. And you're very generous."

I wondered if it was some kind of house rule that Madame Chantal imposed: that every declaration of affection, sincere or insincere, had to be counterbalanced by a gentle reminder of the true–fiscal–nature of the relationship. I was a little hurt.

And, for some reason, after I left–it was early evening–I decided to wait. I hid in a doorway until the Colonel arrived. At about 8 o'clock

*F. Scott Fitzgerald (1896–1940) was in Paris at the time.
†*A Farewell to Arms*.

Anna emerged from Chez Chantal and the two of them set off, word-less, arm in arm. I followed them down to the Métro station and entered the carriage behind theirs at the last second. I saw them get off at Les Halles and, taking care not to be seen, watched them from a dis-tance all the way to their apartment building. I noted the number and the street name. Now, I wonder why I did this. What do I expect to gain?

Describe your state of mind. Insecure. Uncertain. Feverish.

Outline your emotions. Sexual obsession. Guilt. Intense physical pleasure at being alone in Paris. Hatred of time: wanting to be this age on this day in this week, this month, this year, for ever. Can only imag-ine the long slow slide awaiting me. Anna-fever vies with Land-fever. But I can satisfy Anna-fever five times a week if necessary. Which seems to provoke Land-fever.

Why are you so obsessed with Paris? In Paris I feel free.

THURSDAY, 13 JUNE

I go back to London tomorrow. This morning, just before lunch, I went back to Les Halles and waited outside Anna's building for about an hour, hoping she'd come out. I wanted to meet her just once, far from the ambience and implications of Chez Chantal; I wanted us to encounter each other casually in the street and I would raise my hat and we'd say good day to each other and exchange a few banalities about the weather and go our separate ways. I needed to add a different dimension to our relationship, something everyday that had nothing to do with a brothel or paid-for sex. But of course she never appeared, my feet began to ache, and I felt a fool.

I was passing a little *bistro du coin*, looking for a bus stop, when I glanced inside and saw the Colonel sitting there, reading a newspaper, a glass of pastis in front of him. Spontaneously, I went in and ordered a beer and sat down casually at the table beside him. Close to, he looked considerably older than Anna—in his fifties I would guess. His clothes were shabby but clean and he wore a yellow bow tie with a matching handkerchief overflowing from his breast pocket. Something of a dandy, then. His little moustache, upswept at the ends, was more grey than black, as was his hair, sleekly oiled back without a part. As he rose to return his newspaper to the rack, I went to claim it. The head-lines were all about Poincaré's* ill-health.

"Sad to be ill on such a beautiful day," I said in French.

He looked at me and smiled—there was no recognition of course. I felt awkward, realizing I had made love to—had fucked—his wife several dozen times: I wanted to blurt it out—how we both cared for Anna in our own way, how we shared her, about all the tips I gave her that were as much to help him—as if it would make us better acquaintances, somehow.

He made some remark about Poincaré being decrepit, anyway, but I couldn't understand because his French was so rapid-fire and collo-quial—impeccable, in fact.

We went back to our seats and struck up a desultory conversation. He could tell I was English, he said, from my accent—adding, in the polite way all French people do, that I spoke their language remarkably well. I fished a bit, said I thought I could detect a slight accent inflect-ing his own speech. I surprised him: he was a Parisian born and bred, he declared. I steered the conversation round to a report in the paper of Communist riots in Germany and said they should call the army out, asking him, by the way, about his own military experience. He said he had enlisted in 1914 but had been rejected because of his bad lungs. I bought him another drink and learned a little more: he had been a travelling salesman but his firm had gone bankrupt, and since then . . . He looked at his watch, said he had to go, shook my hand and left. Clearly no colonel in the White Russian Army, then.

MONDAY, 24 JUNE

SUMNER PLACE

In my absence mother has redecorated my rooms (what strange com-pulsion is this?) and in the process seems to have mislaid half my books. "Oh, I never touch your books, my darling," she says. "Maybe the painter, he steal them." I find them in a box room—and she has

*Prime Minister of France at the time.

hung my Marie Laurencin in the downstairs lavatory. I retrieve it. We have a new motor also, a Ford.

In the morning I go to Sprymont & Drew and, over lunch in a chophouse, Roderick breaks the news to me that they are obliged to delay publication of *The Mind's Imaginings* until the spring of 1930. Publishing programme's too crowded, too many authors taken on—lame excuses of that order. This is vexing: I feel in a kind of limbo—an author but not truly an author, true authorship being conferred by having a book physically published—a thing you can hold in your hand, purchase in a bookshop. Roderick says he has enjoyed my pieces from Paris—perhaps if I wrote a few more they could be collected between hard covers.

"What about a novel?" I say impetuously.

"Well, we'd, ah, of course love a novel . . ." His caution was eloquent. "Though I have to say I never really had you down as a novelist."

"What do you have me down as, Roderick?"

"An extremely talented writer who could turn his hand to novel-writing in an instant." His suavity was back to full strength.

I think it is his scepticism that really inspires me. I will write my novel while I wait for *TMI* to be published. It will be about a young English writer living in Paris, his relationship with a beautiful but older Russian prostitute and the mysterious "Colonel" she claims is her husband. But what title?

I come out of the underground at South Kensington and who should be on the beat but Joseph Darker. We are both pleased to see each other, shake hands warmly and reminisce about the great days of the General Strike. He tells me he now has two children and invites me for tea—still at the same address in Battersea.

[JUNE]

Darker is relaxed in my company, but his wife, Tilda, is very ill at ease, or so it seems to me. It was the same the first time we met. She keeps apologizing: for the quality of the tea, the noise the children make, the state of the back garden. The little boy is called Edward—"After the

Prince of Wales"—and the little girl is called Ethel. We sit in the garden on deck chairs in our shirtsleeves and watch the toddlers potter about. The sun is warm, my stomach is full of fruit cake, and I feel a kind of suburban peace descend on me. Maybe this is how life should be lived? A modest home, a secure job, a wife and family. All these point-less strivings and ambitions—

"Sorry about the cake, Mr. Mountstuart, it's a bit dry."

"It's delicious. And please call me Logan."

"Would you rather have some sandwiches? Only fish paste, I'm afraid."

When she takes the children inside Darker in his turn apologizes for her, which makes matters worse. "She's a good mother," he says. "Works hard, keeps the house clean." Then he turns to me. "And I love her dearly, Logan. Meeting Tilda was the making of me." I can't think how to respond to this declaration. "You're a lucky man, Joseph," I say, in the end. "I hope I have half your luck." He puts his hand on my shoulder, gives it a squeeze. "I hope so," he says, visibly pleased.

He's a sincere man, Joseph Darker, but I question my own attitudes, not through any doubt about them, but to put them to the test. I'm not patronizing him, not trying to prove what a good egalitarian fellow I am, here, having tea with a humble policeman. I wouldn't brag about this visit—as I know someone like Hugh Fothergill would, wearing such a friendship like a badge. So, why are you here? He invited me and I accepted. I assume I did so because we both derive something from each other's company.

[SEPTEMBER]

Summer travels. July—Berlin with Ben, gallery haunting. On his advice I bought a small jewel-like watercolour by an artist new to me called Klee. Furious street battle between political gangs one night. On by train to, finally, Vienna—travels in the Tyrol—Kufstein, Hall, Kitzbühel. Then Salzburg—Bad Ischl—Gmunden—Graz. August—Scotland, as usual, to Kildonnan by Galashiels. Dick's shooting party larger than ever. I abandoned all pretence and declared myself non-combatant and passed the time walking and fishing or taking bus journeys up the

Tweed Valley to the little solid mill towns set in their gentle hills. Much drinking and merriment in the evening. Angus [Cassell] and Lottie were there. Lottie clearly smitten with me. One evening we were left alone in the drawing room and I—a little drunk—kissed her. I apologized discreetly the next morning but she would hear none of it.

Memory: a day of intense but fresh heat. I walk up the bank of a shallow, rushing, tea-brown river, a tributary of the Tweed, a rod in my hand looking for a pool. Seen from the glare of the sunshine, the shade beneath the riverine trees looks as ink-dark as a cave mouth. I find my pool and stog my beer bottle in an eddy at the water's edge and fish for an hour, catching three little trout, which I throw back. Eat bread and cheese, drink my icy beer and walk home across the fields to Kildonnan with the sun on my back. A day of total solitude, of tranquil and perfect beauty by the river. A form of happiness I must try to recapture more often.

TUESDAY, 22 OCTOBER

Goodish progress on the novel: it won't be long but it should be very intense and moving. Still no idea how it will end, no notion of a title. Proofs of *TMI* arrive. Soon I'll be there—soon.

I go to Hampstead for dinner at the Fothergills'. Land looks tired, says she is working too hard—Lee is very busy in the new government.* She introduces me to a man called Geddes Brown—thirtyish—a painter. Alarm bells ring: he's lithe and muscled like a prizefighter with blond curly hair. Something about his demeanour proclaims huge self-confidence.

I feel very relaxed with the Fothergills—my ideal alter-family. How different would I have been if I had been brought up in this environment? I talk to Vernon about my trip to Berlin and tell him of my purchase of a Paul Klee (Paul who? he asks—the blessed insularity of England's culture). Geddes Brown knows who Paul Klee is, all right, and we get an impromptu ten-minute lecture. He congratulates me on

*Ramsay MacDonald had formed the second Labour government in June.

my taste: suddenly I'm all right in his eyes. Then Hugh talks politics at me and I nod and agree that Mussolini is a monster, reaching across the table to light Ursula's umpteenth cigarette. But where are Land and Geddes Brown? Out on the terrace looking at the stars. Ah-ha.

WEDNESDAY, 30 OCTOBER

Mother seemed a little alarmed by a telegram from Mr. Prendergast in New York. She read it out: "Financial chaos on stock market. Urgent need for cash." "Cash?" she said. "I have no cash." Borrow some from a bank, I said, then went upstairs to work on my novel. And suddenly the title came to me: *The Girl Factory*.

1930

WEDNESDAY, I JANUARY

With a mild hangover I greet the new decade and the new year. (Last night: cocktails at the Fothergills', dinner with Roderick at the Savoy, midnight at the 500 Club. Bed by 3:00 a.m.)

Review of 1929. Love affair with Paris. The bliss of my rooms in the Hôtel Rembrandt. Anna-mania and the Anna/Colonel enigma. Concentration of feelings for Land. "Concentration of feelings." Pshaw! Growing *love* for Land. Acceptance of *TMI*. Beginning of *TGF*. The frustrations of delay. Serious, fairly lucrative journalism.

    Friends made: Alice Farino, Joseph Darker, Lottie Edgefield (?)
    Friends in limbo: Peter, Tess, Hugh Fothergill.
    Friends lost: none.

Conclusion: a year of promise—achievement still frustratingly out of reach. The real start of my career as a writer. Money earned. 1929 proves I can live by the pen.

SUNDAY, 5 JANUARY

Mother announces dramatically at dinner that we have lost the apartment in New York.

ME: What apartment, pray?
MOTHER: My apartment on 62nd Street. Mr. Prendergast say it is lost.
ME: You've mislaid your apartment?
MOTHER: We cannot pay the loan. The bank has taken it.
ME: Shame. How I would have liked to have seen it one day. Why don't you get Mr. P. to sell some of your shares?
MOTHER: This I don't understand. We have all these shares but he say they are worth nothing. Nothing at all.
ME: Shall I mix you a cocktail?

[MARCH]

85A, Glebe Place, Chelsea. My new address. I've rented a furnished garden flat just off the King's Road. Bedroom, bathroom, kitchen, dining room and a spare bedroom that will be my study. I shipped my books and paintings round and now all I need is a few rugs and throws to make the place my own. A Mrs. Fuller comes in three times a week to "do" for me and she says her husband will look after the garden—and all this for £6 a month. I draw the curtains, light the fire and open a bottle of wine. Apparently Cyril Connolly and his wife are near neighbours.* Good progress on *The Girl Factory*.

*Cyril Connolly (1903–1974), critic and writer. He and his wife, Jean, were currently living at 312A, King's Road.

THURSDAY, 27 MARCH

The Mind's Imaginings is published today. As a symbolic gesture I went into town and bought a copy at Hatchard's. A handsome little book with faded purple covers and a small idealized portrait of Shelley by Vernon Fothergill as a frontispiece. Luncheon at L'Étoile with Roderick and Tony Powell—who is working at Duckworth's. On the tube home I kept taking the book out and looking at it, feeling its weight in my hand, opening it at random and reading a sentence or two. I kept going back to the author's notice: "Mr. Mountstuart is a graduate of Oxford University and is currently writing a novel." Why, though, do publishers have to advertise other books on the back cover? I think it sullies the integrity of my own. I don't want to know that Cuthbert Wolfe has written an "arresting and important" new biography of Disraeli. What are you doing on my lovely new book, Cuthbert Wolfe?

This is typical of my current mood: both flat—not a single review so far—and elated—I have the book in my hand; I bought it in a bookshop. But suddenly I want to be with Land, or Anna—or even Lucy. Instead I go round to Mother, who, although she said she would be inconsolable if I left, is already planning to transform my rooms into her studio.

"Studio? To do what?"

"I don't know, my darling. To paint, to sculpture, to dance."

SUNDAY, 13 APRIL

Nice review in last week's *Times Literary Supplement*—"Engaging and spirited." "Shelley as we can believe he truly was"—the *Herald*. "Knocks Maurois into a cocked hat. At last we have an English Shelley"—the *Mail*. I ring Roderick to discover that sales are disappointing—so far only 323 copies sold. "But these reviews," I say. "Can't you take some advertisements?" He mutters something incomprehensible about seasonal budgets and a spring deficit. Letters of congratulation from H-D and, amazingly, Le Mayne. The only problem is that I seem to have lost interest in my novel. I've written around 200 pages. I think I might just kill off the Anna-figure with tuberculosis or some other lugubrious disease.

[APRIL]

First dinner party at Glebe Place. The Connollys, Land, H-D and Cynthia, Roderick and a young poet he's infatuated with called Donald Coonan. Quite a success, I think: soup, leg of lamb, a trifle, cheese. Plenty to drink. And a good deal of flattering talk about *TMI,* as the reviews continue to be good. Connolly says he'll try and review it for the *New Statesman.* He's prickly at first, but mellows soon enough. We were amused to discover we had both left Oxford with a third-class History degree. "Fail early," I said, "then the only way is up."

Land was the last to leave and we kissed at the front door. A gentle kiss—a potential lover's kiss? I walked her up to the King's Road and we hailed a taxi. She said she would be in Paris for the month of August, trying to improve her French. What a coincidence, I said, so will I.

THURSDAY, 22 MAY

Collected *The Girl Factory* from the typists and took it to Roderick at S & D. He seemed surprised to see it completed. "I do like the title," he said, then, his craven caution returning, "but it's not too racy, is it? We can't afford to risk having a book banned." I said it was exceptionally racy but deliberately placed within the bounds of propriety. He suggested I do a life of Keats next—"Shelley's going very nicely," he said.

WEDNESDAY, 28 MAY

I should have said that Wallace was actually irritated that I'd personally delivered the typescript. "It's like taking away my sword and replacing it with a dagger." I said I didn't understand. "I can still draw blood but it's not as easy." Anyway, Sprymont & Drew offered £100 but Wallace managed to bump them up to £150 by saying both Duckworth and

Chapman & Hall were desperate to read it. On the strength of this we lunched at Quaglino's. Wallace has found me more work with the *Weekend Review* and the *Graphic*. We jotted down a list of subjects that I felt qualified to write about: the English Romantic poets, golf, South America, Paris, Spain, Oxford, sex, British History from the Norman Conquest to Cromwell's Protectorate, modern art and corned beef. "What a multifaceted fellow you are," Wallace said, with more than a hint of his usual dryness. The more I know him the more I come to like him. He treats his job, it seems to me, as a kind of amusing challenge, a source of entertainment. His tone is very deadpan, very Buster Keaton. Sales of *Imaginings* beginning to climb—over a thousand now. I have the impression it's being talked about. Cyril [Connolly] introduced me the other evening and said, "You must know Logan's Shelley book."

MONDAY, 21 JULY

Very large party at Lady Cunard's.* I felt a little overwhelmed: my first true social outing. Waugh was there, Harold Nicolson, Dulcie Vaughan-Targett, Oswald Mosley, Imogen Grenfell . . . Waugh congratulated me on the Shelley. I congratulated him on *Vile Bodies*. He pointed out William Gerhardi to me and said he was the most brilliant writer alive. He told me at some length that he was taking instruction with a view to becoming a Roman Catholic and started banging on about infallibility and Purgatory. I had to cut him short, said I knew all about it. He seemed startled to discover I was RC. I assured him I was well and truly lapsed and he scurried off looking sheepish. Why on earth should a man like that want to change his faith at his age?†

---

*Lady Maud "Emerald" Cunard (1872–1945), society hostess, mother of Nancy.
†Waugh was twenty-seven and had recently been divorced from his first wife.

FRIDAY, 8 AUGUST

Paris. Back in the good old, familiar old Hôtel Rembrandt. Unseasonal rain darkens the pavements and a nagging wind makes the shutters bang. Land arrives next week. *Tu ne me chercherais pas si tu ne m'avais trouvé* [You would not be looking for me if you did not possess me. Pascal]. I went out at six, had a drink at Lipp and then strolled down to Montparnasse to meet Ben at the Closerie des Lilas. I was early and hadn't thought of going in to Chez Chantal—thoughts of Land were uppermost in my mind—but, seeing as I was in the neighbourhood, I ducked in none the less. Madame Chantal greeted me warmly and offered me a choice of the three girls lounging around in their satin lingerie. "You know I only like Anna," I said. "But Anna has gone," she replied, explaining that Anna had said she was leaving and didn't need to "work" anymore. She had no idea where she was.

I felt shocked and then saddened. Life does this to you sometimes—leads you up a path and then drops you in the shit, to mix a metaphor. I thought of my days of Anna-mania, of how her story had inspired *The Girl Factory*. I realized I had thought—selfishly—that Anna would always be there, that she couldn't just disappear, as if part of a conjuring trick. I was a little subdued at dinner but Ben was on good form, the gallery beginning to show signs of life, and much talk of Sandrine. Apparently her little boy is charming. I hear the distant chime of wedding bells.

SATURDAY, 9 AUGUST

To Les Halles. I ask the concierge of Anna's apartment block if she still lives here but am told that she and her "uncle" have moved on, destination unknown. I sit in the little *bistro du coin* where I met the Colonel, feeling both bereft and baffled—and also, after some reflection, a little annoyed with myself. Did I expect Anna to forward her new address to her regular clients? To have escaped from that life must be an unmitigated blessing. Anna will be fine, she has her own life to lead. I should concentrate on Land.

TUESDAY, 12 AUGUST

Most uncomfortable. I wonder if what I ate last night is the cause *(blan-quette de veau)*? Whatever it was, when I went to the lavatory this morn-ing it was like shitting sulphuric acid. A burning, itching arse-crack all day that hadn't eased off all that much by the time I turned up at Land's for dinner. She's staying for a month at the home of a business-man and art collector called Émile Berlanger (a great patron of Vernon Fothergill), ostensibly to improve her French. The Berlangers live in a large apartment on the avenue Foch, full of mediocre landscapes amongst which Vernon's did at least stand out. Land's hair is different from the last time: she has dyed it ink black, which, curiously, makes her look a ravishing sixteen. The Berlangers were charming, their excruciating good manners a form of inhibiting social armour—one felt one could hardly move, that a scratch or a sniff would be the ultimate *faux pas*. Consequently, I was achingly conscious of my fiery bum. There was also a man there called Cyprien Dieudonné,* who said he was a writer. "But my day has long gone," he said, in excellent English. "If this was, oh, 1910 you might have been just a little curious to meet me." He was plump and genial with an almost perfectly round face. Wispy fair hair thinning fast. He gave me his card.

[AUGUST]

Took Land to meet Ben at the gallery. It seemed to go well: Ben said to her, "We must compare notes, get my Logan-file up to date." As Land wandered around looking at the paintings, she said, "Geddes would love this. He must come."

"Geddes?"

"Geddes Brown, silly. He's in Paris too."

---

*Cyprien Dieudonné (1888–1976), belletrist and poet. Part of a group known as Les Cosmopolites, which included Valéry Larbaud, Léon-Paul Fargue, Henry Levet, etc.

Now this is bad news. Ben is going to Bandol for two weeks and has asked me to join him—and I'm very tempted. But I can't leave Land in Paris with Geddes Brown.

[AUGUST]

Lunch at the Brasserie Lutetia with Land and Geddes Brown. They seemed very at ease with each other and there was a joke they shared—something to do with Hugh and one of the dogs—that had them weeping with recollected laughter. When I asked them about it, they said it was too complicated to explain.

Later, Land told Brown about Ben's gallery and then added the suggestion that Ben might be the ideal dealer for him—and in Paris, no less.

"Wouldn't that be wonderful, Logan?"

"What? Ah . . . Yes, wonderful."

"Let's go and see him. Now, this afternoon."

All this zeal for Geddes Brown, who sat there chewing placidly on his steak. I told her Ben had gone south, to the Mediterranean. In fact he's due to go in a couple of days, but I was damned if I was going to do Geddes Brown any favours. Instead, we went to his studio, a dingy little place down by the Bastille. All he seemed to be painting were small dark portrait heads of his neighbours: strong angular faces, stylized with lots of black in them. I have to admit they weren't bad.

MONDAY, 25 AUGUST

This is getting ridiculous. Here I am sweltering in Paris in August trying to snatch the odd moment with Land, just wasting my time. The Berlangers have a house in Trouville where they spend August, M. Berlanger returning to Paris for a day or two when business calls, so Land is rarely here. But at least if she's absent I console myself that she's also absent from the loathsome Brown. I think it's his physical combination of svelte muscular presence and cherubic, spilling blond curls that I find so repugnant.

I should say I dined with Dieudonné—a wholly relaxed, sophisticated yet diffident man. He confesses to being *follement anglophile,* but one knows that any liking he has for us is qualified by the shrewdest eye. He talked of Les Cosmopolites and the literary scene in France before the war, of their obsession with foreign travel, their dandyism, their celebration of *le style anglais,* their appreciation of the comforts that a little money could bring, the almost sexual thrill of being out of your own country: an outsider, *déraciné,* worldly, nomadic. I was entranced and envious. He said he would introduce me to Larbaud, who had translated *Ulysses* and was very close to Joyce ("a difficult man to know"). Dieudonné is obviously independently wealthy himself, you can tell that from one glance at his clothes: everything, right down to his co-respondent boots, is bespoke. He writes about "two or three little articles a year," he says, and has abandoned poetry, "a young man's vocation." His life is steeped in culture, self-indulgence and the exotic. He spent half of last year in Japan and said it was a completely fascinating place. I quizzed him more about Les Cosmopolites. Oh, that world has gone, he said, the war changed everything. When I think of my youth, he went on, what we took for granted, what we assumed was for ever certain, for ever permanent. I was captivated: this was the literary life I should have lived; I should have been born two decades earlier. Imagine what I would have done with my £500 a year! I could have had a manservant follow me around. I felt the glimmering of an idea for my next book.

[AUGUST]

Still here in Paris. I've decided to go back at the end of the week. What a waste of a month. I haunt the *bouquinistes* on the quays beside the Seine, buying up anything I can find by Larbaud, Fargue, Dieudonné, Levet, et al. I found Larbaud's *Poèmes par un riche amateur*—utterly captivating. *The Cosmopolitans* by Logan Mountstuart—I like the sound of it. I wonder what Wallace will think? Geddes Brown actually asked me to dinner but I made an excuse—said I had a cold.

[AUGUST]

Viens dans mon lit
Viens sur mon cœur
Je vais te conter une histoire
[Blaise Cendrars]

Sex-dreams of Land. Chez Chantal holds nothing for me now. I wander alone in this dusty, sun-basted, beautiful city, staring at the tourists as if they were alien beings from a distant planet. I carry with me my little pile of slim volumes and read the work of Les Cosmopolites in cafés and at my solitary dinners, lost in a world of *wagons-lits,* the Trans-Siberian express, foggy northern cities, the perfect idyll of under-populated islands in the sun. I dream of being in a sleeping car with Land, lying naked side by side in our bunk, heading south through the night, the champagne bottle chinking in its ice bucket, lulled to sleep by the rhythmic thrum of the wheels on the tracks beneath us. *"Le doux train-train de notre vie paisible et monotone."*

Land has written: she is coming to Paris on Monday for a dental appointment. Any possibility of us lunching together?

MONDAY, 1 SEPTEMBER

So I decided to stay on, just to have the chance of seeing Land one more time. I met her outside the dentist's (on the rue du Faubourg Saint-Honoré), where she had had a large filling replaced, so she told me. We wandered over to the Left Bank and had lunch at the Flore—an omelette, a salad, a bottle of wine. I told her about Dieudonné and Les Cosmopolites. The wine—and the fact that I was going home the next day—emboldened me.

"Land," I said. "I have to know about Geddes."

"What do you mean? He's a friend. And I happen to admire him enormously."

"But do you love him?"

"I suppose I must. In a friendly sort of way."

"And he loves you, no doubt. How cosy."

"I hate it when you're sarcastic, Logan. You seem a different person."

"You can hardly blame me."

She looked at me with resignation and pity. "What's going on?"

"You know how I feel about you," I said, "and yet you flaunt this Geddes Brown at me. If he's the one for you, then make the choice. Don't torture me like this."

She silenced me. "I thought you were meant to be the sophisticated, man-of-the-world writer," she said, trying not to smile. "Geddes is a homosexual."

"A homosexual?"

I will never forget this afternoon. Land and I came back to the Hôtel Rembrandt. The shutters were closed against the heat. The sheets had been changed and we stripped off our clothes and for a minute enjoyed the bed's cool starched crispness on our naked bodies before our sweat besmirched it. Land, with her fringe and her girl's uptilted breasts. Kissing her and tasting on my tongue the metallic spearmint flavour of that morning's dental work. Watching her dress and noting how her buttocks and haunches were heavier than I had imagined. I savour the fact that I am now a familiar of all the singularities of Land. I saw her off on the train back to Trouville, an oratorio playing in my head.

It's only now as I sit here that I wonder if I am the first. There is no small bloom of blood on the sheets. I've no idea.

[SEPTEMBER–OCTOBER]

Movements. After Land I couldn't go back to London. To Bandol to stay with Ben. Then London for a fortnight, then to Vienna, a commission for *Time & Tide*. Leisurely journey back: Berlin–Amsterdam–Brussels–Paris (more research on Les Cosmopolites)–London. Land is sharing a flat with two girlfriends in Islington.

WEDNESDAY, 31 DECEMBER

Land is downstairs. She's told her parents and her flatmates she is going to a house party in Carmarthenshire. We have three days to ourselves. Enough food and drink to last a month-long siege and no plans to venture out.

1931

SUNDAY, 22 FEBRUARY

Spent the day going over the proofs of *The Girl Factory*. I feel curiously distanced from the book: it has a certain melodramatic, low-life allure (my hero Lennox Devane is completely under the spell of Lydia—the Anna-figure—she could make him brand himself if she asked) and I think I have the authentic atmosphere of Paris, but, true to its compositional history, it rather fizzles out. There is a nice hinted-at incest theme: the Colonel is known as "uncle" in the book and he runs a string of "nieces"—hence the title—in other *maisons de tolérance* around town. At the novel's end Lennox manages to turn him in to the police, allowing Lennox and Lydia to flee to Innsbruck (of all places), where Lydia dies of tuberculosis.

Land telephoned this morning to say she's been offered the chance of going to India on some parliamentary fact-finding committee— something to do with Gandhi and the Congress Party.* I magnanimously said she should go, shouldn't let such an opportunity pass by, and all that. I will miss her, of course, but I do need to concentrate on

*Mahatma Gandhi (1868–1948) had recently been released from prison and was participating in the Round Table conference with the Viceroy of India.

my work—I've about four articles overdue, including a long and rather important one on Cubism for the *Burlington Magazine*.

Feeling of contentment pottering around Glebe Place all day. Fire on, proofs spread on the dining-room table. Land was here on Friday and the house still seems redolent of her presence, not least suggested by the powerful scent from the pot of hyacinth she brought—and she left a scarf behind her. Memories of lovemaking on Saturday morning, also, and of our eating toast and marmalade in our rumpled bed, the teapot steaming on the bedside table. After she left I wandered down to the river at lunchtime and had a pint of beer and a steak pie in the Eight Bells. Then back to continue the proofs. I have over £800 in the bank and the prospect of another £50 arriving on publication day (less Wallace's commission of course). I love Land and she loves me, I have published one book and my second is imminent, and I'm not quite twenty-five years old. When I think of all my doom and gloom on leaving Oxford! H-D was right: after a fortnight your degree ceases to have any bearing on your progress through life. Look at Waugh, look at Connolly, look at Isherwood and myself: it would seem almost *de rigueur* to take a bad degree in order to make your way as a man of letters.

[MARCH]

At Sumner Place today I was introduced to an elderly couple, Major and Mrs. Irvine, who, it transpires, are now living in my rooms on the top floor. "Paying guests," Mother says, and she goes on to tell me of other problems engendered by the Crash of '29. Mr. Prendergast, it seems, had invested almost all her capital in American stocks—which are now more or less worthless.

"So what do you have left?" I ask.

"Well, I have the house, but income is low. I borrow a lot from the bank. Like you told me."

I persuaded her to sell the motor and let all the staff go except Encarnación. Apparently she had even borrowed money to pay my allowance. I told her I no longer needed any subvention from her and wrote her a cheque for a hundred pounds to cover any immediate shortfall. I asked for Prendergast's address—he is still in New York, trying to rescue anything from the ruins.

"He is a broken man," she said with tears in her eyes.

"Don't cry, Mother. Everything'll be fine."

"Oh yes, I know. But I keep thinking: what would your father say?"

[APRIL]

Publication of *The Girl Factory*. The success of *Imaginings* prompted immediate reviews. "Tawdry and shameful"—the *Mail*. "A nastily unpleasant little shocker"—*The Times*. "Mr. Mountstuart's manifest talent lies in the field of biography; we suggest he leaves fiction in surer hands"—the *Criterion*. Thank God Land is away in India.

MONDAY, 27 APRIL

Celebratory luncheon at the Savoy Grill: LMS, Wallace, Roderick and Mr. Sprymont of Sprymont & Drew himself, come to see his cash-cow with his own eyes. Wallace and I bask comfortably in the flow of compliments. Almost 11,000 copies have been sold in three weeks, a fifth reprint is in hand. On the strength of this Wallace has sold the book to the U.S. (Decker, Pride & Wolfson) and France (Cahier Noir). Sprymont & Drew are begging for another novel. Wallace cleverly allows them to think this might indeed be a possibility (I let him speak for me on these occasions—grand vizier to my emperor) but suggests that before a novel Logan wants to write a book called *The Cosmopolitans*, don't you, Logan?

"I do like the title," says Roderick.

"So do I," echoes Mr. Sprymont, almost reaching for his cheque book. "What's it about? De luxe travel? The millionaire style of life?"

"It's a study of a group of French poets before the Great War."

By the end of the meal they can see there is no hope of dissuading me and they feign a kind of enthusiasm. As Wallace and I stand in Savoy Court, our cigar smoke thick as ectoplasm in the spring sunshine, Wallace says he's looking forward to the negotiations: he intends to set a new benchmark for the advance paid for a book of literary criticism.

[APRIL]

Land is home but has almost immediately gone–with Lee–up north to Durham or Sheffield or somewhere to speak to the starving families of unemployed miners. £500 advance for *The Cosmopolitans*. *TGF* has sold 17,500 copies and no sign of slowing down. I am despised by my literary peers–but I can cope with their disdain.

THURSDAY, 14 MAY

Lunch with Land at the Ritz. I want to celebrate, but she says she would have preferred a sandwich in Green Park or a pie in a pub–anywhere but the Ritz. She regales me with the horrors of poverty in the north and the mood is rather cool as a result–she seems not remotely interested in my success or my new wealth. She says Lee has warned her that the German banks are on the verge of collapse* and if that happens then the whole of Europe could fall apart. I sit and listen and let her rant on as I drink most of the champagne. She comes home with me to Glebe but it can't be described as a satisfactory night. I am too amorous and, being rebuffed, become clinical. She leaves at six this morning with hardly a word of goodbye. I'll give her some time.

MONDAY, I JUNE

Today I asked Land Fothergill to marry me and she said no.

[The First London Journal ceases at this point for some sixteen months. The Girl Factory *continued to sell. LMS made his first visit to New*

---

*In fact they collapsed in July.

York in September for the American publication and in October he sold the film rights to British Clarion Film Co. for £1,000. He spent June and July 1931 in France, where he continued his researches for The Cosmopolitans. *In the summer he visited Cyprien Dieudonné in his home in Quercy in the Lot. August saw his return to London and, as had become his habit, he went to Scotland to join Dick Hodge's shooting party at Kildonnan by Galashiels. Lady Laeticia Edgefield (Lottie) and her brother Lord Angus Cassell were there also. In the weeks and months that followed LMS began to see much more of Lottie Edgefield–they became a well-known couple in London social circles and were frequently mentioned in gossip columns ("Who's the Girl in Logan's Girl Factory?"). He proposed marriage to her in March 1932. The engagement was to be a short one, the wedding being scheduled for Saturday, 26 November 1932, in the parish church, St. Andrew's, in Edgefield, Norfolk.]*

1932

MONDAY, 31 OCTOBER

To Byrne & Milner* for the final fitting of my dress suit. Seamus Byrne's flattery just fails to convince, as always: "Now that is what I call a perfect fit, Mr. Mountstuart." Still, I've used the visits to be measured for four more suits—a dark charcoal pinstripe, single breasted; a midnight blue, double breasted; a pea-green tweed, three-piece; and a lightweight Prince of Wales check. £300 all in. Lunch with Peter at the Ivy. Tess and the baby† live in a cottage outside Henley and Peter commutes to town, staying up whenever he's on the night shift. I offered

*LMS's tailors in Maddox Street, London WI.
†At some stage in 1932 the two had met again. Peter Scabius was now an assistant editor at *The Times*. Peter and Tess's son, James, was born in 1931.

him my sofa at Glebe but he has an arrangement with a bed & break-fast near Paddington Station. He was full of the joys of married life but for me the pleasure was to note that our old friendship had picked up again quite naturally with no residual reserve or bad feeling. It's true: lives do drift apart for no obvious reason. We're all busy people, we can't spend our time simply trying to stay in touch. The test of a friend-ship is if it can weather these inevitable gaps. He's full of curiosity about Lottie—"An earl's daughter! My God, moving up in the world, Logan"—and Tess, he says, is looking forward to the wedding enor-mously. Peter has to write a third leader on Mosley and the BUF.* I told him I'd met Mosley and had been impressed with the man—mind you, he'd been a Labour politician then. Why do politicians love uni-forms?—all these funny little men in Europe in their pantomime cos-tumes. Still, a fair amount of what Mosley says, in the current climate, can't be dismissed as fanaticism or bombast—he's no Mussolini. Peter is not convinced.

Then on to tea with Lottie and Enid (as I must now learn to call her) at Claridge's. Enid is all smiles—why should it worry me that she likes me so? The wedding looms: how I long for the day to be over and done with. Mother in a panic over what to wear (and I can't explain to her that I won't become a Lord by marrying a Lady). The whole of Norfolk seems to be invited. Dick Hodge said he thought I was making a "grade-A blunder" in marrying Lottie. One expects this sort of brutal advice from Dick but not days before the marriage—he really does go too far sometimes.

FRIDAY, 25 NOVEMBER

Final preparations over. Mother and I are staying in an hotel at Swaffham. We were offered any number of houses, but I couldn't bear to be a guest of some stranger at this particular time. Cold and windy day, the autumn leaves whipped from the trees. Coming back from a walk this afternoon I saw a vast flock of starlings—like a huge shoal of

*The British Union of Fascists, founded in 1931.

fish—darting this way and that, the collective mass shifting and changing all the while, as if there were some single intelligence governing the individual bird-minds.

And I'm assailed by terrible doubts. Lottie is a sweet and lovable girl but again and again I find myself wondering about Land: I want to know more than anything what she must be feeling now. I didn't invite any of the Fothergills, deliberately, but I did invite Geddes Brown—equally deliberately (he couldn't come, but sent rather a nice drawing as a wedding present). I believe—I must believe—that I'm not marrying Lottie simply to wound Land. I'm marrying Lottie because I am ready for marriage and I love her and Land wouldn't have me. It was hardly on the rebound, in any event. Last summer when Lottie and I met again I was completely over Land's rejection.

WEDNESDAY, 30 NOVEMBER

Monte Carlo. Hôtel Bristol et Majestic. Lottie is having a nap in our room and I am sitting in the foyer scribbling these lines. The honeymoon is well and successfully under way. She is so sweet and lovely, my new wife. We spent our first night at Claridge's (Lottie was a virgin—she said she was sore—Land never said this. I must stop thinking and writing about Land). The next day we caught the boat train to Paris and came on overnight on a sleeper to this curious little principality.

The wedding was—all right, I suppose. I made Angus my best man so as not to have to choose between Ben, Peter and Dick (who were all ushers). The strangest thing was seeing Tess again, now so smart and prosperous-looking in her wide hat and fur coat. When we spoke she looked me straight in the eye and every conversation seemed to have its secret subtext. I know she has told Peter nothing, just as I know she is still attracted to me. I must say the locals are a dire bunch. Some of Lottie's friends from London seem more interesting but I dread the thought that when we move this will become our social circle. I've just ordered a brandy and soda. I shouldn't drink this early in the afternoon but, what the hell, I am on my honeymoon.

[DECEMBER 1932–JANUARY 1933]

Movements. Monte Carlo–La Spezia (to see Shelley's last house at Lerici)–Pisa–Sienna–Rome. Rome–Paris (on an aeroplane–this is the way to travel). Paris–London. London–Thorpe Geldingham.

1933

[FEBRUARY]

Thorpe Hall, Thorpe Geldingham, Norfolk. Our home is halfway between Swaffham and Norwich. "Hall" sounds a little grand for what is in fact a perfectly agreeable two-storey, redbrick farmhouse, Georgian, but with bay windows and a porch added in the last century to make it seem more substantial and justify the epithet "Hall." This is our wedding present from Aelthred and Enid. The garden is about two acres and has a stream at its bottom that runs into a large pond–today quite frozen over. We are in dead of winter and one's mood is correspondingly moribund.

Lottie and her mother spend all day buying furniture and meeting decorators while I sit in my study and pretend to work. I had to let Glebe Place go–there was no justifying the expense of keeping up a London house, empty–and all my books and paintings, my rugs and throws, are assembled in this small room with its view of the frozen grey garden. I realize I own very few possessions. Everything we have here in Thorpe, or almost everything, has been provided by my parents-in-law: the house, its furnishings, the motor car in the barn. Lottie is adorable, so excited to be creating this home for the two of us. She's started calling me Logie–which I can just about bear in the privacy of the marital bed–but I heard Enid say this morning, "Perhaps Logie's dressing room should be panelled?" I couldn't stand being Logie Mountstuart to the whole of Norfolk.

I walk around "my" garden. We have a gardener, a cook and a house-maid. I go into my study and spread out my books and dictionaries for *The Cosmopolitans*. I'm planning to translate a sizeable selection of their poetry. After an hour's work I see I've managed to translate two lines—which read and scan very badly. So I go into the drawing room and pour myself a whisky and soda and smoke a cigarette. I can hear the cook and the maid talking in the kitchen. It is 3:30 in the afternoon and already the winter night is gathering outside. Perhaps I'll go to London next week—see Mother, go to the London Library, lunch with Peter if he's free. The vicar is having supper with us tonight, for some reason.

[MARCH]

To Edgefield for the weekend. This is the third weekend we have spent with my in-laws since the year began. I remonstrated gently with Lottie about why we have to stay so often with them when her mother practically lives in our house. Lottie put on her "hurt" face and said that Edgefield is her home—just because I never had a proper home I don't understand. I shut up.

[MAY–JUNE]

Thorpe Geldingham. Well named. I am the gelded writer: the capon, the bullock, the castrato. I simply can't work here. I rise late, I do *The Times* crossword, I have a gin and tonic at eleven, and a bottle of wine at lunch. Then I go to my study and doze over my books. I have a whisky and soda and a stroll in the afternoon, a bath, change, mix a cocktail, dine, drink more wine, finish with a brandy and a cigar. Lottie appears to be in seventh heaven. I am twenty-seven years old and my life seems to have been ambushed somehow. Out there in the world my two books are selling, my name appears above articles in newspa-pers and magazines, but here I stew in this rural purgatory. I see my parents-in-law far too often. Angus comes down from London and stays from time to time, but I daren't invite any of my other friends. We give dinner parties, we are invited to dinner parties where I try to drink as much as possible. I go up to London once a fortnight to see Wallace, Roderick, my mother and those of my friends that are free for lunch. I'm no longer invited to London parties—it's as if my marriage and my move to Norfolk have erased my name from every guest list in the city.

> *Que je m'ennuie*
> *Dans ce cabaret du Néant*
> *Qu'est notre vie*
> [Léon-Paul Fargue]

MONDAY, 10 JULY

Lottie has just returned from a visit to the doctor in Norwich and has informed me that she is pregnant. The child is due in early December— a March conception, then. What were you doing in March, Logan? No idea. How do you feel? Be honest. I feel numb, shocked, panicky, angry. Do you feel happy, knowing you're to be a father? I blame myself—I used no protection, yet I have a drawerful of condoms in my bathroom. I must be calm. There has never been a conversation between us about starting a family.

Lottie was thrilled, but when she saw the look on my face she began to wail. I reassured her, said it was a shock but in fact I couldn't be happier. She stopped wailing and telephoned her mother. She returned to say that Aelthred and Enid insisted on us driving over to Edgefield for a celebratory dinner this evening. I quizzed Lottie gently about her prophylactic. Sometimes she forgot to put it in, she confessed—but it doesn't matter, does it, darling? It must be fate. Fatal fate.

AUGUST

Lottie is unwell. She is delicate. The health of the baby is paramount. The first summer in years with no travel abroad. I writhe in agonies of wanderlust. London is empty, everyone away. Strange dreams of Spain dominate my mind.

Alicante. Cartagena. The road from Seville to Granada.

Cante Andaluz ringing in my inner ear. Oily taste of salt cod and tortilla. That hawk-nosed girl in the brothel at Almería who opened her dressing gown as I passed her doorway to let me see her naked body.

New gramophone. A present for myself. Liszt, Chopin all day. Brahms so beautiful it makes me suicidal. Debussy: terrible *envie de Paris.*

What was the name of that hotel in Juan-les-Pins? Hôtel du Midi? Central-Moderne? Beau Séjour?

All writers should be poor in their youth. The urge to earn produces enormous stamina and resources of energy.

I'm not writing but, thank God, have suddenly discovered the joys of reading.

Authors of the moment: Sterne, Gerhardi, Chekhov, Turgenev, Mansfield.

Moved on to Monteverdi, day and night. Lottie, irritable and tetchy, hates the sound of music in the morning. "Why is that, my darling?" "It's not normal to listen to music before lunch." Define normal.

*   *   *

It is easier to read in the country than in the city. Discuss.

Chekhov: "I am neither liberal, conservative, gradualist, monk, nor indifferentist. I would like to be a free artist and nothing else."

Logan Mountstuart, his moods:
(a) normal—outwardly calm, inwardly stoical
(b) abnormal—drink-induced sentimentality. Everything in life is sweet and lovely
(c) dangerous—outwardly taciturn, inwardly rampant self-loathing

I remember Evelyn [Waugh] saying that Oxford was the worst preparation for adult life. He said he was far more mature at the end of his school career than at the end of his university career. Doesn't apply to me. EW, like Peter, loved Oxford; I couldn't wait to leave the place.

Gracias a la vida que me ha dado tanto. [Thanks to life which has given me so much.]

I am forcing myself to read a page of *To the Lighthouse* each day and am finding it incredibly hard going. It seems such a silly book: compared to Katherine Mansfield, Virginia Woolf is so "girly" in her writing. Silly. Girly. My God, what an impressive critical vocabulary, Mountstuart. I'd better start writing criticism again if this is the best I can do. Must be losing my grip.

First chill in the evening. Urge to have the fire lit in my study. The endless summer is over. This afternoon a late ray of sun hit the vast cloud of midges over the garden pool. The air full of shifting golden dust.

SATURDAY, 9 DECEMBER

Our son is born, here at home in Thorpe, just before midday. I was in the drawing room, fearful and apprehensive, when the midwife came in all smiles and took me up to Lottie. Lottie exhausted but happy. I feel that I have a brick wedged somewhere behind my ribcage making it very hard to breathe. A sense of my life being entirely out of my control—which is not the same as out of control. We are going to call him Lionel Aelthred Mountstuart.

SUNDAY, 31 DECEMBER

Analysis of the year. I can hardly be bothered to write this. No travel. Norfolk–London–Norfolk. Growing hatred of England and its countryside, hatred of railway travel, hatred of church spires glimpsed through windows of railway carriages. Hatred of ploughed fields. Hatred of grass. Hatred of the upholstery in railway carriages. Hatred of _____ (please fill in blank space).

I have a fine house, three servants (four if you count the nurse), a pretty, rich wife, and a new son.

Ambitions: to see Venice, Greece. To finish *The Cosmopolitans*.

Work: two bad chapters of *The Cosmopolitans*. Five articles, two book reviews. Pathetic. Yet my royalty cheques tell me I am a successful writer. *TMI* and *TGF* still flourish and thereby create an illusion of industry and success. How long can it last?

Friends made: none.

Friends lost: none.

Friends renewed: Peter, (Tess?).

Friends in limbo: Angus (he is fundamentally shallow—*un nul*).

1934

THURSDAY, 25 JANUARY

Terrible, awful moment at the font yesterday during the christening when I suddenly realized that no son of mine should ever be called Lionel, let alone Lionel Aelthred, but it was too late. What a legacy, Lionel Mountstuart. I shall have to think up a nickname for him: Budge, Midge, Bobo—anything. Peter was a godfather with Angus; Brenna Aberdeen and Ianthe Forge-Dawson godmothers. Brenna is actually good fun (in small doses). I can't abide Ianthe—Lottie's best friend.

Peter stayed the night. We sat up late with the port decanter and talked. Tess couldn't come as she's expecting child number two to arrive at any moment. Something in Peter's tone of voice—he's in London Monday to Friday, now—made me suspect that the marriage is in difficulties. He told me he was writing a detective novel in his spare time—following my example.

FRIDAY, 16 FEBRUARY

Stood for a good ten minutes at the foot of Lionel's crib watching him sleeping. I tried to analyze my feelings as honestly as possible but could find nothing in me other than banalities: how all babies look similar in their first three months of life; that it is amazing they have such tiny toenails and fingernails; and what a shame it is that speech arrives so late. Perversely, now is the time I would most like to talk to him. Imagine if by some miracle a baby could speak in its first weeks of life—how we would see the world afresh, anew.

At supper Lottie speculated on where we might go this summer and said that we would require a house big enough to accommodate a baby's room and a nurse's—and we'd need at least two spare bedrooms in case "Mummy and Daddy" visited or the Forge-Dawsons came to stay. Cornwall might be fun, mightn't it, Logie?

[FEBRUARY]

Here is my problem, this is why my work stagnates. I spent all afternoon trying to translate five lines of Henry Levet's *Afrique occidentale:*

> *Dans la véranda de sa case, à Brazzaville,*
> *Par un torride clair de lune Congolais*
> *Un sous-administrateur des colonies*
> *Feuillette les "Poésies" d'Alfred de Musset . . .*
> *Car il pense encore à cette jolie Chillienne . . .*

It only works in French, in English it becomes banal, clumping, it loses
all its aching melancholy romance. This is how Les Cosmopolites
haunt me—heat, Africa, literature, *cafard*, sex . . . But it only works in
French. "In the torrid Congolese moonlight/A minor colonial offi-
cial/riffles through the 'poems' of Alfred de Musset." No no no. Give
it up, Mountstuart.

WEDNESDAY, 21 FEBRUARY

Yesterday, after lunch, making no progress with chapter three of *The
Cosmopolitans,* I decided to motor into Norwich to buy a ream of typing paper—at least it was a vaguely writerly thing to do on a Tuesday
afternoon. I told Lottie I'd be back in time for supper and headed off.
Just as I arrived at Norfolk it hailed, briefly, heavily, for a few seconds,
and then the sun came out very bright and clear. Road works—gas
mains—diverted the traffic round towards the station and spontaneously I pulled into the station car park. I sat there for a while thinking about my life and what I was going to do and then went and
bought a one-way ticket to London.

I walked out onto the platform remembering my ends of term at
Abbey and how this station symbolized only disappointment and
defeat to me. But today as I stood there waiting for the London train,
empty-handed, unburdened—apart from my raincoat and my hat—I felt
as free and excited as I had ever been before. Norwich Station: gateway

to the world. It was a wonderfully pure form of selfishness; I was thinking of no one but myself—not Lottie, not Lionel, not my mother. All I
wanted to do was discard the life I had and start another one afresh.

Wallace talked me out of it. I went to his offices on the Strand and
told him what I'd done and asked him to find me a newspaper or a
magazine prepared to send me abroad, anywhere, now. He calmed me
down and asked me what had happened. I told him.

"What about your motor?" he said.

"It's parked outside the station."

"And the keys are in your pocket?"

"Ah . . . Yes." I produced them: evidence of my thoughtlessness.

"Passport?"

"At home."

Good, solid, sensible, pragmatic Wallace. So, we worked out plan B.
I telephoned Lottie and told her I was in London, spinning some tale
about how I'd rung Wallace and he'd summoned me down forthwith
on urgent business. I told her I'd be back tomorrow. Wallace invited
me to spend the night at his home in Wandsworth and there, for the
first time, I met his wife (Heather) and their three sons and two daughters, aged between fifteen and nine years old. Somehow I had never
even bothered to be curious about Wallace's domestic life and I looked
on in some amazement to see him in the middle of this large, genial
family.

After dinner we sat in the drawing room. The room was lined with
bookshelves filled with the various editions of his clients' work. He
asked me where I wanted to go. Africa, Japan, Russia, I said. But where
would you really like to go, he insisted gently? Spain. Right, he said,
that shouldn't be too hard to arrange.

MARCH

Hôtel Rembrandt. Paris. Wallace has managed to contract me for three
articles for the *Graphic:* £5 for 500 words on Granada, Seville and Valencia. No expenses. Slightly under my usual rate but I wasn't in a position to haggle. I also managed to whip up a couple of commissions for

Art Review so I should emerge from the excursion with a little profit. I said goodbye to Lottie and Lionel, managing to keep the silly smile of exultation off my face. Why did I wait so long? I must never let this damaging frustration build up again. I have to recognize that I'm simply not equipped, temperamentally, to stay at home and live a circumscribed, rural, English life. I absolutely need variety and surprise; I have to have the city in my life—I'm essentially urban by nature—and also the prospect and reality of travel. Otherwise I'll desiccate and die.

Yesterday Ben took me to meet Picasso at his studio. Ben doesn't know him that well and Picasso seemed a bit grumpy and uncommunicative until Ben happened to mention I was en route for Spain, at which point he warmed up and gave me the addresses of two excellent restaurants in Barcelona. I asked him what he was working on and he said, wait and see. He spoke French with a thick Spanish accent. He was wearing a shirt and tie—it seemed odd to put on a tie to paint. He seemed a small, aggressive man and I sensed in him a wariness of Ben and me. What were these two young Englishmen doing in his studio? There must be an ulterior motive. I suppose he was right, in a way. Not that I cared: I was just glad to be out of England.

I dined with Pierre Lamartine, my publisher at Cahier Noir. He's a slim, pensive man with a lock of hair draped across his forehead like Herr Hitler. He's given to long pauses in his conversation. I told him about *The Cosmopolitans* and he managed to seem politely interested, though clearly, like all my other publishers, he would like another novel. "Les Cosmopolites sont . . ." Long pause. "Un peu vieux jeu," he said with an apologetic shrug.

Tomorrow I catch the train south from the Gare d'Orsay. I should be in Bordeaux in time for dinner at the Chapon Fin. Then I plan to go Bordeaux–Toulouse–Perpignan, cross the border at Port Bou and from there on down the coast to Barcelona–Valencia–Granada–Seville. I think I may even head on to Lisbon after Seville and perhaps catch a steamer home to Southampton.

> *Là, tout n'est qu'ordre et beauté*
> *Luxe, calme et volupté*
>   [Baudelaire]

WEDNESDAY, 4 APRIL

Metropole Hotel, Lisbon. Yesterday I took the train to Cintra. It was a misty, cool day but the views were all the more enchanting for the general blurriness around the edges. But somehow during the day my coat was stolen, which contained in its pockets both my wallet and my passport. It happened at the Castelo da Pena. I laid the coat on the wall of the exterior gallery and walked out on to a kind of protruding balcony to take a photo of the view south towards the hills of Arrábida. I took my snapshot and when I returned the coat had gone. I wandered around the castle scrutinizing every other visitor, and those in the park outside, but saw nothing or no one suspicious. A mystery, and a damned inconvenient one too. So I went this morning to the consulate and explained my predicament. A temporary passport will be issued this afternoon. I've telegraphed my bank to send me more money.

Later. This is what happened.

I went to the consulate (rua do Ferregail de Baixo) and was asked to wait in an anteroom—a few wooden chairs, a table covered in out-of-date periodicals and copies of last week's *Times*. The door opened and I looked up expecting to see the official but instead it was a young woman. It's amazing how sudden the effect is—it must be the result of a deep atavistic mating urge buried inside us. A glance and you think: "Yes, this is the one, this one is right for me." Every instinct in your body seems to sing in unison. What are the factors that combine to make you feel that way? The arch of an eyebrow? The jut of a lip? The turn of an ankle? The slimness of a wrist? . . . We smiled politely at each other—two foreigners embroiled in officialdom—and I flapped out my newspaper, taking a good look at her over its top edge.

At first glance she had a longish, thin, strong face. The eyebrows were very arched, plucked and pencilled, and she wore lipstick. Her hair was thick and unruly, mid-brown with natural blonder highlights at the temples and the brow. I could imagine her dragging and tugging a brush through it in the morning and then abandoning all further efforts for the day. She wore a linen suit, pale green, quite smart. She took a cigarette case from her handbag and had a cigarette lit before I could spring forward with my lighter. Right, I thought, here's my chance: I could ask her for a light—and was just opening my own case when the consul's secretary came in and said, "Mr. Mountstuart, the consul will see you now." I went into the consul's office and signed for my temporary passport in a daze. I ducked into the anteroom on my way out but she had gone.

I felt an unaccountable, preposterous panic and worry. I raced back to the secretary and asked where the young woman had gone. Seeing another official, came the answer. Apparently she had been travelling by motor car with her father, there had been an accident, her father was injured (a broken leg), and there were complicated insurance problems that needed solving. I went back to the anteroom and waited, the door ajar so I could see the corridor outside.

I spotted her coming out of an office and stepped out as casually as I could manage. I smiled: I had absolutely no idea what I was going to say. She frowned at me, the perfect pencilled arches of her eyebrows buckling.

"Are you Logan Mountstuart, by any chance?"

"Yes, I am." I couldn't believe my luck—a reader.

"I thought so." Then she gave what could only be described as a sneer and strode on past me. I followed her down the stairs to the street.

"Hold on a second," I said. "How do you know? Have we met?"

"Certainly not. But I happen to know you don't come up to London for under ten guineas."

I managed to persuade her to stop in a café with me. I had a glass of *vinho tinto*, she had mineral water and I found out the background to the story. She was a secretary at the BBC in the Talks Department with the responsibility for booking guests; they had tried to have me in for a talk on "New Currents in European Painting" and were informed about my fee. The entire department thought it absurd, she said.

"I mean who do you think you are?" she said. "Stravinsky? Galsworthy?"*

*John Galsworthy had won the Nobel Prize for Literature in 1932.

"Ah, but that would be my agent's fault," I said. "He's always upping my fee without permission. Outrageous."

"He's doing you no favours, I can tell you," she said aggressively. "You went straight on to the blacklist. Ten guineas? Bloody ridiculous. I'd sack him."

I said I'd been thinking of sacking Wallace for ages. Then I asked her name.

"Freya Deverell," she said.

Freya Deverell. Freya Deverell. I have that feeling of heartrace, that bloodheat and breathgasp, just writing her name. And there is something aggressive about her beauty. Her lips are slightly pushed forward, not so much pouting or making a moue, but as if she's on the verge of blurting something out. She's tall and slim and I would say was in her very early twenties, and very sure of herself for one so young. Her father, she told me, has broken his leg quite badly and they think it will be another week before he's out of hospital and fit to travel.

"I'm getting the steamer to Southampton tomorrow," I said, "but can I take you to dinner tonight?—see if I can persuade you to remove me from the Talks Department blacklist."

I sit here writing these words, waiting to go to her hotel to meet her. It terrifies me, the fragility of these moments in our lives. If I hadn't lost my passport. If her father hadn't crashed the car and broken his leg. If she hadn't gone to the consulate at that precise hour . . . The view ahead is empty and void: only the view backward shows you how utterly random and chance-driven these vital connections are.

[APRIL]

SGTM *Garudja*. French ship, Portuguese crew. Half the cabins are empty. I've done my three articles for the *Graphic* and, as an extra, written an account of my visit to Picasso's studio, which I'm sure Wallace will be able to place somewhere. I spent the morning on deck—a sunny fresh day—pacing about, trying to organize and collect my thoughts, attempting to give some sort of shape and coherence to my immediate future.

The dinner with Freya passed off well and I learned more about her.

Her father is a widower who lives with her brother in Cheshire. Once a year Freya and her father take a holiday together. Their favourite destination is Germany or Austria but she refuses to go there now because of the political situation*—hence the ill-fated trip to Portugal. Freya is much further to the left than I am and I realized how disengaged from politics I've become and feel vaguely ashamed of my indifference and apathy. She's twenty-one and has worked at the BBC for two years. She wants to become a producer of programmes in her own right—"Not easy in that place, I can tell you." She disagreed violently with me on certain subjects we talked about. Picasso—"a charlatan"; Virginia Woolf—"our greatest living writer"; Mosley—"a disaster for the country." I walked her back to her hotel and she shook my hand vigorously when we said goodnight. I asked her if I could see her in London and she gave me her address—she lives in a kind of lodging house with eight other young single women in Chiswick. She knows I'm married and have a child. I said I would be in touch as soon as she returned. I gave her my card and she read the address out: "Thorpe Geldingham . . . That sounds very far away." I told her I was looking for a flat in London.

"Have you read either of my books?" I asked her at one stage in the evening.

"No."

"Why did you want me for your programme?"

"I don't know. Somebody had read an article you'd written. I think I was intrigued by your name."

Not the most promising basis for a relationship, but I am completely and utterly captivated by this woman. Freya. Freya. Freya.

TUESDAY, 15 MAY

Back to Chelsea. I've just put three months' rent down on a small semi-furnished flat in Draycott Avenue. A fair-sized sitting room, which can double as my study, a tiny bedroom, a lavatory (no bath) and a narrow galley-kitchen with a fold-down table. I had to buy some furniture—a

*Hitler became Chancellor of Germany in 1933.

bed (single—a double wouldn't fit), a sofa and some pots and pans. A middle-aged Polish seamstress lives above me and below are two civil servants whom I suspect are probably on the "musical" side. The street is darkly anonymous, everyone keeps themselves to themselves. I think it's going to prove ideal for my new life.

Freya loves ballet, so we went to see *Giselle* last Friday. I am a self-confessed ignoramus when it comes to dance (why is that, I wonder? Every other art form fascinates me), but I enjoyed myself—I suppose grace and elegance and lovely music are hard to resist. Freya quizzed me in the restaurant afterwards and was appalled at my ignorance. "What if I said I wasn't curious about art or literature?" she said. "What would you think of me then?" I was happy to admit defeat. Happy to be sitting opposite her admitting defeat.

I've also opened a new bank account into which Wallace will transfer all my literary earnings. Aelthred pays us—Lottie—an allowance of £300 a year, which should be sufficient to keep our Norfolk life going. I told Lottie that I was going to be spending "Much more, considerably more" time in London, but she didn't seem to mind that much—as long as I'm home at weekends, was her only condition. I've used this complacency to quietly shift most of my books and paintings down to Draycott Avenue—I don't think she's noticed. Wallace sold my "Meeting with Picasso" piece to *Life* magazine for $200.

[MAY]

I am paying cautious and unhurried court to Freya. I book our time together solicitously, giving plenty of notice, taking nothing for granted. She enjoys eating in restaurants and drinks as much as me. I've avoided my usual haunts for the time being—so no Ivy, Café Royal, Previtali's—I don't want tongues wagging. We go to the cinema, to art galleries, to the theatre and ballet. Last week before the theatre we had drinks at Draycott Avenue and she admired the flat. There is a "young man" at the BBC who is interested in her but I don't think he's any competition.

FRIDAY, 8 JUNE

Yesterday, one of Freya's bosses in the Talks Department had a cocktail party and she asked me along. She changed at Draycott (she looked suddenly very sophisticated in a navy blue crêpe dress and high heels) and we took a cab to his house in Highgate. His name is Turville Stevens—in his forties, but with a shock of snowy white hair. It was a warm evening and the party spilled out into the garden. For some reason the drink had gone to my head (I drank neat gin before Freya arrived to calm my nerves) and I wandered off on my own, trying to sober up. Then, as I stood in that English garden on that soft early summer night, I felt a surge of pure well-being engulf my whole body. I felt a shivering current of happiness and benevolence flow through me. I looked round and, across the lawn, saw that Freya was looking at me. This is love. This is what love can do to you. We looked at each other and the message passed between us, through our eyes. Then Turville called her name and she had to look away.

I wandered over, like an automaton, to another group of people, I thought I saw Tommy Beatty there. To my vague shock Land was amongst them. We spoke quite amiably: she told me she was going to stand for Parliament at the next election. She asked about Lottie and Lionel, what I was writing and so on, and I in turn asked her about the other Fothergills. It was strange after such intimacy to sense this coolness between us. I suppose if you ask someone to marry you and they turn you down, things can never be quite the same again—too much damage done: humankind can tolerate only so much rejection. Then, as we were talking, Freya came up and I introduced them to each other. There is no disguising these situations: I don't know what tiny signals are given off—perhaps it's something women sense more than men— but I was instantly aware that (a) Land knew how I felt about Freya and (b) that Freya knew that Land was a former lover of mine. The three-sided conversation was very awkward and stiff and we broke off as soon as was polite.

The other aspect of the party that pleased me was to observe how even my small literary splash still sent out ripples. Elizabeth Bowen said, a little cattily, I thought, "Are you enormously rich, these days?"

and I must have been asked half a dozen times when my next book was due. Turville Stevens was very complimentary about *Imaginings* and said he was sure we could do something on the wireless when *The Cosmopolitans* was published.

Freya and I left about nine and hailed a cab in the High Street. I asked her where she'd like to go to eat. "Draycott Avenue," she said.

Freya naked. Even more beautiful. Freckled on her chest and shoulders. Her hip bones jut. I don't know why—we're both in our twenties, after all—but I feel so much older than she. We cling to each other in my single bed. "We must never get a double, Logan," she said. "Never. We must always sleep in a single bed."

She stayed the night and left for work this morning at eight. I sit in the kitchen in my dressing gown writing this on the fold-down table, the uneaten crusts of her breakfast toast on a plate before me, and my heart exults. I think of Lottie, of our life, our child, and I realize what a hideous error I made in marrying her. But the past cannot be undone. I only want to be with Freya: time away from her is time irretrievably lost.

[JUNE]

Thorpe. This summer is going to be very difficult. Lottie has rented a house in Fowey in Cornwall for July and August. I've told her I have to be away in France for much of August to do research on *The Cosmopolitans,* which she accepted, but put on her grumpy face for the rest of the day. She suspects nothing, I know.

Some money worries too. We are overdrawn at the bank, and when Lottie asked for an increase in her allowance Aelthred had a quiet anxious word with me: he couldn't understand how with my income and Lottie's allowance a young couple (with no mortgage) could get into debt. Lottie spends without thinking, I explained, and told him that currently I was earning very little—a writer's life, you know, either feast or famine. Of course none of my earnings go into the joint account. I urged Lottie to economize but the concept is alien to her. My royalties from *TMI* and *TGF* are modest now (though *Girl Factory* did surprisingly well in France) and the money from the film sale seemed to dwindle like snow in the sun. The Draycott flat and the expenses of my London life with Freya eat up most of what I earn through journalism and I won't receive another lump sum until I deliver *Cosmopolitans*—about £150. Until that day arrives I've borrowed against that payment (through Wallace's good offices) to fund our summer. I'm taking Freya to Biarritz.

[NOTE IN RETROSPECT. 1965. Interestingly enough, this was the first time in my life that I became worried about money and was obliged to budget. Until June of 1934, it's fair to say that I never gave a thought as to how I—or someone else—might pay any bill presented to me.]

[JUNE]

Lionel has croup. He seems a sickly baby. I sat him on my knee the other day and he stared at me with a baleful, sullen, unknowing eye.

Wallace says there is a job on offer as chief book reviewer on *artrevue* (yes, all one word) at £10 a month. Extra for any features I may write. Apparently my Picasso piece impressed them. It's a pretentious, expensive magazine (supported, aptly enough, by some pretentious, millionaire philanthropist) but at least it concedes that people make art outside this little island. I accept without thinking—even though I know I must finish *Cosmopolitans* as quickly as possible. It's an expensive business leading a double life. And after *Cosmopolitans*, what next?

MONDAY, 30 JULY

Back from Fowey. Christ, what an ordeal. When we were alone as a family I could just about tolerate it but when there were guests it was insupportable. I felt I was undergoing some sort of elaborate prison sentence. Angus and Sally,* then Ianthe and family. Luckily I'm going to miss Aelthred and Enid. I came up to London on the earliest train and went straight to Broadcasting House to meet Freya. We went round the corner to a pub and held hands and drank gins and tonic. She can only come away for two weeks—she has to save some of her annual holiday for her father.

I go to visit Mother. There are now four sets of lodgers in Sumner Place. Mother and Encarnación occupy the ground floor and have rented out the other three, including the basement. No sight or sound of Prendergast for over a year. I made her bring out every document relating to her financial transactions. Father left her the house in Birmingham and assets of almost £15,000. Even after buying and decorating the house in Sumner Place there should have been more than enough to provide her with a handsome income for life (at least £1,000 a year) and me with the legacy Father promised. I can hear his words: "You will both be well provided for." Both. This was not just Mother's money, it was mine as well. And taking into account the extravagances—the motor cars, the servants, my allowance—I calculate that the Crash has cost us almost everything. Prendergast, through his reckless investments in U.S. stocks, has lost us £8,000—a fortune—not to mention the 62nd Street apartment. I suppose I should feel anger but it's always hard trying to imagine the loss of something you never had. At least Sumner Place is hers, however sad it is to see her sharing it with strangers, and she has enough income trickling in from the rents to look after herself. I notice an empty gin bottle in the kitchen—I will have a quiet word with Encarnación. Endless moans, needless to say, about not seeing enough of her grandson.

I'm writing this in Draycott Avenue: Freya has been living here while I've been away in Cornwall. There are flowers in vases, the place feels and smells clean. Our narrow little bed has fresh sheets on it. I hear Freya's key in the lock. On Wednesday we leave for France.

*Sally Ross, his fiancée.

TUESDAY, 31 JULY

Meeting at *artrevue*. I like Udo [Feuerbach, the editor], a swarthy, sophisticated German refugee who taught briefly at the Dessau Bauhaus, and I think he's pleased with my pieces. Udo's evaluative criteria are summed up in only two phrases: an artist, or a work of art, is either *ganz ordinär* (very ordinary) or displays *teuflische Virtuosität* (devilish virtuosity)—I've never heard him elaborate further. Does make judging simpler, I must say. He's commissioned a long article on Juan Gris*—my suggestion, and not prompted by the fact that I own a couple of charcoal drawings. Gris is very underrated—and now he's dead the twin refulgent beams of Picasso and Braque confine him unjustifiably to the shadows. Udo also wants me to interview Picasso, if I can set it up through Ben. I warm to Udo's Bauhaus egalitarianism. The *artrevue* office is one large room with a refectory table down the middle around which everyone—editor, secretary, designer, proofreaders and visiting writers—sits. No magazine in England would ever organize itself in this way.

I jumped off the bus on the Brompton Road and was just about to turn down Draycott Avenue when I heard someone shout my name. I looked round and saw Joseph Darker climbing out of a police car. We chatted a bit and I told him about Lottie, Lionel and the move to Norfolk and apologized for losing touch.

"How's the family?" I asked.

"We had a bit of a blow, there," he said, looking down. "Tilda died last year. Diphtheria."

I don't know why the news shocked me the way it did. I even staggered back a pace or two as if I'd been pushed. I remembered that diffident woman, always apologizing, now dead and gone for ever. I muttered something bland, but he could see how buffeted I'd been. We exchanged a few more words and I gave him my new address. I came home and felt genuinely saddened. I told Freya how I had reacted and she said, "We're not ready for it—for people of our age to die. We think we're safe for a while, but it's a dream. No one's safe."

*Juan Gris (1887–1927), painter.

She ran her hands through my hair, put her arms around me and stood on my shoes. Then she hooked a leg round and through mine. It's something she does, one of her quirks—a "leg-hug" she calls it—"Got you," she would say, "clinging on for dear old life."

FRIDAY, 3 AUGUST

Biarritz. Ben has taken a large villa between Biarritz and Bidart, set back about half a mile from the coast, with a big overgrown garden with many trees and a concrete swimming pool. The party consists of Ben and Sandrine, Alice and Tim Farino, me and Freya, Cyprien Dieudonné and his girlfriend, Mita, a dancer from Guadeloupe, and Geddes Brown (now one of Ben's artists) and his friend, an Italian—also a painter—called Carlo.

Every day a picnic lunch is served beside the pool for those who are staying at the house, but we are free to come and go—to the beaches at Saint-Jean-de-Luz and Biarritz, or up into the mountains to walk.

There was a memorable moment yesterday at lunch—Geddes and Carlo were absent, and Cyprien had gone into Biarritz to get his spectacles repaired. We'd all eaten and drunk a great deal when Alice suddenly unhooked the top of her two-piece swimsuit, moved her chair into a patch of sunshine and sat there bare-breasted.

"Are you all right, darling?" Tim said, wholly unperturbed.

"You know I like to do this," she said. "So much nicer to feel the breeze on your tits."

At which point all the other women around the table looked at each other and spontaneously removed their various tops and we finished lunch with all these shapely and beautiful breasts on display. I found it quite arousing at first but after ten minutes it seemed the most natural thing in the world. I caught Freya's eye—she was striped like a tiger from sun and shadow cast by the bamboo lattice beneath which we were sitting. She reached back behind her head to adjust a clip in her hair and I watched her breasts rise and flatten as she did so, the shadow-stripes shifting to accommodate the new contours. When the party broke up for a game of boules we slipped away to our room.

THURSDAY, 9 AUGUST

Geddes and Carlo have gone up to the mountains for a few days to paint. "Too much ocean light," Geddes said. I think he has talent—he certainly works hard—and I quite like him, a blunt and dour fellow, though I think he's a little wary of me. He still sees Land, he told me, and implied she was having an affair with Oliver Lee.

It was a little overcast this morning, so Tim Farino and I went to play golf at the Plateau du Phare Club in Biarritz. Tim's not a bad player, but we were both rusty with lack of practice. I had just birdied the ninth hole and was teeing up at the tenth when a man in white flannels and a blazer approached us, announcing himself as secretary of the golf club, and asking if we would mind allowing a distinguished visitor the opportunity of playing the back half ahead of us. Our green fees would be reimbursed, he added by way of incentive, and gestured at a couple of men walking down the gravel path from the club house, followed by caddies.

"Are you English or American?" the secretary asked.

"I'm English," I said.

He leant forward and whispered, "It's the Prince of Wales."

And of course I recognized him immediately as he drew near. He's a small, delicately made man and was wearing immaculate plus fours with ankle boots. He was carrying a flat tweed cap and his blond hair was thick and oiled in an immaculate part. He was with a taller, older, slightly untidily dressed man who was not introduced—an equerry, I supposed.

The secretary, bowing and scraping, explained that these English gentlemen had kindly agreed to give way.

We shook hands: I introduced myself and Tim.

"Awfully good of you," said the Prince. "We just want to get in a quick nine holes before luncheon. Don't want to keep the ladies waiting."

We stood back and watched them drive off. The Prince had a stiff, awkward swing—not a natural sportsman, I would say. They strode off— and then the Prince came jogging back, an unlit cigarette in his hand.

"Got a light?" he said. I took out a box of matches and lit his cigarette.

"Couldn't spare the box, could you?" he said and gave me his famous smile.

"All yours, sir," I said, handing them over.

"Thanks. What was your name again?"

I told him. Logan Mountstuart, sir.

Later. Ben says the Prince has taken a house here and that the American woman, Mrs. Simpson, chaperoned by her aunt, is with him. Some ribald speculation ensued. Tim says he knew her vaguely before she married Simpson—knew her first husband, a terrible drunk, by all accounts. Freya didn't understand our innuendoes, so we explained about Lady Furness being supplanted and the new favourite. She was amazed: she knew nothing of all this. I realized I'd heard all the gossip from Angus Cassell. Ben said it was common knowledge in Paris.

Worth noting these encounters, I think, however nondescript—the gift of a box of matches to the future King of England. We forget, otherwise. What else? He was wearing no tie.

FRIDAY, 17 AUGUST

Freya goes back tomorrow and I intend to stay on until the end of the month—perhaps go on to the Lot and stay with Cyprien. "Think of me on Monday morning walking into the BBC," Freya said, as we lay in bed, giving a half groan, half scream. "And think of me thinking of you lot down here. IT'S NOT FAIR!"

"You've got to give up your job," I said, reaching for her.

"And what would I do then?" she said. "Become a writer?"

SATURDAY, 18 AUGUST

Freya off on the train to Paris. I begged her to stay on in Draycott Avenue, to think of the flat as hers and she promised to consider it. "If

I move in," she said, "I'll be paying my share of the rent." I demurred half-heartedly—every little helps. "I'll not be your kept woman, Logan," she said sternly. How I'll miss her.

These have been magical days down here on the coast. I am burnt brown but Freya, my northern goddess, doesn't like the sun as much as I do. To remember: wading hand and hand into the big surf at Hendaye. Standing naked at the window, looking out on the garden at night, feeling the cool air on my body, listening to the drilling noise of the cicadas, Freya calling me back to bed. Long conversations around the lunch table—as extra wine is fetched to see us through the afternoon—Cyprien, Ben and me arguing about Joyce; Geddes making the case for Braque against Picasso; talking about the spitefulness of Bloomsbury—Freya stoutly defending Mrs. Woolf against all comers; analysing Scott Fitzgerald's new novel* (apparently his wife is insane, Alice says). Nights in the casino, dancing to the jazz band. Freya winning a thousand francs at blackjack—her unmitigated joy at this unearned gift of money.

Ben has been a discreet and true friend, given he was an usher at my wedding. I tried to explain the situation vis-à-vis Lottie but he didn't want to hear. "I don't care, Logan. You live your life and I'll live mine. I won't judge you—just as long as you're happy. I'd hope you'd do the same for me." I assured him I would.

He told me a lot about Gris and how ill he had been at the end of his life. He said, if I were interested, he could lay his hands on a small "but exquisite" late still life. How much? I said. £50, he said, cash. I can't afford it but something in me made me say I'd take it. He went off immediately to make a telephone call to Paris.

Vague ideas rove around my head about setting a novel here, around such a summer house-party as this.

[NOVEMBER]

The Juan Gris, "Ceramic Jar and Three Apricots," hangs above the fire-place in Draycott Avenue. The walls are covered with my other drawings and oils. In August Freya painted the room dark olive and on these

---

* *Tender Is the Night.*

gloomy evenings, with winter coming on, the lamps seem to glow with an extra warmth, backed against the earthy greenness that surrounds them.

Freya has decided to live here on condition that she contributes something to the rent (£5 a month). She punctiliously hands me a fiver on the first day of each new month (I'm not ashamed to say every little helps—but I see I've already mentioned that above—which doesn't make it any less true). I've now borrowed to the full extent of my *Cosmopolitans* advance. All the money I made from *The Girl Factory* is tied up in blue-chip shares and insurance policies, which I can't cash without alerting Lottie, or Aelthred, even worse. Wallace urges me to deliver *Cosmopolitans,* but I keep telling him I haven't the time to spare as I'm doing so much extra journalism these days, to make ends meet. I suggested doing a monograph on Gris, but Wallace shot that down at once—saying I'd be lucky if I got £10.

At lunch the other day:

WALLACE: I thought you said you had an idea for another novel.
ME: Just a vague idea. About a group of young people, couples, sharing a villa at Biarritz for the summer.
WALLACE: Sounds excellent. I'd read that.
ME: I thought of calling it *Summer at Saint-Jean*.
WALLACE: You can't fail with "Summer" in the title. I could get you £500 tomorrow.
ME: Wonderful. But when am I meant to write it?
WALLACE: Write a synopsis. Two pages. A few lines. Time's running out, Logan.

That sounded ominous—clearly my *Girl Factory* credit is all but used up. So I sat down and tried to put something on paper. As a simple experiment, I took our situation at Biarritz, changed everyone's names, created extra tensions, external pressures (wives, ex-lovers). Suddenly, like Wallace, I could see the huge potential in this idea—the sex appeal, abroad, the freedom of summer heat by the ocean—but I couldn't unleash it, no matter how I tried.

1935

[JANUARY]

Snowed-in at Thorpe. Snow piled up to the window ledges. It would be rather beautiful and romantic if I were here with Freya and not Lottie and Lionel, who seems to have whooping cough. I hear the raucous mocking call of the rooks in the elms—Freya-Freya-Freya—they seem to cry.

Udo Feuerbach has asked me to do a piece on the Bauhaus and lent me photographs from his collection. I marvelled at the pictures of the girls in the weaving rooms—beautiful and free. One of them looked like Freya. I can't escape.

TUESDAY, 5 MARCH

We dined at Luigi's and went on to the Café Royal. It was busy, full of unfamiliar faces. Spotted and spoke briefly with Cyril and Jean who were with Lyman? Leland? [unidentified]. They left shortly after. Then Adrian Daintrey* came in with a party in evening dress—which included Virginia Woolf,† smoking a cigar. I let them have our table and during the general milling around that took place I introduced Freya to Woolf. "Are you two here alone?" she said to Freya. "What a ghastly crowd. How it's changed."

"We were here with Cyril Connolly, a moment ago," Freya said.

"Was his black baboon with him?" VW asked.

Freya didn't know what she was talking about.

"His little gollywog wife."

*A painter friend of Duncan Grant.
†See *The Diary of Virginia Woolf. Volume IV: 1931–5.*

I turned to Freya. "Now you understand Mrs. Woolf's reputation for charm." Back to VW. "You should be ashamed of yourself."

We strode out and when we reached home had our first serious row. Freya was a little shocked at VW's spite. I said you would never imagine the person who wrote all that lyrical breathy prose was steeped in such venom. "At least she writes," Freya said, without thinking. But it cut and so we looked around for something to argue about and duly found it. Now I'm writing this, about to go to sleep on the sofa, and I can hear Freya sobbing next door in the bedroom.

WEDNESDAY, 20 MARCH

To a dull exhibition of collages and photographs at the Mayor Gallery. Enlivened only by being cut dead by Mrs. Woolf—positively spun on her heel to avoid me. Clearly I am not forgiven.

Went on to *artrevue* offices and drank wine with Udo. He listened patiently while I raged at the mediocrity of English art. He told me they have signs up in every German town now saying *Die Juden sind hier unerwünscht* [No Jews wanted here]. You can hardly believe it possible. But Udo said it put things in perspective: we could tolerate a moribund art scene without too much pain, he said: there were other consolations for living in London.

[MARCH–APRIL]

Movements: Norfolk–London–Norfolk. Paris–Rome (for Easter. Three days with Freya). We plan our summer: Greece. What do I say to L. this year?

[APRIL]

Heroic efforts see *Cosmopolitans* finally completed. I took it into Roderick, who commented, a little acidly, on its brevity: it will come out at under 150 pages. (I explained I had planned, then abandoned, the idea of an anthology of translated poems appended, which would have bulked it up.) Well, at least you've got it out of your system, he said. Now what about this rather sexy novel Wallace has been tempting me with? I let him believe it was a possibility.

Freya follows the development of the P. of Wales/Mrs. Simpson affair with fascinated interest—she can read about it in the American newspapers they have at the BBC. She thinks it utterly disgraceful that the population at large remains in near total ignorance. "I tell everyone about it," she said, "everyone I meet." I must admit to a curious interest in it myself since my encounter with the Prince on the golf course. Angus is a reliable source—he must know somebody in the inner circle—he says the Prince is utterly besotted with Mrs. S.—follows her around like a dog.

[JULY]

In the end I lied. Said I was going to France to work. Freya and I met in Paris and flew to Marseilles. Then from Marseilles by boat to Athens. Hired a car and motored: Delphi—Nauplia—Mycenae—Athens. Intense heat: we longed for rain and cool weather. We resolved never to spend our holiday like this again, constantly on the move. Last year in Biarritz was an idyll. And I just can't take a constant diet of ancient culture—guided tour after guided tour of individual ruins, however beautiful, however freighted with history. In my mind Greece is reduced to one vast pile of shattered marble, shimmering in a heat haze. Dust-mantled olive groves, sweltering hotel bedrooms, flies. We vowed to come back one spring. Mind you, it was incredibly cheap. Flew Athens—Rome. Then train to Paris, London. Exhausted, irritable, not the success we had imagined. And now I have to spend a month with my family. I think Freya will relish her solitude.

[AUGUST]

Dick [Hodge] comes to the rescue. A quiet month at Kildonnan with Lottie and Lionel. Angus and Sally for a fortnight also. I golfed at Gul-

lane and Muirhead with a friend of Angus from the City, Ian Fleming.*
He was off to Kitzbühel. I told him about the scorching heat of Greece
and he recommended the Alps in the summer–loves the Austrian
Tyrol. I wrote to Freya and told her to pick her favourite mountain for
next year.

THURSDAY, 26 SEPTEMBER

At lunch today Peter [Scabius] presented me with a copy of his
thriller–or his "Teccie," as he referred to it with disparaging modesty.
It's called *Beware of the Dog*, published by Brown & Almay next week.
Just a bit of fun, really, he said, not in your league. We drank rather a
lot to celebrate and Peter confessed he was having an affair with the
wife of another journalist who works on *The Times*. He said he had
fallen out of love with Tess but would never leave her because of the
children. "She's a dear thing and a good mother, but I was far too
young to marry her." He asked me how things were with Lottie and I
said wonderful. Lucky man, he said: it's not always "marry in haste
repent at leisure." I was on the point of telling him about Freya and
then resisted: the idea of telling Peter, here and now, would cheapen
my relationship with her. My life with Freya is no "affair," no fling.
And I felt obscurely hurt for Tess; felt her betrayal and resented Peter
for including me in his duplicity. And all this has, of course, made me
reflect on my own situation. I feel nothing for Lottie. And I feel nothing negative about her either. Sexually our life is at a virtual standstill–
though I notice that lately she has started talking about a little brother
or sister for Lionel. Since Lionel's arrival I always make sure I wear a
condom on our rare fucks. The last time (in Scotland) she said: "Must
you, darling? Not tonight." I said we couldn't afford another child. She
started to cry and the need for prophylaxis was over.

In parallel, Freya and I lead this curious, loving, cocooned life at
Draycott Avenue. When I'm not with her she picks up her old bachelor-
girl ways with her friends–none of whom I've met. When I'm with her

---

*The writer (1908–64). Creator of James Bond.

we lead the selfish, self-absorbed existence of a newly married couple. She goes off to work in the mornings and I set about my London business: have meetings, visit the offices of the magazines I work for, do research in the London Library, lunch with friends. I'm always home by the time she returns from the BBC. At some stage in the day I ring up Lottie and we chat for a few minutes. Lottie seems quite content and unsuspecting—she doesn't really like London anyway.

But I realize that this state of affairs has been going on now for over a year and I think it's wrong of me simply to let it drift in this way. Something will change suddenly—something will break or alter course—and before it does I should really make my own move.

FRIDAY, 11 OCTOBER

Lunch with Fleming at the Savoy Grill. I should have said that I'd golfed with him again at Huntercombe—he called out of the blue to ask me to make up a four. He had an ulterior motive, I think. He's unhappy being a stockbroker and is curious about my writing life. He asked me if I was interested in pornography and I said not particularly. He has quite a collection, he said proudly. Then for some reason, as if it would explain my essential indifference to erotica, I told him about Freya, the flat and our secret weekday life. I now feel rather disgusted with myself for confessing this to him, and I don't really know why I did. I think it's because he's one of those men—a man's man, clubbable, arrogant, seemingly impregnably sure of himself—that makes you want to impress them somehow. And he *was* quite impressed, which made it worse. My God, he said, you've a wife in the country and a mistress in town. I said I didn't see it quite in that light and to change the subject I suggested he read Peter's new book (which is not bad, actually—I read it in a two-hour sitting). Then he asked me if I'd like to come to his flat to play bridge that evening; I reminded him that I had to return to Thorpe to my wife and child. "So your girl's at a loose end tonight," he laughed, to show he was joking. "Perhaps she'd like to come round instead." I smiled: Freya would loathe Fleming. I can't put my finger on his essential nature. He's quite a handsome man—dark, lean—but it's the sort of handsomeness that vanishes on a closer look and you see the flaws: the weak mouth, the doleful eyes. He's affable, generous, appears interested in you—but there's nothing in him to *like*. Too spoiled, too well connected, too cosseted: everything in life has come too easily.

[NOVEMBER]

Freya—suddenly—asked me to meet her father. Why? I said. So he can get to know you, she said. Why would he want to get to know me? Because you're going to be his son-in-law one day. I laughed, but Freya kept on looking at me in that unflinching way of hers. I have to do something.

1936

TUESDAY, 21 JANUARY

The King died last night and Kipling* died last week. It seems old England's gone all of a sudden and I feel vaguely fearful, for some strange reason. I suppose you grow accustomed to these old men being around, always aware of their presence in the background of your life. Then they're gone and there's a bit less noise in the room, you look around to see who's missing.

Strange to think of the Prince as our King—that slight figure on the golf course at Biarritz.

*King George V and Rudyard Kipling (1865–1936). The Prince of Wales now became King Edward VIII.

THURSDAY, 27 FEBRUARY

Le trentième an de mon âge. Thirty years old, my God. I should be in London with Freya but Lottie has arranged a surprise for me—a dance at Edgefield. She's managed it all with great covert skill: Ben has travelled over with Sandrine and their child; Dick Hodge has come south; Angus and Sally of course, my mother, Aelthred and Enid and a host of locals. Peter and Tess couldn't make it, which is just as well, because it's awkward enough being aware that Ben and Sandrine know about Freya and I feel uncomfortable and guilty. Well, so what? It's your fault, isn't it? You can't introduce Freya to your friends and then complain that it's embarrassing when you're all in the same room with your wife. It was your choice—live with it—stop moaning.

So, thirty years old and the inevitable sense of disappointment, of being unfulfilled creeps through me like a virus. Two books published, a third imminent, a journalistic reputation of sorts. I am healthy, I have enough money to live comfortably (a house in the country, a flat in town), I am married and I have a son. And I love a beautiful woman who loves me in return. But two things nag at me, repeatedly. First, no real, good work done these last years. I feel the boundless energy of my twenties hasn't been capitalized on. *The Girl Factory* was a fluke and *The Cosmopolitans* practically had to be dragged out of me word by word. And second, all my true happiness depends on Freya, but that happiness is compromised, corrupted, by the world of lies and evasions, duplicity and betrayal, that surrounds it. It's like hanging a beautiful picture in a dark room. What a waste, you think—what's the point?

[MARCH]

The Cosmopolitans was published last week to a deafening silence, so far. I sense the literary world taking stock, not knowing what to make of this book—they can't fit the author of *The Girl Factory* to this affectionate, unscholarly examination of half a dozen obscure French poets. Is it a hoax? Who are Larbaud and Levet, Dieudonné and Fargue? And I wonder if it's all been a waste of time, all the effort it took to produce this little *jeu d'esprit* . . . No, it hasn't. I've always urged myself to do what I want to do, not what I think I ought to do. Which is a lie. Wallace sold the unwritten *Summer at Saint-Jean* in advance to Sprymont & Drew for £1,000–£500 on signature, £500 on delivery. An enormous sum, worryingly large, and suddenly I feel alarmed, wondering if I can produce the thing. Of course I immediately feel wealthy again–well, wealthier. Lottie knows nothing about the deal. I said to Freya: what shall we do with all this money? And she said, why don't we buy a lovely little house?

I bumped into Peter at Quaglino's yesterday. He was with a young woman whom he introduced as Ann Wise. When she left us for a moment to powder her nose, I asked him if this was the affair he had told me about. Oh no, he said, that one was over, this was somebody new. *Beware of the Dog* has sold almost 10,000 copies. He's nearly finished another called *Night Train to Paris* and if that does as well he's going to give up journalism. He said he'd much enjoyed *The Cosmopolitans* and had no idea I was so sophisticated–everyone's terrified by its recherché learning, he told me, ashamed to admit this gap in their cultural knowledge. It was nice of him to be so praiseful and I would have liked to have stayed in his company but I was meeting Udo–and Peter's girlfriend was about to reappear. Peter, the lucky bastard. I think I would have told him about Freya if we'd lunched alone. Two worldly authors together, two old friends–how revolting.

[In July of 1936 Spanish generals mutinied against Spain's legitimate but left-wing government and a bloody civil war ensued that, on the surface, seemed to be a classic conflict between the forces of the left–the Republicans–against the right–the Royalists. The left–the Popular Front–was always more divided than its opponents, being made up of many factions (Communists, Anarchists and Trade Unionists to name but three), not all of whom saw eye to eye. As the war advanced and Spain became geographically divided the fragile coalition of the left began to show signs of weakness and strain. The Fascist right, as it was perceived, enjoyed military support from the dictatorships of Italy and Nazi Germany. France and Britain maintained a position of non-alignment. Only the Soviet Union sent aid to the beleaguered Republicans.*

Many young committed Europeans enlisted in an International Brigade*

to fight against Fascism and there was almost universal support amongst
writers, artists and intellectuals for the Popular Front's cause.

Not long after the beginning of the war Wallace Douglas contracted
LMS to an American press agency, the Dusenberry Press Service, which
commissioned him to travel to Spain and explain the conflict to American
readers. The terms they offered were handsome, and LMS was only too
happy to accept. In the event he made two journeys to Spain to cover the
war, one in November 1936 and one in March 1937.]

MONDAY, 2 NOVEMBER

Barcelona. Maddening confusion at the Bureau for Foreigners. They
offered me a trip around a hospital: I said I had been to the hospital on
Friday, what I wanted was a trip to the front. Come back tomorrow
they said—the fourth day running they've made the same suggestion.
So I sit in this café on the Ramblas, drinking vermouth and seltzer,
watching the girls.

It's strange to see this city I know at war. Each window in every
building is criss-crossed with sticky tape to prevent them shattering in
air raids. The red and black flags fly from balconies. One in two street
corners boasts its huge poster of Marx or Lenin or Trotsky, and everywhere the grafitti of initials—CNT, UGT, FAI, POUM, PSUC. But here
in Barcelona, at any rate, CNT and FAI—the Anarchists—dominate.

And the mood on the streets is one of febrile enthusiasm. The people seem almost sick with excitement at this new society they've created—you'd think there was a revolution going on rather than a civil
war. The problem with Barcelona is that it's distant from the war, so
everyone has far too much time to talk and analyze, plot and intrigue.
And all the words take audible form in the endless hectoring announcements issuing from the loudspeakers on the buildings and in the trees.
I look about me at the young men swaggering by in their leather jerkins,
their revolvers on their belts like gunslingers. And the girls, equally
confident, hatless, with their red lips and brazen looks. Barcelona *en*
fête: more like a street party, a fiesta, than anything more serious—or
deadly.

Back at the hotel. I'm staying, aptly enough, at the Majestic de

Inglaterra on the Paseo de Gracia. It appears to be full of journalists, mainly French and Russian. I avoid the British if I can. What is it about British Communists? *Ganz ordinär,* I would say. They seem to possess a smugness and arrogance out here that would never succeed in London. Very, "See? I told you so."

I write my piece for the Dusenberry Press Service—1,000 words on the atmosphere in the city—and take a tram to the post office to send it off. I must reach the front before I leave.

WEDNESDAY, 4 NOVEMBER

I've been appointed my own special liaison officer (that's what happens when you write for American newspapers). He's a man in his forties called Faustino Angel Peredes. When I met him at the Ministry of Information he was wearing the standard Anarchist uniform of denim overall and short leather jacket, but I have to say he looked a little ill-at-ease in them. His greying hair is oiled back from his brow in neat furrowed waves and he has a handsome pitted face as if he's suffered from smallpox early in his life. I spoke to him in Spanish and he answered me in fairly good English—an intellectual, then, not a worker. I told him I wanted to go to either the Madrid front or the Aragón front, whichever was practicable. He politely said he would do the maximum to see that my wishes were fulfilled.

Met Geoffrey Brereton, *New Statesman* correspondent. He said Cyril Connolly was due out any day now.

THURSDAY, 5 NOVEMBER

Faustino, as he insists I call him (we are all brothers now), said he'd obtained clearance for us to go by train to Albacete. To celebrate I treated him to lunch. He's a droll but reserved man. I asked him what he had done before the war and he said he had been an administrator at La Lonja, the School of Fine Art. An administrator, he reminded me, not a teacher. We talked about contemporary painting and I told him I had met La Lonja's most famous alumnus. "Ah Pablito," he said, with little warmth. "How is he? Still safe in Paris I suppose." He explained to me something of the complexities of the Popular Front who are fighting Franco and the Fascists. Forget about the different trade unions, he said, that will just confuse you further. Basically the Republican side was made up of Anarchists, Communists and Trotskyists. "Here in Catalonia," he said, somewhat ruefully, "we are very Anarchist. And unfortunately we are all very suspicious of each other. Factions inside factions inside factions. In Valencia, the Communists call us Fascists here in Barcelona. And we call the Communists in Valencia Fascists also." He shrugged. But you're all united against the Fascists, I said. "Of course. And it is a most useful term of abuse." What do you think of the Communists? I asked him (I was taking notes). "Buenos y bobos," he said with a smile. Some good ones, some stupid ones.

I typed all this up and mailed it to the Dusenberry office in New York. There seems no point in cabling—I'd need some sort of a scoop to justify the expense. So far in a week I've made $300 from Dusenberry—the most lucrative journalism ever. At this rate I'm making $100 every two days, and I'm on expenses.

FRIDAY, 6 NOVEMBER

To the railway station at first light to be told by the militia that our documentation is not in order. I suggested to Faustino that we go to Valencia and see if we have better luck with the Communist authorities there. It is the Republican seat of government after all, I reasoned, and it might be easier to reach Madrid from Valencia than Albacete from Barcelona. You may well be right, he said with his polite smile. "En el fondo no soy imbécil, Faustino," I said [In the end I'm not a fool]. He actually laughed at that and patted me on the shoulder. I think I've broken through.

SATURDAY, 7 NOVEMBER

We reached Valencia last night after a train journey of about ten hours. Faustino had changed out of his Anarchist overalls and wore the shabby black suit of a functionary. Valencia was thronged with people but it lacked the slightly crazed zeal of Barcelona. You see more soldiers than militia and armed civilians, and there is a regular traffic of army lorries up and down the streets. Many buildings are sandbagged: the front is only sixty miles away, after all. We are staying at the Hotel España and last night ate a huge meal of steak and fried potatoes at a restaurant called, bizarrely, the Ideal Room. The place was packed with well-dressed men and women. No shortages in this city, clearly. We went to the government offices and I was told I could go to Madrid with a party of other foreign journalists in ten or fifteen days. Which is no good to me. At luncheon we stuffed ourselves again—mussels and shrimps washed down with a pitcher of beer. Faustino caught an afternoon train back to Barcelona. He said he felt uncomfortable in Valencia and the realization seemed to disturb him: "And this is my own side," he said. We said goodbye with some affection and I told him I would be back in a month or so. I'm going to take a steamer from here to Marseilles and fly from there to Paris. I'll file my Valencia story for Dusenberry and try to organize things better from London. I could be waiting here fruitlessly for weeks otherwise.

Went to the Museo Provincial in the afternoon. Closed. I wanted to see the Velázquez self-portrait. Sums up my trip, rather.

FRIDAY, 27 NOVEMBER

On the train heading for Norwich and Thorpe for the weekend. Heart like a stone. Very depressed to be back in London after the sheer passion and fervour of Barcelona. Those young men and women held sincere beliefs, had clear values and a cause and wanted to change the world they lived in for the better. To walk the streets of London after that and see our pinched, grey-faced, downtrodden populace makes me despair.

It was exacerbated by meeting Angus for a drink in White's.* He asked me if I wanted to join (he would put my name down, he said). I said no, instantly, then—to undermine his surprise—said I couldn't afford it. Evelyn [Waugh] was in the bar with some people and, in conversation, I let him know I'd just been in Spain and told him how impressed I'd been with the Republican spirit. He looked at me pityingly, his pale blue eyes wide and bright. "Spain has nothing to do with you or me, Logan," he said. And then immediately contradicted himself by asking if I'd seen any burnt-out churches. I'd seen locked ones, I said, but no signs of anti-clericalism. Then he changed the subject and started asking me questions about Aelthred and the Edgefields. Sometimes I think I'm only of interest to Evelyn because I married an earl's daughter.†

All the conversation in the bar was about the King and his American girlfriend, and there was a lot of ribald and actually quite disgusting speculation about the King's "sexual difficulty" and Mrs. Simpson's skill in being able to resolve it. Why do I feel ashamed on his behalf? I feel some sort of absurd bond with him because of our brief meeting and my giving him my matches and his asking my name. I'd be no good as an Anarchist in Barcelona, evidently.

MONDAY, 30 NOVEMBER

I was cast down and depressed all weekend, and Lottie, unusually for her, asked me what was wrong. I told her I was out of sorts, hated England and wanted to live abroad, as far away from Britain as possible. I ran through the possibilities: Australia, Canada, Malaya, South Africa, Hong Kong . . . But we're everywhere—there's no escape.

*The club in St. James's.
†Waugh was currently engaged to Laura Herbert, whom he later married.

TUESDAY, 8 DECEMBER

Nothing but the Royal Crisis in the newspapers. It makes me sick. Let him abdicate for her, I say—good for him. They would understand him in Spain: he's decided to be ruled by his heart, not his head, and our little bourgeois world is appalled.

Very nice review of *The Cosmopolitans* (anonymous, of course) in *The Times Literary Supplement*, which has cheered me up. The reviewer seems to understand why Les Cosmopolites provoke such a strong feeling in me. They are all about romance, about life's excitement and adventure and its essential sadness and transience. They savour everything both fine and bittersweet that life has to offer us—stoical in their hedonism. An admirable code to live by, it seems to me. Sales stand at 375 copies. Talk about falling "stillborn from the press." Roderick side-steps around the book when we meet, as if it were a turd on the pavement, and talks only of *Summer at Saint-Jean*—of which I have written only a few hurried pages. I feel I can forget it for the moment, financially buoyed as I am by all my dollars earned in Spain. I'm planning another trip in March. *Life* has commissioned a long piece on the International Brigade ($350). Sold one of my Barcelona articles to *Nash's Magazine* for £30.

MONDAY, 14 DECEMBER

I thought the King's broadcast* was very moving, very sober and pitched exactly at the right level of personal regret, mingled with a sense of duty and conscious sacrifice. You could hear the strain in his voice. The ex-King, I mean, now that we have George VI. What a year, 1936: at the very least it can go down in British history as a year when three kings reigned, however briefly. Freya's opinion about the abdication is, without any prompting on my part, exactly the same as mine—Lottie's is absolutely opposed. So what should he have done? I asked

---

*The King, having abdicated, became Duke of Windsor. He broadcast his reasons for his decision to the nation on 11 December.

her on Sunday (we were lunching at Edgefield–the whole table turned on me). It was impossible that he should even think of marrying her, Lottie said. You can't have a Queen of England who's been divorced twice–what kind of example is that? No, no, Aelthred said: he should have shipped her back to America for a year, pretended it was all over, then everyone would have forgotten about her and then he could have quietly set her up in a discreet place in London–have her back in his life with no fuss at all. "Isn't that a bit cynical?" I said. "A bit ignoble, perhaps?" Aelthred was genuinely puzzled. "What on earth do you mean?" he said. "He's the King. He can do what he damn well pleases." They make me sick–the lot of them.

1937

[WEDNESDAY, 10 MARCH]

Toulouse airport. I'm waiting for the flight to Valencia–delayed one hour. Today is Wednesday–on Monday evening I left London. I think I'm still suffering from aftershock: I've no idea what I left behind. Wrong–you know exactly what you left behind. What you don't know is what you'll discover when you go back.

It happened like this. I spent the weekend at Thorpe as usual. Came up to London on the early train and shopped at the Army & Navy Stores for a few items that would be useful in Spain (powerful torch, 500 cigarettes, extra warm clothing). I was back at Draycott Avenue after luncheon. I laid out my clothes on the bed and was about to start packing when there was a ring at the doorbell. I went down the stairs to open the door and found Lottie and Sally [Ross] standing there–gleeful to have surprised me like this. Lottie said something like: "You left your manuscript behind and we were bored so decided to have a day trip to London." She handed over the folder (twenty-four appalling pages of *Summer at Saint-Jean*–I had no desire to take it to Spain and had deliberately left it at Thorpe). Sally said: "Well, come on, Logan, aren't you going to ask us up?"

What could I say? What could I do? In the flat Sally realized instantly and started talking like a machine gun. It took Lottie a few seconds longer and I saw her stiffen and her "Isn't this a nice . . ." die in her throat as she looked around her. They didn't go into the bedroom, kitchen or bathroom—there was no need. They had recognized the effect a woman has on a dwelling place. Whether a palace or a mud hut, it is palpable and unmistakable—a presence, a kind of order quite different from something that even the tidiest man living alone produces. They had been expecting something basic and functional—which is how I described Draycott Avenue to anyone who was curious—one level above a monk's cell. Our dark, warm, cherished, lived-in few rooms were eloquent testimony to the kind of secret life I lived in London—my books, my paintings, the odd, interesting bits of furniture. Lottie became very quiet while Sally's camouflaging prattle intensified, with her finally blurting out, "Do you know, darling, if we run we'll make the 5 o'clock." It was the perfect exit line and allowed us all to bustle downstairs. Lottie rallied and managed to say, "Do take care in Spain," and I was able to kiss them both goodbye and wave them off up Draycott Avenue.

I sat in a chair for half an hour letting the clamour in my head settle down: the warring suppositions, courses of action, ways of escape, excuses, lies . . . Freya came home and I told her what happened. It really startled her and then she gave me her look and said, "Good. I'm glad. It's time we stopped hiding."

And now I sit here in Toulouse thinking of potential consequences and I see that, in general, Freya is wise and right. But I feel—what?—that it has been forced upon me, that it should never have happened this way. I could have lied my way out of my sham marriage to Lottie in a manner that would have spared her feelings better and hurt her pride less. Not to be. They have just announced a three-hour delay for our 'plane.

MONDAY, 15 MARCH

Valencia. Hotel Oriente. Things have changed here even in a few months. The Communists (the PSUC) seem to have consolidated their hold and consequently things are being run better: at the Foreign Press Bureau I was presented with my passes to the Aragón and Madrid fronts. British journalists protested vainly at this favouritism: they go to the back of the queue—the Republican government is incensed by our non-intervention policy. One of them told me that Hemingway was here, staying in a vast suite at the Reina Victoria. I shall go and pay my respects.

Later. Hemingway was very cordial—he said he was on his way to Madrid to make a documentary film. He'd never heard of the Dusenberry Press Service. "Are they paying you? That's the only criterion." Like clockwork, I said. He's also on a contract for something called the Newspaper Alliance. He's paid $500 for each cabled story and $1,000 for each mailed one—up to 1,200 words. Jesus: almost a dollar a word. Rather puts Dusenberry in perspective. "Rack up the expenses," Hem advised. He was at his most likeable, in expansive, genial mood, and we drank a lot of brandy. The Hotel Florida in Madrid, he told me, was the only show in town. I said I'd see him there later in the month. I head back to Barcelona tomorrow to meet up with Faustino. I realize I'm happy to be back in Spain and not just because it has its own excitement. It stops me thinking—and caring—about what Lottie may be doing or saying. Wrote a loving letter to my Freya, saying all would be well—but specifying no particular course of action.

THURSDAY, 18 MARCH

Faustino and I caught a troop train this morning and chugged slowly up onto the Aragón plateau. It's damn cold and I'm wearing my Army & Navy long johns. We've billeted for the night in a little village called San Vicente about a mile from the front. My supply of cigarettes makes me a very popular man. We had a big tortilla each and as much wine as we wanted in exchange for a pack. Faustino warned me to ration them: "All Spanish tobacco comes from the Islas Canarias." I realized: Franco holds them—soon there'll be no cigarettes for the Republicans.

Barcelona has changed too: that exhilarating revolutionary fervour seems to have vanished and in its place the city seems merely to have reverted to its pre-war state. The poor are everywhere and the rich are correspondingly obvious. The big expensive restaurants are busy, yet there were huge queues for bread and the beggars and the urchins were back outside the shops of the Ramblas. At night you could see the prostitutes lounging in the doorways and on street corners and the nude cabarets were being advertised again. All that had gone last year. I asked Faustino what had happened and he said the Communists were slowly taking control from the Anarchists. "They're more interested in governing," he said, "they're better organized. They put their principles to one side in order to win this war. While all that we have are our principles. That's our trouble: we Anarchists only want liberty for the people—we crave that—and we hate privilege and injustice. We just don't know how to achieve this." He laughed softly and repeated his words like a private incantation: "Love of life, love of humanity. Hatred of injustice, hatred of privilege." It was actually strangely moving to hear the heartfelt way he said these words. "Who could disagree with that?" I said. I quoted him Chekhov's two freedoms: that all he asked for was freedom from violence, freedom from lies. He said he preferred his formula of two loves, two hatreds. "But you left one out," I said. "Love of beauty." He smiled. "Ah, yes; love of beauty. You're absolutely right. You see how romantic we are, Logan—deep down." I grinned at him: "En el fondo no soy anarquista." He gave a genuine joyful laugh at that and to my surprise he held out his hand. I shook it.

FRIDAY, 19 MARCH

We are led up to the front. In the misty early morning light we can see that San Vicente is a huddle of stone and mud buildings, somewhat knocked about, the narrow lanes between the buildings churned into a quagmire by the passage of vehicles, men and animals. It's freezing cold. We plod up a path between small mean fields showing the first acid-green shoots of winter barley rimed with frost. We are making for the ridge ahead. The countryside is bleak and virtually treeless—a wind-battered scrub (I can identify rosemary bushes) covers the sierra and the escarpments beyond.

The trenches are on the ridge of the hill—scrapes behind piled rocks and sandbags—or else more substantial caves dug into the lee side of the hill. Beyond the trenches (which only extend a hundred yards) there is a line of barbed wire and then the hillside falls steeply away to the valley bed beneath. On the crest of the hill rising up on the opposite side of the valley I can see some emplacements and an orange and yellow flag flying—the Fascist position, over half a mile away, and I can even spot the ant-figures of soldiers moving about. The absence of threat is very present—nobody is bothering to keep his head down. Faustino introduces me to the *teniente,* who turns out to be English—a sullen, suspicious man who says his name is Terence, pointedly not giving me his surname. He used to work at Chatham Docks, he says. He takes me on a cursory tour of the position: the men huddle around little smudge fires, unshaven, filthy and demoralized, their weapons muddy and ancient. Terence explains that this area of the front is manned by the POUM militia—the Trotskyites. Only the Communist forces receive new Russian weapons. "The Russians won't supply us because we're anti-Stalin," he says with real vehemence. "Make sure you write that in your newspaper. I'm sure Franco's most grateful." He spoke of the government in Valencia with more disdain than he expended on his enemy opposite.

We clamber over the trench and advance as far as we can to the wire. Peering down the slope, I can make out what I take to be a dead body lying there. "A Moroccan," Terence says. "They attacked us in January. We beat them off." Then I hear a few dry reports, almost like two stones being hit together. "Are we being shot at?" I ask. "Yes," Terence says, "but don't worry, they're too far away."

When I leave I give him two packs of cigarettes and he manages to produce his first smile.

[SATURDAY, 20 MARCH]

I realize I've seen everything I'm likely to on the Aragón front so we arrange to leave. Faustino and I spend the morning waiting for a truck to take us back to the railhead. We are both dispirited by what we've seen—but, as Faustino points out, it's worse for him: I'll be going away in a matter of days—this is his war and he has to stay. These are the images of the struggle against Fascism that he has to subsist on.

We squelch along the main street and wander into the church. It is empty of all furniture (all burnt as firewood) and is now used as a stable for mules and shelter for chicken coops. I take out my *Baedecker* and read out loud: "San Vicente has a small Romanesque church that is worth a detour." We sit on the floor and smoke and sip whisky from my flask. How long will you be in Madrid? Faustino asks. A week, ten days—I don't know, I confess, I really should return home as soon as possible. I smile at him: my marriage is in difficulties, I say. I tell him about Freya, our double life, my London/Norfolk set-up. My wife found out, I say, just before I came to Spain.

He makes a rueful, sympathetic face. Then, as if this small confession has reassured him in some way, he scribbles an address on a scrap of paper. "If you could visit this person when you reach Madrid—he'll give you a parcel for me. And then when you return to Valencia I'll come and collect it. I'd be most grateful." He can see from my expression that I'm somewhat reluctant to become involved in anything clandestine. "Don't worry, Logan," he says. "This has nothing to do with the war."

MONDAY, 5 APRIL

Hotel Florida, Madrid. Air raid sirens tonight but it must have been a false alarm—I heard no bombs falling. Then I dined with Hemingway and Martha.* Tiresome Russian journalist joined us halfway through. Sore

*Martha Gellhorn (1908–98), journalist. Later became the third Mrs. Hemingway. In Madrid she was working for *Collier's Weekly* magazine.

head this morning, so Martha took me to the Bar Chicote and had the barman make up Hemingway's favourite hair-of-the-dog concoction— rum, lime juice and grapefruit juice—and I felt marginally better.

Then we caught a tram out to the University Quarter to "have a look at the war," as Martha put it. It was strange to leave your hotel and journey through a city that, although on a war footing and somewhat knocked about, gave the signs of being a normal Monday—shops open, people going about their business. And then suddenly you find your-self on the front line.

Here in the University Quarter there is much more rubble on the streets, buildings have been destroyed and there's not a pane of glass left unshattered. We showed our press passes and were led into an apartment block where we climbed to the top floor and found a room that had been turned into a machine-gun emplacement. Through the sandbagged windows there was a good view of the ugly concrete blocks that were the new university buildings. The mood was one of lethargy: soldiers sat around smoking and playing cards. It has been stalemate here for months—since the big Fascist attacks were repulsed last November.

A young captain in the militia (with a patchy, soft, boy's beard) lent us his binoculars and we peered over the sandbags piled in the window embrasure. We could clearly see the lines of trenches and strong posts, barricaded streets and barbed wire. There were piles of earth thrown up by the shelling, and the concrete façades of the buildings were pocked and scarred by bullets and shrapnel. Off to the west I could see the shallow valley that marked the course of the Manzanares River and the San Fernando bridge. It was a slightly hazy sunny day: springtime in a civil war.

Martha had some questions for the captain who had come from Guadalajara and she wanted to know some details about the Popular Front's victory there last month. I translated for her. Martha is a tall leggy blonde, not spectacularly pretty, but good fun and bracingly sure of herself, in that particularly American way. She and Hemingway must be lovers by now, though they are very discreet in public. I know there's a Mrs. Hemingway and children back in the USA somewhere. Martha's wiry blond hair reminds me of Freya's. Hemingway is busy with his film* and I've not seen much of him. Strange to think of us both in similar state of amatory duplicity.

Once she had her information Martha left me, but I stayed on, wondering if I could write this up for Dusenberry, somehow. They had cabled asking me to stop sending them so much material—I sense interest in the war is dying down. Then, as I was scanning the landscape beyond the university, I saw what looked to be some kind of armoured staff car coming along the road from Moncloa. It was painted grey and its windows and windscreen had been replaced by metal plates with slits and firing holes in them. I pointed it out to the captain and he said, "Let's give them a fright." I had the impression that the urge to relieve boredom was the motive here, rather than anything more bellicose. So they ratcheted up the machine gun to its highest elevation—the car must have been a mile away—and the captain gestured to me, as if offering me a seat at a table, and said, "Why don't you have a go?"

I sat down on the little bucket seat fixed to the gun's tripod and peered through the sights. There was a pistol grip on the gun, and beside me a soldier stood feeding the belt of bullets into the breech. Through the sights I drew a bead on the car that was pottering down an embanked lane towards one of the university buildings. I squeezed the trigger and fired off a long burst—a split-second later the bank on the side of the road erupted in a cloud of dust. I fired again, traversing slightly, and watched the bullets chew up the tarmacadam in front of the car—which had stopped abruptly, and was now reversing. My God, this is fun, I thought. I fired again, "walking" the bullet strikes up the road until I could see I was hitting the car. A cheer went up. The car backed around a corner and was gone.

I sat back. The captain patted me on the shoulder. The man on the ammunition belt grinned, showing me his silver teeth. I felt all trembly and tense at the same time. "That'll teach them," the captain said. "What do they think this is? Some kind of—"

He never finished because suddenly the room was full of flying metal, falling plaster chunks and brick dust. The wall opposite the windows had fist-sized holes punched in it, stripping the plaster in seconds down to the lathes. Everyone flattened themselves to the floorboards

---

The Spanish Earth, a documentary, directed by Joris Ivens.

and crawled into the lee of the outer wall. I threw myself to one side as the sandbags in front of me seemed to explode. The man holding the belt screamed as a bullet hit it and ripped the belt out of his grasp. Blood flicked from his hand onto my jacket.

There must have been two or three machine guns that had zeroed on to our position and had let fly simultaneously. They kept up an almost consistent fire for what seemed like an hour but was probably only five minutes or so. I lay on the floor, my arms wrapped around my head, repeating to myself over and over again "Fish in a pond, fish in a pond" (my mother's advice for calming any panic attack). A sizeable lump of plaster dropped on my leg, giving me a terrible shock for a second or two. To my right the man who had been feeding the bullets into the machine gun whimpered in pain. It looked like the little finger of his right hand had been almost ripped off. It bled copiously, forming a little dust-mantled pool on the floorboards until the captain managed to bandage it up.

When the firing became more desultory the captain and I crawled to the door, wrenched it open and wriggled out onto the landing. I stood up and dusted myself down: my throat was parched and I was shaking all over. "You'd better go," the captain said, in a brusque unfriendly way, as if it had all been my fault.

I sit here in my room writing this and realize I have filed my last dispatch from the war zone. I have to go home now. This is as close to death as I've ever come in my life and it terrifies me. My clothes smell of plaster dust, my head is still full of the clanging ripping thudding noise of the thousands of bullets that poured into that room. Fish in a pond, fish in a pond. While I lay there the only other thought in my head was of Freya and of Freya receiving the telegram announcing my death. What are you doing here, you fool? You've been pretending you're needed but you're secretly delaying your return. What's the Dusenberry Press Service to you? Go home, you fool, you idiot. Go home and sort out your life.

FRIDAY, 9 APRIL

Valencia. On my last night in Madrid I was packing up my bits and pieces when I came across the scrap of paper Faustino had given me in San Vicente. It was an address, nothing more, in the Salamanca district. I decided to do the favour he'd asked of me and went down to the lobby to ask the concierge if he knew where this place was. Hemingway arrived with Ivens as I was peering at a city map and wandered over to see what I was up to. I explained and I could sense he was immediately intrigued.

"There's no name? No contact?"

"Just an address. I'd be expected, he said."

"Let's go, Logan," he said, and steered me out of the hotel to where his car and driver were waiting.*

We drove down the Calle Alcala to the Retiro Park and then motored north into the Salamanca district where, after a few false turns, we found our street and pulled up outside a large nineteenth-century apartment block.

"You wait here," I said to Hemingway.

"Out of the question."

The concierge showed us up the stairs to Apartment 3 and I rang the bell. An old servant opened the door. Beyond him the apartment seemed huge, barely lit, a few pieces of furniture covered in dustsheets.

"We thought you wouldn't come," the servant said. "Who is Señor Mountstuart?"

I showed him my passport.

"Who's he?" the servant asked.

"Never mind. I'm a friend of his," Hemingway said.

The servant went away for a moment and returned with what looked like a small Persian rug rolled up and tightly secured with string. We took it from him and left.

Back in my room in the hotel I untied the bundle and unrolled the rug. Hemingway was as excited as a child. Inside the rug were seven unstretched oil paintings that I spread out on the bed.

*Provided exclusively for Hemingway by the Republican government.

"Joan Miró,"* I said.

"Miró," Hemingway said. "Fuck me."

"Aren't they appalling?"

"Hey, he happens to be a friend of mine," Hemingway said, some of his geniality deserting him. "I own a big early one of his—not like these, though."

"They're just not to my taste," I said. The canvases were all on the small side, about three feet by two, typical Mirós of his post-realist, surreal phase. I rolled them up again.

"Who owns seven Mirós?" Hemingway said.

"And why am I chosen to be courier?"

"So many questions," he said. "Let's go to the Chicote and try and figure them out."

MONDAY, 12 APRIL

Back in Barcelona again, having heard nothing from Faustino. Telephone calls and telegrams to the Press Bureau and the FAI headquarters brought no response, so I thought it would be better if I tried myself.

.Accordingly this morning I go to the Bureau of Foreigners, the people who first attached him to me as press liaison and they tell me he no longer works there. Faces are heavy with suspicion and few words are wasted. Nobody seems to know where he is. I leave the building and a young man with prematurely grey streaks in his hair follows me out and leads me to a café. He won't tell me his name but says that Faustino was arrested about ten days ago. "Arrested by whom?" I ask. "By the police." "On what charge?" He shrugs. "It's usually treason: it's the easiest." I ask if Faustino has a wife or family. Just a mother in Seville, I'm told—which is no good to me, as Seville is behind Fascist lines. His family came from Seville originally, the grey-haired young man tells me, and maybe that was bad luck for him. Then he leaves: I don't know what he means by that—all I know is that Seville fell early to the Generals in this war.

*Joan Miró (1893–1983), Catalan artist. Hemingway owned *The Farm*, purchased in 1925 for $250.

*   *   *

Later. There was an unsigned printed note waiting for me at the hotel when I returned this afternoon. It reads: "F. Peredes was shot by the police while resisting arrest. He had been accused of being a Fascist spy. Don't stay long in Barcelona." After the initial shock I begin to wonder if this is true. Perhaps it's some kind of hoax? Or maybe Faustino is really the victim of some kind of Communist-Anarchist feud. Or was he a spy? The mistrust, the doubt, the elusiveness of the real facts seem typical of this war. Somehow I can't believe he has gone. I think of Faustino and our brief acquaintance and the wry scepticism he brought to his Anarchist calling: "Lover of life, lover of humanity. Hater of injustice, hater of privilege." Not the worst epitaph a man could have. But now I am the possessor of seven paintings by Joan Miró—and which almost certainly didn't belong to Faustino. What am I meant to do with them?

[*LMS returned the next day to Valencia and five days later he was in London once again, the seven paintings with him, wrapped in their Persian rug. He went up to Thorpe as usual on the next weekend. Later in the year he wrote up the events that followed his return as a form of aide-mémoire.*]

[SEPTEMBER]

After these endless months of lawyers and meetings and emotional upheavals it seems wise to try to write a coherent account of events, and not rely on scrappy notes I kept at the time.

When I came back from Spain in April I spent some wonderful but increasingly apprehensive days with Freya. Lottie had no idea that I'd returned and I wanted to go back to Thorpe in a manner, at least initially, that implied everything was as it had always been. Freya said no one had tried to make contact with her, though for two or three days she had had the feeling that the flat was being watched: she'd seen the same man on the street two days running when she returned from work.

I telegraphed Lottie that I was back and boarded the train for Norwich with a feeling of nausea and dread. It was the recriminations ahead that made me feel pre-emptively weary and sick, not what I was about to do. Freya and I had spoken at length and we had decided the only course of action was to tell Lottie everything and then ask for a divorce. But when I reached home the house was empty and dark. No sign of Lottie and Lionel–I knew that my telegram had driven them to seek refuge at Edgefield.

So I rang Edgefield and was very surprised when Angus answered. His voice was cold and flat and he said he would be round to see me in the morning.

"I'd like to speak to Lottie, please," I said.

"She's too ill to speak. She never wants to speak to you again. That's why I'm here: anything you want to say, say to me."

"For heaven's sake," I began. "This is no way to "

Then he practically screamed at me: You disgusting piece of filth! You set yourself up with your whore–I hung up, cut him off.

The next day was exceptionally uncomfortable. In the morning Angus arrived with the family solicitor, one Waterlow, and this man informed me that I was to be out of Thorpe by nightfall, that our joint bank accounts were frozen (by court order), that I was to be sued for the upkeep of Lottie and our child and that if I wished to see Lionel I would be granted one day a month but would have to give ten days' written notice of my intention. Angus sat glowering at me silently while this went on. I ordered them both out of the house.

At the front door Angus took a swing at me but I ducked and managed to punch him hard in the chest, so hard that he fell down. Waterlow had to hold me back from giving him a good kicking. Angus looked as if he was about to cry as he was helped into the motor, screaming threats and insults at me all the time. He really is a grade-one CAUC.*

*The initials stand for "Complete And Utter Cunt"–LMS's ultimate term of abuse.

And so we entered the war of the solicitors. I found a good man called Noel Lange—recommended by Peter Scabius—and Lange and Waterlow set to. I agreed to offer no defence to the petition of divorce, but I refused to concede to their other demands. And as usual it all came down to money. I thought I owned half of Thorpe Hall, that it had been a wedding gift from Aelthred and Enid to Lottie and me, but in fact it turned out it was held in a trust under Lottie's name. So much for the Earl's faith in the durability of his daughter's marriage. I used this information to free some of the money I'd earned from *The Girl Factory*, which was tied up in investments and joint savings accounts. We ding-donged to and fro. Lange did a fine job but he didn't come cheap. I found myself doing more journalism than ever.

And then at the end, just when we seemed to have everything sorted out, they insisted that I had to go through the motions of being caught in flagrante. I believe absolutely that this was Angus Cassell's doing. I became very depressed at the tawdriness all this would involve: the hiring of a prostitute, the booking of a hotel room, the complicity of a member of the hotel staff who would "discover" us and sign an affidavit. I told Freya what they were demanding and she said, "Wonderful, let's have a dirty weekend together."

So we went to Eastbourne and the hotel maid delivered us breakfast in bed with both of us actually in the bed, much to her consternation. Freya called out: "Morning. By the way, I'm not married to him!" and the poor girl left the room to our delighted laughter.

The decree nisi came through last week and the announcement appeared in *The Times* under the headline: EARL'S DAUGHTER GRANTED DECREE NISI AGAINST BESTSELLING NOVELIST. It read: "There was no defence to the petition of Lady Laeticia Mountstuart, of Thorpe Hall, Thorpe Geldingham, for the dissolution of her marriage with Mr. Logan Gonzago Mountstuart on the grounds of his adultery with Miss Freya Deverell at the Westminster Hotel, Eastbourne. Costs were granted against Mr. Mountstuart."

I feel exhausted, poor, but exultingly happy, now that it's all over. Another of those moments in my life—a sloughing away of the past, the old, mottled dull skin gone; gleaming, glossy new scales on display. Now my life with Freya can truly begin. But there remains one problem: the guilty ache in my heart—Lionel. What do I do about Lionel? I love him; he's my son. I can't argue against the truth inherent in these words, but, to be truthful again, they have no real meaning for me. But what exactly is Lionel to me beyond my flesh and blood? Be honest, Logan—you only see him as a sickly, irritating child. Ten minutes of his company is demanding: your mind wanders, you want him to be taken away. Yes, I admit it, maybe I'm not good with infants, but for all that I cannot, will not, let him go. I have to save him from the Edgefields. He's only a baby: he might change as he grows older and I have to be there in his life, however awkward, however unpleasant for me, as a key and lasting influence. I will not abandon Lionel Mountstuart to that hellish crowd.

1938

FRIDAY, 7 JANUARY

Freya and I were married yesterday at the Chelsea Town Hall. Present: the bride and groom. Mother, Encarnación, Freya's father, George, her brother, Robin. Afterwards we went up the road to the Eight Bells and had a few drinks. It was a low-key affair, but our happiness was complete. Mother, however, was subdued; she says she likes Freya very much but added that "you cannot forget a person like Lottie in just one day." I reminded her that Lottie and I had been separated for eight months by now. "It seem like one day to me," she insisted.

Then they all went their separate ways and Freya and I went home to Draycott Avenue. We had lunch, we went for a chilly walk in Battersea Park, came back and read and listened to music on the gramophone, then ate our supper.

"I'm so happy," I said to her as we held each other in bed, "that I think I might explode."

"Boom!" she said. "Young marrieds disintegrate simultaneously in Chelsea flat."

THURSDAY, 17 MARCH

I pick up this journal again to note that (a) I have finished Chapter 3 of *Summer at Saint-Jean* and that (b) Freya announced this morning that she was pregnant. We had talked about trying for a child but I never expected it to be so suddenly successful. And of course the news made me think of Lionel, whom I've seen only once this year. He was brought to a hotel in Norwich (where I'd rented a room for the day) in the company of a nanny and I spent a few hours with him, trying to play with him, trying to entertain him. He was suspicious of me and kept going to his nurse. It was an embarrassing exercise. Poor Lionel—is he going to be the biggest casualty of our loveless marriage? Somehow I feel the child Freya and I will have will fare better. One thing is clear: we have to find a new place to live.

[APRIL]

Can there have been a filthier spring than the one we have had this year? Cold and rain—rain and cold. Wallace has managed to contract me to the *Sunday Referee:* ten articles, £500. Since Spain my stock and my rate have gone up, gratifyingly.

Freya is well, no morning sickness to speak of. Another day this last week in Norwich with Lionel. This is now establishing itself as the pattern. I rent a room for a day—on neutral ground—and Lionel is brought down from Thorpe in a taxi with the nanny. He stays until it's obvious that he's tired or bored—or both.

Enjoyable supper with Turville Stevens last night. Turville said he knew war was inevitable as far back as 1936—before Spain. And the news is bad from Catalonia—Franco's troops advancing fast, every day. My God, Spain. It seems like some crazy dream. And what am I to do with Faustino Peredes's Mirós? I shut my mind to Turville's warnings of the coming war with Germany. I think we've found a house in Battersea that we can just afford.

[JULY–AUGUST]

32, Melville Road, Battersea. We moved in July and have spent the summer putting the place together. I was sorry to say farewell to Draycott Avenue but we both love Melville Road. "Do you think it's named after Herman Melville?" Freya said. "I'm sure it was," I said, "and what better place for a fellow scrivener to reside." Melville Road is a curved row of three-storey, redbrick, Victorian terraced houses. Each one has a small patch of lawn or gravel at the front and, behind, there's a long thin garden that backs onto the fence demarcating the gardens of Bridgewater Street, which runs parallel. We have a sitting room, dining room and kitchen on the ground floor; two bedrooms and a bathroom on the floor above and, under the eaves, an attic room with a dormer window. This I've transformed into a book-lined cell to act as my study. Through the window I can see the chimneys of Lots Road Power Station on the other side of the Thames.

Yesterday we went for a walk in the park and watched machines digging lines of trenches. War is in the air and will come from the air, it seems, even to tranquil Battersea. Freya is fat and uncomfortable now: the baby is due in October.

WEDNESDAY, 31 AUGUST

Hitler has a million men under arms, it says in the *News Chronicle*. Meanwhile, I write a review of a mediocre book on Keats for *The Times Literary Supplement*. A dry hot summer, one almost entirely of hard work and pleasurable domesticity. Freya's nipples are the colour of Bournville chocolate. We papered the second bedroom in canary yellow for "Baby" as we call it—it, not he or she. We are superstitiously vague: we say we don't care, but after Lionel I long for a little girl. I think Freya wants a boy.

And I had another odd trying day with Lionel. He was fractious and whingeing, "alive with prickly heat" the nurse said. So I took his clothes off and let him play in the room naked, much to the nurse's shock. "I shall have to tell Lady Laeticia, Mr. Mountstuart." "Please do," I said. I haven't seen Lottie since the divorce—it's curious how your old life, or a life you abandon, can just fall away so quickly. Lionel is our only connection, now. From time to time I would soak a flannel in cold water, wring it out and lay it over the worst of his rashes on his thighs and under his arms and for a minute or two he would calm and seemed to look at me with gratitude. "Thank you, Daddy," he said. "That feels nice." My guilt grows as our baby approaches. I wept on the train back to London—a rare event for me—but nothing brings tears to my eyes like Lionel. How can I do any more for him? And what will it be like when "Baby" arrives? Hitler has a million men under arms, according to the *News Chronicle*—I see I've already written that.

[SATURDAY, 1 OCTOBER]

If I'm honest with myself I completely understand the relief people feel over Munich.* Our child is due any day now and, although—polit-ically, intellectually—I condemn our cowardly concessions, and I feel a desperate sorrow for the Czechs, I say to myself that surely it's better that we have peace than go to war over an insignificant disputed part of a distant small country? Remember I have seen war at first hand in Spain, all its absurdity and malevolent chaos, and I know that war has to be the absolute, final, last resort. The brutal truth is that the Sude-tenland issue would never be sufficient reason to set the countries of Europe at each other's throats. So, are you an appeaser, then? No: I see the threats these madmen pose, but I know also that all I want to do is live my life in peace like the rest of the world. Hitler doesn't want war—what he wants are the spoils of war, which is why he's so clever and

*Europe came close to war in the autumn of 1938 as Hitler threatened to march into German-speaking Czechoslovakia, the Sudetenland. Neville Chamberlain, the British Prime Minister, flew to Munich and there, in a four-power meeting (Germany, Italy, France, Britain), it was agreed that the Sudetenland be ceded to Germany. The Czechs were not invited to be present. Chamberlain returned triumphant from Munich bearing a piece of paper signed by Hitler expressing the desire "of our two peoples never to go to war together."

which is why he keeps on seeming to succeed. The spoils of war without war. Perhaps this is what Chamberlain understands and is why he has given this final concession but cleverly extracted peace as its price. As I wander about Battersea I sense a real palpable lightening of mood—laughter from a pub, women chatting on corners, a postman whistling as he does his round. These clichés tell us something: we came to the brink and we pulled back. The trenches can be filled in, the gas masks returned to the government warehouses. I'm sure my German equivalent—the writer in his thirties, with a wife and a child on the way—can't feel any different from me, can't want to see his cities bombed, his continent ravaged by war. Surely it's a matter of common sense? But then I say to myself: how much common sense was on display in Spain?

Turville rings, almost in tears, talking about the shame and betrayal, of how Chamberlain and Daladier [the French prime minister] gave away too much and Hitler will be back for more. Is he right? I sit here in my little house, a sudden autumn rainstorm beating down outside, and pray that he is wrong.

Oliver Lee on the wireless this evening, predicting death and destruction unless we stop Hitler now. But we have stopped him, haven't we? Hearing Lee, I find myself thinking of Land and, in the way one automatically does, imagining the alternative life I might have led if she had agreed to marry me. Futile, pointless speculation. I'd have never met Freya. Perhaps Land did me the greatest favour she ever could.

I walked out this evening to the bottom of the garden and smoked a cigarette. Last week I planted an acer in the furthest bed from the house, in honour of our new baby. The sapling is as tall as me and, by all accounts, it can grow forty feet tall. So, in thirty years' time, if we're still here I can come back and see this tree in its maturity. But the thought depresses me: in thirty years' time I'll be in my mid-sixties and I realize that these forward projections that you make, so unreflectingly, in your life are beginning to run out. Suppose I'd said in forty years' time? That would be pushing it. Fifty? I'll probably be gone by then. Sixty? Dead and buried, for sure. Thank Christ I didn't plant an oak. Is that a good definition of marking the ageing watershed? That moment when you realize—quite rationally, quite unemotionally—that the world in the not-so-far-distant future will not contain you: that the trees you planted will continue growing but you will not be there to see them.

FRIDAY, 14 OCTOBER

We have a little girl. Born at 8 o'clock this morning. I had a telephone call from the hospital and went round immediately. Freya was exhausted and dark-eyed. The baby was brought out for me and I held her in my arms, a little angry red thing, tiny hands beating the air as she screamed her lungs raw. We are going to call her Stella—our personal star. Welcome to the world, Stella Mountstuart.

1939

SATURDAY, 14 JANUARY

Distressing letter from Tess Scabius, addressed to me alone and marked "Personal and Confidential." In it she tells the story, as she sees it, of Peter's constant infidelities and the appalling strain they put on the marriage. She asks for my help: "I never suspected this of Peter when I married him and I know you would never imagine him capable of this sort of behaviour. Quite apart from the harlots in London he is now seeing a woman in Marlow. He still regards you as his closest friend. He admires you and respects you. Logan, I cannot ask you to make Peter love me again as he used to, but for pity's sake he has to be asked to stop these shameful affairs. I am at the end of my tether and I know everyone in the village is aware of what is going on. Can he not be a gentleman and spare me and our children this cruel humiliation?" And more of the same. Poor Tess.

FRIDAY, 20 JANUARY

I rang Peter and he asked me to luncheon at Luigi's to celebrate the publication of his third thriller, *Three Days in Marrakesh*. I should have said he left *The Times* last year. He is, by all surprising accounts, a far more successful writer than I am. I'm glad to say I do not possess a scintilla of envy for him.

Later. We lunched, and it was most enjoyable. He has changed, Peter— there is a worldlier, coarser streak in him. In mid-sentence his eyes would follow a young waitress as she walked across the room and he endlessly passed remarks about the other women in the restaurant: "That's not her husband," "She could be a beauty if she dressed better," "You can smell the sexual frustration coming off her" and such like. Maybe this is the effect of constant adulteries. Though he confessed he felt more relaxed with prostitutes: he says he's a regular with two or three. He recommended the practice to me—pleasure without responsibility, he said. I reminded him I was extremely happily married. "No such thing," he said. It was the perfect cue, so I told him about Tess's letter. That shook him: he went very silent and I could see there was a fury building in him. "Why would she write to you?" he kept saying. I didn't enlighten him. But at least I've done my duty by Tess. I wrote to her telling her what I'd done. Those days in Oxford seem centuries ago, now.

Newspaper placards in Soho as I catch a bus home: FRANCO AT THE GATES OF BARCELONA.

[MARCH]

Well, that's it, I suppose, now Hitler's in Prague.* Oliver Lee was right, and now "Czechoslovakia has ceased to exist." My sentiments of last

---

*Hitler's troops entered Prague on 15 March ostensibly "to protect" Bohemia and Moravia from the newly seceded Slovakian state.

October look like foolish wistful desperate dreams. And Franco has all Spain now—which will please Mother. I write this at the kitchen table as Freya holds the baby to her breast. In the cupboard beside her the gas masks sit in their cardboard boxes—never returned. War must come now and Danzig will be the next crisis. And what will you do in this coming conflict, Logan? What will Daddy do in this war?

Roderick has offered me the job of reader at Sprymont & Drew at £30 a month. I asked for £40 and he told me Plomer* at Cape gets the same, so I could hardly argue. I suspect Roderick is trying to tie me into the firm as I had told him *Summer at Saint-Jean* was almost finished. One has to wonder at his logic: journalism is so time consuming, and now that I have to read manuscripts all week and compile reports on them, it is going to make it virtually impossible to write anything else.

Small but sustained success of *Les Cosmopolites* in France. Cyprien writes to say he is being fêted again as if it were 1912 and he was an eminent man of letters, "grace à toi." I must go back to Paris before Armageddon arrives.

[JULY]

Aldeburgh. We've rented a small house in the town here for July and August—forever drawn back to Norfolk for some reason. I go up to London when business demands but I've relished our first two weeks here and am reluctant to move. The fresh silver light off the North Sea, the lure of vanishing horizons. I work all morning, writing journalism or, more than likely, reading manuscripts for S&D (which seems to be taking up more and more of my time). Then if the weather's fair we have a picnic on the beach—take a travelling rug, a thermos and sandwiches, sit on the shore and watch the waves roll in onto the pebbly strand. Stella is a beautiful, round-faced, plump-cheeked, blue-eyed, golden-haired stereotype of a baby girl. Curious and jolly. We sit her

*William Plomer (1903–73). South African writer and reader at Jonathan Cape Ltd. for many years.

down and put a pile of pebbles in front of her and we watch the baby pick up, examine and let fall pebble after pebble while we sit and chat. Freya's started to help with the reading of some of the S&D manuscripts—I think she rather misses the BBC.

I managed to persuade Lottie to let us have Lionel for a weekend, given we were close at hand. It was not a success. Lionel seemed terrified of Freya and I began to wonder what nonsense Lottie had put in his head—or that bitch Enid more like. He seemed more relaxed with me and I tried to do the right sort of Daddish things. We kicked a football around the garden for an hour and eventually he said, "Daddy, how long do we have to play this game?" To be blunt he seems an average child with nothing remarkable in any area as far as I can see—not bright, not charming, not funny, not cheeky, not handsome. And to make matters worse he has all the worst aspects of the Edgefield physiognomy. Once he asked me if I was married to Freya. Of course I am, I said. He frowned at this and said, "But I thought you were married to Mummy." I explained. "Does that mean you're not really my Daddy?" he asked. I'll always be your Daddy, I said and, God help me, almost started to cry.

[JULY]

Fleming asked me to lunch at the Carlton Grill. It seems he's still a stockbroker but now has some sort of clandestine role in the Admiralty. He said "a lot of people" had been very impressed with my articles on the Spanish War. I told him that 90 per cent of what I'd written had been published in America. "I know," he said, "those are the ones that impressed us." He talked about the future war as if it were already taking place and asked me what my plans were. "To survive," I said. He laughed and leant across the table and said—very cloak and daggery—that he would count it a personal favour if I "would hold myself in readiness for a special post." He said the job would be based in London but would be a vital one for our war effort. Why me? I asked. Because you write well, you've seen war at first hand and you have no illusions about it. On the way out, and I'm sure this was arranged, we bumped into an older man, in a grey suit of very old-fashioned cut, who was introduced as Admiral Godfrey. I was being quietly evaluated.

MONDAY, 7 AUGUST

Tess Scabius is dead. She drowned in the Thames, Peter told me—incoherently—over the phone. She hadn't returned home at tea time after a walk and Peter wandered down to the river to look for her. He saw a crowd of people and police about half a mile downstream and strolled over to see what the fuss was all about—to find they had just dragged Tess out of the water. She'd been gathering flowers and slipped on the bank. And she couldn't swim. "A terrible ghastly accident," he said.

What a hellish awful shock. Dear Tess. I think back to our stolen Sundays in Islip and the intense storm of emotions that was generated in that hard damp bed in the little cottage. And I acknowledge what you did for me, Tess. Accident? I doubt it. I think she had had enough. Thank God, thank Christ, at least I bearded Peter about his rutting and fucking. I told Freya, who could see how upset I was, and I told her something of our shared history: the challenges at school; Tess's audacious following of Peter to Oxford. I said I thought I'd been a bit in love with her at the time and jealous of Peter. I thought it best not to tell her of our affair.

SUNDAY, 3 SEPTEMBER

Battersea. A warm hot day. Freya and I listen to the prime minister's broadcast announcing that we were now at war with Germany.* Stella crawls about the kitchen floor making little high-pitched yipping sounds, which signal intense and almost insupportable pleasure. I hug Freya and kiss her brow. Don't join the army, she whispers, I beg you. So I tell her about Fleming's offer and we pray it holds good.

---

*Hitler had invaded Poland on 1 September. Britain had issued an ultimatum that the German forces had to have withdrawn by 11:00 a.m. on the 3rd. Hitler had not complied.

*   *   *

Later I walk out into the garden alone and look up at the blue sky and the few cruising clouds. It's steamy and warm. Church bells are ringing. I feel strangely relieved: like a seriously ill patient suddenly being diagnosed—"It's serious, Mr. Mountstuart, but there is no need to despair." The confirmation of the worst news does, paradoxically, clear the mind: at least the way ahead is obvious and people know what they have to do. But as I stand in my narrow garden this warm summer day I wonder if it will end in oblivion for the three Mountstuarts and I feel fear seep through me like icy water.

THE SECOND WORLD WAR
JOURNAL

True to his word, Ian Fleming was in touch during the first week of the war and Logan Mountstuart was offered a job in the Naval Intelligence Division. This celebrated intelligence service was housed in the Admiralty Buildings off the Mall and was run, in 1939, by Admiral John Godfrey (Fleming was his assistant). Mountstuart was created a lieutenant (special branch) in the Royal Navy Volunteer Reserve. Within the organization of NID he was attached to the propaganda department with particular responsibility for monitoring intelligence coming out of Spain and Portugal and was also instructed to come up with clever schemes to ensure that both countries stayed neutral. At first this involved no more than the placing of anti-German stories (which had relevance to Spain and Portugal) in as many press outlets as possible. Mountstuart also advocated leafleting the populations of the key cities, Lisbon, Oporto, Barcelona and Madrid. He liked NID: it was a relaxed, faintly raffish but proudly efficient institution. He also thought he looked very smart in his navy blue uniform (handmade at Byrne & Milner) with its undulating gold bands at the wrist.

Initially Freya and Stella went to stay with the Deverells in Cheshire but, as the foreseen mass bombing of London never occurred, they moved back in early 1940. Peter Scabius volunteered to serve in the Auxiliary Fire Brigade. Ben Leeping and his family left Paris in October 1939 and he set up a small gallery (still Leeping Frères) off Duke Street in St.

James's. The keeping of a diary during wartime by serving men and offi-
cers was forbidden. LMS seems to have been aware of this and the nar-
rative flow is often interrupted until something of genuine interest
happened to him.

1940

MONDAY, 10 JUNE

I took Faustino's Mirós into Ben's gallery today and laid them out on
the floor of his viewing room. He practically had to grab a chair to stop
himself falling over. "Have you any idea what a collection like this
means?" he said. I explained their strange provenance. "Well, I suppose
possession is nine tenths of the law," Ben said. "You've no idea who
they belonged to?" I told him it was a mystery, but such aspects of the
story that could be established would be vouched for by Ernest Hemingway.

Ben seemed all a-quiver, as if his brain were working too fast. He
kept saying that this was the sort of thing that happened once or twice
in a dealer's lifetime. I said I was short of money, that they'd sat in a
cupboard in my house for three years and something had to be done.
In the end Ben paid me £300 for them but said he would sell the
biggest one on my behalf—when, he wasn't sure: he would wait until
the market was right or the perfect buyer or buyers came around. He
was almost overpoweringly grateful to me but not so grateful that he
couldn't spot a bargain. Paul Klee* is very ill, he said, and offered me
an extra hundred pounds for my little Klee. I said I'd hold on to it for
the moment, thank you very much.

Lunched in a restaurant by the BBC—liver sausage and salad. Is

*Klee died on 29 June.

rationing beginning to bite already? Did my talk on Joyce with Geoffrey Grigson (prickly, chippy man), but I was very complimentary
about *Horizon** and he was mollified, somewhat.

WEDNESDAY, 26 JUNE

One of our new commanders in NID turns out to be James Vander-
poel†–who I was at school with. Still the same powerful stocky figure
but now with a pointed ginger beard. A navy man through and
through and, I think, a little discomfited to find me amongst his
underlings. We went for a walk in Green Park and reminisced about
Abbey. He told me some news about my coevals and I realized I'd lost
all interest in them. Telephone call from Dick Hodge this evening.
Great excitement: he's joined the Royal Marines. I told him I was in
the Wavy Navy. Doing what, he asked? Very hush-hush, I said. How
wonderful to be able to use that expression in all seriousness.

MONDAY, 8 JULY

Godfrey and Fleming called me and Vanderpoel in and asked if either
of us knew Lisbon. I said, yes; Vanderpoel, no. "At least one of you
does," Godfrey said. "Anyway, that's where you're heading." I inquired
why. The Duke of Windsor has arrived there, Godfrey said, in flight
from his house in France and the advancing German and Italian
armies, and we need to keep an eye on him. Can't the embassy do
that? Vanderpoel said (I sensed he was reluctant to go). Apparently the
ambassador is a bundle of nerves and the MI6 man there is a dipsoma-
niac and hated by all the staff. The position of the Duke was very delicate, Godfrey went on: he can't come back here (because of the family)
and we can't risk him falling into the hands of the Nazis. I said: "I met
him once, in Biarritz, 1934." Fleming looked at Godfrey as if he'd just

---

*The magazine, recently launched and edited by Cyril Connolly, to which
Grigson contributed.
†See p. 36.

won a bet. "I told you Mountstuart was our man," he said mysteriously.

I went back to Freya to relay the news. I said I'd be in no danger—but, because it was Lisbon, she didn't seem to mind so much. "Will you go to our restaurant?" she said. I told her I'd drink an entire bottle of wine to us both.

WEDNESDAY, 10 JULY

Lisbon. Vanderpoel and I flew out in a Coastal Command Sunderland flying boat from Poole Harbour. Smooth, trouble-free flight. Lisbon seemed crammed with well-off refugees, all the riff-raff of Europe looking for safe passage out. For the first time I felt strangely aware of Lisbon and Portugal being on the very edge of the Old World. Here at its extremities the terrified transients gathered, gazing out at the vast refulgent ocean for some sign of security.

We reported to the embassy, where we were coolly received by a man called Stopford—the so-called "Financial Attaché" but actually the head of MI6 in Portugal—and were grudgingly briefed. The Duke and Duchess had fled their villa near Antibes on the 19th of June as the collapse of France gathered pace and had travelled by road with their staff and some consular officials to Madrid. There, they had spent nine days being wined and dined before coming on to Portugal. They were living in the house of a Portuguese millionaire called Ricardo Espírito Santo in Cascais, about an hour's drive from the city. "I don't know what NID think they can do that we can't," Stopford said nastily. "We've got our people in the house, the grounds are hotching with Portuguese police. He can't fart without us hearing about it."

As we left, I said to Vanderpoel: "What a boozer, very comforting." "I thought he seemed very decent," Vanderpoel said. I don't think our Vanderpoel's cut out for intelligence, somehow. We went back to our seedy hotel, which was all we could find, aptly called the London Pension, and Vanderpoel took to his bed saying he thought he was coming down with flu.

THURSDAY, II JULY

Vanderpoel running a temperature. This evening I went to a drinks party at the embassy and met a man called Eccles* who seems to be some kind of *éminence grise* out here—very much in the know; highly sceptical about the abilities of the embassy staff. He sees the Duke regularly and I gained the impression things were not going well. The Duke won't leave until he has his future sorted out and certain guarantees have been delivered about his and the Duchess's status. "All very petty," Eccles said, "given the appalling situation we're in."† I repeated my old line about meeting the Duke in Biarritz and Eccles practically embraced me. He immediately invited me out to dinner at the villa tomorrow night. "It was a very fleeting encounter," I said. "Couldn't matter less," Eccles said. "He's surrounded by dubious financiers who're all talking to the Germans. You'll be a breath of fresh air."

Just popped in to see Vanderpoel to tell him the latest development. He's outraged and has forbidden me to go. I said only Godfrey had that kind of authority. Wrote to Freya and told her I was to dine with David and Wallis. That should be some story to tell.

FRIDAY, I2 JULY

To reach the Duke's villa—the Boca do Inferno—you drive almost to the furthest western point of Europe, or so it seems. He's staying in a big pink stucco house on a rocky promontory surrounded by pine trees. Ahead stretches the whole Atlantic Ocean. We passed through Belém and Estoril and followed the coast road to Cascais. Approaching Cascais (set back on a hill above the villa) we were stopped twice by police. They are clearly well guarded. As we drove through the gates Eccles

*David Eccles, on secondment to Lisbon from the Ministry of Economic Warfare.
†France had surrendered on 22 June. Britain now stood alone against the Axis powers.

reminded me that a "bow from the neck" was suitable for the Duke but the Duchess should receive nothing more than a smile and a handshake. On no account was I to refer to her as "Her Royal Highness." I said I understood.

The villa itself sits behind high stone walls and is large and comfortable with a swimming pool. Ricardo Espírito Santo and his wife, Mary, greeted us on the terrace, where we were served drinks. There was another couple there by the name of Asseca. Then we waited. And waited. There was a lot of covert watch-glancing and Mary Espírito Santo kept disappearing to whisper to the staff until eventually the Duke and Duchess of Windsor came down from their room.

First impressions. They were both immaculately dressed. The Duke looked like a miniature American film star, slim and dapper, with his grey-blond hair swept back, a perfectly cut dinner suit, a cigarette casually poised in hand. The Duchess, who must be in her mid-forties, was equally petite. A beautifully matched porcelain couple. You wanted to put them on your mantelpiece. I towered over them both. The Duchess was heavily made-up and heavily bejewelled. She has an expressionless, mask-like face and a rather protuberant mole on her chin. Eccles introduced me when my turn came and mentioned Biarritz.

"We met on the golf course, sir."

"You're a golfer, thank God." He turned to the Duchess. "Darling, Mr.–um–this dear fellow–was at Biarritz in '34. Do you remember that holiday? Wasn't it fun?"

"I adore Biarritz," she said.

"So do I," I said, "In fact I think–"

"And he's a golfer," said the Duke.

"David, don't butt in like that. Mr. . . . . Mr. ?"

"Mountstuart."

"Mr. Mountstuart was going to tell us something fascinating about Biarritz."

Then we were interrupted and ushered into dinner. I sat beside Senhora Asseca and Mary Espírito Santo (who was rather attractive in that cold, hard way certain rich European women have). Senhora Asseca spoke Spanish and broken French. Mary E.S. was fluent in English. Eccles and the Duchess laughed together a lot: they seemed very gay. I thought at the time: store this one away, Logan–the Duke and Duchess of Windsor, a lovely house on the sea, hot-and-cold running servants, good food and wine. The world at war.

As we were leaving the Duke came up to me and asked if I was free for golf tomorrow afternoon at the Estoril Golf Club. I said indeed I was, many thanks, etc. He lingered a bit and I said it was good to see him in such fine form after his epic drive across Europe. His face slumped, sulkily, and he lowered his voice: "I'm a virtual prisoner here," he said. "Nothing but blocking on all sides and mountains of red tape." I commiserated and we agreed to meet at the club tomorrow at three o'clock.

On the drive back to Lisbon, Eccles was intrigued to learn of the appointment. He thought for a while and said, "I'd appreciate it, Logan, if you'd let me know anything that goes back to NID." Of course, I said, then added: "You haven't any idea where I can lay my hands on a set of golf clubs, have you?"

SATURDAY, 13 JULY

His Majesty's Government has generously procured me a new set of golf clubs, which is very decent of it (them?) and thus equipped I set out to the Estoril Golf Club for my game. The Duke, Espírito Santo and another man called Brito e Cunha turned up half an hour late and with them were about a dozen Portuguese detectives. The Duke said he would prefer to play a two-ball with me and urged the other two to tee off first. The day was warm with a slight breeze from the sea. The course was baked hard and the grass burnt tinder-dry. My first drive leapt along the fairway as if it were bouncing on concrete for practically 300 yards. But the greens were watered and played well, if fast.

The Duke was a twelve handicap and played a sober and risk-free game. At the third tee we stopped for a cigarette as Espírito Santo and Cunha played on. I bounced my ball on the ground and it made a crack like a marble on asphalt. "I'm told this is what golf's like in the tropics," I said.

"Well, I'll get plenty of practice soon enough," the Duke said glumly.

"I don't understand, sir."

"They're sending me to the Bahamas. I'm going to be governor."

"Bahamas? Should be wonderful."

"D'you think they said that to Napoleon when they packed him off to St. Helena?"

The Duke was in a bad mood but was playing good golf—and I was careful not to challenge his early two-hole lead. As his golf improved so did his demeanour and his indiscretions. I sensed his relief at talking to a fellow Englishman and golfer.

Some of the things he said:

His brother, the King, was an amiable fool completely dominated by his wife. It was the Queen who was preventing him and the Duchess returning to Britain. "Doesn't want us there," he said. "Thinks we'll steal their thunder. Very jealous of Wallis."

He was sick to death of Portugal and longing to leave but would only go "on my conditions."

Two problems appeared to preoccupy him more than anything else. One was the recovery of certain possessions left at their houses in Antibes and Paris (clothes, linen), and the second was the refusal of the British government to release his soldier servant from active service so he could become his valet in the Bahamas.

"Do you have a valet?"

"Alas, no," I said.

"You should get one. People don't understand that someone like me just can't function without a valet. I want Fletcher,* and I won't leave till I have him."

I said, without really thinking, "Perhaps I might be able to help."

He turned to me and grabbed my arm. "Believe me, Mountfield, if you could do anything—"

"Mountstuart, sir."

"Mountstuart. I'd be most grateful."

"Why don't I see what I can do."

After golf (the Duke won, three and two, and I wrote him a cheque for £3) I went straight to the embassy and had a cable encrypted and sent to Godfrey at NID. I said that if Piper Alistair Fletcher could be

*Piper Alistair Fletcher was in the Scots Guards.

released from active service I felt sure that the Duke would become far more amenable to all suggestions.

Vanderpoel running a temperature of 103 degrees. He still managed to dress me down for sending a cable without his permission. "I'm your senior officer," he coughed. I have a feeling Vanderpoel will soon attain CAUC status if he carries on in this way.

SUNDAY, 14 JULY

Drinks with Eccles. He's a smooth, plumply handsome man, who apparently made a fortune from Spanish railways before the war. I told him about our day on the golf course and the Fletcher moan.

"It seems to be bothering him more than going to the Bahamas," I said. "If we could get him Fletcher and his trunks from Antibes he'd be putty in our—in your hands."

Eccles looked at me—not very kindly. "Interesting point," he said. "I'll get on to it."

We talked circumspectly about the Duke. It's clear that he behaves like a spoilt child and all one's dealings with him are conditioned by this attitude. If he's in a good mood, all's well. If he's in a bad mood, then he sulks and stamps his foot and won't come out to play.

MONDAY, 22 JULY

Invitation to dine with the Duke and Duchess on Wednesday. Vanderpoel insisted that he go in my place, protested to Eccles, who told him not to be ridiculous. So it's non-speaks with Vanderpoel—about as adult as the Duke. Vanderpoel seems more or less recovered and spends all day at the embassy sending cables and trying to look busy. I sit in the sun and read ancient detective novels from the pension library. Wish Freya were here. Depressed by the news that Vichy France has severed diplomatic relations with us. Was there ever a better example of the lunacy of this war? And here I am hobnobbing with an ex-king.

WEDNESDAY, 24 JULY

On the way to Boca do Inferno Eccles warned me not to sign the Duke's visitors' book if I were asked. Also he said not to breathe a word about the NID. Apparently German agents have been putting about the rumour that the British secret service are plotting to have the Duke assassinated.* Eccles said he was paranoid and very jumpy.

But in fact he was the soul of good humour and fun—laughing, chatting non-stop, pouring people's drinks. I had a sense of him as he must have been as a young man and the charisma he wielded so effortlessly. And the Duchess herself was suddenly far more attentive to me—Eccles quite abandoned. When she talks to you she puts her face about two inches closer than is normal. As a result even the most banal statement has a quality of intimacy and when she speaks you feel her breath on your face. It is a fantastically effective trick. She is no beauty but somehow this special proximity makes you feel chosen—she has eyes only for you. I saw her at close range and I must say her teeth are immaculate. Impossible to get any idea of her figure under the haute couture. She's very skinny but is she flat-chested? She called me Logan.

It was a big party full of Espírito Santo's Portuguese friends. The Duke and Duchess feel they have been cold shouldered by the embassy, and Eccles and I were the only British there. It was a warm night and we took brandy and coffee out on the terrace. There was a great booming and crashing of surf in the darkness. The Duke, smoking a cigar, led me onto the lawn to the edge of the circle of light cast by the house. I said how enjoyable the evening had been and what a pleasure it was to see the lights of Estoril blazing along the coast after the blackout in London. I didn't add this, but, standing there in the warm night, it seemed to me as if we were in a never-never land for rich and beautiful people where war was unknown. But the Duke wasn't listening.

*This was a plot by the Germans to lure the Duke to Spain and "safety."

"I had a telegram from Winston* today," he said. "We've got Fletcher—he's coming to join us."

"Excellent news, sir."

"All thanks to you, Mountstuart."

"No, really, I—"

"You're too modest. I know you must have pulled a few strings. We're really grateful."

"Don't mention it."

"Trouble is we still can't get those trunks of clothes and linen from Antibes. We desperately need them for the Bahamas. If there was anything you could do . . ."

"I'll try, sir."

As we strolled back to the terrace the Duchess called me over. She put her face very close to mine and for one mad instant I thought she was going to kiss me on the lips. But she said, "Would you sign the visitors' book, Logan?" and showed me where it was on the side table in the hall. "Thank you for everything you did for David," she added in a quiet voice, and touched my arm. I picked up the pen, pretended to write my name, but she had drifted away.

Back at the London Pension. Vanderpoel has left me a note. I'm to take a flying boat back to London tomorrow while he stays on. Miserable jealous little bastard.

[*The Duke and Duchess of Windsor left Lisbon on 1 August on board an American liner to take up the Duke's appointment as Governor of the Bahamas. In London LMS wrote up his account of the Lisbon trip and his meeting with, and impressions of, the couple (in more circumspect terms than he employed in this journal). This long confidential memorandum† (some sixty pages) was circulated in NID. It was highly regarded.*]

*Churchill had cabled: "I have now succeeded in overcoming War Office objections to the departure of Fletcher."
†PRO FO 931 33/180 in the Public Record Office.

When the bombing of London and other British cities began in September of that year (the Blitz), Freya and Stella once again decamped to the Deverells in Cheshire until the summer of 1941. LMS's mother remained in Sumner Place, now home to some eighteen paying guests, Mercedes Mountstuart and Encarnación occupying one large room on the ground floor. LMS's work continued routinely in NID and he wrote regular bulletins for the Spanish language service of the BBC.]

1941

WEDNESDAY, 31 DECEMBER

Summary of the year. Freya and Stella are asleep. I sit in my little study under the roof with the blackout curtains drawn, whisky bottle in front of me.

The war. The war, the war. My mind can't take it in. Depressed by the news in the East.* Elated by Pearl Harbor. This will finally bring the Americans in and for the first time I allow myself to think this war will end—with victory. Thank you, Hirohito.

Mrs. Woolf committed suicide in March—drowned herself in the River Ouse, à la Tess. Death by water. And Joyce died this year in Zurich, a sick, blind, prematurely old man, by all accounts. Talking of which:

Health: good in the main. Two teeth removed, flu in September. Drinking too much.

Family: Freya and Stella both startlingly well. I've seen Lionel three times this year—shame on me.

Work: Vanderpoel a grade 1 CAUC. Many hours expended on the Spanish bulletins. Freya has taken over my reading duties at S&D for £20 a week. I pointed out that this was the same work I did for 30 per

---

*The British battleships *Repulse* and *Prince of Wales* had been sunk by the Japanese in December. Hong Kong was occupied. The Japanese raid on Pearl Harbor occurred on 7 December 1941.

cent less money. Roderick wouldn't budge—he's punishing me for the non-delivery of *Summer*. I wrote a long article on Verlaine for *Horizon* (Cyril very complimentary but it has yet to run). Some reviewing for newspapers, but with £55 a month from NID, plus Freya's salary, plus my Miró windfall we are better off than ever.

Home: solid new doors and windows on Melville Road*—we sleep more securely. Dreams of Spain. Who drinks at the Chicote now? I try to imagine Paris full of Nazi soldiers.

A wasted year, in the end. I asked Fleming for a move to another section, but he said I was too valuable to the Iberian peninsula.

Friends: Ben (as always); Peter (more distant); Ian (can't really make him out); Dick (lost to view). But I don't really need friends because I have Freya.

General reflections: I am in uniform, I am making a tiny contribution to the ending of this interminable war. My profession—writer—is in temporary abeyance. I am solvent, thanks to the RNVR and Joan Miró (and Faustino), but my French royalties are unobtainable. I must read more. I finally got round to Hemingway's Spanish book [*For Whom the Bell Tolls*]—an embarrassing disaster. What could have possessed him to write so badly?

Resolutions: to drink less. I fear this war is driving me to alcoholism. To find a book I truly want to write (in other words abandon *Summer at Saint-Jean*, you fool).

Favourite place: Melville Road.
  Vice: procrastination.

*Melville Road had been damaged by a near-miss in April. Before repairs could be effected the house was burgled.

Faith: love for Freya and Stella.

Ambition: to come through this war and write something of value.

Fantasy: driving south from Paris to Biarritz and the Atlantic with Freya by my side and a suite booked at the Palais.

1942

FRIDAY, 20 FEBRUARY

Lunch with Peter [Scabius]. He looks gaunt and ill. He says his children are living with his parents. He can't stay in the house at Marlow—haunted by Tess. He had a terrible row with her father, Clough, who shouted and screamed at him and they almost came to blows. I commiserated: awful business, ghastly tragedy. Then he told me he was taking instruction to join the Roman Catholic Church.

ME: Why on earth would you want to do that?
PETER: Guilt. I think I drove Tess to her death in some way.
ME: Don't be absurd. She didn't commit suicide, did she?
PETER: I can never be sure. But even if it was an accident, once she was in the water I'm sure she welcomed her death.

I said that what he needed was a psychiatrist, not a priest, but he wouldn't be told. He said he wanted God back in his life. I said, well what's wrong with the God you grew up with, your Anglican God? He's too soft, he said, too reasonable and understanding, doesn't really want to interfere—more like the ideal next-door neighbour than a deity. I need to feel God's terrible wrath, his retribution waiting for me, he said. My Anglican God will just look sad and give me a ticking off.

"Look at us," I said, growing exasperated. "Here we are, two highly educated, worldly writers talking about God in heaven. It's all complete mumbo-jumbo, Peter, all of it. If you want to feel better you might as well sacrifice a goat to the sun-god Ra. It makes just as much sense as what you're saying."

He said I didn't understand: if a person had no faith it was like talking to a brick wall. I recognize that his "conversion" is a form of penance—some punishment he needs. Then he told me he was writing a book about Tess and their life together.

"A book? A biography?"

"A novel."

FRIDAY, 27 FEBRUARY

I'm thirty-six years old today. Does that make me middle aged? Perhaps I can hold off the designation until I'm forty. Freya baked me a cake, a sponge (she found some real eggs somewhere) and stuck three red candles and six blue ones in it. Stella insisted on blowing them out. "How old are you, Daddy?" she said. I counted the candles for her: "I'm nine," I said. Freya looked at me: "Who's a big boy, then?"

Take away this war and I suppose you could say I was as happy as a man could be. Only two worms in my particular bud—Lionel and my work. I see Lionel less and less—partly because of my job and also because Lottie remarried.* Lionel is almost nine now and nearly a complete stranger to me. And my other concern: I sense my *métier* slipping away. No urge to write beyond occasional commissioned journalism. Perhaps I need this war to be over before I can start again.

WEDNESDAY, 15 APRIL

Today Peter is received into the Roman Catholic Church. He asked if I would be his godfather but I declined on the grounds that it would be insincere. I think he was a little hurt, but too bad. He asked me if he could send me the manuscript of the Tess novel "to verify the facts." It

---

*Lady Laeticia had married Sir Hugh Leggatt (Bart.), a widower and neighbouring landowner twice her age, in 1941.

seems nearly finished by all accounts. The prospect of reading it makes me feel sick, to be honest.

MONDAY, 4 MAY

To the BBC for yet another broadcast to Spain—to pre-empt fears of a German invasion of the Canaries, apparently. On the way out I met Louis MacNeice,* whom I scarcely know, but who was embarrassingly complimentary about *The Girl Factory*. He asked me what I was doing and I said nothing—and blamed the war. He said he knew how I felt but we had to keep writing, that this war might last another five or even ten years and that we couldn't just live in a kind of artistic deep-freeze. "What about our life to come? 'What did you write in the war?'—we can't just say nothing." He talked vaguely about adapting *The Girl Factory* for the radio, but worried that it might be a bit strong. Anyway, he inspired me—I'm always inspired after meeting another writer, and I realize we have our own secret brotherhood, even if it just comes down to sympathizing with others' moans and complaints. I came home and read through my chapters of *Summer*. They were appalling. I went down to the bottom of the garden and burnt everything I'd written in the incinerator. I have no regrets—in fact I feel relieved. However, I worry a little about what Roderick might say about my advance, spent many years ago . . .

THURSDAY, 28 MAY

Ian [Fleming] wandered into our office today with a file in his hand and looked at me rather intently. Plomer was in the room and said, "Watch out, Logan, Ian's got his hey-I've-just-had-an-idea look on." I asked him what the file was and he said it was mine. "So 'G' is for Gonzago," he said. "So what?" I said. "And you're half Uruguayan, born in Montevideo—how fascinating. How good's your Spanish?" I said I

*Louis MacNeice (1907–63), poet, then working as a talks producer at the BBC.

could speak it all right, though indifferently. Ian looked at me and
nodded. "I don't think we're exploiting you to the full, Logan," he
said. I felt a little unsettled by this for a while but now don't think it's
worth pondering further—just Ian with too much time on his hands,
trying to come up with one of his mad ideas.

[JULY–AUGUST]

Movements. Freya and Stella to Cheshire. I joined them for a week.
Then ten days in Devon with the Leepings. A dragging August. Sudden
depression realizing that we'd been at war for three years, almost. I
think back to our lives in the fretful, worried thirties and it seems a vanished, golden age.

[AUGUST]

Back from Devon. I took Stella to see Mother—who suddenly looked a
lot older. She is sixty-two, after all. She started to reminisce about
Montevideo, which is not like her: she was always thrilled to come to
Europe, even Birmingham seemed exotic. But today she moaned on at
me as we sat in their cluttered room, Encarnación washing up the tea
dishes in the single sink. Logan, she said, I have become *una patróna* [a
landlady]—is not dignity for me. I wanted to point out that if she hadn't
let Prendergast squander the small fortune that Father had saved both
our lives would have been a great deal more comfortable—but I hadn't
the heart. I realized she'd lost weight and that was what had aged her—
she was always "ample." Not any more. She loves Stella and this has
reconciled her to the loss of Lionel and her aristocratic daughter-in-
law. Both she and Encarnación revel in Stella's fair skin, blond hair
and blue eyes, as if she is some kind of genetic joke. They stare at her,
fascinated, and point out the most ordinary things: "Look how she
opened the cupboard"; "See, she sneeze again"; "Watch her playing
with her doll." It is as if no child in history has ever mastered these
challenges. When they pick her up, they kiss her repeatedly: kiss her

hands, her knees, her ears. Stella is composed and tolerant, permitting this licence. When we leave and I close the door I hear wails and sobbing.

THURSDAY, 17 SEPTEMBER

A letter from Roderick, hinting at a law suit, demanding the repayment of my advance on *Summer*. Simultaneously, the arrival of Peter Scabius's novel in typescript, ominously entitled *Guilt*. The first line reads: "Simon Trumpington never thought he would associate shire-horses with a beautiful girl." I can't bear to read on: there will be something truly disgusting and upsetting, I know, in this exploitation of Tess's short, unhappy life.

FRIDAY, 18 SEPTEMBER

I wrote to Peter—lying—saying I had read the novel in one sitting and that I thought it "masterly" (very useful word) and that it was a "fine tribute" to Tess and praising him for the courage it must have taken to write such a harrowing etc., etc. I made one suggestion: that he change the hero's surname—it sounded too P. G. Wodehouse. I said I would read it again in a calmer mood—I hope I may have bought myself some time.

MONDAY, 12 OCTOBER

Fleming and Godfrey came in today looking very pleased with themselves and told me to pack my tropical kit. "You're off to the sunny Caribbean," they said, "lucky so-and-so." Most amusing, I said, save your jokes for the new boys. But they weren't joking: the Duke of Windsor is about to re-enter my life.

FRIDAY, 30 OCTOBER

New York City. I have been temporarily promoted to commander and
sit here in my downtown hotel waiting to go and take up my new command. I suppose—not to put too fine a point on it—that I have become
a spy and I have been sent to spy on the Duke and Duchess. Feel a little
ill-at-ease.

Fleming and Godfrey explained the background. The Duke has settled reluctantly but diligently into his new role as Governor of the
Bahamas. He became friendly with a Swedish multi-millionaire who
lived out there called Axel Wenner-Gren (the founder of Electrolux), a
man who has made a vast fortune from vacuum cleaners and refrigera-
tors and who, like most of the wealthy denizens of Nassau, does not
want to pay any taxes on his fortune. Not only does the tax-free status
of the Bahamas suit Wenner-Gren, but its location also places him
close to his burgeoning business interests in South America. He and
the Duke had become close—they dined together, Wenner-Gren leant
him his yacht—but then in July of last year Wenner-Gren was black-
listed by the United States and declared a Nazi sympathizer. The
British followed suit and the Duke was obliged to inform his friend
that he could not re-enter the Bahamas.

Word had reached NID from an agent in Mexico City that Wenner-
Gren was involved in massive currency speculation and was making
huge profits. The fear is the worry is—that the Duke is in some way
involved in this speculation also. The Duke's private income, including his salary as governor, is estimated as being between £25,000 and
£30,000 a year. His assets are tied up in England and France, so where,
if he is indeed speculating with Wenner-Gren, is the money coming
from? This is what I have to try to find out. The unspoken fact behind
all this is that if the Duke is guilty, then his actions are treasonous.

These are high stakes and I feel somewhat uneasy about the job. I
have nothing against the Duke and Duchess—on the contrary, they
have been kind and friendly to me. I think my long memorandum
after Lisbon has made me the departmental Duke-expert. So the plan is
that I turn up in the Bahamas as the commander of an MTB [Motor

Torpedo Boat] posted there on submarine-hunting duties. I must try to reingratiate myself with the ducal couple and find out what I can.

SATURDAY, 31 OCTOBER

Not an MTB as it turns out but a Harbour Defence Motor Launch— HDML 1122. We are heading south at steady speed, the New Jersey coast on our starboard side. Now doubly worried. I met my ship and crew, who had come over from Bermuda, in Brooklyn harbour. The 1122 is commanded by a taciturn young Scot called Sub-Lieutenant Crawford McStay. I handed him over my orders (signed by the Admiral of the Atlantic Fleet) and he made no attempt to conceal his reactions—incredulity and then disgusted resignation—as he read them. He asked me what my last command had been and I told him something of the "honorary" nature of my rank in the RNVR. "The Bahamas?" he said. "And just what the hell're we meant to do there?" "You'll follow my orders," I said, very coolly. He practically spat on the deck. No love lost there, I'm afraid. The 1122 is a big new wooden boat—armed with depth charges and a couple of Lewis machine guns—with a crew of ten. I share a small cabin with McStay (bunk beds, I'm on top) which is also where we eat. We are to make our way down to Florida and thence to the Bahamas. I think what really disgusted McStay was the amount of luggage I had loaded on board (I know there will be formal receptions and I'll have to dress accordingly) and the fact that I had my golf clubs with me.

WEDNESDAY, 4 NOVEMBER

Nassau, New Providence Island, the Bahamas. McStay and the crew are billeted at Fort Montagu, about a mile east of the town, while I have a room in the British Colonial Hotel—which seems full of American engineers and contractors apparently here to build the new airfields. Went for a walk through the town—throngs of American GIs and RAF trainees. If you don't look too closely Nassau appears pretty rather than shabby. It's a small colonial town, population 20,000 or thereabouts. Wooden buildings painted pink, plenty of shade trees. The centre of town is a neat little square with a statue of Queen Victoria flanked by the government offices and the law courts. From the harbour front the ground rises to a ridge on whose crest sits Government House (colonnaded front, also pink). The main street is called Bay Street, about five blocks long with a shaded boardwalk and lined with souvenir shops selling fancy goods and tat for tourists. There is a yacht club to the east and, west of the Colonial Hotel, a golf course and country club. Wenner-Gren owns an island, Hog Island, forming the seaward edge of the harbour lagoon.

I hired a taxi and was driven around: here and there are large houses set in tropical gardens and, inland, two big airforce bases where they train pilots. We passed Government House and I saw the Union Jack flying. I tried to imagine the Duke and Duchess in this curious, dead-end, tropical nowhere. "Small town" takes on a new meaning out here. He's been quartered in Nassau, out of harm's way, for as long as is possible, that much is obvious. To have been King—and have come to this—is as close to a blatant insult imaginable. Three invitations to dine already. I go up to GH tomorrow to pay my respects.

THURSDAY, 5 NOVEMBER

The reception at Government House was for some visiting American general. The rooms were prettily decorated, chintzy, full of plants and flowers, photographs on polished tables. I was served a gin and tonic and mingled with the other guests—military types in the main with a few local dignitaries sweating in their suits. I felt bizarrely presumptuous in my smart white uniform with my commander's stripes. The Duke's aide-de-camp* introduced me: "You'll remember Commander Mountstuart, sir." The Duke, very tanned, in a fawn suit, wearing a pink and yellow checked tie, looked blankly at me. "Lisbon, 1940, sir," I said. "Ah, yes," he said vaguely and then darted off. He went straight to the Duchess: they spoke quietly together and the Duchess looked over at me, she said something to him and he came straight back, smil-

*Major Grey Philips—the Duke's comptroller.

ing now, and clapped me on the shoulder. "Mountstuart," he said. "Of course! Brought your golf clubs?"

Later I spoke to the Duchess. Her hair and make-up were as immaculate as they had been in Lisbon. She looked thinner, however, though perhaps it was simply the short sleeves on her dress exposing her bony, meagrely muscled arms. She was very friendly and lowered her voice to say, "What brings you to this moron paradise? Watch out or you'll die of boredom before you know it." I smiled. "Hunting submarines," I said. "We must have you to dinner," she said, "right away. Where are you staying?" I sense I am back in the swim again.

TUESDAY, 15 DECEMBER

I've been to three dinners at Government House, the last occasion actually sitting beside the Duchess. I've golfed with the Duke too, played half a dozen rounds, but always as part of a four-ball. I've visited every bar and club and, it seems, most of the private houses and have met enough RAF personnel to last me a lifetime.

This small town, like any small town, is rife with rumour and gossip, intrigue, resentments, vendettas, slights, alliances and misalliances, cliques and sets, both amongst the so-called establishment and the parvenus. As far as I can tell Nassau society is divided roughly along these lines. At the top the governor and his entourage. Second, the politicians—the "Bay Street Boys (or Bandits)"—local merchants, bigwigs and wealthy men who sit in and control the House of Assembly. Then there are, somewhat apart, the military transients and visitors. Then there are the elderly tax-exiles—British and Canadian in the main—stuffy and conservative, who look with disdain on a younger, more raffish crowd: dubious entrepreneurs, divorcées, relatively rich talentless young men and their girlfriends. They sail, they have parties, they drink too much, they swap partners easily. In the tourist season, December to March, they are enhanced by their American equivalents looking for winter sunshine and la dolce vita. Another subgroup, which may overlap with any of the above, are the few wealthy and powerful men who wield a publicly unacknowledged influence because of their fiscal clout. Wenner-Gren was in this category and I have to say it's hard to find anyone with a bad word for him. Rumours do swirl around the mention of his name: that he was a personal friend of Goering; that he was building a Nazi U-boat pen on Hog Island; that he owns a bank in Mexico City. I pass it all on, duly tagged as speculation, to NID. Finally there is another world—one that is the most populous and, in a paradoxical way, the most invisible: the native Bahamians themselves. Most of them are poor labourers or fishermen who live in a sprawling shanty over the ridge from Government House called Grant's Town. The colour bar is almost absolute in the Bahamas—certainly in social terms (even the Duchess's "canteen for the troops" is segregated). I'm told the code is as rigid as in the southern states of America. Any softening of attitudes here in the Bahamas, it is argued, would discourage the American tourists. Even in Government House no black is allowed through the front door.

All these worlds interact to a certain degree—most obviously at Government House receptions (though the only blacks are serving canapés). I'm a regular at these functions and I watch the crowd carefully and discreetly glean information—people are very forthcoming. I have to say the Duke and Duchess move through their guests serenely and smilingly, as if there were nowhere else on earth that they would rather be, and in no other company. The acting is flawless.

They are away at the moment in Miami. McStay is begging to be allowed to put out to sea. The 1122 is the smartest, cleanest, most polished boat in Nassau harbour.

SUNDAY, 20 DECEMBER

We ride at anchor off a small island in the Exuma chain. On deck the men fish and swim. The sun beats down out of a washed-out blue sky. We seem very far from the war. Freya writes to say we have retaken Benghazi and Soviet forces have encircled the German army at Stalingrad. The unhappiest man in the world is Crawford McStay.

1943

FRIDAY, I JANUARY

Last night I went to a New Year's party at Cable Beach given by a young widow called Dorothy Bookbinder (American). There was a band and champagne from 8:00 till midnight and beyond. Dorothy— in her forties, blowzy, a drunk, I suppose—is living with the "Marquis" de Saussay—of French extraction, I would say, rather than French. Dorothy has a daughter (nineteen? twenty-two?) called Lulu who made a beeline for me as the clock struck twelve and planted a long wet kiss on my lips. I shook her off and went down to the beach and looked at the stars and thought about Freya. Lulu found me and candidly propositioned me: "Why won't you fuck me, Logan?" "Because I don't fucking want to," I said. Then she fell over, dead drunk. So I carried her back and laid her on a cane sofa on the terrace and slipped away.

News from Government House is that the Duchess is unwell— exhausted, tormented by her ulcer. I think I'll let McStay take the 1122 off to the Out Islands for a few days. Nassau is beginning to get to me as well.

THURSDAY, 14 JANUARY

I wrote up my third report for NID and took it out to Oakes Field and gave it to [Squadron Leader] Snow (he flies it to Miami and someone takes it to New York and from there it reaches NID). Snow says the Duke will be offered the governorship of Australia as a sop. I felt my heart lighten at the prospect. I've only been here a few weeks and already I feel I'm rotting. I'm putting on weight, drinking heavily, I spend too much time in the bar of the Prince George Hotel talking to nobodies. My intellectual life is non-existent: I read and write nothing (except letters from and to home). I begin to understand what the Duchess meant by "this moron paradise."

My report was a diligent account of the latest rumours. I have been

told, in confidence, by de Saussay that Sir Harry Oakes* has advanced
the Duke two million dollars and Wenner-Gren is using this to specu-
late on the currency markets through his bank, the Banco Comercial†
in Mexico City—all profits to go to the Duke. No doubt NID can see if
this can be confirmed or denied: it would certainly explain where the
money came from. I can't really believe the Duke would take such a
risk, however: too many people in London, New York, the Bahamas
could trace the money if he suddenly starts making payments to Oakes
or some subsidiary.

SATURDAY, 27 FEBRUARY

Thirty-seven years old. I celebrated with a morning masturbate. Visions
of Freya, naked, on top—her round, slightly pendulous breasts judder-
ing as she rode me. I've coped with absence and abstinence before in
this endless war but something about this scurrilous town seems to
have increased my sex-drive. An RAF wife touched my cock under the
table at dinner last night—I can't even remember her name.

Threatened to report McStay on a charge of insubordination. He practically called me a coward in front of [Petty Officer] Dignam. The men
make no complaint about their posting: they recognize a cushy number when they see one. Only McStay's martial instincts are frustrated.
Perhaps I'll let him drop a depth charge tomorrow.

MONDAY, 22 MARCH

Intense pangs of loneliness: missing Freya and Stella so much it is like
an ache in the gut. I suppose this is the soldier-on-active-service's lot—
and the world must be full of millions of men missing their loved ones.

*Oakes, who had discovered the world's second-richest gold mine in Canada,
was the wealthiest man in Nassau and the colony's biggest benefactor.
†Actually the Banco de Continente.

Such collective yearning is almost impossible to imagine. Still, I feel slightly fraudulent: a pseudo-sailor spying on an exiled duke in a tropical island resort . . . Would I feel better if I were in a trench in the North African desert?

Feeling sorry for myself, I telephoned McStay and offered him dinner at the Prince George. I could practically hear his astonished mind working. Eventually he managed to say yes and we agreed to meet there at 8:00.

The season is ending here in Nassau—the rich American tourists are closing their villas and beach cabanas and returning home. Walking from the hotel down Bay Street to the Prince George, you could sense the island returning to its normal comatose self—the shops empty, the horse carriages standing idle, only the occasional large car cruising along looking for some indication of fun to be had.

McStay was stiff and overly formal at first (maybe he thought this was a prelude to him being sent home?), but as I called for more drink he began to unwind somewhat. I have to remember he is only twenty-three—he must look on me as an irritating older man who has stepped in to bugger up his promising career. He comes from Fife, his father is a farmer. McStay has one of those "carved" faces—not an ounce of flesh on him—which is not so much handsome as noteworthy, as some statues or gargoyles are. He might suit a beard.

Towards the end of the meal, a little tight, he leant forward and said, "I mean, Logan, what the fuck're we doing here? It's been nearly five months." I suppose I shouldn't even have dropped the smallest hint but I thought I owed it to him. "Who's the most important Englishman this side of the Atlantic?" I said. He knew, of course, who I was talking about. "Let's just say we're keeping a close eye on him," and I tapped the side of my nose, as one does. He nodded, his face serious. I think he'll be more relieved to know there is a purpose, a mission—but probably no less frustrated.

As we left, de Saussay came in with some of his chums and two really incredibly beautiful girls I'd not seen before. They seemed to know McStay, and de Saussay convinced us to join them for more drinks. I found myself talking to a tall, handsome, foreign-looking man who let it be known early in the conversation that he was Harry Oakes's son-in-law. He invited me to lunch at his house on Sunday. I asked McStay how he knew these people. "Sailing," he said. "I've got nothing to do, so I go sailing with them."

SATURDAY, 10 APRIL

Golf with the Duke at the country club. Just the two of us—and his detective stayed at the club house. It was humid, hot and quiet—all the tourists gone. The Duke seemed troubled until he sunk a 25-foot putt at the third to win the hole and then visibly brightened. I let him win the fifth and eighth, which put him three up at the turn and in a much better mood. He became very chatty.

Things we talked about:

His desperation to leave Nassau—ranting on about "this lousy little island." He'd asked Churchill for a job in America—he has no interest in any other governorships, however grand. He's proud of what he's achieved here—"the worst posting in the British Empire."

The familiar antagonism directed at the court. Finds the King and Queen unbelievably petty and vindictive. I think what irks him more than anything is their denying the Duchess her HRH appellation (shades of his servant Fletcher problem). "A wife takes her husband's rank," he kept insisting. "Regardless of anything." I sense much of the blame directed at the Queen (easier than blaming his brother, I suppose). "She can't bear Wallis."

Finds the House of Assembly difficult and selfishly obstructive, filled with "grasping, common little men."

Says he likes Churchill but no longer counts him as a staunch ally. "Winston knows who butters his bread."

On the seventeenth he chipped in from a bunker and spontaneously invited me back to GH for supper. I handed over his winnings and he went to tell the detective to call ahead. So I had to pay for his caddie as well as mine. He does not like spending his money, our esteemed governor, however paltry the sum.

Back at GH we were served drinks at the pool cabana. The Duchess looked well, her dark hair caught up in a kind of silk turban. She bemoaned the coming hot season, saying to me, "You've no idea how hard it is to get permission to go to the States. All the to-ing and fro-ing, the bowing and scraping: 'Please Mr. Churchill ask the King if we can go to Miami for the weekend.'" The Duke looked thoughtful, pulling on his pipe and fussing with one of his cairn terriers. Then to my astonishment the Duchess asked me a question about myself—about what I'd done before the war—and I told her I was a writer. They both flashed a glance at each other and the Duke asked me if I knew Philip Guedalla,* a friend of his. I said I'd met him once or twice and they relaxed: it was a little moment of caution and alarm that soon passed.

When it grew dark we went into the dining room and had chilled soup and scrambled eggs to follow. They have a French chef, a butler and the Duke has his valet and the Duchess her maid—plus innumerable Bahamian staff. We reminisced about Biarritz and Lisbon. It was as relaxed and intimate as I've ever been with them, the Duchess calling me Logan, the Duke rising from his chair to show me the special stance he'd adopt to fade a long iron into a green. Inevitably the court came up again, the King and Queen and their tedious vendetta. The Duchess, laughing, said, "Oh, they can't stand me. But it's David they're really worried about. She has to keep him as far away from Bertie as possible."

The Duke remonstrated vaguely, but I could see that the line the conversation had taken was not displeasing.

"No, no," said the Duchess. "They couldn't have you in England. Bertie'd be ignored, forgotten, if you were there. All eyes would be on you, darling." Who knows, she may be right. I sensed the Duke wanted to rush across the room at that moment and take her in his arms.

"At least we still have friends, powerful friends who won't desert you. Even Winston will do his best for you, darling, you know he will. We can always call on them if it's a real emergency." There was something in her eyes as she said this that rang true: the power and influence of even an ex-king must be substantial, must reach into the very heart of the establishment. I sensed her ruthless, her absolute determination.

*Philip Guedalla (1889–1944), writer, a friend of the Windsors who wrote a pro-Windsor account of the Abdication Crisis, *The Hundred Days* (1934).

As we left the Duchess drew me aside and, putting her face close to mine, said, "Logan, we would like you to think of yourself as *un ami de la maison.*" Some kind of honour, I suppose. She does exude a strange sexual attraction, given that she's not physically beautiful or alluring: the ideal dominatrix—if one were that way inclined.

MONDAY, 17 MAY

The Duke and Duchess are away in the USA, due back in June sometime, and a kind of lethargy has settled on the colony that is highly contagious. I cabled to NID asking for a recall but was told it was out of the question. Even my letters to Freya are becoming boring, I sense, as very little changes the rhythms of my life. Once a week I report on all the gossip and innuendo. (Does someone find this useful? Who, exactly, wants to know all this tittle-tattle?) I golf with Snow and other acquaintances from the base; I go to moderately interesting dinner parties; twice a week McStay and I take the 1122 out on a run and McStay puts the men through their paces. Meanwhile, round the world, the war staggers on day by day.

THURSDAY, 27 MAY

Yesterday was one of our days out in the 1122. It was unseasonably clear and there was almost a sense of crispness in the air at first light. I enjoy these brief voyages more and more—maybe there is something intrinsically naval in me after all. We chug slowly out of the harbour—I stand on the bridge with McStay—and all the dockworkers and idlers stop to watch us pass by. The 1122 does look exemplary, flags and pennants cracking in the breeze, the men on deck in their tropical whites. Everyone instinctively waves at us. And then as we reach the harbour mouth McStay gives the order to increase speed and beneath your feet you feel the latent power of the twin engines thrum into life. The angle of the boat tilts as the stern goes down, the screws biting, and we grab the handrail around the bridge. Suddenly there's a spumy white bow wave and we surge into the blue Atlantic, cheers from the quayside echoing distantly.

Sometimes we go up to Grand Bahama, sometimes to Andros or Abaco, but our favourite run is down the chain of the Exumas—tiny, scrubby, low-lying islands with small bays and crescent beaches of pure white sand. We know there are no submarines but we pretend to look for them. At midday we anchor off some islet and have lunch. The men swim or sunbathe. Occasionally we let off a depth charge or fire the Lewis guns at an empty oil drum we set floating, just to remind ourselves that there's a war on and that we are a small component in the struggle to defeat Nazi Germany.

Yesterday, because it was so still and clear, I decided to have a swim after our lunch. I stripped off and dived in from the prow and swam the 150 yards from the 1122 to the small island. The water was cool and astonishingly translucent. I waded ashore and wandered along the small beach, picking up the odd shell or piece of driftwood, pleasurably conscious of my nakedness on this uninhabited island, thinking—as one inevitably does—of castaways, Robinson Crusoe, unaccommodated man.

The highest part of this island couldn't have been more than ten feet above sea level and the vegetation that covered it was a form of succulent scrub, low gnarled bushes with fat olive green leaves, a few cacti here and there and some patches of blond marram grass.

Then I became aware of a commotion on the 1122 and looked round to see men running about the deck and heard the grating, clunking sound of the anchor being weighed. "Hoy!" I shouted. "What's going on?" But no notice was taken of me. I waded into the water and was waist high, about to start swimming back, when, with a roar of diesel engine and a puff of exhaust smoke, the launch surged off and within seconds was lost to sight around a headland.

I waded back on shore, cursing, wondering what the emergency was, what signal had been received and what the hell McStay was playing at, forgetting I was no longer on board. I wasn't worried: I knew I would be missed eventually and at some stage they'd be back for me. Mind you, I thought, it depended what the urgency was. It might be some hours . . . And then I heard a rustling, a small commotion in the bushes a few yards from me and slowly, hesitantly, a lizard, an iguana about three feet long waddled on to the beach and, tongue flicking, headed towards me. Within seconds, it was joined by four or five others. I moved down the beach away from them, instinctively and stupidly cupping my hand over my genitals. The afternoon sun felt hot on my salty shoulders. I threw some shells and pebbles at the advancing lizards and they stopped. As soon as I showed no sign of aggression they began to plod towards me again. Then some more iguanas appeared at the other end of the beach. I charged at these, shouting, and they backed off clumsily, in some disarray, before regrouping and advancing again.

Within a few minutes there were twenty or thirty iguanas on the beach, tongues flicking, looking at me with their dead eyes, as if they expected something of me. I stood there, a stick in each hand, wondering what I would do if I wasn't rescued by nightfall. They weren't frightening; they seemed no real threat; this was merely a form of temporary enforced coexistence. Naked man and three dozen primeval lizards on a deserted island. How were we going to get along?

And then the 1122 roared back into the little bay and I felt my heart lift. She chugged in as close as she could and a small ladder was let down the side. I waded out and swam the few strokes necessary to reach it, leaving my non-swimming friends behind. McStay helped me aboard, trying to keep the grin off his face, and handed me a towel.

"Very funny, McStay," I said.

"It's great you have a sense of humour, sir."

We headed back to Nassau, everyone in good spirits, including me. I wasn't in the least put out by McStay's prank. Images of myself alone on the island with the iguanas dominated my mind (and what will I dream about tonight, I wonder?). It was one of those moments that you recognize, after the event, as epiphanic—charged, numinous in some way. I think McStay was bemused at how easygoing and benign I was about it all.

MONDAY, 28 JUNE

Real, humid, enervating heat. A day of prickly irritability. McStay put in for a posting in the morning, I accepted, and he withdrew the request in the afternoon. I cabled NID: "See nothing to gain from my staying on. Banking problems non-existent. Please advise future course of action." The reply came: "Most useful your presence there. Carry on."

TUESDAY, 6 JULY

The D&D are back. Govt. House reception tonight for some Foreign Office grandee touring the Caribbean. Even the Duke couldn't disguise his low spirits, which is unusual for him—no one "puts on a face" better. The Duchess said that he'd been very cast down by a meeting with Churchill in Washington, D.C. "They want us to rot out here for the duration," she said with some bitterness. "We had some hope that after three years . . . David tried everything. They won't budge."

THURSDAY, 8 JULY

I went down to the harbour at about 10:00 this morning and McStay said at once, "Sir Harry Oakes has been murdered." My God, I thought, alarm bells ringing. But who would want to kill Sir Harry? McStay didn't need to be asked. "Everyone says it was Harold Christie." I suppose McStay must have got this from his sailing chums. I only know Christie by reputation: big in real estate, here in the House of Assembly, an unattractive blunt-looking man, reputedly an ex-bootlegger. A political power and a close friend of Sir Harry. In a Bahamian context, Christie murdering Sir Harry is akin to Lord Halifax [Foreign Secretary] murdering Bendor [the Duke of Westminster].

I've met Oakes a few times: a small chunky boorish man with a surly expression, the corners of his mouth permanently turned down. A self-appointed "rough diamond," calls a spade a spade. Fabulously wealthy too, by all accounts, but one of those men whose grotesque excess of money only seems to make him more troubled and tormented, rather than the reverse. He hated paying tax in Canada, which is why he moved here. Now that there are rumours of introducing an income tax in the Bahamas, he was planning a move to Mexico. Funny how Mexico keeps cropping up.

At lunch I went to the Prince George and the place was humming like a hive. It was a voodoo murder; Oakes's genitals had been burned off; it was robbers looking for the gold he kept in his house; and so on. Now the prime suspect is his son-in-law, de Marigny. Christie had actually spent the night in Oakes's house and had slept through everything. Oh yes: the Duchess had been having an affair with Oakes and the British secret service had killed him to protect the Duke's honour (this was as outlandish as it got).

I was walking back to the British Colonial when a car pulled up and one of the Duke's equerries, Wood, asked me to meet the Duke in his cabana at Cable Beach at 5:00 this afternoon.

Later. I met the Duke. We were alone; he smoked constantly and seemed very worried. He told me he had been profoundly, utterly shocked by Sir Harry's death. At first he had been led to believe it was suicide but afterwards news that it had been a murder emerged. A blow to the head with some sort of blunt instrument, then there was an attempt to set the body and the house on fire, which had failed.

"I've asked the Miami police to send two of their detectives," he said. "They arrived this afternoon. They're taking over the investigation."

"But why, sir?" I said spontaneously. "What about Erskine-Lindop?" Erskine-Lindop is Chief of Police in the Bahamas.

"He's entirely in agreement with me," the Duke said, a little snappily. "This is too big for the local force. I don't think you realize the consequences of Sir Harry's death—the ramifications. It's a disaster. We have to have experts. Real experts. And this has to be wound up, solved, as quickly as possible. Minimize damage to the colony. Complete disaster."

"I understand." I didn't really.

The Duke lit another cigarette. "It's become clear—crystal clear—that the murderer was de Marigny. Do you know him?"

De Marigny, the good-looking son-in-law. I said I'd lunched at his house once and occasionally bumped into him at the Prince George. McStay knew him well.

"Good," the Duke said, allowing himself a quick smile. "That's very good." I was now more in the dark but let it ride. Then he said: "I want

you to meet the two detectives from Miami—Melchen and Barker—
tonight. Could you manage that?"

"Of course, sir. My pleasure."

Later. I must write all this down. Melchen and Barker have just left my
room. Melchen is fat and bespectacled, untidy. Barker is lean with
cropped grey hair, tough, fit-looking. They had just come from de
Marigny's house (with evidence, they said) and there was absolutely no
doubt at all that de Marigny had murdered Oakes. Oakes and de
Marigny loathed each other, de Marigny had threatened violence in
the past. Oakes had never forgiven de Marigny for eloping with his
daughter, Nancy (Nancy was eighteen, de Marigny thirty-six). De
Marigny was broke and with Oakes dead he would inherit Nancy's
share of the fortune. De Marigny had given a dinner party last night
(Wednesday) and had no alibi between 11:30 when he drove two guests
home—near Oakes's house, Westbourne—and 3:00 a.m. Between these
times the murder was committed. He had both motive and means and
no alibi.

I said: "He gave a dinner party and then went out and murdered his
father-in-law?"

"It happens," Barker said. "Believe me."

"What about Christie?" I said.

"Slept through it all."

"I thought they set the place on fire."

"It was a small fire. It didn't take."

"He didn't hear anything? Smell anything burning?"

"No."

I told them I thought de Marigny wasn't the murdering kind. I said
he was one of those hugely self-satisfied narcissists whose main interest
in life is figuring out who might next sleep with him.

"You can never tell a killer," Barker said patronizingly.

Then Melchen said: "The Duke speaks very highly of you, Commander Mountstuart."

I said I was gratified to learn that this was so.

"We need someone to get close to de Marigny and the Duke said
you would be ideal."

"Get close?" I said.

Barker said: "We'd like you to have a drink with de Marigny, some time tomorrow."

"Why?"

"And, you know, just slip anything he touches into your pocket—a glass, book of matches, ashtray. Then bring it to us—we're in the hotel here."

I stood up and told them to get out. They looked at each other wearily.

"The Duke is going to be very disappointed," Barker said.

I said: "Wait till he learns what you just asked me to do. I'd book your seats on tomorrow's plane back to Miami, if I were you."

They sauntered out, unperturbed. And I sat down and wrote all this up.

FRIDAY, 9 JULY

I am sitting in the back of a taxi outside Government House scribbling this on a piece of paper [later transcribed in journal]. It is 9:13 in the morning. I had urgently requested an interview with the Duke and had been ushered into his study. He was standing stiffly in front of the bookcases.

"Thank you for seeing me, sir," I said. "Those two inept fools from Miami have actually—"

"They told me you'd been most unhelpful."

"'Unhelpful'? Do you know what they asked me to do?"

And then he seemed to go a little mad. His voice became a high, semi-throttled scream and his face flushed red.

"If I cannot ask a friend and a British officer to be of assistance in the worst crisis this island has ever seen! . . . I told them they could count on you, Mountstuart. They said we need a trustworthy man and I said, instantly, Commander Mountstuart. And this is what you do to me! This is how you let me down! I'm deeply hurt and disappointed in you."

"Just one second, sir. They were asking me to incriminate—"

"They are highly professional police investigators who know exactly what they're doing and exactly what they have to do to bring this sordid affair to a rapid and proper conclusion. De Marigny killed Sir Harry Oakes—full stop. The sooner that man is behind bars the happier this island will be."

"With great respect, sir, you're mistaken. Those men are utterly cynical and corrupt. They're not what you think."

"Don't you dare tell me what I think! Get out! Get out! You're useless to me."

And so I left. These are, verbatim, the words we exchanged.

Friday night. The news is all around Nassau. De Marigny was arrested this evening for the murder of Sir Harry Oakes. His fingerprints were found in the murder room. Barker and Melchen have got their man.

SATURDAY, 10 JULY

Still a bit stunned by all that has taken place. I can't quite piece it together yet, but all is not well. Today there was a Red Cross fundraising drive in Victoria Square. The crew of the 1122 had laid on lucky dip, skittles, a coconut shy and all manner of games, so I went down to see how they were coping.

The Duchess, who is patron of the Bahamian Red Cross, had opened the fête and was wandering around meeting people and examining the stalls and exhibits, being her usual gracious and friendly self. As she approached the 1122 stall she saw me and checked her stride momentarily. She avoided my eye but could hardly ignore us. She shook my hand and gave me a thin smile. "How wonderful you British sailors are," she said and was about to move on.

"Your Grace," I said quietly, "how is the Duke?"

Then I saw the depthless lake of hatred in her eyes.

"Judas," she whispered, and turned her back on me.

[NOTE IN RETROSPECT. December 1943. These notes have been compiled with help from Sq. Leader Snow—who sent me newspaper accounts of de Marigny's trial (in October)—and from Sub-Lt.

Crawford McStay, who visited de Marigny in gaol in July and August.]

Some time in the early hours of Thursday, 8 July 1943, Sir Harry Oakes was murdered in his bedroom in his house "Westbourne" as he slept. He was hit on the head with some sort of spiked instrument that caused four deep puncture wounds, triangular in shape, in front of and behind his left ear. His skull was badly fractured. Then his body was significantly burned, most of his pyjamas being consumed by flame, as was the mosquito netting above his head. There was further scorching on the mattress, on a folding Chinese screen near his bed and on the carpet. Feathers from a ripped pillow were scattered over his body. On the walls of the room, low down, were blood stains and bloody hand-prints.

Harold Christie, a friend and business associate, who was sleeping in a guest bedroom two doors away, found the body in the morning and summoned help. The local police and other interested parties moved more or less unchecked through the house and the murder scene.

De Marigny, informed of the death of Sir Harry, turned up at the house on the Thursday morning but was not allowed admittance to the upper floor and did not see the body.

In the early afternoon the two detectives, Captains Melchen and Barker, summoned from Miami by the Duke, arrived and began their investigation. Barker did not dust for fingerprints, as he regarded the conditions in the murder room as being too humid. Sir Harry's body was moved to the Nassau morgue for autopsy at around 4:00 p.m.

At dinner time de Marigny was instructed to go to Westbourne, where he was interrogated and physically examined by the two detectives. Clippings of singed hair were taken from his beard and arms. Then Melchen and Barker, accompanied by local police, went with de Marigny to his house, where the clothes he had been wearing the previous night were taken away as evidence (it was after this that the detectives visited me in the British Colonial Hotel). During that night a local detective stayed with de Marigny.

The next day, Friday, 9 July, de Marigny was escorted back to West-bourne. He went upstairs to a seating area on the landing where he was interrogated by Melchen. During the course of his questioning Melchen asked de Marigny to pour a glass of water from a carafe on a nearby table. Then he offered de Marigny a cigarette and when he accepted tossed him a pack of Lucky Strikes. De Marigny lit a cigarette and returned the pack. At this juncture Barker appeared and asked if everything was "OK." Melchen said it was, the interview was termi-nated and de Marigny was allowed to leave.

At about four o'clock that afternoon the Duke of Windsor arrived at Westbourne and went upstairs. He had a confidential, unwitnessed conversation with Barker that lasted twenty minutes.

At six o'clock that evening de Marigny was escorted to Westbourne yet again and was arrested and accused of the murder of Sir Harry Oakes. A clear fingerprint from the little finger of his left hand had been found on the Chinese screen.

During de Marigny's trial it was established by the defence counsel that (a) Barker showed astonishing incompetence for a so-called finger-print expert and that (b) the fingerprint offered in evidence—that placed de Marigny in the murder room—could not have come from the Chinese screen as alleged. It must have been lifted from some other surface (A glass? The cellophane from a cigarette pack?) and planted as incriminating evidence. The case against de Marigny effectively col-lapsed and he was declared not guilty and acquitted.

I make only these observations.

Barker and Melchen were determined to solve this case in record time. They clearly believed de Marigny was guilty and decided to implicate him by fair means or foul. I was intended to supply the nec-essary print (it would have saved having to go through the charade with the carafe and the cigarette pack). When I refused on Thursday night they realized they would have to retrieve the "evidence" them-selves. Barker's question—"Is everything OK?"—actually meant "Do we have clean prints?"

*   *   *

I ask only these questions.

Why did the Duke of Windsor call in detectives from Miami (one of the most corrupt forces in the USA) when he had a completely competent police department on his doorstep?

What did the Duke and Barker talk about during their private conference on Friday, 9 July? (This question was deliberately and pointedly not asked during the trial.)

Why, when de Marigny was acquitted, was the case closed when the murderer was still at large?

Why did no one investigate Harold Christie?

Here is an interpretation of what actually went on—as unprejudiced as I can make it.

The Duke—a nervous and insecure man—was thrown in complete panic by Sir Harry's death. For some reason he had no confidence in his own police force and dreaded the affair running on for months. One has to wonder why there was this need for a rush to justice. Was there anything else that might be uncovered? Anyway, whatever the reason, the Duke called in Melchen, whom he knew from previous Miami trips. It's not clear if he asked for Barker also, but Barker, not Melchen, effectively ran the show.

The Duke did not like de Marigny—this was common knowledge—but he was fond of Sir Harry. The quick gossipy consensus on the island was that de Marigny was the likeliest suspect. This would have been very clear to the Miami detectives early in their investigations—hence de Marigny's swift summoning to Westbourne.

At some stage (probably through Christie, who kept the Duke informed of developments) the Duke was told that there was a way that the crime could effectively be pinned on de Marigny beyond reasonable doubt. All the detectives required was a trustworthy person who could supply them with clean fingerprints from de Marigny. The Duke may well not have known why they wanted this person: all he was asked to provide was someone unimpeachable. How about a commander in the Royal Navy? And so the detectives came to meet me and made their request. I refused and so they did the job themselves, as they had no doubt done many times before in Miami. The tossed cigarette pack trick has the air of a familiar ploy about it.

However, once they had the clear print, they had to let the Duke know the case against de Marigny was now convincingly made. They had motive, means and could now "place" him in the murder room. When the Duke came to Westbourne on the Friday afternoon this must have been the substance of his conversation with Barker. I am sure the language employed would have been highly euphemistic but the implication would have been clear. He only needed the Duke's nod—his tacit permission—to go ahead. And the Duke must have given it. He was doubtless highly relieved and would have put his own proper gloss on proceedings: "Well, Captain Barker, if you're sure of your facts I see no point in lingering further." And so de Marigny was arrested.

The Duke would not know the details and therefore could place all blame on the detectives. The less he actually knew the better. This was why he was so furious with my refusal and why he cut me off in a rage when I tried to tell him what Barker and Melchen had asked me. He didn't want to know. He could not know.

But the Duke of Windsor is not a guileless fool. He would have been aware that some sort of set-up was under way, however vaguely he was conscious of it, a set-up that was humiliatingly exposed during the trial (the Duke and Duchess were conveniently out of the Bahamas in the USA while the trial took place).

At the very least you have to accept that the Duke colluded in the implication of de Marigny. At the very least, the Duke of Windsor, the Governor of the Bahamas, the ex-King of the United Kingdom and the British Empire, was guilty of conspiracy to pervert the course of justice. At the very least. This, as I say, is the kindest interpretation one can make. Many other, darker questions arise. McStay told me de Marigny's version: all to do with money, Mexico and Wenner-Gren, but the allegations are completely unverifiable. For the moment these are the facts behind the arrest and the trial of Alfred de Marigny.

But I still keep thinking about the Duchess's parting word—"Judas." Why did she call me Judas? I hadn't betrayed anyone. I was acting honourably and assumed a similar honour on the Duke's part. The more I think about it the more I sense that "Judas" was a reference to a *future* betrayal. I now knew a secret about the Duke of Windsor–a dangerous and damaging secret about his tangential involvement in the placing of false evidence. The Duke and Duchess–consumed with paranoia, anyway–assumed I would reveal it, or threaten to reveal it one day. Now I was another enemy to add to the growing list: I could cause them harm–and that was why I had to be so resolutely spurned.

MONDAY, 12 JULY

Cable from NID. I am to be recalled immediately. I fly to Miami tomorrow. Someone has moved very fast.

> [*LMS was back in England by the end of July. He was granted a month's leave before resuming his normal duties at NID. Interestingly enough, he was not officially asked to write up the account of his eight and a half months' association with the Duke and Duchess or express his doubts about the handling of the Harry Oakes murder. The Duke and Duchess remained in the Bahamas for the duration of the war.*]

THURSDAY, 18 NOVEMBER

On the train to Birmingham, a sleety rain smearing the windows. A small boy sitting opposite asks me if I'm an officer and I say, yes. Are you in the navy? Yes. Well, where's your ship, then? Good question. His mother shushes him up: stop bothering the gentleman. He would be amused to learn that this RNVR officer is off to an RAF base to learn how to jump out of aeroplanes.

It was Vanderpoel who announced last week that I was to go on this course. "May I ask why?" I said. "We think it might be useful," was all he would say. I asked Ian if anything special was afoot but he said he knew nothing. Perhaps in preparation for the invasion? He's not nearly so *au fait* with the department's secrets since Godfrey left.* Anyway, it's a change and I'm glad to get out of the office.

Freya and Stella came to Euston to see me off, which was sweet of them. Stella asked me if I would be brown when I came back and I reassured her I wouldn't. She was hugely intrigued by my tan when I came home in July. And I must say when I pressed myself up against Freya's pale freckled torso I did look like some dusky octoroon. After the long months away from each other it was as if our sex-drives had been renewed. Freya used to pull back the sheets and stare at me—as if my naked brown body obsessed her. We kept sneaking off for quick fierce passionate fucks at all hours of the day. Five-minute specials, we called them. "Fancy a five-minute special?" Freya would say after lunch. Stella would beat on the locked door and shout, "What are you doing?" "Daddy's a bit tired, darling," Freya would call as I humped away, a stupid grin on my face.

It seems strange to be heading back to Birmingham again, twenty years on: how I used to dread my end-of-term returns home. I'm to report to RAF Clerkhall for a two-week course in parachuting: a few days' training, then a succession of five jumps in order to qualify. Something tells me this is not Vanderpoel's idea—it seems more like something cooked up by Rushbrooke [the new head of NID] or some other brain. Ian said NID was trying to widen its *modus operandi*. "We're going to be on the continent of Europe soon," he said. "We can't just sit on our laurels." Ian seems glum: he's a moody so-and-so anyway, but since I returned he appears withdrawn, fretful. *Cherchez la femme?*†

I had a month's leave when I came back from Nassau but I didn't want to travel away from home: I wanted to stay in Melville Road and lead as ordinary and sedate a life as possible. I read, with pleasure—for the first time in months; I tended our vegetable garden; took Stella for walks. Freya and I would go out to a pub for a drink from time to time. I caught up with my friends and acquaintances.

*Godfrey was sacked in 1942.
†Fleming had fallen in love with Ann O'Neill, later Ann Rothermere, and later still Mrs. Ian Fleming.

Guilt has been a huge success, critically and commercially:* Peter Scabius is hailed as a new and important novelist. I still haven't been able to read the book and when I met Peter just talked about it in the vaguest generalities. Peter didn't notice, anyway: his head has been well and truly turned by all the money and acclaim. He has bought a large house on Wandsworth Common where he lives with Penny, his new wife (they married on publication day). He wears Tess's death like a stigmata—a badge to demonstrate how much he has suffered. He said one truly revolting thing: "You know, Logan, since the news of Tess's death, women seem to find me amazingly attractive." He's probably cheating on Penny already.

And I had a strange blunt letter from Dick Hodge announcing he had his leg blown off at the thigh when he trod on a land mine in Italy. He's back at home in Scotland, "learning to walk," and he added, "Since I don't ever intend to move from here again you'd better come and visit me." He signed himself off as, "Yours, Dick. Legless but not, in case you were wondering, dickless."

I read in the papers that de Marigny has been acquitted at the trial. Some justice at least—but who did kill Sir Harry Oakes? The Bahamas, the Duke, the Duchess, seem like another world to me now.

WEDNESDAY, 8 DECEMBER

RAF Clerkhall. This place is a base for training Bomber Command crews and is filled with aircrew. We have our first real jump tomorrow and I am actually quite looking forward to it. We—the non-aircrew—form an odd little group in the mess: six Englishmen, a Pole and two edgy Italians. None of us talks about why we are learning to parachute—perhaps, like me, none of us knows. I'm the only naval officer.

In the evening after dinner we're free to go to local pubs or into Birmingham itself. I've been revisiting my old haunts, wandering around Edgbaston. Perhaps it is a post-Bahamas feeling, but I find I relish Birmingham's stolid unpretentiousness. A big no-nonsense city.

---

*It was published in June 1943 by Murray Ginsberg Ltd. By November sales were over 30,000.

My schoolboy loathing of the place reflects badly on me. After the last six months everything about Birmingham seems reassuringly true and real—however grimy or knocked-about. One night I stood outside our old house and thought of Father, wondering what he would make of his son now, nearly twenty years having gone by. My two marriages, his two grandchildren, some sort of career and reputation as a writer cut short by the war. Would his ghost recognize this ageing naval officer? . . .

Actually, this train of thought has rather been dominating my mind since I set it running. At NID it's an open secret that all our work is now beginning to focus on the forthcoming invasion of Europe—the "Second Front." Conceivably this war could be over in a year—and a kind of panic sets my heart beating as I try to imagine "normal" life again, with my forties approaching fast and the need to start up my old career once more. Can I do it? It's funny: the war, much as I moan about it, has meant that all decisions have been held in limbo. And sometimes a limbo is a tolerable place to be stuck.

Last night I went into a pub on Broad Street and ordered a pint of bitter. The place was quite busy and the thick blackout curtains made it feel unnaturally closed off from the world. I lit a cigarette and drank my beer and let my head empty of thoughts, only half aware of the chatter around me, entering a warm, particularly English type of trance, allowing time to stop for twenty minutes or so. When I tried to pay, the publican refused my money but his wife contradicted him. "He's always doing that," she said crossly. "Anyone in uniform. I tell him: they all get well paid and we've got a living to make. No need for charity." The man shrugged his shoulders and looked sheepish. I said she was absolutely right, paid up and left a tip. Quite what the significance of this anecdote is, I don't know. I rode the bus back to RAF Clerkhall in a calm mood. Very Birmingham, I thought, which is why I've grown so fond of the place all of a sudden.

THURSDAY, 9 DECEMBER

After all the training, the gymnastics, the jumping off the tower in the harness, finally the real thing. About twenty of us filed into an old Stirling bomber specially fitted out. I sat next to one of the Italians, who looked very jittery as we hooked the clips of our ripcords on to the cable that ran the length of the fuselage roof. *"Buoni augurii,"* I said, and he looked at me with pure panic in his eyes. Perhaps he knows where he'll be jumping into. Who were we, the odd-bods, the non-aircrew? We seemed the most unlikely sort of secret agents.

The Stirling took off and we made a long slow series of ascending circles before we were at the correct height. As the drop zone approached a hatch was opened in the floor of the aircraft and the sergeant-instructor stood by it. "Whatever you do, don't look down," he kept saying. "You look at my handsome face and when my hand falls, just step forward."

Half a dozen dropped out of view before my turn came. I felt nothing: I had managed to shut down all emotions—and I had an absolute trust in the efficacy and strength of the webbing and equipment I was wearing; had no doubt at all that my parachute had been properly packed and that the ripcord, when tugged, would see its easy and flawless release. The sergeant-instructor dropped his hand and said, "Go, seven," and I stepped through the hatch.

There was a substantial physical blow from the rush of the slipstream and it seemed to me as if my parachute opened almost immediately. I looked up first into its dirty grey canopy and then looked down at the Staffordshire countryside. I saw that the first man to have left the plane was already on the ground, gathering the billowing folds of his parachute into his chest; the others who had preceded me were floating down in a rough line below me. I was savouring the feeling of suspension—not quite weightlessness (whatever that may be like: I didn't feel like a piece of featherdown), more a sense of being dramatically out of your element, something I'd experienced once before in the Bahamas when I swam out beyond a reef and the ocean floor suddenly deepened beneath me, the water around me abruptly turning blue-black from pale blue—when I was aware of someone shouting at me from the ground: "Keep your feet together, number seven!" I glanced down and saw another instructor called Townsend bellowing instructions at me through a megaphone. Christ, I thought, if I can recognize him as Townsend I must be bloody close to—

Thud. I hit the ground and rolled over, automatically rather than as instructed. It was exactly as we had been told it would be: the same effect as jumping off a twelve-foot wall—quite a height, actually, if you've ever tried it. I stood up, a proud grin on my face. "Not too bad, Mr. Mountstuart," Townsend said, jogging up to me. "Only four more to go."

1944

FRIDAY, 7 JANUARY

I was covertly reading Plomer's autobiography*—which has done aggravatingly well—and wondering if anyone would guess from its pages that its author was a promiscuous homosexual. Rhetorical question: the answer is no. Which then begged another—so what level of truth did this book contain? I was musing over this paradox when Vanderpoel came in and called me through to Rushbrooke's office. Rushbrooke was waiting for me with another man whom I didn't recognize but who was introduced as Colonel Marion (he was wearing civilian clothes). I felt a sudden pressure build in my body when I realized I was going to be given the assignment that my parachute course had prepared me for—and I wanted to say, "Before you go any further, Admiral Rushbrooke, I'd like to request a transfer to the Catering Corps"—but said nothing, of course, and meekly sat down when Rushbrooke waved me to a chair. He smiled at me.

"Don't look so worried, Mountstuart. We've bought you a couple of tramp steamers. You're a shipowner. Now we want you to go to Switzerland and buy a few more."

Switzerland? I felt a warm rush of pleasure in my lower abdomen and for a horrible moment wondered if I'd wet myself in my relief. My

*Double Lives (1943).

bowels had indeed loosed but my dignity was preserved. Switzerland was neutral, I was saying to myself, safer even than the Bahamas. It seemed odd to go to a landlocked country to buy ships but that was none of my business.

And so "Operation Shipbroker" was born. The job, as it was explained to me, seemed quite straightforward—only the actual getting into Switzerland was complicated. The strategy was that I was to pass myself off as a Uruguayan businessman looking for funding in Portugal, Spain and Switzerland to increase the size of my merchant fleet, two of which were currently moored in Montevideo harbour. I wondered if this was credible and was reminded that not the whole world was at war. Take South America for example. Citizens of neutral countries were free to come and go, providing they had the necessary documentation and visas. Swedes could travel to England, Mexicans to the USA, Spaniards to Australia, if they could get permission.

I was to visit certain banks in Geneva and Zurich and see if I could secure a loan to purchase my ships (all this would be detailed in a series of briefings over the next few days). "We don't actually expect anyone to lend you money," Rushbrooke said, "we just want you to be out there trying." I asked why. Then Marion spoke. "You'll be approached, covertly, by Germans, or by the representatives of important Germans. They will want to know how much it'll cost for you to take them to South America on your boats." Why would they want to do this, I asked? Because the war is going to end soon and the rats are already preparing to leave the sinking ship, Marion said. These people will approach you and you will take down their details—such as they are—and try to identify them. A man called Ludwig will contact you and you will pass that information on to him. How will I know Ludwig? I asked. He'll know you, don't worry, Marion said. How do I get to Geneva? I asked. "Why do you think you learned to parachute?" Vanderpoel said, with an unpleasant smile. I was told I'd learn all the rest in the coming briefings. I had one more question: how long would I be in Switzerland? Until allied troops reached the border—either from France or from Italy—probably, Rushbrooke glanced at Marion, some time in the summer.

SUNDAY, 9 JANUARY

I hinted to Freya about "Operation Shipbroker"—said the department had another job for me in Lisbon. This was Rushbrooke's idea: he knew that a wife had to be told something. You're not doing anything dangerous, are you? Freya asked. No, no, I said, it's not dangerous. Just a question of information gathering—some scheme dreamt up by NID. Which started me thinking: whose idea was this? And who was Colonel Marion? I have a week full of briefings ahead of me, largely to make my cover story complete. They asked me to choose a name for my papers and visas and I came up with Gonzago Peredes—a little bit of me; a mark of homage to Faustino. Cables are being sent from Montevideo to bankers in Zurich and Geneva requesting appointments for Señor Peredes. A room has been booked for me at the Hôtel du Commerce in Geneva. I have a file full of details of merchant ships for sale.

SUNDAY, 13 FEBRUARY

Tranquil domestic weekend with Freya and Stella. We bought a puppy, a black Labrador bitch, on Saturday for Stella. Stella said she wanted to call it Tommy, so Tommy she shall be. Tomorrow I begin the long journey out to Italy. KLM from Bristol to Lisbon. Then by boat to Tripoli. Then military plane to Cairo and on to Naples. Everything seems well organized in true NID fashion. I've told Freya I'll be gone a month or so and that she can always receive news of me through Vanderpoel. She seems calm about it: she looks on it as a business trip, she says. And I was away for eight months in the Bahamas, of course, so the white lie seems quite tolerable. Last night I bought a bottle of Algerian wine, which we mulled with some sugar and some ancient cloves and spiked with rum. We lay in each other's arms on the sofa and listened to Brahms's second symphony on the gramophone, then we went to bed and made love with due and tender seriousness—two old hands who knew what they were doing. Today we will take Tommy for her first walk in Battersea Park.

MEMORANDUM ON "OPERATION SHIPBROKER"

On Wednesday, 23 February 1944, I boarded a Liberator bomber at an airfield outside Naples. With me were two Frenchmen—whom I'd just met—who were going to be dropped in occupied France. Our Liberator, loaded with supplies for the French Resistance instead of bombs, was to form part of a bombing raid destined for southern Germany. During the raid we would divert from the main bomber group and fly over western Switzerland, at which point I would parachute out. I had no idea of the Frenchmen's destination.

Under a zip-up overall I was wearing a grey flannel suit and tie. The label on the inside of the jacket was from a Montevideo tailor. I had with me a suitcase full of clothes and various documents of my trade—including a photograph of my wife and daughter back home in Uruguay. In my wallet I had a wad of Swiss francs and stamped visas and train tickets that recorded my journey from Lisbon to Madrid and on across occupied France to Geneva. I had letters of introduction to banks in Lisbon, Madrid, Geneva and Zurich. Everything about me said, with absolute authenticity, that I was a Uruguayan businessman in neutral Europe looking for a bank loan to buy ships.

I shook hands with the Frenchmen and my trepidation abated somewhat. They were dropping into occupied France; I, at least in theory, would land in a neutral country whose inhabitants would not regard me as the enemy. I kept telling myself that: I was not falling into the arms of my foes. The dropping-officer was an Englishman, Flight-Sgt. Chew.

We took off at dusk. Our squadron of Liberators joining up with others from nearby bases gathering in a group above the Bay of Naples before heading north in formation, making for Bavaria. "Ball-bearing factory," Chew whispered confidentially. Chew was a talkative fellow (perhaps it was part of his brief) and he was glad to be dropping an Englishman for once ("Keep themselves to themselves, the Frenchies do"). He kept asking questions to which he knew I wasn't allowed to respond. "Been in London lately, sir?—Sorry, sorry." "Miners still striking back home, are they? Sorry, sir, haven't been back in months, you see."

After about two hours I felt our bomber bank away from the

bomber group and begin to descend. Chew told me to prepare myself, so I went and stood by the side door and attached the long webbing strap of my suitcase to my ankle and clicked my ripcord on to the roof cable. I dug a balaclava out of my pocket and put it on.

This was the moment my fear reached its purest form and I heard a voice inside my head screaming, "What the fuck do you think you're doing, Mountstuart? You have a wife and a child. You don't want to die. Why did you agree to this?" I let it rant on, it was distracting, and in any case I had no answers. Chew looked out of a small porthole and said, "Nice clear night for it, sir." Then an American voice said, "Five minutes," and a red light came on above the doorway. The two Frenchmen gave me V for victory signs and muttered good luck.

Chew hauled the door open and the cold air whipped around us. Through the door I could see searchlights stiffly probing the sky. "Good old Swiss," Chew said. "Occasionally they throw up some ack-ack for form's sake. Always switch on the lights, though, just so we can see where we are." Above the door the green bulb went on. Chew slapped me on the back and I picked up my suitcase, clutched it to my chest and stepped out into the night for my sixth parachute drop.

It was an icy wind that hit me and I heard the whumph as my parachute opened above me, as simultaneously my suitcase was snatched from my arms by the slipstream and, as it fell, it jerked painfully on my right leg. For one horrible moment I thought I had lost a shoe. It was most uncomfortable with the dangling suitcase tugging beneath me like some animate being attached to my ankle. I heard the noise of the Liberator's engines surge as it climbed away to rejoin the other bombers.

There was a half moon that night and scudding clouds. Beneath me I could see the fields in a uniform grey-blue light with larger, whiter patches of unmelted snow. In the distance I could see the flat sheet of Lake Geneva and the not very efficient blackout of the city itself. I seemed to be approximately in the right place.

I had a bad moment as I came in to land, just missing a small copse of trees, hit the ground awkwardly and was dragged along by my 'chute for thirty yards or so. I caught my breath and methodically gathered in my parachute, slipping off the harness and my overalls. In my suitcase were an overcoat, a scarf and a Homburg hat. I put them on: it was cold. I then spent half an hour looking for somewhere to hide my parachute and overalls and eventually ended up burying them in a drift of snow by a stone wall, patting down the disturbed snow as best I could, reasoning that by the time anyone discovered them I should be lost in the city.

I knew in which direction Geneva lay and followed the line of the field's edge until I came to a gate that gave on to a small lane. I walked along this until I reached a junction where there was an obliging sign-post: GENÈVE, 15 KMS. This was the most dangerous time for me, I knew, out alone in the countryside in the middle of the night—a businessman with a suitcase—if I were challenged I would have no way of explaining myself and what I was doing. I needed to reach the city as quickly as possible and blend anonymously with its denizens. I kept on walking: the roads were quite empty, free of traffic. After about an hour I came to the edge of a village. A signpost gave its name as Carouge. It was by now 4:00 in the morning.

I found an old wooden barn not far off the road and decided to wait there until it was light and the village began to stir, reasoning that with a few people about I might attract less notice. And perhaps there would be a railway station or a bus. I had a hip flask with me and a few biscuits—so I sat shivering in the angle of two walls, nibbling oatmeal and sipping whisky.

When it grew light I took some care cleaning myself up, wiping the mud off my shoes and trouser bottoms. Dirt is the great give-away when you're trying to be unobtrusive. Then at about half past seven I strolled into the village, hoping I looked like someone who was going to catch a train. Luckily it was a sizeable place—there was a roadside inn and a post office and the cafés and the boulangeries were open: I wandered through without attracting any unusual glances. I joined a queue at a bus stop and asked a teenage boy if this bus would take me to Geneva. He said yes, my French seeming to pass muster.

The bus came, I boarded it, bought my ticket and took my seat. For the first time I relaxed slightly and I felt a small satisfying wash of justifiable pride course through me. Phase one complete. I looked out of the window as the suburbs of Geneva flashed by: the dangerous bit was over. Now I just had to get on with my job.

I left the bus in a small square in what seemed the centre of town and using my street map found my way to the Hôtel du Commerce.

By now I was just one of hundreds of coated, hatted office workers hurrying to start their day. I walked into the lobby of the Hôtel du Commerce and walked right out again. Two policemen were talking to the receptionist.

It could have been purely routine, a coincidence, bad luck. Perhaps I should have just strolled up to the desk and announced myself but it seemed a foolish and unnecessary risk. I walked round the corner and saw a parked police van with half a dozen men in it, waiting. This looked more ominous. I moved on through the nearby streets searching for another suitable hotel—nothing too grand, nothing too shabby. Then I found one: the Hôtel Cosmopolitan—I took it as a good omen.

I spent most of that day in my room, calming down, taking stock. I slept in the afternoon. When I woke I called the Hôtel du Commerce and cancelled my booking, saying that I had been detained in Madrid.

In the evening I went to a restaurant and ate a veal chop with fried potatoes washed down with a glass of beer. It was unusual wandering the streets of Geneva. There was a blackout after 10:00 p.m. (the street lights were switched off), but it was instigated more, one felt, out of a sense of duty than necessity. Life was constrained—even the meal bore signs of that: the beer was watery and I had to leave half the potatoes as they were inedible—but there was, none the less, an atmosphere close to normality. The war was elsewhere, even though near at hand, and there was no sense of that latent stress amongst the populace, that constant nagging worry at the back of your mind that you were so aware of in London. I went back to my hotel and slept well.

In the morning I telephoned the Banque Feltri to confirm my appointment for Monday morning. "Ah, oui, Monsieur Peredes," the secretary said. "C'est noté." So far so good.

I went down and strolled by the lakeside at lunchtime and had a cup of coffee and a slice of apple pie. I remember thinking how bizarre all this was, my being here in Geneva, pretending to be a Uruguayan shipowner. I felt a laugh rise in my throat and sensed for a moment—and maybe this is the allure the true spy feels—the element of sheer play underneath all the risk and the seriousness of intent, and how intoxicating it was. All things said and done, I was here playing a game of hide and seek.

Back at the hotel the girl at reception said there was a message for me. I unfolded the slip of paper: *Café du Centre, midi. demain. Ludwig.* I handed it back. "There must be some mistake," I said. "This is not for me." But he was here, she said, the man, only twenty minutes ago, he asked for you, Señor Peredes. No, no, I said, trying to be calm. I asked her to make up my bill—I said I had to go to Zurich urgently.

I went upstairs to pack and when I opened the door to my room found four men waiting for me there: two uniformed policemen with sub-machine guns and two detectives. One of them showed me an identity card and said in Spanish, "Señor Peredes, you are under arrest."

I was taken to a police station in the suburbs and shown into a room. On a table were my parachute and overalls and I was asked to identify them as mine. In French, I said I knew nothing of these things, I'd come from Spain on business. The detective who had spoken to me in Spanish complimented me on my French but said nothing more.

I was left in that room until nightfall. I was allowed to go to the lavatory and was served a mug of unsweetened black coffee. My mind was a rowdy, shouting confusion of ideas, suppositions, guesses and counter-suggestions. I tried hard not to come to conclusions—it was too early, perhaps they'd let me go? But one question kept coming back to nag at me: how did Ludwig know I was at the Hôtel Cosmopolitan? The only person in Geneva, in Western Europe, in the world, who knew I'd checked in there was me.

In the evening I was taken from the room and led out of the rear of the police station. There I was helped into the back of a van and the door locked. There were no windows. The van moved off; after about three hours travelling we stopped and the engine was cut.

I climbed out to find myself under the porte cochère of a sizeable villa at whose front door two armed soldiers stood guard. The detectives then handed me over to bona fide prison officers, as far as I could tell. I was taken into a changing room and asked to remove my clothes and was given, to replace them, a set of underwear—drawers and a vest—a pair of black serge trousers, a collarless grey flannel shirt and a crude grey tunic that buttoned up to my neck. On my feet I wore some thick socks and, most curiously, a pair of heavy wooden clogs. I felt like a cross between a Dutch peasant and a komissar in revolutionary Russia.

Thus attired, I followed my gaoler along a corridor and up some stairs and was shown into a large, barely furnished room. There were some traces of its former decoration remaining—a curtain pole, a painted cornice—in stark contrast to the functionality of the furniture it contained. An iron bed (made up with blankets), a table and chair and a chamber pot. The one large window was heavily barred and against the wall was a central-heating radiator—warm.

As the guard left he said, "Buenas noches." He locked the door behind him.

This was to be my new home and I couldn't help wondering how long I would be staying here.

Life at the villa. From my window I had a fine view of the end of a lake and snowy mountains beyond. Lake Lucerne, I later discovered. Every morning a guard unlocked the door at seven and I was escorted to a washroom where I emptied my chamber pot and could shave and wash at a basin. Once a week I was allowed a shower, when I could wash my hair. I received a complete change of clothing once a fortnight. When I returned to my room, breakfast would be waiting: bread and cheese and an enamel mug of warm coffee, never hot. The next interruption was at noon—lunch: always some kind of vegetable soup with more bread. In the afternoon I was allowed into the interior courtyard of the villa, where there was a patchy lawn surrounded and quartered by gravel paths. Under the eyes of a guard I was allowed to stroll around or sit in a patch of sunshine if the day was clement. When I was ordered inside I would catch a glimpse of another inmate (dressed identically to me) emerging into the courtyard for his period of exercise. As time went by I concluded that there could be only half a dozen of us in the building and widely dispersed among its three floors—rarely did I hear the clattering clump of clogs along my passageway. Then it was back to the room and at seven the evening meal was served, a plate of stew or a chop, always with potatoes and more bread and cheese. The lights went out at nine. The guards seemed to change constantly and always attempted to speak to me in bad Spanish—"Hola," "Vamos," "Está bien?"—no matter in what language I addressed them—and they always called me Peredes.

It was a very simple, very efficient and very secure regime. Very

Swiss, you might say, and at first my mood was strangely relieved. All bets were off: "Operation Shipbroker" had foundered all too quickly. I had been caught and there was nothing more I could do—the game was over and they had won. The Swiss were neutral, after all: I wasn't going to be tortured by the Gestapo, and it was surely only a matter of time before I was transferred to a proper internment camp (I knew there were about 12,000 Allied soldiers and airmen already interned in Switzerland). Somewhere, wheels would have been set in motion and the creaking bureaucracy that governed wartime prisoners would eventually seek me out and deal with me. But as the days and the weeks went by (the guards would always tell me the date) I began increasingly to worry. This routine seemed as if it could go on forever and I was bored to insensibility: no books, no newspapers, no writing material. But I was exercised and well fed—in fact I was putting on weight what with all the bread and cheese I was scoffing daily.

After about six weeks I asked to see the governor—I said I had a confession to make. Some days passed. Then one evening I was led downstairs to one of the big drawing rooms on the ground floor. It was half empty but here and there were some tatty but rather fine pieces of furniture. A tall lean man in his fifties, with hair so severely combed it looked painful, stood before the fireplace in a light grey double-breasted suit.

"Habla inglés?" I asked and, on being assured that he did, I told him everything: that my name was Logan Mountstuart, that I was a lieutenant in the RNVR attached to Naval Intelligence and that I had been sent to Switzerland to pre-empt the flight from Europe of important Nazis at the end of the war. All I asked was to be put in touch with some consular official who looked after British interests or even Allen Dulles, head of OSS in Bern. Everything could be quickly sorted out.

The man looked at me and smiled. "You really don't expect me to believe this nonsense, do you, Señor Peredes?"

"My name is Logan Mountstuart."

"Who is Ludwig?"

"He was my contact in Geneva. I never met him."

"That is a lie. Who is Ludwig? Where is he?"

I protested I knew nothing more of this Ludwig-person. Guards were called and I was taken back to my room.

And so my life continued. I never saw this man again, although I made regular requests (I now believe he was Colonel Masson, head of the Swiss Military Intelligence). Boredom reached new levels of intolerability. My one distraction was that I began to keep a small farm of insects that I found in my room—silvery woodlice, a cockroach, some small brown ants—which I herded together in a small packet made from a corner of the blanket of my bed. I named them all (though the ants were hard to tell apart) and during the day I would let them roam, closely supervised, about the room. It passed the time quite effectively. They kept escaping, of course, and I kept having to replenish my stock, but each escape was a small moment of vicarious freedom for myself, as if it were me wriggling through a crack in the floorboards or under the skirting when my back was turned. From time to time I made requests to see figures in authority, but all in vain.

I descended into a form of tolerable apathy—which I believe all prisoners experience. You surrender your individual spirit to the routine of the institution. I had no idea where I was, what I was being held for (apart from spying, I suppose) or what benefit accrued to the Swiss nation from my expensive incarceration. I had faith—almost as naively trusting as religious faith—that efforts were being made to release me and that Freya knew what had happened to me and that I was alive and well. I realized I would just have to wait.

And then suddenly, in the late summer, I was given smoking privileges. A few ounces of loose tobacco and some cigarette papers. I learned to roll the thinnest cigarettes, thin as cocktail sticks with a few shreds of tobacco tightly packed. When I wanted a light I had to call a guard. I began to hoard my spare cigarette papers. In the washroom was an old sooty stove used to heat the water for the showers and the baths. On my way out I would scrape some flakes of soot off the outside with my nails. This soot, when mixed with urine, formed an acceptable if pungent ink. I had a safety pin holding my trouser fly together—my pen. I had pen and ink and paper. And thus began "The Prison Diary of Logan Mountstuart." It took me hours to write a few sentences, scratched in laborious minuscule handwriting on my slips of cigarette paper, but for the first time since my arrest my old spirit began to stir and ease itself. I was a writer again.

October. Peregrine (one of my woodlice) has died. Found him in the morning curled in a tight ball and when I tried to unwind him he broke in half. Poor Peregrine, he was the most docile and least adventurous of my insect crew. Lurid, fiery sunset over the lake. Terrible pangs, a physical ache, missing Freya and Stella. Surely they must know I'm alive, at the very least. My request for writing materials turned down again with no explanation. The guards accept your requests without demur and always apologize when they return empty-handed. NID must be aware I was taken. The mysterious "Ludwig" knew where I was staying. (How? Was he outside the hotel, saw me arrive and followed me to the Cosmopolitan?) He would have reported I was picked up. At night I sometimes hear the drone of heavy bombers heading north to Germany. Intense gustatory memories of the apple pie I had at lunch the day I was arrested—the last sweet thing I ate. The taste of freedom? Apple pie.

14 November. Hugo told me the date today. I call him Hugo but have no idea if that is his real name. He won't tell me. All the guards now refer to me as Gonzago, despite my protests. Hugo seems to be on duty every three or four days. I ask him in French how the war is going and he smiles and nods and says "très bien." One has a sense of the guard rota being as well organized as everything else in this place. This afternoon I banged on the door for five minutes until a guard came. I demanded to see the governor. Request denied.

Today I went downstairs to meet "someone from the embassy." Interestingly, it was three days since my vain demand to see the governor. You think you have been refused, but it's just that they operate very slowly.

The man introduced himself as Señor Fernandez and said he was from the Spanish consulate in Lausanne and was responsible for Uruguayan affairs. He said I was only the fifth Uruguayan to visit Switzerland since the war began. I told him my story and my true name. But if you are British, he said, looking disappointed, you are no longer my responsibility. Can you get a message to my wife? I asked. Of course, he said, your wife in Montevideo? No, I said, in London. He spread his hands, "es muy dificil." I told him Freya's name and begged him to write down the address, which he did, eventually. "Just write one line," I said. "Tell her I'm alive, that's all. Can you do that?" He gave a nervous smile and said he would try.

1945

January. The new year passed in solitude and silence. I wrote a poem to Freya on a slip of this paper, then rolled some tobacco in it and symbolically smoked the cigarette. I've been in this place nearly a year now and am beginning to be tormented by some unpleasant suspicions. I'm growing convinced that there is a link between my arrest and incarceration and what happened in the Bahamas. I'll never forget the Duchess's words: we still have powerful friends. For example, why was I recalled so quickly after the de Marigny arrest? And just who is this Colonel Marion who dreamt up "Operation Shipbroker"? How come Ian knew so little of what was going on? I mull over the chain of events and dislike the questions that are raised: what about the police who were waiting for me at the Hôtel du Commerce? Or the speed with which my parachute was found? Just filthy luck or some darker force operating?

This life is like a slow but gentle torture and for me the most terrible aspect of my imprisonment is the loneliness. For the first time ever I feel truly lonely: I'm without the comfort afforded by others, my loved ones, my friends. It's not a question of solitude: one can bear solitude, but no one likes to feel lonely.

Sexually my libido is subject to some crazy rhythm. Sometimes I masturbate six or seven times a day with all the unreflecting prowess of an adolescent schoolboy. Then three weeks will go by without a lascivious thought entering my head.

I've abandoned my insect ranch: they die from cold—or when I put them near the radiator they die from heat.

It's most peculiar possessing so little in the world. You could say that the clothes I wear, my bed and its bedding, my table and chair, my chamber pot (and its rag for arse wiping), my tin of tobacco and my thin sheaf of cigarette papers and my safety pin represent the sum total of my worldly goods. And they can't really be described as my possessions—they've been lent to me. I think of my cluttered house in Battersea, my thousands of books, my paintings, my papers, my crammed drawers and wardrobes . . . Suddenly to have my world, my stuff, reduced to this meagreness makes me feel without ballast, without identity.

The lake as I see it from my window has many moods and this modest view has become the focus of my aesthetic being. All beauty, all transcending thoughts, all stimulae and evaluation derive from this circumscribed panorama of Lake Lucerne. I think if they were to brick up this window I'd go mad within hours. Today the angle of the sun makes the lake a sheet of burnished silver. High thin clouds mist the sky's blue ever so slightly. I can see half a field of corn shading from pale green to the first hint of ripening sand-yellow. I wish there was a road and some human traffic. I can watch the birdlife for hours and once, just once, I saw a small steamer with a thin scarlet smokestack come into view, turn and sail back beyond the window edge.

Hugo let slip today that there is a new director of the prison. I asked to see him. Request denied.

August. At about two in the morning I was wakened by the rise and fall of a siren and I thought at once it was an air raid. Two guards came in and ordered me to get dressed. I was hurried downstairs and pushed through the front door and on to the gravel. Three other prisoners were there: we blinked and stared at each other like Victorian explorers meeting in the jungles of Africa, shy and tongue-tied. Others joined us, fetched out from the various floors of the big house: eleven in all, identically dressed in grey tunic, black trousers and heavy clogs. The alarm was genuine—there was a fire in the kitchen. Some sort of fire appliance was driven round the back of the villa and we could hear shouts and breaking glass. It was the most excitement we'd had in months and the guards were restive and curious. While they were distracted by the fuss, I turned to the man next to me and said, in English, "What's your name?" "Nicht verstehen," he whispered, "Deutsche." So this was the enemy. "Englander," I said. He looked at me, baffled, then pointed at another man: "Italiano," he said. A guard shouted to silence us. Who are we, I thought? What are we doing here in this villa by Lake Lucerne so strictly and solicitously guarded? What have we done?

August. As usual my denied request to see the new director produced its familiar tardy results. I was led down to the drawing room and introduced to a young American with round horn-rimmed glasses. "I don't exactly know what to do with you, Mr. Peredes," he said apologetically. I went through the rigmarole of explanation again. "This is a security—intelligence—matter at root," I said. "If you could get the OSS to pass this on to London, then I'm sure something could be worked out." Then he told me that Dulles had closed down the OSS. "Since when?" I said. He blinked at me, surprised: "Since the end of the war in Europe." He told me the war was over, had been over for some months, and I felt both sudden panic and huge relief. The end had to be in sight now—but why were we still being held incommunicado like this? I gave him Freya's name and address and implored him to send a message saying I was alive and well. He said he would do his best. Please, I said, as the guard led me to the door, just do that one thing for me. "Battersea, England?" he shouted after me as the door closed. "Battersea, London," I shouted back. I hope he heard.

I catch fewer and fewer glimpses of my fellow prisoners (glimpses were all I ever had), and this infrequency means that I'm beginning to worry that I'm left alone in this villa. I asked Paulus (another guard I've christened) what was going on now the war was over and he said, "Oh, they keep us busy." I asked to see the director but was told that the director was now based in Bcrn. I said that if I didn't get to see the director I would go on hunger strike. "Hey, Gonzago," he said, looking hurt. "Tranquilo, hombre."

15 December 1945. I left the villa by the lake last night dressed in the freshly laundered clothes in which I had been arrested. I was supplied with official-looking documentation, a form of temporary identification paper issued by the Ministry of the Interior, which announced that I was one Gonzago Peredes, citizen of Uruguay. I was driven in a truck to a railhead at the Italian border, where I joined a group of two hundred other displaced persons (mainly Croats and Romanians) and we were put on a closed train for Milan. We were interned awaiting interrogation in an internment camp (campo 33) near Certosa. My days in the villa by Lake Lucerne were over. Finally I was on my way home.

[NOTE IN RETROSPECT. 1975. My recent reading has now convinced me that the circumstances of my arrest and incarceration in Switzerland 1944–5 were complicated by a moment of panic that occurred in Swiss military intelligence. From the beginning of the war the Swiss had a spy planted at the heart of the Nazi regime and received a flow of first-rate intelligence material from this source. In 1943 a security blunder had put this secret link at risk and the Swiss became increasingly uneasy that they were being fed compromised information and that a German invasion of Switzerland was growing more and more likely, with the aim of making the country an impregnable lynchpin in the Germans' wider plan of "Fortress Europe." This state of high sensitivity did not really begin to subside until after D-Day on 6 June 1944. My clandestine arrival in the country in early '44 could not have come at a worse time. I had parachuted into a snake pit of paranoia, military trepidation and raw nerves. Everything about me—the Uruguayan connection, the mysterious "Ludwig," my own admission that I had come to contact high-ranking Nazis—made me the object of massive suspicion. Whoever betrayed me could have had no idea of the consternation I would cause.]

WEDNESDAY, 19 DECEMBER

Campo 33. Certosa. Strange to be accumulating possessions again. My own suitcase, a change of clothing, a shaving kit, some American magazines—signs of my re-entry into the real world. I managed to speak to a British liaison officer called Crozier this afternoon. An intelligent man, he could see that my story was true, however fantastical it seemed on first hearing. I almost wept with joy when I saw credulity replacing scepticism in his eyes. He said he would cable London immediately. I asked him to cable Freya also and handed him a letter I'd written to her. He promised it would be delivered and gave me a notebook and pen and ink. He suggested that I write everything down in the form of a memorandum while the details were relatively fresh and warned me there would be some strenuous debriefing and interrogation up ahead before I would be sent back home. So tonight I will write down all I can remember about the ill-fated "Operation Shipbroker." But after my conversation with Crozier my heart was distinctly lighter: I walked back through the swarming camp towards my hut, through the riff-raff, the dispossessed and *les misérables* of Europe, looking about me with a fond and benevolent eye. Hitler is dead, evil vanquished, we have won the war. Logan Mountstuart's life can begin again.

THE POST-WAR JOURNAL

The post-war journal is a strange and often disturbing document, not surprisingly, given the desperate circumstances that met Logan Mountstuart on his return to England in late January 1946.

The brutal facts are these.

When LMS did not check into the Hôtel du Commerce in February 1944 and was arrested the next day he effectively disappeared from the surface of the earth as far as NID was concerned. The last person who could testify to having seen him alive was Flight-Sergeant Chew—who had watched him step out into the night air through the hatch in the side of the Liberator bomber. The contact "Ludwig" reported that LMS had never gone to the hotel as arranged. All attempts at discovering what had happened to him were fruitless. (This makes one wonder who the "Ludwig" was that sent the message to the Hôtel Cosmopolitan—giving some credence to LMS's persistent accusation that he was betrayed.)

In NID, after a few weeks of total silence, it was assumed that LMS had met with a fatal accident or been killed—a fate that befell many agents who parachuted into Europe. The parachute could have failed to open; he could have made a landing on a mountainside and broken a leg, fallen into a lake or been dropped in the wrong place—in occupied France rather than Switzerland. None of these could be discounted and as the days went by NID feared the worst.

In March, Freya Mountstuart was visited by Commander Vanderpoel, who informed her that her husband was missing, presumed dead. He *told her only that LMS was an NID agent and had parachuted "some-where in Europe" on a secret mission. The effect on Freya can be imag-ined. The devastating news was confirmed when she was awarded a war-widow's pension. To all intents and purposes Logan Mountstuart was dead. LMS's mother was informed and so was Lionel. A mass was held in Brompton Oratory attended by a few friends (Peter Scabius, notably) and some colleagues from NID (Plomer, Fleming, Vanderpoel).*

Freya and her young daughter now had to cope as best they could. Some months later, probably in August, she met Skuli Gunnarson, twenty-nine years old, a member of the Icelandic Liaison Committee based in London. They began to see each other socially and in October they became lovers. Freya's letters home to her father and brother mention Skuli with increasing frequency. Stella also liked him a great deal, it was reported.

In December, Freya married Skuli Gunnarson and he moved into Melville Road. Mercedes Mountstuart was a witness to the wedding and toasts were drunk to LMS's memory at the small party held afterwards in a room above the Builder's Arms, Battersea.

In late January 1945 Freya discovered she was pregnant. Two days later she and Stella were killed by the blast from a v-2 rocket as they were walking home after infant school. Thirteen other people were killed in the explosion.

In October 1945 Gunnarson sold Melville Road and returned to Ice-land.

LMS arrived from Milan at an RAF base in Wiltshire in January 1946. He cabled Freya and went straight to London, to Melville Road–where he discovered his house was now owned and occupied by a Mr. and Mrs. Keith Thomsett and their three children. It was Mrs. Thomsett who inadvertently set the sequence of appalling discoveries in motion when she remarked to a frantic and worried LMS that it was "a terrible shame about that poor Mrs. Gunnarson and her daughter."

The post-war journal is the hardest of all in which to fix the month, let alone the day. LMS's random and inaccurate datings are all that can be relied upon. Even the years may be suspect.

1946

Hodge is a cunt, *soi-disant* and says he has every right to be one, having left a leg in Italy. I am a cunt for letting him rile me, poor pathetic bastard.

Walked the river, seeking beauty. Saw it but felt nothing. We drank a bottle and a half of whisky between us last night. Hodge stinks: I told him to have a bath. He says he hates the sight of his scarred stump.

FreyaFreyaFreyaFreyaFreyaFreyaFreyaFreyaFreyaFreyaFreyaFreya
FreyaFreyaFreyaFreyaFreyaFreyaFreyaFreya
FreyaStellaStellaFreya
Freya
Stella
Freya
Stella

FREYAFREYAFREYAFREYA

Free
Right
Everloved
Young
Always adored

Stella, my daughter. Freya, my wife. Stella Mountstuart. Freya Mountstuart

[The journal is full of these anguished doodlings.]

Took Dick out on a drive up the Tweed Valley to Peebles. Cool blustery day, the first fatigued leaves ripped off the trees. All the way he talked about the mistake he had made in never getting married. "Look at me now," he said. "Who'd take me? A one-legged drunk." Tonight, sitting by the fire, I began to weep quietly—couldn't help myself, came on with absolute spontaneity—thinking of Freya and Stella. "Stop blubbing," Dick said. "You're only feeling sorry for yourself, it's got nothing to do with Freya and Stella. They're fine, they're atomized dust blowing in the breeze. Free as air. They're not thinking about you. I can't abide self-pity, so shut up or get out." I almost hit him. I went to my bedroom. Can't sleep.

Is this worth recording? I experienced what can only be described as a spasm of happiness—the first since I heard the news—when I managed to work out (with a toothpick) a shred of mutton that had been stuck in a crevice between two back teeth. It had been resistant to everything it was so firmly wedged. I grinned spontaneously. Must have been real pleasure. My mind forgetting. Am I healing?

Hodge lectured me again on Freya and Stella. Thirteen other people died when that explosion happened, he said. Thousands of Londoners died from bombs or rockets, many of them women and children. Millions of people died in the war. You could have been a German Jew—lost your entire family in the gas chambers—wife, children, brothers, sisters, nieces and nephews, parents, aunts and uncles, grandparents. It's an awful bloody terrible tragic thing but you have to see them as victims of a global armed conflict, like the millions of other victims. Innocent people die in a war. And now we're casualties too. I said, you can't equate my wife and child with your fucking leg. Yes I fucking well can, he bellowed at me. To me—to me—my lost leg is more important than your lost wife and child.

Couldn't sleep so I pulled on a coat over my pyjamas, put on a pair of gumboots and walked around the gardens. One of those light, star-filled, northern nights. An owl hooted and I walked through a cloud of perfume from some scented shrub, almost palpable, it seemed to flow round me carried by the breeze. I urinated, hearing the patter of my urine on the gravel clearly, like a fire crackling. I mooched around, not thinking, just taking in the information my senses provided, not cold, until the first birds began to sing and the dawn-light began to restore the colours to the old house and its unkempt garden.

Lucy [Sansom]* took me to an old café she knew in Leith while we waited for the boat. She's much stouter and her hair is greying but, beneath the accumulation of flesh, you can still see the pretty girl I used to fantasize about. She was very sweet to me: the perfect antidote to Dick's brusque rationalizations. We drank tea and ate toast and jam. Outside Edinburgh rain turned the grey sooty stone black, like velvet. Lucy has a cottage at Elie in Fife, which she offered to lend me if I "needed some peace and quiet to work." What work? I said. You're a writer, for God's sake, she said. You've got to keep on writing. She asked me if I was sure I was doing the right thing. I said I had to. I said that it was the only chance of a purging—a sense of it finally being over.

SEPTEMBER 1ST

We should dock at Reykjavik tomorrow. It's been good being at sea these last few days. The voyage calming and restful. I stand at the rail for hours and look at the sea and the sky. Why does the sea induce these feelings of transcendence in us? Is it because an unobstructed view of overarching sky meeting endlessly stirring water is as close as we can come on this earth to a visual symbol of the infinite? I feel more at peace than I have for months.

Reykjavik. Impressions of a town of painted concrete and corrugated iron and of various-sized, tarpaulin-covered things. When in doubt the

---

*She was now a lecturer in Medieval History at Edinburgh University.

Icelanders seem to cover anything with a tarpaulin. It was raining heavily when we docked and in the hour it took me to disembark, find a taxi rank, wait in the queue and be driven to the hotel, the rain stopped, the sun shone fiercely, it rained, hailed and the sun shone again. If this is the norm it will drive me mad. I'm staying at the Borg. I had a lunch of German sausage, pickled cucumber and smoked salmon and a plate of small sweet cakes as a dessert. Now I begin my search for Gunnarson.

It has taken me two days to find Gunnarson; everyone has been politely helpful in answering my inquiries. There's a pretty girl on reception who has translated when required (her name is Katrin Annasdottir). Gunnarson turns out to be a civil servant in the Icelandic equivalent of the Ministry of Agriculture. I wrote him a letter and handed it in at the door, telling him who I was and that I was staying at the Borg. Tonight comes a message saying that he, Gunnarson, has no reason or need to meet me.

The price of alcohol in this hotel beggars belief.

I went down to the ministry early in the morning before the staff arrived and waited. I stopped a young man who seemed to be about the right age and asked him if he was Gunnarson. No, he said, you couldn't mistake Gunnarson, he was exceptionally tall. Look, he pointed, here he comes. I watched Gunnarson go into the building: he glanced at me, half curiously. He was tall and athletic-looking, his blond hair so fair it was almost white. I thought: this is the man Freya wanted after me . . . I felt quite sick.

I waited outside until lunchtime and when Gunnarson emerged went up to him and introduced myself. He was a good half-head taller than me. He had a large hooked nose and looked fit and burly—which is not an adjective you usually associate with exceptionally tall men. He looked like someone who could climb mountains all day long. He

seemed more irritated to meet me than anything else, though he
perked up a bit when I offered to buy him lunch.

He took me to a nearby restaurant and ordered some kind of fish
stew served with a creamy gravy with cooked radishes and sodden hot
lettuce. I could eat nothing and sipped at a hilariously expensive beer
while he shovelled food into his mouth as if he were stoking a boiler. I
can only think it is his sheer height and bulky energy that attracted
Freya. Physically he is the opposite of me in almost every detail. I'm
tall and slim enough, but my posture is bad and nothing about my
demeanour and comportment suggests urgency. I never walk fast, for
example, if I can help it.

When he finished his stew he ordered the inevitable plate of sweet
cakes. As he wolfed these down, he looked at me curiously.

"It's strange," he said. "I feel I know you." He spoke good, almost
accentless English.

"You've probably heard a lot about me."

"I've seen so many photographs of you, yet I didn't recognize you."

"I don't take a flattering photograph."

"No. I think it was because for me you've always been dead. And
now here you are in front of me alive. Strange."

"And Freya and Stella are dead."

At this he clenched his jaw and took a few deep breaths.

"She was very beautiful," he said. "I loved her very much."

"So did I."

"Stella was a lovely child."

I asked him not to talk about Stella. It wasn't so bad talking about
Freya—because my time with Freya had been far longer than his—but I
had missed the last two years of Stella's short life and I couldn't bear
the fact that this stranger had known her when she was five and six and
I had not.

"Why did you want to meet me?" he asked. "It must be . . .
painful."

"It is," I admitted, "but I had to see you, see what you were like. To
try to understand. Fill in the gap."

He scratched his head and frowned. Then he said, "You mustn't
blame her."

"I don't."

He ignored me. "She was convinced you were dead, you see, it was as simple as that. It was the absolute silence that convinced her. She said if you were alive there would have been something—a word, even. She was lonely. And then I came along."

I knew what it was like to be lonely. "I don't blame her," I said, almost stupidly, as if repeating the words were enough to convince myself. "How was she to know I was still alive?"

"Exactly. She thought you were dead, you see. She had to get on with her life."

"Yes—I can see that."

We talked on in a series of random questions and answers and I was able to piece together a picture of Freya's life while I was away. I realized Gunnarson had his own problems too: he had his own grief; and he had to reconcile himself, now that I was alive and sitting opposite him, to the fact that he was and would always be Freya's second choice, that her heart had really belonged to me. I was more like the cuckolded husband confronting the lover—and my mind kept forming pictures of Freya and Gunnarson, naked, making love in our bed. I had to curb my imagination violently. It was nobody's fault, just too desperately, hopelessly sad.

He said he had to be back at work.

"One more thing," I said. "You sold my house. I'd like the money."

He paused. "It was my house. Freya left it to me in her will."

"I bought that house. That is my house, by natural law."

"Luckily we don't live by natural law."

"You're a thief," I said.

He stood up. "You're upset. I won't hold it against you."

There is a small artificial lake at the centre of this ramshackle town called the Tjörn that is populated by many wild ducks. I bought a bottle of Spanish brandy at the hotel and went down to the lake to drink myself insensible. The brandy tasted like marzipan-flavoured cooking oil and I could only manage a few mouthfuls.

[OCTOBER?]

NORTHWICH (CHESHIRE)

George Deverell seems crushed by his loss. His manner is polite but dazed, as if he's just come round from being knocked unconscious. He seems unperturbed by his ex-son-in-law's return from the dead. "Wonderful to see you, Logan," he will say from time to time and pat me lightly on the shoulder as if to confirm that I am indeed flesh and blood. Then you see him inwardly withdraw and shrivel up—I've come back and am alive but his daughter and granddaughter have gone forever.

Robin has taken over the running of the timber yard completely and is worried by the quiet depth of his father's misery. He, by contrast, was intensely curious about my experiences. Muttering oaths and expletives as I told him about my parachute jump, my arrest and long months in the villa, going, "Bloody hell," "That's barbaric!," "Jesus Christ" and the like.

Two days ago a letter arrived from Iceland containing a banker's draft for £400. Gunnarson, the honourable Icelander.

All my belongings are here, boxed and stored—my books, my manuscripts, all my paintings. Even pieces of furniture that the Thomsetts didn't purchase. I have no home but all the ingredients of home.

1947

[MARCH]

It was my forty-first birthday last week. I see I forgot to note the arrival of my fortieth last year—small wonder. For the record, then, I who once had a wife, a child and a perfect family home now, in my forty-first year, have none of these and live in a damp and fusty room in my mother's decrepit house. I am rich enough, financially speaking: two years' back pay screwed out of the Ministry of Defence (with the help of Noel Lange [LMS's lawyer]), plus the money Gunnarson sent from the house sale. I gave my mother a hundred pounds and told her to spend it on Sumner Place—fresh paint, new carpets, etc.—but I think she's lost the energy. The house is not exactly a rat-infested slum but hundreds of careless paying-guests have left it grimy and knocked-about. Mother and Encarnación, both arthritic and wheezy, bicker at each other in Spanish. I go for meandering strolls through Chelsea and South Kensington, wondering what to do with myself.

In Battersea I found the crater made by the v-2. The end of a terrace of houses gone, wooden hoardings round the huge hole. It would have been sudden. The rocket falling silently out of the sky as the two of them walked along, hand in hand, heading back home from school. Just the flash, the noise and then oblivion.

I can see nothing of myself in Lionel. Perhaps something around the eyes. My eyebrows. The boy has your eyebrows, sir. And he had my hairline: the sharp prow of a widow's peak. Lottie was cool—I don't think she can ever forgive me. And Leggatt seems a dotard, not long for this world, I would say. He asked me where I served in the war and I said the Bahamas and Switzerland. "I said where did you serve, not where did you go on holiday." I told him I had been in the navy and that seemed to shut him up.

Lionel and I managed to wander round the garden alone for half an hour. He is a quiet diffident boy, nearly fourteen now (Christ!), his eyes always cast down, stiff fingers pushing constantly at his forelock. I asked him if he was happy at Eton. "Yes, sir, pretty much . . . Sort of." Please don't call me "sir," I said. Call me Father or Daddy. He looked anguished. "But I call mummy's husband 'Father' now," he said.* Call me Logan, then, I said. Never call me "sir."

*During the years of LMS's disappearance and presumed death, Lionel had been formally adopted by Leggatt as his son and heir. LMS made no recorded objection to this state of affairs.

*   *   *

State of literary play. *The Mind's Imaginings*—out of print. *The Girl Factory*—out of print. *The Cosmopolitans*—out of print (except in France). Income from journalism—nil.

Wallace says it takes two to tango. I have to help him find me work. I said I'd been silent too long, everyone thinks I'm dead. Then Wallace had a bright idea: what about your old friend Peter Scabius? What about him?

Peter [Scabius]'s piece on me in *The Times* ("One Writer's War") seems to have done the trick: people know I am around once more and I've had a small flurry of congratulatory postcards, letters and telephone calls. Roderick has renewed my old job as reader on a piecework basis (£5 per report); Louis MacNeice has invited me to give a talk on "Post-War French Painting" and the Swiss Ambassador has written a letter to the paper denying the existence of the villa by Lake Lucerne and effectively accusing me of being a dangerous fantasist. Many magazines have invited me to write about the Harry Oakes murder, but I've declined—I'm keeping my powder dry.

Peter was—what?—impressed, astonished, admiring? when we met. Somewhat in awe by what I'd been through. His own war was uneventful: fire watching, then the Ministry of Information and another novel—*Iniquity*—to follow up the success of *Guilt*. "You've got to use all that stuff," he said to me. "It's heaven sent. Money in the bank." I humoured him and said I was writing a memoir to be called "From Nassau to Lucerne," although I remained resolutely uninspired. If I had no money it might be different, I realize, but I've more than enough for the next year or so. I spend almost nothing, living very quietly, though I've started to go to pubs again, the bigger and more crowded the better.

Mother says her varicose veins cause her continual pain. Encarnación is suffering from piles. I go to the optician to be fitted for reading glasses. The house of mirth.

I have had no sexual contact, no intimacy of any kind, since February 1944 (my last days and Freya). Only sporadic bouts of masturbation testify to the fact that the libidinous side of my brain has not shut down entirely. What sick Victorian cleric dubbed the practice self-abuse? Self-help, more like, self-support, self-solace. Auto-eroticism keeps you sane. I should record this for curiosity's sake; the image in my mind as I pleasure myself these days is not Freya (too achingly sad) but Katrin Annasdottir, the receptionist at the Borg Hotel in Reykjavik. Obviously something more must have registered in me during our few encounters apart from her helpfulness and efficiency. Funny, these sensual fingerprints left on your imagination, only revealing themselves much later. Like invisible ink emerging when warmed by a light bulb or candle flame. What was it about Katrin that sneaked its way into my sexual archive?

[JULY–AUGUST]

In the George with MacNeice and Johnnie Stallybrass from the BBC. MacNeice banging on at me to write a radio play about my months in the villa. Make it a monologue, make it mythic, make it a dream, he says, you can do anything on radio. Good money too: with one radio play—broadcast three times—he says I can make as much as a school-teacher does in a year. MacNeice is off to India to report on the Partition.* I envy him. Sudden desire for travel. Buxom girl behind the bar in the George. Tight blouse flattening her fat breasts. The sap may be rising at last.

FRIDAY, 10 OCTOBER

Dinner at Ben's. About a dozen of us crowded round two pushed-together tables in his dining room. Five of my Mirós hanging on the wall. A mixture of friends, potential buyers, artists and family. Ben uses

*India and Pakistan were formally separated on 15 August 1947.

these dinners as a kind of informal private view, changing the pictures on the wall according to who is coming and how deep their pockets are. As he welcomes each guest he says, "Don't be shy. If you like something, speak up. Everything on the walls is for sale."

Sandrine never stirs from her seat: Ben does all the clearing and serving, aided on this occasion by Marius. He's twenty now—a handsome boy in a sulky, brooding way. Clothilde [Leeping—Ben and Sandrine's daughter] is away at boarding school. I sat beside Sandrine and she indicated a dark, delicate-featured, good-looking man. She whispered, "Ben thinks he's the only real talent in English painting. The only one he wants to buy." I asked her what his name was. Southman,* she said. I should keep a note. Ben tells me he thinks he'll sell the Mirós soon but not until he's back in Paris—he's asking huge sums. They move back to Paris at the end of the year. Ben has found new premises for a gallery. "The Americans are coming back," he says. "I'm going to make you a lot of money."

[DECEMBER]

Baldwin† dead. Makes me think of the Duke and Duchess—how they hated him. I'm laid up with a bad flu that has gone bronchial—cough like a sea lion's, throat-tearing. As I lie here shivering, despite the two bar-radiators pointing at me on either side of the bed, I have a vision about my future life. It's a question, it seems to me, of "who travels lightest, travels furthest." Huge desire to be as free of "things" and possessions as possible. All that stuff I have packed up in boxes . . . What bliss it would be not to have to think about it all anymore.

*Probably Graham Sutherland (1903–80).
†Stanley Baldwin, Prime Minister at the time of the Abdication Crisis.

1948

[JANUARY]

I have bought a basement flat in Pimlico. 10 B, Turpentine Lane. It has a bedroom, sitting room, kitchen and bathroom. You descend steepish steps to the front door. From the back bedroom there is a view of a small garden to which I have no access. The sitting-room window looks out onto the deep basement well. All the essentials seem in good running order and there are new gas fires in the bedroom and sitting room. I am having it painted white distemper and the floor will be lined throughout in rubberized cork tiles. I need only the most essential furniture: two armchairs, a bed and bedside table, a long table and chair for me to work at. I sold (almost) all my books to Gaston's in the Strand and will sell my paintings to Ben.

It strikes me now that I may have picked up a *façon de vivre* at the villa on Lake Lucerne. Less is more. We shall see.

WEDNESDAY, II FEBRUARY

Paris. Ben took me as his guest to a grand dinner at the house of a man called Thorvald Hugo, a great collector of modern art. Picasso was there and his new muse, Françoise [Gilot]. Very pretty girl—mind you, so was Dora Maar (more my type). Picasso is quite bald now and the hair on the side of his head is grey. Face seamed and belligerent. He was full of energy and humour: the more he appeared to be enjoying himself the more Françoise became moody and on edge. He had no memory of meeting me before (why should he?), but when Ben told him I had been in Madrid in 1937 he became very curious and moved round the table to sit beside me. I said I'd been there with Hemingway, whom he knew a bit. He had seen Hemingway in Paris after the Liberation and told me how Hemingway claimed to have killed an SS officer. "That man killed a lot of animals," he said, "but animals don't shoot back." He wants to take me to dinner, he says, and talk some more.

Ben thinks I'm mad to sell my paintings. I said, just because I'm selling these doesn't mean I won't be buying some more. He'll give me a fair price. His new gallery is on the rue du Bac but from the way he talks it seems to me he sees Paris purely as a springboard to propel him into New York. He's planning to rent space there for a show next year. That's where the real money is, he says. That's where he'll sell the Mirós.

Back to days and nights of walking through my favourite Paris *quartiers*—a *flâneur* and a *noctambule* once again. On the surface Paris looks unchanged, as beautiful and as transporting as it always has been, untouched by whatever went on during the war. But there are food shortages and darker currents flow beneath the surface. Everyone not a Communist seems terrified by the Communists. A jangly, hysterical atmosphere.

I was sitting in the Flore watching the tourists trying to spot Sartre (he doesn't come here anymore because of the tourists trying to spot him) when I had the glimmerings of an idea for a novel. A man goes to his doctor and is told he has a week left to live. The novel is about the last seven days of life he has left to him and what he does in them: an attempt to encapsulate all forms of human experience in one week. Everything from impregnating a woman to committing a murder . . . To be pondered. For the first time in ages a quiver of literary excitement. There is something in this.

To the Brasserie Lipp. Me, Ben, Sandrine, Marius, Picasso, Françoise. Picasso talks a great deal about Dora [Maar], which doesn't seem to bother Françoise. I asked how she was and Picasso said she was going mad. We talked about my visits to Spain in the Civil War, and Picasso was very intrigued by my story of the machine gun, to the extent of

making me act it out. Did you hit the armoured car, he asked? Yes.
Did you kill them? I doubt it, I said. But you saw the bullets strike the
car? Indubitably.

Picasso seems to me one of these wild, stupid geniuses—more Yeats,
Strindberg, Rimbaud, Mozart, than Matisse, Brahms, Braque. It's quite
tiring being with him.

We parted at midnight and walked homeward, Ben, Sandrine, Marius
and I—relieved to be out of the Picassian pressure-cooker. Ben cock-a-
hoop: Picasso has agreed to sell him directly (not through Kahnweiler
[his usual dealer]) two pictures for his New York show. He put his arm
round my shoulder: just keep talking about Spain, he said. Marius was
unable to understand how someone as young and pretty as Françoise
wanted to be with a man forty years older than her. We all laughed. As
we gently teased Marius for his naivety, I felt simultaneously the ineffable sadness of my loss and also a growing comfort, a warmth—a realization that these old friends of mine, the Leepings, were in a way my
true family, that my life was and would always be bound up with
theirs, whatever happened.

Turpentine Lane. Back from Paris. All the work in the flat is finished
and the place looks like a cross between a laboratory and a stage set for
some experimental play. There is nothing "modern" about it at all—no
glass or chrome or leather, no curved wood or abstract wall hangings. It
is about the absence of adornment, the non-existence of clutter. The
light struggles to reach the sitting room and I leave the lamps on all
day. This is my bunker and I will be happy enough here, I think.

[SEPTEMBER]

I ran into Peter [Scabius] at the London Library and he invited me to
join him for a drink. He was meeting a "friend," he said. In the pub the
friend was already there: a young woman, in her early thirties, I would
say, sitting on a stool at the bar with a gin and tonic in front of her and
smoking a cigarette in a holder. "This is Gloria Nesmith," he said.
"Ness-Smith, Petey," she corrected him, then to me: "Pleased to meet

you," though it was immediately clear she wasn't. I could tell that I was a deliberate gooseberry—Peter had brought me along to pre-empt some row. She was a small, pretty woman with prominent cheekbones. Her voice was curious, almost stagey, and she was wearing very high heels to give herself a few more inches. She smoked her cigarette, finished her drink and then said she had to leave. As she kissed Peter goodbye I saw her dig her nails into the back of his hand. After she'd left he held it out: three little crescents welling blood. "She's incredibly dangerous," he said. "I should give her up but she fucks like a stoat." I said I wasn't familiar with the simile. "You wouldn't be," he said, pleased with himself. "I made it up, just for Gloria. You'd have to fuck her yourself to know what I mean." He looked at me slyly. "Maybe you should," he said. "Get her off my hands." "How's Penny?" I asked. "You bastard," he said, laughing.

[NOVEMBER]

Vanderpoel is no longer in the navy—he's the headmaster of a girls' boarding school near Shrewsbury. I took the train down to meet him and we had an edgy uncomfortable lunch together in his ugly new house. He's removed his gingery matelot's beard—which is a mistake aesthetically—but maybe it's required that the headmaster be clean-shaven. Lunch was served by his young wife (Jennifer, I think) who promptly disappeared and I could hear a baby crying somewhere. Perhaps a wife and a child are also necessary elements for headmastering. Who knows? Who cares? Vanderpoel was not particularly pleased to see me, but he had read Peter's article in *The Times* when it had appeared, so was at least familiar with the abrupt failure of "Operation Shipbroker" and the consequences that had befallen me. He was hardly curious, I have to say. But I had plenty of questions, the first being: whose idea was the whole thing?

"That chap Marion's," he said. "He was seconded to us for a few months."

Who was he? Where had he come from?

"Not sure. Could have been from Supreme Headquarters, now I come to think of it. Maybe the Foreign Office. I think he was a diplomat before the war. He was very well connected anyway." He looked at me patiently. "It was a long time ago, Mountstuart. I can't remember all the details. And, anyway," he went on, "even with a little bit of hindsight you have to admit 'Shipbroker' was a first-class idea. Who knows how many Nazis we might have caught."

"First class or not," I said, "I was betrayed. I was set up like a sitting duck. The police were waiting for me at the hotel. Only NID had all the details on me. You, Rushbrooke and Marion."

"I resent that."

I showed my exasperation. "I'm not accusing you. But somebody sent me on that mission knowing I'd be arrested almost immediately. You must see that."

"It wasn't me and it certainly wasn't Rushbrooke."

"Where's Marion now?"

He said he had no idea. He, Vanderpoel, was a member of a dining club of ex-NID staff and he promised he would ask around, discreetly. I had one further question.

"Do you know if Marion had any connection to the Duke of Windsor?"

Vanderpoel actually laughed at this, a strange wheezy sound, and he covered his mouth with his hand.

"Really, Mountstuart," he said, "you are priceless."

1949

[SATURDAY, 1 JANUARY]

Saw in the New Year at Peter's home in Wandsworth. Quite a large party, forty or so, most of whom I'd never met. Peter's wife, Penny, is sweet and jolly, plumper since her two children. I was surprised to see Gloria Ness-Smith there and told her so. I think she liked my bluntness, liked the implication. There was no need for any pussyfooting

between us. "He wouldn't dare not invite me," she said. "I'd kill him."
She used to be a nurse, she said, and now worked as a secretary in
Peter's publishers. "But not for long," she added. I suspect Penny's role
as Mrs. Scabius hasn't much longer to run.

Gloria was drinking gin and had her drink topped up twice as we
chatted. At one stage she leant into me, her pushed-up breasts flattening against my arm. "Peter envies you," she said. I asked what on earth
for? Peter was the paradigm of the successful novelist—why should he
envy me? "He envies you your glamorous war," she said. "He can't buy
that. He can buy everything else, but he can't buy that, and he envies
you." There was pure glee in her chuckle. Jesus Christ, I thought. Then
she leant into me once more, before wandering off to look for Peter,
leaving me with an unequivocal erection. At midnight, I told myself
that, even if I wasn't happy, my load of unhappiness was maybe beginning to diminish, ever so slightly.

[FEBRUARY]

Letter from Vanderpoel. Colonel Marion died in April 1945, in a
"motor vehicle" accident in Brussels. According to Vanderpoel there
were two other fatalities. He had asked his old NID contacts, but as far
as he could establish there was nothing suspicious in Marion's death
and he had no apparent connections to the Duke of Windsor.

So much for my great vendetta, so much for the tireless hunt for my
betrayer. Isn't this how life turns out, more often than not? It refuses to
conform to your needs—the narrative needs that you feel are essential
to give rough shape to your time on this earth. I wanted to hunt down
Marion, wanted to confront him, but instead am left with the banal
conclusion that, more than likely, there was no conspiracy, and that
the Duke and Duchess had not plotted with their powerful friends to
have done with me. Hard to live with, this: hard to come to terms with
the fact that it was just another botched operation, another baffling
run of bad luck . . . Feelings of depression; feelings of frustration; feelings of emptiness in the face of all this randomness—done down by the
haphazard, yet again.

[APRIL]

Hôtel Rembrandt. Paris. I've come here to work on my novella, *The Villa by the Lake*. It can only be a novella, I've decided, a cryptic, Kafkaesque, Camusian, sub–Rex Warnerish parable of my bizarre incarceration. I've no idea how to end it, however. Perhaps Paris will inspire me. Wallace said he could obtain a large advance if I wanted, but I persuaded him not to. It's one of those works that will have to find its own voice and conclusion—and even then I won't know if it has succeeded. It seems to be going relatively well. All I do is try to recapture the routines and atmosphere of the villa with maximum fidelity, but I'm aware that the reality was so strange that readers will think it all profoundly symbolic and metaphorical. That's my fond hope, anyway. Also I realize that any hint of pretension, any effort to turn up the significance, will be fatal. The more I make it resolutely true to life, the more all metaphorical interpretation will be unconsciously supplied by the reader.

There is a pretty girl called Odile who works in Ben's gallery. In her mid-twenties, dark, with short untidy hair and big eyes. She wears black all the time and gold strappy sandals on her unabashedly grimy feet. Ben told her I was writing a book about my time in prison during the war and I could tell she was intrigued. If I can't have Gloria Ness-Smith, perhaps Odile will consent to be my passport back to the world of human sexual relations.

My routine is straightforward. I wake up, take two aspirin for my hangover headache, and go out for a breakfast of coffee and croissant at a café. I buy a newspaper and my lunch—a baguette, some cheese, some *saucisson* and a bottle of wine. By the time I come back my room has been cleaned and I sit down at my work table and try to write. I eat out in the evenings, usually at the Leepings—it's open house, Ben says— but I like to give them some time without me so I take myself off to Balzar or Chez Lipp, or other brasseries for a solitary meal. I don't mind a day spent entirely in my own company but I do drink a lot in compensation: a bottle at lunch, a bottle in the evening, plus *apéritifs* and *digestifs*.

*   *   *

I asked Odile if I could take her to dinner and she said yes, immediately. We went to Chez Fernand, a little place I've found on the rue de l'Université. Odile dreams only of going to New York when Ben opens his gallery there, so we speak English to each other to help her practise. It strikes me that this may be the real nature of my appeal: her own pet anglophone. She has brown, long-lashed eyes; downy olive skin.

I walk Odile back to her Métro station. I lean forward to kiss her on the cheeks and she moves her face so that our lips meet. We kiss gently, the tips of our tongues touching and I feel that old familiar weakness spread at the base of my spine. We agree to see each other later in the week.

FRIDAY, 15 APRIL

Odile was here last night. We ate at the Flore and came back to the hotel. She has a lithe, girl's body. I was useless, incapable of maintaining a semi-erection for more than a few seconds. My mind was swarming with images of Freya—she might as well have been in the room watching us. Odile patiently masturbated me and, when that had no prolonged effect either, generously bent her head to take my cock in her mouth, but I told her not to bother.

She sat up and lit a cigarette as I tried to explain how my wife had died in the war and how I still couldn't get over it. In the war? she said. But the war was a long time ago. I agreed it was and apologized. She said, "Maybe I better go," and dressed and left me. I slept a few hours of a sound and dreamless sleep.

But when I woke—an hour ago now—I felt a quality of despair and darkness grip me that was entirely new. Three years on I am living as vividly with the loss of Freya as I have ever done. And the rain is falling outside. The melancholy drip, drip, drip.

*   *   *

I have taken my two aspirin for my morning headache and have taken two more and two more and two more and two more and two more and two more. I fetched my bottle of whisky out of the cupboard and put out the DO NOT DISTURB sign. I have begun to drink my whisky, slowly washing down the remaining aspirin in my pill bottle.

I know what I am doing but somehow the situation seems quite unreal—as if I'm on stage acting in a play. I just feel—I don't know what I feel. The decision came to me this morning and I don't think it has much to do with the humiliation of last night. I know it must be done. It's a rainy, grey morning in Paris. All over the city there must be other people dying, on the point of death or dead. I'm another to add to their number. I don't fear death, I simply think for me here, now, it's the best and only solution. The decision came to me, quite matter-of-factly. I drink more whisky. I will keep on writing. People will say: did you hear about Logan Mountstuart? He killed himself in Paris. I drink more whisky. There are no more pills. I begin to feel drunk—or is this the beginning? I am committing suicide. It seems absurd. Forty-three years was long enough for me. I wasn't a complete failure. There is some of my work that will

[At this point the words become an illegible scribble and stop.]

THE NEW YORK JOURNAL

Logan Mountstuart was discovered an hour later by Odile, who popped by the hotel on her way to work to recover her cigarette lighter–a prized silver Zippo–which she'd left on the bedside table. LMS was rushed to hospital, where his stomach was pumped, he was sedated and put on a saline drip. Two days later he left to spend a month with the Leepings before returning to Turpentine Lane. No one in London, including his mother, ever seemed to have learned about the suicide attempt.

He began a process of psychiatric care and analysis at Atkinson Morley's, a neuropsychiatric hospital in Wimbledon, where he was a patient of Dr. Adam Outridge. Dr. Outridge prescribed a mild sedative and sleeping pills and advised LMS to cut down on his drinking. Dr. Outridge also encouraged him to proceed with his novella, The Villa by the Lake, *which was published in 1950 to serious and enthusiastic acclaim ("One of the most haunting and unusual novels to have come out of the last war"* –Listener*) and very modest sales.*

Meanwhile Ben Leeping opened his New York gallery, Leeping Fils, in May 1950 on Madison Avenue between E. 65th and 66th Streets. Marius Leeping moved to New York to run the gallery. At the core of Leeping Fils's business would be the "classic" modernists of twentieth-century European painting, but Marius's brief was to be on the lookout for new talent emerging in New York. Artists like Jackson Pollock, Franz Kline, Willem de Kooning and Robert Motherwell were starting to create a stir and the "Abstract Expressionist" movement, as it shortly after became known, was beginning to turn the attention of the art world away from Paris to New York.

Ben Leeping felt that Marius's age (he was twenty-three) and inexperience demanded that he have an older associate director of the gallery whom he could trust and, just as importantly, one on whom Ben Leeping could rely as well. LMS, now fully recovered, and his novella published, was the obvious choice.

Thus it was, at the end of 1950, that Ben Leeping offered him the job of associate director of Leeping Fils at a salary of $5,000 a year. The real purpose of the appointment was to have someone keep a close and guiding eye on Marius. LMS did not need much persuading: he closed up Turpentine Lane and sailed for New York in March 1951.

When LMS arrived in New York he spent a few days in a hotel before renting an apartment on E. 47th Street between First and Second Avenues (the first of many New York addresses he was to occupy in a peripatetic existence). It was not the most salubrious of areas but was a convenient twenty minutes' walk from the gallery.

He and Marius then began a thorough and comprehensive trawl of all the established and new galleries in New York as well as the transient co-op galleries showing the younger artists' work. Ben Leeping had provided a $25,000 acquisition fund for them to make their initial purchases, money furnished by the final sales of the Peredes Mirós (of which LMS's Miró netted him some $9,000).

At a party, about two months after he arrived, LMS met a divorcée called Alannah Rule who worked in the legal department of NBC. She had two young daughters, Arlene (eight) and Gail (four). LMS began to see Alannah socially. Their affair began—with perfect timing, as LMS always said—on 4th July 1951.

The New York Journal commences in September of that year.

1951

FRIDAY, 21 SEPTEMBER

So here I am in New York, writing again, working again, fucking again, living again. I decided to restart this journal largely because I'm beginning to grow worried about Marius and want to have some aide-mémoire about his actions and behaviour. Ben has absolute faith in him but I'm starting to wonder if it's somewhat misplaced. I also think his taste is bizarre, not to say dangerously skewed. We argue constantly about what is good and bad and what artists we should try to patronize. I have a horrible premonition about Marius and this gallery and want to have all the evidence I might need well documented and to hand.

For example: I'm always the first here in the morning, even before Helma (our receptionist). More often than not Marius doesn't show up until after lunch. My whole strategy, agreed with Ben, was to add to our core European stock as shrewdly as possible and not worry about making a splash. The town is full of galleries and co-ops—Myers and de Nagy, Felzer, Lonnegan, Parsons, Egan—to name our obvious rivals. Reputations flare up and die away within the space of a few weeks and we need to make sure that anyone we show—given our pedigree and the Parisian clouds of glory that we trail—has some legs. Marius—let's be blunt, and this has nothing to do with his charm—has no aesthetic judgement as far as I can see. He seems to react on a whim, or worse, the whim of the last person he was talking to. Anything that Greenberg* suggests he takes up uncritically. I keep telling him: don't board a crowded train leaving the station, let's find our own with lots of empty seats where we can stretch our legs. He doesn't listen—any bandwagon rolling by will do.

Still, I enjoy these mornings in the gallery before the clients and Marius turn up. We are on the first floor—rather, the second floor, in

---

*Clement Greenberg (1909–94). The most influential art critic at the time, credited with "discovering" Jackson Pollock.

American parlance—and I stand in the window looking down on Madison watching the people and the traffic going by. Helma brings me a cup of coffee and I smoke my first cigarette of the day. At moments like these I think I'm dreaming—I can't believe I'm living and working here, that this opportunity turned up in my life.

To Alannah's tonight. A whole weekend together, as the children are away with her ex-husband. We're going to look for somewhere for me to rent in Greenwich Village. I think I need to be closer to the action.

SUNDAY, 23 SEPTEMBER

We found a small apartment on Cornelia Street, off Bleecker. It's a basement of a brick row house (What is it about me and basements? Why do I like the semi-subterranean life?), unfurnished, with a bedroom, sitting room, tiny kitchen and shower room. An Italian family occupy the two floors above.

It was an agreeable bonus to have Alannah's whole apartment to ourselves this weekend. I find Alannah very sexy: there's something fiercely alluring about her astonishing teeth and her perfect, groomed blondness. Yet her pubic hair is glossily dark brown—seeing her naked, wandering into the bedroom with a pitcher of Martinis and two glasses, I wonder if it's that dramatic contrast that so stimulates me. Everything about our sex is very orthodox, condom-clad, missionary position, at the moment, but there's something about her that makes me want to go totally debauched. She's tall and big boned and has a sharp lawyer's mind. Very concerned about her children and how they will get to know me (why should I want to get to know them?). She's witheringly dismissive about her ex-husband ("a weak, pathetic man")— another lawyer, as it turns out. Alannah is thirty-five. She has a big apartment on Riverside Drive with a live-in maid. What with her salary and her alimony she's well off. I'm just glad to be sexually functioning again after the disaster of Paris. I thank the U.S. of A. and its fine confident women. Coming here was the best thing I ever did.

*   *   *

Outridge described me as cyclothymic—a small-scale manic-depressive—
which is why, he says, he didn't give me any electro-convulsive therapy. He's given me the name and address of a psychiatrist in New York
if I feel in need of counselling. But I think his diagnosis is wrong: I'm
not a manic-depressive, neither small nor large scale. In Paris I think I
was suffering from a long-term, building, nervous breakdown that
started when I returned from Switzerland and discovered that Freya
and Stella had died. After some three years it was finally detonated
by Odile, or rather, was detonated by my failure with Odile. (What's
become of Odile, by the way? I thought she was coming to New York.
Must ask Ben.) Now I'm here in New York it's as if the blinds that had
been lowered on my life have all been lifted. Sunlight floods the house.

THURSDAY, 11 OCTOBER

Crisp perfect New York day. In the sharply defined shadow and strong
sunlight these huge buildings look magnificent—so defiantly non-
European. We don't need your cathedrals and castles, your moated
manors and Georgian terraces, they seem to say—we have something
entirely different, we speak in a different language, we have our own
version of beauty. Take it, or leave it. Comparisons are meaningless
and redundant.

Marius turned up at 3:00 this afternoon, having bought four worthless canvases (smears and slashes in primary colours) from some charlatan called Hughes Delahay at $500 a piece. For that amount of
money I could have bought a Pollock—if I'd wanted. I remonstrated,
gently—our float is dropping rapidly and I haven't bought a thing—
pointing out that in a month or two we wouldn't be able to give away
a Delahay. Logan, he said, patronizingly, you're too old-world, like
Papa, you've got to move fast or you won't ever fit in here in this city.
I managed to keep my temper. Ironic comment, given my rhapsody
above. I'd better let Ben know what's going on.

I go to Janet Felzer's co-op on Jane Street tonight. I kept the invitation from Marius. Tomorrow I move into Cornelia Street.

FRIDAY, 12 OCTOBER

Saw the first picture I wanted to buy in New York, by a man called Todd Heuber. Janet is keeping it for me. Somehow—we were both very drunk and Janet had given me a pill of some kind—we both managed to end up in bed together at 47th Street. I woke up feeling hellish and heard someone in the bathroom. Then Janet wandered in, naked, and slid into bed. I had a hill-cracking hangover. She snuggled up to me and I realized what had happened. She's small and bony with a completely flat chest—not really *mon truc*—but there's something impish, mischievous and plain *bad* about her, which is exciting. I went to the ice-box and took out a beer. She said, hey, give me a beer too, I feel like shit as well. So we sat in bed and drank our beer and chatted for half an hour. Neither of us was prepared to vouch for events of the night before, but, in any case, the beer worked and we made love. The sound of traffic on 47th Street. Our beery, belchy kisses. Janet's funny little monkey face below me, her eyes screwed shut. As I came, she said: don't think you get any discount on Heuber.

TUESDAY, 23 OCTOBER

Cornelia Street. Wallace cables to say he has a U.S. publisher for *Villa*—Bucknell, Dunn & Weiss. He urges me to telephone Mr. Weiss himself, no less, who is delighted to find that his author is currently residing in New York. Only a $250 advance, but beggars can't be choosers.

I bought the Heuber for $100 and then bought it again for myself for $300 (our usual 200 per cent mark-up—at least Leeping Fils has finally made a profit on a piece of contemporary art). "Earthscape No. 3," it's called. A long picture of heavy brown and black slabs of paint, scraped and scored, smoothed and patina-ed. At one of the angled congruences of the slabs there is a rough rhomboid of dirty cream. Maybe it's because he's German (his real name is Tabbert Heuber), but Todd's work has real weight and presence. It has composition. It is completely abstract, however its title encourages a form of figurative interpretation. Only Heuber and a Dutchman called de Kooning really impress. They can both *draw*. It helps.

TUESDAY, 13 NOVEMBER

First really bitterly cold day. Snow flurries and a wind off the icecaps. Cold burning, numbing my cheeks on the walk to the subway. Marius didn't come in at all yesterday and when I phoned him he said he was working at home. I said, thanks for letting me know—and he replied that as it was his gallery he could decide where he wanted to work, thank you very much. I think Ben has to step in now; things are getting decidedly unpleasant. I can't sack Marius or give him a barracking—though I make it quite clear what I think. He's changed since he came to New York—maybe it's simply because he's removed from his father's—stepfather's—presence. Whenever I saw him in Paris he seemed charming—a bit lazy and feckless, sure—but he's nothing like that now. He's cool with me, arrogant and self-satisfied. And yet he does no work. God knows what he gets up to—probably the same as the rest of us—drink, sex, drugs—but at least I show up at the gallery every morning, Monday to Friday. There is a dangerously corrupting element in this city for the unwary: you have to stay on your guard.

Lunch with Ted Weiss. He wants to publish *Villa* before the end of the year. They've bought sheets from England so it's just a question of binding it up and putting a new jacket on. Weiss is a lean, shrewd, bespectacled intellectual—very dry. "We're going to sell it as an 'Existential' novel," he said. "What do you think?" "Isn't it all a bit old hat?" I said. "No. Very new hat over here," he said.

MONDAY, 3 DECEMBER

I slept with Janet again last night. I had to spend the weekend alone—Alannah's sister and her children were staying with her. So I went to a party at de Nagy's and Janet was there (and the usual crowd). At the end of the evening, as people were drifting away, Janet said, "Can I

come home with you?" And I said, yes, please. Why do you take these
risks, Mountstuart? But it's not a risk. Alannah is a girlfriend, just like
Janet: I've made no vow of fidelity to either one. But look at you, making all these excuses. You're blustering—you feel guilty about sleeping
with Janet. I'm a 45-year-old, unattached man—I don't have to hide my
love-life or my sex-life away from anyone. So why don't you tell Alannah all about it, see how broadminded she is? There is no crisis here.

FRIDAY, 14 DECEMBER

I gave a small party at the gallery for the launch of my book. BD&W
invited a few writers and critics along. I asked Greenberg and Frank
O'Hara* and some other literary acquaintances to leaven the art world.
I felt oddly proud to see my book stacked up on a central table. *Villa*
has a very simple jacket here: lower case sans serif letters in midnight
blue on a coarse oatmeal ground—very Bauhaus, somehow. Frank was
taken with the title. "*The Villa by the Lake*. Like it," he said. "Very simple
but with a kind of ring, a resonance to it. Could be a painting by Klee."
Actually I'm not sure it could, but it was nice of him to make the asso-
ciation. He had another writer friend with him, Herman Keller, who
looks like a weightlifter (broad shoulders, thick neck, cropped hair) but
in fact teaches literature at Princeton. I thought he might be one of
Frank's "fag" friends, but someone told me he wasn't. Frank likes to
make plays for heterosexual men, apparently.

What was interesting was to see how people's perceptions of me
changed as a result of the book being published. No longer another
smartly suited Englishman dabbling in the art world but a published
author of some longevity (the title page listed my other works). Keller
was curious about *Cosmopolitans* and asked if I was interested in reviewing books for some little magazine he's involved with—they need
someone who can read French. He said he knew Auden and asked if I
wanted to meet him. I said I'd love to—but in fact I'm really not that
bothered. My old literary world seems so remote now from my New

*Frank O'Hara (1926–66), poet, then working at the Museum of Modern Art.

York perspective. Such a small festering pond, with hindsight. And I rather enjoy keeping my distance from it.

Udo Feuerbach came—it was good to see him again. Portly and grey now, his face seamed and jowly. He's editing a magazine called *Art International*, which I said sounded like an airline. He picked up *Villa* and riffled through it. Another book, he said, *teuflische virtuosität*. We laughed. He has a satyr's goatee, streaked with grey—makes him look avuncularly evil.

Alannah has asked me to spend Christmas with her family. Her father, a widower, is a retired professor from some women's university in Connecticut and has a big house on the coast. When I found out that the party would include her sister and her husband and their children I begged off. Said I had to go back to London to see my mother—so I suppose I'd better now.

Ted Weiss said there were good reviews for *Villa* coming up in the *New York Times* and the *New Yorker*. How does he know so far in advance?—but gratifying none the less.

1952

[JANUARY]

Spellbrook, nr Pawcatuck, Conn. I got here on the 3rd—I'll go back to the city on Monday. Alannah's father, Titus [Fitch], has a large white clapboard house up here in Spellbrook, about five miles from Pawcatuck. It's set in a grove of larch and maples and is about a twenty-minute walk from the ocean. The sun was out this morning and we strolled down through the meadows towards the shore (there was about three inches of snow on the ground). There are nine of us: me, Titus, Alannah, Arlene, Gail, Kathleen Bundy (Alannah's older sister), Dalton (Kathleen's husband) and their children Dalton Jnr (seven to eightish) and Sarah (a toddler). We meandered along the shore, looking in rock pools, a good surf was running, and the kids ran around. Back at home a housekeeper was preparing us a huge lunch. An idyllic morning, marred only by the fact that it is quite plain to me (though to no one else) that Titus Fitch doesn't like me. He dislikes me for generic reasons, not personal. I am English and he is a dyed-in-the-wool, unapologetic, grade-A Anglophobe. If I'd been a Negro and he the Grand Vizier of the Ku Klux Klan the animus couldn't have been more clear cut. I think he's appalled that his younger daughter has taken up with an Englishman. For the first time in my life I feel the victim of race hatred, like a Jew in Nazi Germany. He refers to me as "our English friend." "Perhaps our English friend prefers his steak well done." "Perhaps our English friend would rather take tea than coffee. Is that the phrase? To 'take' tea?" "Our English friend isn't used to sitting down to dinner with young children. The green baize door and all that." The unfriendliness is palpable but the rest of the family just chuckle away. I pointed out this offensive *froideur* to Alannah and she pooh-poohed it. "Nonsense. Daddy's just like that. He's a professional crusty old man. Don't be so sensitive, Logan. Don't take it personally."

In any event, it was good to see Alannah out of the city: she loses some of her hard edge out here, her gloss and grooming. Her hair is curly, she has less make-up, wears jeans and big sweaters. The severer planes and angles of her handsome face seem to relax and soften. I find this semi-rural Alannah just as attractive as the New York version.

Fitch is irked by the success of *Villa*, which, as Ted Weiss predicted, garnered excellent reviews. The Bundys were fulsome. I gave Fitch a copy when I arrived and he put it down on a side table without even glancing at it. He's a rangy, strong-featured old man in his early seventies, with a thick mop of unruly white hair. He smokes a pipe with pedantic and practised affectation, favours a bow tie and wears tweed jackets with ancient khaki trousers. Sometimes when I glance quickly round I see the undisguised loathing in his eyes before the prickly "mein host" mask is fixed once more.

London was grim. Dark, filthy, cold weather, the population unsmiling and downtrodden. Still like a city at war, somehow. I saw my mother (endlessly complaining) and took her for Xmas lunch at the Savoy. Dick asked me up to Scotland for Hogmanay but I thought it wiser to give my liver a rest and caught the first plane out on January the 1st.

I telephoned Ben from London about the Marius issue and the potential problems I saw ahead and he said he would come over himself as soon as possible. Peter was on his honeymoon in the Caribbean with Gloria Ness-Smith, now the third Mrs. Scabius. I had a fairly solitary time. The bunker was warm enough when both gas fires were blazing and I felt as at home there as anywhere. The agency which looks after the place in my absence appears to be doing a competent job.

Talked to Gail Rule for an hour after lunch. A delightful, chatty, open little girl who loves telling jokes—which she can hardly get out, she laughs so much at them herself. I was entranced and then realized why: Stella was about her age when I last saw her and I was miserable again from my awful loss. You think it begins to diminish with time, the pain, then it comes back and hits you with a rawness and freshness you had forgotten.

I wanted to make love (I wanted to hold someone, really) and asked Alannah if I could sneak into her room tonight but she thought it was too risky. So we went out for a drive and had some hurried and unsatisfactory sex on the back seat of her car down some lane. I said it was the first time I'd done it in the back of a car. Welcome to America, she said. Obviously a key *rite de passage.* What pleased me more when we returned home was to imagine Fitch sniffing the air like a bloodhound, nostril full of the scent of English spunk. Old bastard. It gave me a warm glow all through dinner.

FRIDAY, 7 MARCH

To Todd Heuber's studio on E. 8th Street. Bought another, a small "Earthscape," for $75. Almost all shadowy, bending browns but scored by a hard horizontal band of lemon at the top, like a bilious stormy dawn light. Talked of Emil Nolde, de Staël and other artists. Heuber knows his stuff. He's strong, like a young peasant or longshoreman, with a square jutting jaw, pale blue, myopic-seeming eyes.

We went to the Cedar Tavern to drink, not my favourite place—it's so blazingly brightly lit—but he wanted to celebrate another sale. Pollock, steaming drunk, called him a Nazi but Todd just laughed and said that every now and then he had to beat the shit out of Jackson, just to keep him in his place, but tonight he was feeling benevolent. There were a lot of young women come to gawp at the lions: Heuber, Pollock, Kline, that fraud Zollo—all flaunting their brawny manliness like dunghill cocks. Because of the glaring light everyone looks exhausted, hollow-eyed. The women—Elaine [de Kooning], Grace [Hartigan], Sally [Strauss]—were putting back as much booze as the men. It was a sweaty, edgy, sexy atmosphere that had me eyeing the girls like some lecherous satrap. O'Hara came in with Keller. Maybe they are fucking each other? Keller said he'd read *Villa* twice. "Complex, but I'm getting there," he said. Phoned Alannah and asked if I could come by for a nightcap—she said Leland was there with the girls but she was free for lunch tomorrow. Phoned Janet—out. So I tried to pick up one of the girls myself but as soon as they discovered I wasn't a painter they lost interest. There was a dark, thin-wristed one with very long hair that I really fancied and I drunkenly refused to be put off until she said, "Beat it, old man." Old Man? Jesus, forty-six years old isn't old. I feel I haven't even started living properly, yet. That fucking war took six years away from me. So I came home, drank some more and wrote this.

THURSDAY, 8 MAY

Good reunion at the Waldorf: me, Ben and Peter. The old gang. Peter is over here promoting his new novel *The Slaughter of the Innocents*. We talked—inevitably, old school chums—about Abbey and our time there. I don't think Peter and I have physically changed that much—we could still be recognized from schoolboy photos—of course we are all heftier, broader in the beam, but Ben is heavy now, with a round belly and a plump double chin flowing over his collar and looks older than we do. Or so I hope: each one of us is probably thinking identical thoughts about the other. Gloria joined us for coffee. She was looking . . . rich. Sexily rich. Her voice is strange, over-polite: thet men in a het. Like these English film stars that have been to charm school or had elocution lessons. She said, "I'm not spoiling you boys' party, am I?" I was glad to see her. She's one of these people whose entry into a room immediately makes the place more interesting. And she was more than welcome—fond though I am of Peter, he has grown increasingly pleased with the sound of his own voice. He boasted to Ben that he's bought a Bernard Buffet for £3,000. Ben, diplomatic as ever, congratulated him on his wise investment. Ben was a bit preoccupied: he has promised to resolve the Marius situation over the weekend.

Towards the end of the evening Gloria fixed me with her sceptical ever-so-slightly mocking gaze and said, "So what are you up to, Logan?" I told her I'd just had a book published too. "It's tremendous," Peter chipped in, "meant to say. Best thing you've done." He hasn't read it of course and I can't complain as I haven't read any of his since he abandoned his rather good little thrillers for the New Portentousness. "Will you send me a copy?" Gloria asked. "We've got one at home, darling," Peter said. "But that's inscribed to you," she said. "I want Logan to inscribe one for me, specially." I said I'd rather she bought one—I needed every royalty I could get. But as she left she reminded me: "Don't forget that book now." I wonder if Peter has finally met his match.

Ben had gone and Peter and Gloria had ascended to their, doubtless, vast suite and for a moment I was alone in the lobby, putting on my raincoat, when I thought I saw the Duchess of Windsor coming in through the revolving doors. I went rigid—until I realized that it was just another thin New York matron with an over-elaborate hair-do, set like cement. She and the Duke have an apartment here, I remembered. I would have to bear that in mind—give the Waldorf a wide berth in future.

MONDAY, 12 MAY

The Marius situation is resolved—on paper anyway. I now run the gallery; Marius reports to me and has to refer all purchases of over $500 to me for approval. He has his own fund to draw on of $5,000—which will be topped up by Ben. This was all spelt out at a frosty meeting this morning—Marius sulky and aloof. Ben was very firm, almost harsh, and I remembered that, of course, Marius was Sandrine's son, not his. I hope this pseudo-independence and pseudo-autonomy will satisfy him. I'm a little worried still.

I had an early supper with Alannah and the girls. Gail told a series of jokes that she claims to have made up herself. The best one, which had us aghast for a second, was, "How do they tell the alphabet in Brooklyn?" Recite the alphabet, dear, Alannah said. OK, so how do they recite the alphabet in Brooklyn? "Fuckin' A, fuckin' B, fuckin' C," Gail said. Alannah was outraged but I was laughing so hard she couldn't even feign anger. Gail did admit she hadn't made that one up.

Alannah begged me to come up to Spellbrook for another weekend. I said that quite apart from the fact that her father detested me I resented being treated like an adolescent and being made to sleep apart from her. We were mature adults, we were lovers, why shouldn't we be in the same room? "I'm his youngest daughter," she said. "He thinks I don't have sex outside marriage." I said that was nonsense. Then I had an idea. If she had to see him regularly, why didn't we rent our own place nearby? She could pop over to him and we could sleep together. Not a bad idea, she said.

FRIDAY, 11 JULY

Alannah is in Connecticut with the girls for the summer vacation. Marius has gone to Paris and so I watch the stock in sweltering July, thanking the gods for the invention of air-conditioning. No business at all this month: every painter in New York seems to be on Long Island. Maybe I should sniff around there.

Janet is back, however, and had a party at her gallery last night. Frank [O'Hara] was there too, impish and irritating, drunk as a skunk and deeply tanned. For half an hour he had me pinned in a corner, yodelling on about some barbarian genius called Pate he had unearthed in Long Island. "At last an artist with a brain, thank God." Back to Janet's place. I never plan to sleep with Janet but when she's in the mood it's very hard to resist. You've got to see my tan, she said. It's an all-over tan.

SATURDAY, 16 AUGUST

Spellbrook. Alannah thinks she's found a house about two or three miles from her father near a village called Mystic. I said I liked it already. We drove out this afternoon with Gail and Arlene. It's a small shingle-walled bungalow set back from the coast road and surrounded by dwarf oaks. It has a gently pitched roof and there's a long sun porch at the front and a rubble-stone chimney at the side. Two bedrooms, a bathroom, a big living room with an open fire. The long thin kitchen at the rear looks out on a scrubby unkempt garden. It could be sixty years old, Alannah said, imagining—sweetly—that this would swing it for me, the European, with his centuries of culture. Everything works inside, water, electricity, heating—so we could use it in the winter too. I could see myself in it—effortlessly—but a little alarm bell was ringing in my brain as the four of us walked around it with the Realtor. Logan with his proto-family . . . "Look, Logan," Gail shouted, "there's a room up here, this could be your den." There was a little attic room under the eaves with a shed dormer giving a distant view of Block Island Sound. I thought suddenly of my room in Melville Road and the roof-scape of Battersea from its window. My eyes filled with unexpected tears, remembering my old life. Alannah saw and slipped her hand in mine. "You're right. We could be happy here," she said. Gail took my other hand. "Please, Logan, please." "It's a deal," I said.

I've insisted on paying all the rent—$1,200 a year—which I can't really afford but it makes the place notionally mine, rather than Alannah's and mine. Who am I kidding?

Gail said to Fitch tonight, "Logan's renting a house for us at Mystic." He looked at me darkly: "Once a colonial . . ." The old bastard was in a sour mood this evening. He and I sat together in silence—the girls in bed, Alannah tidying up in the kitchen—as he fiddled with his pipe kit, scouring the bowl of his preposterous pipe, thumbing in shag.

Then he said, "Do you know Bunny Wilson?"*

I said I knew who he was, that I'd read a lot of his books. Another fully paid-up member of the Anglophobe club.

*Edmund Wilson (1895–1972), eminent critic and man of letters.

"A brilliant mind," Fitch said, blowing blue scented smoke ceiling-ward. Then he pointed the stem of his pipe at me. "When was the English revolution?"

"1640. Oliver Cromwell. Execution of Charles I. The Protectorate."

"Wrong. It was here in 1787. This is when the Anglo-Saxon bourgeoisie formed a new society. You're still *ancien régime*, always have been since Charles II. The revolution you should have had actually happened here, on the other side of the Atlantic. That's why you resent us so."

"We don't resent you."

"Of course you do. That was Bunny's point. You now have two distinct anglophone societies that split from a common root in 1785. Ours is revolutionary and republican; yours is for status quo and royalty. That's why we can never get along."

"I'm sorry, but—with the greatest respect—I think that's utter nonsense."

"That's exactly what I'd expect an Englishman of your class and education to say. Don't you see?" He barked a laugh at me. "You've just gone and made my point."

I let him ramble on. He really is an objectionable old CAUC.

SUNDAY, 17 AUGUST

I love to use these phrases—"with the greatest respect," "in all modesty," "I humbly submit"—which in fact always imply the complete opposite. I bombard Fitch with them constantly when we argue (it's beginning to drive Alannah mad) as it allows me to disagree categorically beneath a smug façade of good manners. We had another row about manners at lunch. I said that, in America, good manners were a way of furthering and promoting social contact, whereas in England they were a way of protecting your privacy. He refused to accept my reasoning.

Went into New London to sign the papers on the Mystic house and make the down payment. Alannah is taking over the costs of furnishing, decorating and refurbishment. So much for my independence.

Gail and Arlene wrote me a letter saying thank you, which they posted under my door. They're great girls. I'm very fond of them.

WEDNESDAY, 5 NOVEMBER

To Janet's gallery for her big show. Heuber has three paintings there, which we should have had but I wouldn't pay his prices. The inflation in the last six months is worrying—one senses a sudden scramble beginning for these really untested, untried young artists. Anyway, Janet has Barnett Newman and Lee Krasner as well. Smart girl. It was a real party too: Gunpowder, Treason and Plot. Annoyingly the show looks like being a wild success. Frank was raving about his new discovery—Nat Tate, not Pate—all of whose work was sold in a flash. I met this prodigy later: a quiet, tall handsome boy who reminded me of Paulus, my Swiss guard. He stood quietly in a corner drinking Scotch and wearing a grey suit, which I was pleased to see. We were the only two suited men in the room. Heavy dark blond hair. Janet was on fire and said she had been smoking heroin (can one do this?) and urged me to try some. I said I was too old for these games. I bought a Heuber and a Motherwell. No Nat Tates to be had, though I rather liked them—bold, stylized drawings of bridges inspired by Crane's poem.* I see what Frank means by brains.

Bumped into Tate as I was leaving and asked if he had anything for sale privately and he replied, most oddly, that I would have to ask his father. Later Pablo [Janet Felzer's dog] shat copiously in the middle of the room, so Larry Rivers told me.

Looks like Dwight D.† is strolling home.

---

*Hart Crane (1899–1932), poet. His long poem *The Bridge* was published in 1930.
†Eisenhower was elected President by a landslide. Richard M. Nixon was his Vice President.

THURSDAY, 25 DECEMBER

London. Turpentine Lane. Glum and depressing lunch at Sumner Place with Mother and Encarnación. Mother seems to be fading–alert enough, but now markedly thinner and scrawnier. We ate turkey and sodden grey Brussels sprouts. Encarnación had forgotten to cook the potatoes, so Mother shouted at her, Encarnación said that this English food was disgusting anyway and started to cry–and I made them apologize to each other. I drank the lion's share of two bottles of red wine (which I'd wisely supplied–the only drink in the house was white rum). I didn't tell them about Alannah.

I asked Alannah to marry me before I flew here. She said yes, straight away. Tears, laughter, generally overcome. I rather feel she's been waiting for me to ask for months. On that day, Saturday, I had taken Arlene and Gail for a walk in Central Park. Arlene wanted to go skating. Gail and I sat on the bleachers watching her (she was quite good) and ate pretzels. Gail said, in a serious, considered voice, apropos of nothing, "Logan, why don't you marry Mommy? I'd really like it if you would." I huffed and puffed and changed the subject, but that evening over supper (we were alone) I popped the question. It's true I am very attracted, physically, to Alannah, and I like her but I can't say, if I'm being honest, that I love her. If you loved her would you still be fucking Janet Felzer? Alannah says she loves me. The problem is that I don't think I can truly love anyone again, after Freya. But I'm happy, I suppose–more than that: I'm pleased, delighted that we will be married. I'm used to being married; I'm not used to being on my own– being on my own is not a state I welcome or enjoy. The thought lingers, however, that I'm marrying Alannah because it means I'll have Gail in my life. Perhaps the one I'm in love with is Gail . . . This is probably very foolish of me: she won't stay the enchanting, funny five-year-old forever. Still, *carpe diem*. Of all people, I should be living by that axiom.

[*LMS married Alannah Rule on 14 February 1953 at a quiet civil ceremony attended by a few friends and the children. Titus Fitch had influenza and could not travel, so he claimed.*]

*The New York Journal falls silent now for over two years until it
resumes in early 1955. LMS had left his Cornelia Street apartment for
Alannah's on Riverside Drive. The house in Mystic (Mystic House, as he
referred to it) proved a much loved contrast to New York. He carried on
running the Leeping Fils gallery but the uneasy truce between him and
Marius Leeping was showing signs of strain.]*

1955

SUNDAY, 10 APRIL

Mystic House. Warm sunny day. Could be a day in summer. Dogwood
in full bloom. I pretend to be reading in the garden but in reality all
I'm thinking of is my first drink. Just before 11 a.m., I go into the
kitchen and open a beer. No one around so I take a couple of big gulps
and top the can up again with bourbon. Back outside into the garden
and suddenly the newspaper seems more interesting. "Drinking already?"
Alannah says in her best caustic, disapproving voice. "It's just a beer,
for Christ's sake," I protest. This keeps me going until noon, when I
can legitimately mix a pitcher of Martinis. Alannah has one, I have
three. I open a bottle of wine for lunch. In the afternoon I snooze, then
go down to the shore and wander around the rocks with the kids. By
the time we return home it's time for a pre-prandial Scotch and soda or
two. More wine with the evening meal, a brandy afterwards, and pretty
soon it's time for bed. This is how I survive a Sunday in the country.

    Why am I drinking so much? Well, one reason is because on Sun-
day I know I have to go back to New York on Monday morning. Spirit
of place is something I profoundly believe in—which is why I love Mystic House—and the spirit of place of the Upper West Side is just not for
me. I hate our apartment; I hate its location and it's beginning to sour
the entire island of Manhattan for me. What combination of factors
provokes this? The narrowness of the north-south avenues on the West

Side. The unremarkable buildings that line them. The height of said buildings. And there are always too many people on the Upper West Side. We're too crammed in, the sidewalks always too busy with pedestrians. And then there's the cold wide expanse of the Hudson. It's just not for me—my soul shrivels. I've suggested moving many times to Alannah but she loves this apartment. Maybe I'm not used to living with two young girls. Maybe I'm not happy.

[JUNE]

Drove out to Windrose on Long Island—Nat Tate's stepfather's house, a big neoclassical pile. Peter Barkasian (the stepfather) buys 75 per cent of his stepson's output, acting in a way as an unofficial dealer. Which has good and bad consequences for Nat—a charming (there must be a better word—can't think of one) but essentially guileless young man. Good, in that it provides him with a guaranteed income; bad, in that as an artist of talent you don't want your stepfather controlling your professional life.

I bought two of the "White Buildings" series—big grey-white canvases with blurry charcoal markings emerging through the gesso (as if through a freezing fog) that, after a little scrutiny, reveal themselves as houses. Barkasian is inordinately proud of Nat, who diffidently bats away all compliments as if they are buzzing flies. I like him—Barkasian—he has all the unthinking self-confidence of a rich man without the attendant, shrill egomania. You sense he looks on the art world as a schoolboy does a well-stocked sweetshop—here is a world to revel in, full of potential fun and self-indulgence. He went drinking with Nat at the Cedar and was raving about the women: "I mean, the boy practically had to fight them off!" I suspect Nat's taste doesn't lie in that direction.

[JULY]

Mystic. God, what a great place this is. I've managed to cut down on the booze and out here all tensions between me and Alannah subside. I look at her on the beach: tanned, her big, lissom frame, the girls laughing and shrieking at the ocean's edge, and I say to myself: Mountstuart, why are you making life so hard to enjoy? I taste the salt on Alannah's breasts when we make love. I lie in bed beside her, listening, when the sea is high, to the wash of surf and the occasional zip of a car on Highway 95, and I suppose I feel at peace.

Out here, just a few miles away, the River Thames runs from Norwich to New London. Close at hand are the townships of Essex and Old Lyme. Fitch couldn't have chosen a worse place to let his hatred of old England stew.

[AUGUST]

The girls are with their father. Alannah and I have spent a week on Long Island with Ann Ginsberg. Herman Keller is here and the ubiquitous O'Hara. Thank Christ our summer house is in Connecticut—the New York art world seems to have decamped here to a man and woman. Keller took us to dinner at Pollock's but Lee [Krasner, his wife] wouldn't let us through the door. She said Jackson "wasn't well." We could hear jazz music coming from the back of the house at tremendous, ear-shattering volume. So we drove on to Quogue and ate hamburgers. Keller and O'Hara kept referring to Pollock as a "genius" and I had to interrupt. I'm sorry, but you can't just bandy that word around, I said. It applies only to a handful of the very greatest artists in history: Shakespeare, Dante, da Vinci, Mozart, Beethoven, Velázquez, Chekhov—and a few more. You can't put Jackson Pollock in that company and call him a genius—it's an obscene misuse of language, not to say totally absurd. They both disagreed violently and we had an entertaining row.

[SEPTEMBER]

Today I discovered that Marius has embezzled close to $30,000 from Leeping Fils. I don't know quite what to do. Somehow he has been siphoning off small amounts, always under the $500 that he is entitled to spend without referral, for paintings he has bought. I went down into the picture store to do an inventory and found almost thirty canvases with his name on them: I'd be surprised if he'd paid more than ten or twenty dollars for them, yet the invoices read $250, $325, and so on. An elementary fraud—but hard to prove. And a situation that has to be handled with extreme delicacy.

I met Alannah after work and we had an early dinner and went to see a movie—*Long Time Gone*. I hardly watched what was on the screen. But later, in bed, we made love as if we were on our first date. Was it because half my mind was elsewhere? She seemed to spread her thighs wider so that when I pushed down into her it was as if I went deeper than ever before. I felt hugely swollen and potent and seemed to be able to go on and on without coming. Then when she came, she gripped me in such a way that I spurted immediately and with such a feeling of release, of purgation, that I thought at once of Balzac—"there goes another novel." The idea made me laugh and, hearing my laughter, Alannah joined in, both of us experiencing a form of delightful, mutual, sexual mirth. When I withdrew, my erection had only half subsided and I felt I was in some kind of animal rutting fever, ready to go again. "Jesus Christ," Alannah said, "what's gotten into you tonight?" We took a shower together and touched each other and kissed gently. We dried off and went back to bed. I opened some wine and we caressed and played with each other, but lazily, as if we had both tacitly decided not to make love again. Something had happened that last time and we both wanted to hold on to that memory.

I woke at 4:00 and am writing this down now, a dull ache in my balls. But my mind is still full of Marius and his fraud.

THURSDAY, 29 SEPTEMBER

Paris. Hôtel Rembrandt. I decided to come to Paris partly to talk over the Marius issue with Ben, face to face, and partly because Mother says she is unwell, on death's door according to her. And also because I need to renew my passport.

Before I left I tracked down one of the artists Marius had bought from. On the invoice he claimed he had paid $200 for an infantile daub of a yacht at sea (described as "in faux-naïf style"). Paul Clampitt was the artist's name and I discovered him at a dubious private college in Newark called the Institution of American Artists, where he was doing some sort of course in graphic design. I asked if he had any paintings for sale, a friend of mine had bought one, which I'd liked. Sure, he said, and spread out a dozen on the table—$25 dollars each. I bought one and asked for a receipt.

Ben was distressed and angered when I presented him with this evidence. "He has to go," he said, with real bitterness. He asked if I thought I could run the gallery on my own and I said, of course. Ben said he would deal with everything: Marius would be gone by the time I returned. He shook me warmly by the hand and said he was very grateful. "It's rare in this stinking business to find someone you can trust," he added, with some vehemence. I'm a little concerned, myself, about the eventual outcome of all this.

Dined with Cyprien Dieudonné, the picture of the handsome, distinguished man of letters. White hair just slightly on the long side, curling over his collar. A cane with a silver handle—the little gesture towards *dandyisme*. He has just been awarded the Légion d'honneur and is candidly proud, claiming that I had had something to do with this recognition (*Les Cosmopolites*, amazingly, is still in print, selling a few dozen copies a year). I said it told you more about France and its innate respect for writers. This septuagenarian, a minor poet who hadn't published a line of verse in decades, whose heyday had been before the Great War, was still regarded as a cultural asset by the state. We raised a glass to each other, toilers in the same vineyard. I doubt there are a dozen people in England—outside my family or circle of friends—who know who I am and what I have written.

MONDAY, 3 OCTOBER

Mother is bedridden, coughing, pale, weak. Encarnación administers to her as best as possible, but she's an old lady too. The house is grim and condemnable. Two teenagers and their baby son live in the basement, the last of the paying guests. I call a doctor and he prescribes antibiotics. Bronchitis, he says, lot of it about. It's not so much that Mother is ill, it seems to me, but that she's weary from the effort of struggling on. I go to her bank and discover that the loans taken out with the house as collateral effectively mean that the place is owned by the bank. I pay off her £23 overdraft and deposit a further £100. I'm not a rich man myself—when I subtract Alannah's salary—and I can't really afford these altruistic gestures.

Reading Ian [Fleming]'s novel, *Live and Let Die*. An impossible task, knowing Ian as I once did—I can only see him in it: suspension of disbelief quite impossible. Can he have any idea how much of himself he is exposing? Still, it whiled away an hour or three.

To the passport office to collect my new passport, valid for another ten years. In 1965 I'll be fifty-nine and the thought makes me feel faint. What's happened to my life? These ten-year chunks that are doled out to you in passports are a cruel form of *memento mori*. How many more new passports will I have? One (1965)? Two (1975)? Such a long way off, 1975, yet your passport life seems all too brief. How long did he live? He managed to renew six passports.

THURSDAY, 6 OCTOBER

Turpentine Lane. I telephone Peter. Gloria answers. Peter is away in Algeria researching his next novel. Algeria? You know, the uprising: he thought it might be a good background to his book. Why don't you come round for a drink? Gloria says. So I go. Peter now lives in Belgravia in a large flat in Eaton Terrace. Gloria very *soignée*—a lot of plump cleavage on show for 6:30 in the evening. We flirt uncontrollably. When I leave we kiss and I am allowed to squeeze those breasts of hers. "Shall we start our affair here," she says, "or at your place?" I suggest Turpentine Lane—more discreet. "Tomorrow night," she says, "8 o'clock."

FRIDAY, 7 OCTOBER

Gloria has just left. It's 11:15. "What a curious little den you have, Logan Mountstuart. Like a monk's cell. A randy monk I hope." She had a bottle of gin with her: she was not to know the old Tess-associations that I would make. Her small curvy body is surprisingly firm—you expect her to be all soft and plump but she's actually tense and rubbery, like a gymnast. I notice that between us we've drunk the best part of a bottle. It was good, energetic, no-nonsense, mutually satisfying sex. However, I'm quite pleased to be going back to New York tomorrow.

[When LMS returned he discovered that Marius had already left the gallery. Ben's stern ultimatum had been softened somewhat and Marius had been given the opportunity and the money to start up his own gallery and see if he could redeem himself in the eyes of his stepfather. With little delay he had opened the ML gallery on E. 57th Street. LMS took over the running of Leeping Fils. He had no further contact with Marius, each taking care to keep out of the other's way.

In August of 1956 Mercedes Mountstuart died as the result of complications following pneumonia. She was seventy-six years old. LMS flew back to London to attend the funeral. He took advantage of being in Europe and went on a brief clandestine holiday with Gloria Scabius. They met in Paris and motored south in easy stages towards Provence and the Mediterranean.]

1956

SUNDAY, 5 AUGUST

Movements. Paris–Poitiers. Dire hotel. Poitiers–Bordeaux. Hôtel Bristol–fine. Then two days in Quercy with Cyprien at his chartreuse. Cyprien seemed untypically daunted by Gloria ("Elle est un peu féroce, non?"). Back to Bordeaux for a night. Row in the Chapon Fin. Back in the hotel Gloria threw a shoe at me and it broke a mirror. She refused to speak to me all day until we reached Toulouse. "Where do you want to eat?" I asked. "Anywhere you aren't, you bastard-cunt," was her reply. We ate at the Café de la Paix–excellent. Both drank a bottle of wine each, then several Armagnacs. Friends again. In the morning Gloria telephoned Peter–he thinks she's travelling with an American girlfriend, called Sally. It seems very risky but for some reason I don't care. I feel–and this may be self-delusion–that this is Gloria's affair and not mine. I could be any old gigolo. Toulouse–Avignon. Gloria, quite drunk at lunch, dug the tines of her fork into my thigh and drew blood. I said one more act of violence and I'd be on the next plane back to London. She's behaved quite well since.

MONDAY, 6 AUGUST

Cannes. Lunch with Picasso at his new house, La Californie. Vulgar, but with vast rooms and a spectacular view of the bay. A young woman called Jacqueline Roque *in situ* as resident muse. Picasso very taken with Gloria. She sat between him and Yves Montand while I lusted after Simone Signoret at the other end. ("Looks like a barmaid," bitchy Gloria said. I agreed: "Yes, a fabulously beautiful French barmaid.") Gloria very amorous tonight, said she's never had a more enjoyable holiday in her life. Picasso said to me that he thought she was *typiquement anglaise–au contraire,* I said. He did a quick sketch of us both while we stood on the terrace after lunch–took him about thirty seconds–

but he signed and dated it and unfortunately presented it to Gloria. No getting it back now.

WEDNESDAY, 15 AUGUST

I fly back tomorrow so I went to Brompton Cemetery to look at Mother's grave. Encarnación has gone to live with a niece in Burgos and Sumner Place has been claimed by the bank. Mother died with an accumulation of small debts, some of which I will pay. Everything has been left to me in her will, but there's not a penny to pass on. All of Father's small fortune that he left us both utterly gone—and I find I'm still upset by the fact. Not so much because some of that money was meant for me, more because I know how appalled he would be at such fiscal irresponsibility.

Gloria has "loaned" me the Picasso drawing. ("I can hardly hang it in Eaton Terrace, darling, really. Even Peter might smell a rat.") I had it framed and it now hangs above the gas fire in the sitting room, the only picture on the wall. Peter's Algerian novel, *The Red and the Blue and the Red,* is selling furiously and Gloria seems happy to help him spend his royalties. She kissed me goodbye at Le Bourget and said, "Thank you, Logan, darling, for a super holiday, but I don't think we should see each other again until 1958." She leaves me with a clear conscience: she told me Peter has an endless succession of girlfriends, whom he refers to as his research assistants. Clear conscience vis-à-vis Peter—but what about Alannah?

To my tailors for a final fitting: one pinstripe, charcoal; one lightweight grey flannel for the summer; and my standard midnight-blue double-breasted. Apparently I've put on five inches around the waist since 1944. "It'll be all those hamburger sandwiches, sir," Byrne said.

THURSDAY, 23 AUGUST

Jackson Pollock has killed himself and a girl in a car crash on Long Island. Sadness, but no real surprise in the art world: everyone agrees he would have killed himself one way or another very soon. Ben telephoned me from Paris and told me to buy any Pollock I could lay my hands on. But they're rubbish, I said. The man was a hopeless artist and he knew it—that's why he had a death wish. Who cares? Ben said, just buy them. And he was right: prices are already climbing. I picked up two of the appalling later stuff for $3,000 and $2,500. Herman Keller says he knows someone who has a drip painting from 1950 but he wants $5,000. All right, I said, with huge reluctance. Ben is delighted.

FRIDAY, 19 OCTOBER

I bumped into Marius Leeping on Madison Avenue today. He was coming out of a hotel and looked flushed and unsteady on his feet—too many cocktails. It was 4:00 in the afternoon. I smiled politely, nodded hello and tried to pass by but he grabbed my arm. He called me a "petit connard" and a "goddam creep" who was trying to come between him and his father. I said that if anything was going to come between a son and his father, then the son stealing $30,000 from his father might explain it. He took a swing at me and missed. I pushed him away. I'm fifty years old and can't be brawling with young men in the streets of New York anymore. "I'm gonna get you, you fucking prick!" he yelled at me. "Yeah, yeah, yeah," I said and wandered off. A few New Yorkers stopped for a second to smile: no big deal, a couple of crazy foreigners having an argument.

1957

SATURDAY, 13 APRIL

Mystic House. I walked into the girls' bedroom today and Arlene was standing there naked. Small sharp-pointed breasts, downy shading of pubic hair. Sorry! I said breezily and about-turned. Of course, she's fourteen, but I still think of them both as the little kids they were when I first met them. I took the precaution of mentioning the incident to Alannah, just in case Arlene did. "My, she's growing," I remarked, or something innocuous like that. "Just don't make a habit of it," she said. I said I didn't like her tone or implication. She told me to go fuck myself. I said I'd rather do that than fuck you—though the chance would be a fine thing. And so we had a nasty spiteful little row saying the most wounding words we could think of. What's going wrong? For one ghastly moment I thought she might have found out about Gloria, but that's impossible. Gail senses this tension between us: "Why are you and Mommy always fighting?" "Oh, we're just getting old and ornery," I say. Arlene can't look me in the eye since my intrusion.

MONDAY, 3 JUNE

Curious meeting yesterday with Janet [Felzer]. It was about business, she said, not pleasure, but she didn't want to meet in either of our offices. All right, I said, how about the steps of the Metropolitan Museum? No, no, she said, too obvious. We eventually plumped for a bookstore on Lexington Avenue.

Janet asked: did I know Caspar Alberti? Yes, I said, he's a client—he bought a little Vuillard off me. He's broke, Janet said. How do you know? I just do: he's going to auction off his entire collection. How do you know? I repeated. A little bird told me, she said—he's had a valuer round. He needs money fast, she said knowingly, and then, she added coyly, can you raise $100,000? Why? Because if you can, and I can, and someone else I know can, then we can buy Alberti's collection for $300,000. What do we do then? We sit on it for a year and sell it off, split everything three ways. You'll double your money—guaranteed.

I telephoned Ben in Paris and he wired me the money right away. I was surprised and vaguely ashamed: somehow I felt I was being brought down to Marius Leeping's level—as if I occupied a world where the underhanded thrived and the dishonest man flourished.

[JUNE]

I get up at 7:00 usually—not sleeping so well these days—shower, dress and go through to breakfast. Shirley [the maid] has everything ready for me and the girls. I eat scrambled eggs on toast. The girls arrive, eat their cereals, drink their milkshakes, munch on cookies. I pour some coffee and smoke my first cigarette of the day. Gail is indefatigably chatty; Arlene seems always in some kind of a fuss or crisis to do with clothes or homework. Alannah arrives, prompt at 8:30, looking immaculate, has a coffee and a cigarette before Shirley takes the girls off to school. Sometimes I share a taxi with Alannah but I always like the city at this time of the morning and usually choose to walk a few blocks, buy a newspaper and pick up a cab to the gallery.

I'm always the first to arrive. I open up, switch on the lights, collect the mail and then settle down in my office with the binoculars waiting for the girl to show. From the back of our building we have a good view of the rear of a Fifth Avenue apartment block. There's a girl who lives on the fourth floor who seems to get up between 9:30 and 10:00 most days and draws back her curtains. She must feel she's not observed from directly opposite but she's forgotten about those of us who can see into her room obliquely.

Being a part-time voyeur like this has made me develop a concept I call "Voyeur's Luck." I can sit at my desk, binoculars fixed on her two windows, and the phone will ring and that's the moment she'll take her nightdress off. By the time I have dealt with the call, snatched up the binoculars again, she'll have her bra on. These missed opportunities used to aggravate me cruelly, but now I console myself with my concept. Voyeur's Luck will see me all right, one way or another.

Such as last Friday, when I was with an early client and so thought I'd miss out completely on the show. But I popped back into the office for a second and there she was, naked in the window, standing in front of her closet, wondering what to wear. I'm now quite reconciled to the role that chance plays in all this. I come in each morning, I check her curtains, I look through my binoculars, I give it a minute or two, and if nothing's happening I continue with my day. I suppose that over the two years or so I've been aware of her I must get a good look at her body once or twice a month.

She's no beauty this girl: slightly overweight with wiry corkscrew hair, a jutting chin and a weak mouth. I bumped into her once in a deli on Madison Avenue and almost said, "Hi." It was strange to be standing in line beside her at the checkout, knowing her as I did, watching her make her selection of clothes each day from her wardrobe. I wanted to say, "I love the red brassiere." She bought some menthol cigarettes, I noticed. I know when she goes on vacation and I know when she returns. She is, in a curious way, "my girl." The relationship is wholly one-sided but that's how I refer to her when I pick up my binoculars: "Wonder if I'll see my girl today?" I don't want to learn her name or anything more about her.

[JUNE]

I told my psychiatrist, Dr. John Francis Byrne, about the girl. "Does she excite you?" he asked in his flat voice. "Do you masturbate afterwards?" I said no, which is true, and tried to explain what measure of excitement I derived from my casual, opportunistic voyeurism. After all, as I said to Byrne, I don't creep around spying on women. There I was sitting in my office and this girl across the way opens her curtains and walks around her room with no clothes on. But you bought some binoculars, Byrne said. That was curiosity, I said, I was interested in the details. What I liked about this ritual was that its candour and intimacy provided the frisson rather than anything more overtly sexual—it's like a Degas or a Bonnard, I tried to explain: you know, "Woman Drying Her Hair," "Marthe in the Bath." Byrne thought about this: "Yeah," he said. "I know what you mean."

Dr. Byrne had been recommended to me by Adam Outridge, but I didn't make contact until earlier this year—out of boredom rather than neurosis. All was not well between Alannah and me, and I suddenly felt the need for someone to talk to.

Byrne is a sardonic, world-weary fellow in his sixties. Sharp mind, well informed. He's a tall man who carries his excess weight well. I asked him if he knew he had the same name as the man who was the model for "Cranly" in James Joyce's novels—J. F. Byrne. I'm aware of that, Byrne said, but so what? It's not a particularly remarkable coincidence. That's true, up to a point, I said—I had a tailor in London called Byrne. But to have exactly the same Christian names—that *is* a coincidence. Byrne was unimpressed: look at you, he said, you've an unusual surname but it's the same as the man whom Boswell accompanied on his Grand Tour. Does that make you feel any more different? Any better? But there's another twist, I said, I've met Joyce, I've read his books, I've read Byrne's memoir of him and now you're my psychiatrist. Don't you think the serendipity is getting a little out of hand? I don't think this is a fruitful line to explore, Byrne said. Tell me about this girl: is she stacked?

When I first met Byrne I asked him what his professional persuasion was—Freudian, Jungian, Reichian, whatever. None of the above, he said. I'm basically a good, old-fashioned S&M man. S&M? Sex and Money. He explained: in his experience, if you were not clinically ill—like a schizophrenic or a manic depressive—then 99 per cent of his patients' neuroses were generated by either sex or money, or both. If we get to the bottom of the sex problem or the money problem, then these sessions can be quite productive. He smiled his wan smile: know thyself, sort of thing. So, which category do you fall in? he asked. I think I'm one of your sex-men, I said.

[OCTOBER]

Janet and I have restarted our affair in a desultory way. I wonder why? Perhaps because I rather miss Gloria and the fun we had. I drove Janet back from Windrose the other day (we'd been out to see Tate) and she asked me in for a drink and what with one thing and another . . . We were celebrating, anyway, partners in crime. We look set to more than triple our money on the Alberti collection. So easy.

Went to meet Charlie Zemsche [a client] at the Plaza. It was a warm day and the stink of horse-piss and horse-shit from the ponies and traps on Central Park South was as thick as felt. I never come by here in summer because of the stench but had thought I was safe in October. It is an interesting history lesson: if three dozen horses can make this stink, imagine what the pungent reek of a nineteenth-century city must have been. Not to mention the thousands of tons of horse manure deposited on the streets each day. I find my gorge rising as I skirt round—how would I have survived in Dickens's London?

Charlie is as engagingly morose as ever: he hates New York, hates his new house. "I'm through with contractors, architects. You don't lead a life. You got to live in a hotel—I'm selling all my houses. You live in a hotel, it's another person's problem, not yours." Charlie's theory is that if you minimize the fuss and hassle in your life, you appreciate life all the more. I asked him how he could abandon New York for Miami. "A bad day there is better than a good day here." All the same, he's interested in my little Bonnard. It'll fit in a suitcase, I told him, take it from hotel to hotel.

1958

[MAY]

A weekend at the Ginsberg house in Southampton. Todd Heuber was there with his sister Martha, also a painter: a redhead with odd slanting blue eyes. She paints crude stripey abstracts like Barnett Newman's. Todd is quite keen for Leeping Fils to take her. "Marius is very interested," he said, to spur me on.

Gail spends all evening until her bedtime "looking for the Sputnik." I join her on the lawn, a bit stoned, on a perfect night and stand with her peering up at the stars looking for the moving point of light. I feel empty-headed, vertiginous, and lose my balance. Gail helps me up off the lawn. "Why did you fall over, silly Daddy?" she says, then adds, "Silly Logan." I was glad she couldn't see the tears in my eyes.

[JULY]

Mystic House. Watching Alannah, naked, shaving her armpits this
morning, brought on a little quiver of lust, like the old days. I slipped
out of bed and went into the bathroom and let my hardening cock
nudge against her buttocks. "Honey, it's my period," she said. But I
know it's not.

[JULY]

I slug gin direct from the bottle at 10:00 in the morning, just wanting
that buzz, that little kick. The fog burns off to leave a day of hazy blue,
the water in the Sound oddly opaque, like milk. I'm bored, which is
why I reach so early for the bottle: Alannah is in the city for three days.
Shirley has come up to help with the girls and their two friends. Four
young girls in the house—they're either fighting or giggling together,
there seems no other form of behaviour available to them.

[AUGUST]

Looking at my face in the shaving mirror, I note its roughening texture:
the nodules and pigment shadows, the burst capillaries, the lines and
the slackening skin, all the small accruing damage of ageing. My hair
seems to be receding, the promontory of my widow's peak very marked.
I experiment with different ways of combing my hair but don't like the
result. I'm fifty-two for God's sake, no point in pretending.

[AUGUST]

NYC. Todd called, very excited, asking me to come and see Martha's
new paintings. It's strange being in the apartment on my own. It seems
so big without the girls and Alannah. I have a couple of extra meetings
and so have decided to stay on over the weekend till Monday.

I went to Martha's studio. Peculiar, haunting work. The paintings are big—eight feet by four, ten by five—charged, Turneresque swirls of colour. Light and shade, impressionistic brush work. But they seem to be flawed by marks, as if tiny drops of dark paint have been spilled or the weave of the canvas is showing in some way. Then when you peer very closely—very close, just inches—you can see that these dots are in fact minute figures or animals—I would say never more than a tenth of an inch high. The sudden change of scale this brings about when you step back is startling. Perceptual gears change automatically, almost audibly, in your head. You look again at the picture and it's altered. Suddenly these vague, misty coronas and supernovas of colour are vast unearthly wildernesses with tiny people moving through them, beneath astonishing weather and light effects. I sign Martha up for a show. We had a boozy lunch in the Village to celebrate.

[AUGUST]

Today, Sunday, a bit hungover, I went to see a movie in the afternoon—*Gigi*. Even this ersatz Hollywood version made me long to be in Paris, in Europe, the old world. As I came out I was thinking: maybe I should take Alannah and the girls to Paris—and thinking how much they would love it—or even if they didn't love it, how it would be good for them to go, part of their education.

And so I was strolling up Lexington looking for a cab, my head full of Alannah, when a woman came out of a coffee shop across the street who looked exactly like her. It was her. I shouted, but she didn't hear me. I ran across the street but she'd turned the corner. I think it was 44th. I saw her go into a hotel. The Astoria. I went into the lobby—no sign. Then I saw her in the bar sitting with another man, her back half turned towards me. He looked to be in his thirties, dark, attractive, with heavy, black-rimmed spectacles. You can tell from the way two people sit beside each other in a bar how intimate they happen to be. There was no doubt in my mind. I waited outside the hotel for half an hour and then went back in. They weren't in the bar anymore and they hadn't come out.

[AUGUST]

When I returned to Mystic, Alannah told me she'd had to go into New York on Sunday—some crisis with her sister. She'd called the apartment but there was no reply. I was at a movie, I said: *Gigi*. It made me want to take you and the girls to Paris. She was full of enthusiasm for the idea and we talked of Paris all through supper. I wonder who her lover is?

[In October, Alannah told LMS about her affair and asked for a separation. She was in love with a colleague at NBC, a producer called David Peterman. LMS said that if she broke off the romance he was sure he could find it in himself to forgive her. Alannah replied she had no intention of ending the affair. So LMS moved out of the Riverside Drive apartment and crossed the city to the Upper East Side, taking the top floor of a townhouse on E. 74th Street between Third and Second Avenues–an easy stroll from the gallery. They agreed to share Mystic House on alternate weekends. LMS continued his visits to Dr. Byrne.]

1959

[FEBRUARY]

It's pathetic. I was standing outside Gail's school in the afternoon waiting for her class to come out. I missed her and I wanted to see her, just go to a diner for half an hour and chat. Alannah's man was there too, also waiting. I said: What the fuck are you doing here, Davidson? Peterman, he said, David Peterman. He was here to meet Gail and take her home. I said I'd bring her home. He thought Alannah wouldn't like that. I said I had been part of Gail's family for six years and as far as I was concerned she was still my stepdaughter. He looked at me: Just beat it, Mountstuart. It's over. Accept it. I wanted to hit him, haymaker his square jaw and stamp on his heavy framed spectacles. Then I thought of Gail coming out and seeing these two men she knew fighting over her. Not fair. I left, found a bar and got drunk.

[APRIL–MAY]

Got this banal song in my head—"Gonna do the jailhouse rock"—won't go away, I've been hearing it for days. I listen to Bach and Monteverdi and as I change records it starts up again: Gonna do the jailhouse rock.

   Coincidentally, a sweet letter from Lionel saying he is working in the music business in London as the manager of a band called the Greensleeves. He says he has changed his name to Leo—Leo Leggatt— and doesn't want to be known as "Lionel" anymore. "Leo" sounds good to me: Lionel-Leo. Christ, he must be twenty-six by now.

THURSDAY, 23 APRIL

Went round to Nat Tate's studio at 6:00 to collect my "Still Life No. 5." He was already quite drunk and kept repeating that Janet was to know nothing about this sale. I reassured him. He offered me a bowl of Benzedrine pills—as if they were peanuts—but I declined. He took a couple and washed them down with a slug of Jack Daniel's. We went into the studio and I watched him work for an hour or so. He was painting a triptych and the final panel was primed and ready on the big easel. We listened to music (Scriabin, I think) and talked aimlessly about his forthcoming trip to France and Italy—where he should go, what he should see. Amazing to think a man—an artist—of his age has never left the U.S.A.

   Nat seemed content to drink and talk until he reached a certain plateau of drunkenness, waiting for the booze to trigger the precise moment. Suddenly he threw the dust sheets off the other two completed panels of the triptych. There was, first, a nude, an orthodox odalisque, more yellow than flesh-toned, and then, in the second panel, was another version of it, more stylized and crudely flashy—very sub–de Kooning. Nat stood staring at the two panels, drinking, and then, putting the bottle down, literally attacked the big canvas with a wide brush and tubes of cadmium yellow, laying on great swathes of colour. He seemed almost deranged to me. I left after an hour with my still life and he was still at it, rubbing off most of what he had done with a rag, then going at it again, this time with black and green.*

He has some talent, Nat, but he seems unduly tormented. One wants to say: relax, enjoy life a little more, creation need not always be so apocalyptic—look at Matisse, look at Braque. It doesn't have to be all *Sturm und Drang* to be good. However, this is hardly a message to be heeded in New York in this day and age. The Jack Daniel's had given me a thirst so I stopped off in a couple of bars. Drank more whisky when I came home. I realize I'm alone again and drinking too much. I'm unhappy: it's not my natural state—I need to be married, or living with someone. Mind you, I have to say I drank as much when I was with Alannah and the girls.

FRIDAY, 5 JUNE

I told Byrne I was feeling depressed and he prescribed me some tran-quillizers and Seconal to help me sleep. He advised me not to mix them with excessive amounts of alcohol. Define "excessive," Dr. Byrne. I can have a couple of Martinis, some wine—that sort of level. Any amount of beer is fine.

Byrne asked me about my sexual fantasies and pronounced them pretty banal. I suppose they must be, given the stories he hears in this place. He seized on one that I mentioned, however: the idea that's always tempted me of going to bed with two women at the same time. You should try it, he suggested. His theory is that it is a fantasy associ-ated with my married, familial life. Now that I'm alone, my indulging in it will be a form of liberation, a watershed, a sign that I had moved on—a sense that my time with Alannah was truly over. Fine, I said, but how do I set about realizing it? You got a girlfriend? Byrne asked. I

*For a fuller account of Nat Tate's life, see *Nat Tate: An American Artist* by William Boyd (21 Publishing, 1998).

mentioned Janet. So tell her to bring a friend on your next date. I told him that wouldn't work. Byrne shrugged: well, I guess you're just going to have to pay for it.

SATURDAY, 6 JUNE

My mood has lifted. Perhaps Byrne has a point: I've been thinking seriously about his theory. Anyway, this evening, after 10:00, I go down to Times Square and take a stroll around the streets that lead west off it. There are a lot of hookers and a lot of worrying-looking men. I am offered the opportunity to buy drugs at least a dozen times.

On 47th and Eighth I see a girl standing by a small neon-lit bar. My first thought is that the image could be from an Edward Hopper painting. The girl must be in her late twenties, quite heavy, with a pronounced bosom. Her cheap clothes are creased tight on her and she has a curious coppery glint to her hair that catches as highlights the flashing neon of the beer signs—blue, yellow, green and blue again—above her head. She's wearing a matching jacket and skirt, high heels and a red satin blouse. I go up to her. "Hi," I say, "can I buy you a drink?" "What do you want, mister?" "How much for a whole night?" I feel curiously calm: this takes me back to my youth—mine was a generation that unreflectingly went to prostitutes, almost in the same way as one would go to the theatre. She looks me up and down and I know she's making calculations based on my clothes, my manner, my accent. "A hundred," she says, "and any extras are extra." I ask her if she's here most nights. Yes and no, she says. I say I'll be back on Wednesday. "Oh, sure," she says disgustedly.

I keep walking and end up on Sixth Avenue, where I find a medium-sized, medium-priced hotel. It has a big lobby—good for discretion—and there's a bank of ten elevators to take you to the rooms above. No one should notice a couple of hookers coming in and out of a place like this. I book a junior suite for Wednesday night.

THURSDAY, II JUNE

It's over. It's done. Write it down quickly while I remember.

I have everything ready in the room. Scotch, gin, mixers, some beers, six packs of cigarettes—different brands—peanuts, pretzels, chewing gum.

At about 10:00 I go back to the corner of 47th and Eighth but the girl isn't outside the bar. Then I see her across the street. She's wearing the same clothes as on Saturday. I saunter over, my heartbeat audible to passers-by, it seems to me.

ME: Hello, remember me?
GIRL: No.
ME: I'm the one who asked you for a whole night.
GIRL: Oh, yeah . . .
ME: I'm ready now but I have another request. Can you bring another along?
GIRL: A guy?
ME: No, no. Another girl. A hundred dollars each.
GIRL: Extras are extra.

I give her the address of the hotel and my room number and hand her a $20 bill as a token of my sincerity. I return to the hotel, where I sit in my junior suite for an hour and a half, becoming increasingly angry with myself—how naive can you be? The easiest twenty bucks she's ever earned. I switch on the TV set and the doorbell rings. It is my girl, with another in tow: smaller, darker, with a nervy, shifty gaze. They come in, I pour them a drink and we introduce ourselves: Logan, Rose (my girl) and Jacintha (her pal). In the light of the room I have a better look at them. Rose is buxom, hefty. Jacintha is grubbier, her print dress stained, her cardigan has a hole in the elbow. They both smoke.

ME: Do you two know each other?
ROSE: I seen her around.

JACINTHA: Yeah. This is the whole night, yeah? Hundred bucks?
ME: Absolutely. Help yourself to a drink.

They do and sit down with their drinks on the two available arm-chairs while I perch on the edge of the bed. I switch on the radio and try to find a jazz station. The girls drink, smoke and munch peanuts—Rose asks about the room rate. I suggest we all take our clothes off.

When we are naked the girls go automatically into a different mood, one of routine coquettishness. I'm glad to see I have the makings of a respectable erection. Jacintha asks about rubbers and I tell her I have a drawerful. I go over to Rose and take her in my arms as if we are going to dance to the crackly jazz emanating from the radio. I try to kiss her and she says, "No kissing." We agree on $5 for a proper kiss with tongues and I get my five dollars' worth. I'm very aroused now and Rose and I fall on the bed as I fumble for a condom. Rose could be a pretty girl—prettier, anyway—if she lost about twenty pounds. The fat she's carrying distorts her face, plumps her cheeks unattractively. We fuck and I come very quickly. Meanwhile Jacintha has switched on the television. Rose asks if she can take a shower and disappears into the bathroom. I sit on the rumpled bed, looking at Jacintha, then I look down at my flaccid dick—I feel not an ounce of sexual interest in my entire body. Jacintha turns round.

JACINTHA: You know, you look a bit like one of those guys in *Sergeant Bilko*. The dark one—what's his name?—Paparelli.
ME: Thanks a lot.
JACINTHA: You from out of town?

I wander over to her. She can hardly tear her eyes from the screen but she reaches out and gives a few tugs to my cock. I cup her breasts. Close to, her body looks unhealthily pale: I can see the fragile fluted cage of her ribs, the grey square screen of the TV set reflected in her dark eyes. I turn away and go to pour myself another drink. Rose comes out of the bathroom, all steamy and pink, a towel around her waist. "They got great soap," she says. So Jacintha goes to take a shower in her turn. Rose pours herself a big gin, lights another cigarette and looks squarely at me. "So, how's it goin', Logan?" "Fine," I say. "The night is young."

We watch a movie, a western, the three of us lying on the bed at my request—me the meat in the hooker sandwich. Occasionally I grab one of their hands and place it on my cock and they jerk away desultorily for a while. I get hard and reach for Jacintha but she says she's enjoying the movie and we've got all night. I nuzzle Rose's big bubs and she pushes my head out of the way.

After the movie Jacintha gives me a blow-job ($15) and when I'm hard I whip out a condom. I stay hard but I heave away for what seems hours without coming. Eventually I withdraw.

JACINTHA: It's better with two guys and a girl. Free advice.
ME: Why?
ROSE: Two guys can always be doing things—more variation.
JACINTHA: Yeah. You got two girls—one of them is always sitting around, twiddling her thumbs. Unless they got a lesbian thing going.
ROSE: And think about it: you have another guy in here, you split the price and you only pay for one girl.
ME: I think it's the idea of another man in the bed with us—a stranger with a hard-on—it would put me off.
ROSE: Don't be so squeamish.
ME: Prudish.
ROSE: Whatever.
JACINTHA: So, how long're you in town, Logan?
LOGAN: I live here.
ROSE: Can we order room service?

We order some sandwiches (the girls hide in the bathroom when they're delivered). We eat, talk, drink (I'm fairly drunk, by now) and smoke. Then we all admit we're kind of tired and clamber into bed. When Rose and Jacintha are asleep I do actually feel a sensual thrill—feel I've achieved a form of sexual revelation. Their flanks touch mine, I hear their breathing, smell the soap, booze and cigarette smoke on them. Outside on Sixth, the traffic roar waxes and wanes, the sirens yip, the night gets on with its business. It is over. Alannah is past—I can start again.

In the morning Rose shakes me awake. It's very early—not yet 6:00—

and she's dressed. "I got to go," she says. I haul myself out of bed—
Jacintha sleeps on—and find my wallet (hidden behind the radio in the
bedside cabinet). I give her $150—I'm truly grateful. "Can I take these
cigarettes?" she asks. "Leave a couple of packs for Jacintha." At the
door she says, "See ya—any time, Logan." She blows me a kiss. I leave
the door open a crack and watch her saunter off down the corridor.

I pull on my robe, order up breakfast (taking the tray at the door)
and pour a slug of gin into my orange juice to help my headache. I sip
my coffee and watch the sun climb the façades of the buildings opposite. Jacintha wakes and I bring her some coffee. "Want a shot?" I say
and top up her coffee with whisky. I explain that Rose left early.

JACINTHA: Want to fool around?
ME: What've you got in mind?
JACINTHA (lighting up): Want to do something weird?
ME: What do you mean?
JACINTHA: Well, I figure this must be some kind of big orgy-thing
fantasy—right? Seems to me you must want to do some more
stuff.
ME: How about a passionate kiss?

So Jacintha kisses me ($5) with lots of tongue work and little grunts
and groans of ersatz passion. Then she runs through various options:
in the ass, doggy-fashion, 69, spanking. But suddenly I feel weary, my
brain busy analysing the events of the past few hours, wondering why
the occasion has been so straightforward, so unerotic, unexciting. So
clear-eyed in its ordinariness. It's my fault, I decide: it's precisely
because I over-analyze, am too observant, am too interested in the
details, savouring the quiddity of the two girls. A true punter would
have just got on with the job and satisfied himself—do this, do that—
while I'm noting what brand of cigarettes Rose smokes and that
Jacintha has got a scab on her knee. Sweaty, brusque Rose with her
weight problem; thin, damaged Jacintha, with her preposterous name.
I should be more selfish, less curious, less—

JACINTHA: By the way, my name's not Jacintha. It's Valerina.
ME: That's a nice name. Is it Russian?

JACINTHA: My dad was Russian. I think. You think it's OK?
ME: Sure.
JACINTHA: I don't think a Russian name will work in America.
These days.
ME: It's a point.

She slips out of bed and goes to the breakfast tray to butter toast. "Nice hotel," she says for about the fortieth time. Then her eyes brighten. "I got an idea," she says. "I could piss on you if you like. Some guys like that."

ME: They do?

We agree on a rate of $30—it's a new day, Jacintha says: last night was last night. She leads me through to the bathroom and I take off my robe.

ME: How exactly does this work?
JACINTHA: Lie down in the bath. I was thinking: I need to take a piss. Shame to waste it, you know, maybe he likes that stuff.
ME: (lying down in bath) You never can tell. I just don't want it anywhere near my face.
JACINTHA: I'll be careful.

Jacintha straddles me, says, "Ready?" I look up at her body, very foreshortened from my unique point of view. I nod and she lets fly. I keep my eyes open and instruct every sense to record and evaluate in minute detail. This is a first. This night has yielded something new. This is real, true experience. It's oddly humbling to know that life can still surprise you after fifty-three years.

When she finishes and steps out of the bath I draw the shower curtain and shower off. Lots of soap. When I come out—actually beginning to feel a bit frisky—Jacintha is already back in her sad dress. "I got to go," she says, "I got to pick up my kid from my sister." I give her $200.

"Thank you, Jacintha," I say. "It was amazing, the whole thing. Really."

"Yeah. Any time, Logan," she says when she leaves, managing to inflect her voice with some fictitious enthusiasm—but she can't do anything with her dead smile. "It was swell."

SUNDAY, 9 AUGUST

Mystic House. I tell myself I enjoy being up here on my own but I'm always half conscious of Alannah and the absent children, now that they never come here anymore. Peterman has a place up the Hudson River. I should probably pack it in. Alannah and Peterman, it turns out, had been sleeping together for nearly a year when I caught them out. This is the knowledge that really burns—twists the gut. Again and again you go back over that time, charting and logging the lies and duplicities that you missed; acknowledging and realizing that those moments of fun, of peace, of happiness, of sex, were feigned and fraudulent, and that the affair was running like a pestilence through your ordinary life, poisoning everything. I read back through these journals, thinking: she was seeing Peterman then, and then, and then. So much for your fabled powers of observation, Mountstuart. Yes, but it's also clear from these pages that I was busy betraying her too, my own lies blinding me to hers. Alannah wasn't as complacent as I. When I blustered, outraged, about her infidelity she said, "Save it, Logan, I know you've been fucking Janet Felzer for years. Don't bother preaching to me."

Writing a piece for Udo about Rauschenberg. This second generation seems to me more interesting, more depth: Rauschenberg, Martha Heuber (I don't think Todd will make the first grade), Johns, Rivers. There seems more intellectual weight here: an acknowledgement of art's traditions, even as they turn away from them, or cast them anew to fit their purposes.

Walked down to the shore this evening and stood on the rocks, looking out on the Sound and swigging gin from my hip flask. A warm sunny evening, the plash and gurgle of the waves in the rock pools, the rush of the cold gin. I thought for the first time of my novel, abandoned, all these years, and I came up, unprompted, with the perfect title. *Octet. Octet* by Logan Mountstuart. Perhaps I will surprise them all, yet.

I should note down here another strange development in my career as a gallery director. Jan-Carl Lang [of the Fulbright-Lang Gallery] came to see me on Friday of last week and asked if we had any Picassos. We had three, as it turned out, but his real interest was for the worst and most recent. It was a big stylized nude in front of a window with a bay and palm trees beyond. Very fluent, some texturing of the oil with the handle of the brush, but too facile, in the end: you feel he could churn these out all day, one every hour or so. Price-tag $120,000. Jan-Carl said to me that he had a client who would buy it for $300,000. Was I interested in learning more?

Jan-Carl is a tall balding blond man in his forties, vain, charming, impeccably dressed in every season. We went to the Carlyle Hotel for a drink and he explained his plan more fully. The "collector," whom he wouldn't name, is European, domiciled in Monte Carlo, but clearly some vastly wealthy merchant prince. The plot goes like this. Leeping Fils sell this Picasso to collector X for a record sum—announcements in trade journals, press releases, interviews—but no money actually changes hands. However, the picture, *Nude by a Window,* has now become famous, celebrated, notorious and, more important, its provenance is highly respectable—a notable French gallery operating out of New York. And it has a ludicrous price-tag. A year later, two years later, the picture turns up at auction somewhere in the world. Ah! Picasso's *Nude by a Window.* Wasn't that the one that, etc, etc. The art market being what it is, an indifferent famous picture is worth more than an excellent unknown one. The reserve is set at $500,000. It could go higher. 50 per cent for Leeping Fils for providing the picture and the provenance; 25 per cent each for Jan-Carl and collector X (who, I suspect, is not as rich as all that). Everybody makes a *lot* of money and a new buyer is very happy with his celebrated painting.

Jan-Carl lit his cigarette with delicate precision. "All we do is create renown. Or call it notoriety, if you must." I smiled at him: "I'll call it dishonesty. All we do is commit fraud." He chuckled: "Don't be so precious, Logan. We're exploiting our market. We do it every day. You do it every day. If a rich man only wants to buy a famous painting it's hardly our fault." I said I'd get back to him; I needed to talk it over with Ben. No hurry, said Jan-Carl. Take all the time you want.

FRIDAY, 4 DECEMBER

Nat Tate came round to my apartment last night, unannounced. Not drunk—indeed, quite calm and composed. He offered me $6,000 for the two paintings of his I owned—far too much. I said they were not for sale. All right, he said: he only wanted to rework them (an idea inspired by his visit to Braque's studio*) and explained what he had in mind. I let him take them away with some reluctance. Before he left he offered me $1,500 for my three "Bridge" drawings; I said I would swap them for another picture but I didn't want to sell. He became rather tetchy and incoherent at this point—banging on about artistic integrity and its conspicuous absence in NY, etc.—so I gave him a stiff drink and unhooked my two canvases off the wall, keen to see the back of him.

Then Janet called this morning with a report of the same "reworking" notion. She'd let him take away all the work she had in the gallery—she thought it was a neat idea.

I asked her for a date but she said she was seeing another man. She was in love with him. Who is it? I asked. Tony Kolokowski. But he's a queer, I said, you might as well fall in love with Frank. Don't be so cynical, Logan, she said: he's bi, anyway. These New York women.

SATURDAY, 19 DECEMBER

I go down to 47th and Eighth hoping to spot Rose or Jacintha. Am I crazy? How many tricks will they have turned in the six months since our night together? I can't find them, anyway, and clear off with some relief. Times Square and those side streets give me the creeps. Am I so preposterously sentimental to think that I have shared something meaningful with those girls? That we could meet, reminisce, that there is some sort of a bond between us? Yes, I am that preposterously sentimental. There's no fool like an old fool, Mountstuart.

*Tate and Barkasian had visited Braque in his Varengeville studio in September 1959.

The Jan-Carl situation has resolved itself. I finally received a very cryptic letter from Ben in which he said that the "Swiss adventure" might be worth exploring. Then there was a very circumlocutionary passage: "If the Swiss holiday is taken, then it can only be taken by you. I would not be coming on the trip. However, if you had a successful time, then I might, anecdotally, pretend I had been there too. If, on the other hand, you don't enjoy yourself, then that would be a disappointment you alone would have to cope with." I assume all this means is that if it goes wrong I will take the blame—the mud will stick to me. Ben wants "deniability" as I believe they call it. But if we make a pile, he'll take it. I have to think further.

THURSDAY, 31 DECEMBER

I'm going to Todd Heuber's party later tonight and I find myself depressed by the prospect, and not just because my jaw is aching. I had three molars removed yesterday. And my dentist says I'll have to be careful: my gums are retreating, I could lose the lot. Funny how the idea of losing your teeth chills the soul. I send my tongue out to caress the raw void where my teeth were, then sluice some whisky round my mouth. Ouch! A new decade and a terrible premonition of the body beginning to decay; the old reliable machine beginning to malfunction. New Year's resolution: resolve to get fitter, to cut down on the booze and the pills. Perhaps I should take up golf again.

1960

FRIDAY, 15 JANUARY

Janet called in at the gallery in huge distress. It seems that Nat Tate has "gone missing," though all the evidence points to suicide. A young man, looking very like Tate, jumped off the Staten Island Ferry on Tuesday [the 12th]. Janet then discovered that all the work Tate had reclaimed had been systematically destroyed—burned in a great bonfire at Windrose. She asked me to come down to the studio, where Peter Barkasian was meeting her.

At the studio, Barkasian, you could see, was only just holding himself together by massive wishful-thinking. Nat would never do such a crazy thing—it's just a breakdown—he'll be back, start over. We wandered around: the place was immaculate, tidy and ordered. In the kitchen, glasses were clean and stacked, waste-paper baskets had been emptied. In the studio there was just one canvas placed against the wall, obviously recently started, a crosshatched mass of bruised blues, purples and blacks. Its title, *Orizaba/Return to Union Beach*, was scrawled on the back but neither Janet nor Barkasian picked up the reference. I told them that "Orizaba" was the name of the ship carrying Hart Crane [Tate's magus-poet figure] back from Havana on his last, fatal journey in 1932. "Fatal?" Barkasian said. "How did Hart Crane die?" Janet shrugged—no idea. I felt I had to tell him. "He drowned," I said, "he jumped overboard." Barkasian was shocked, driven to tears. The painting, inchoate and mystifying, was suddenly the only suicide note available. If poor Nat could not continue to live his life as an artist, he at least ensured that the symbolic weight of its end was apt—and to be duly noted.

All very sad, of course, but he was in a desperate state—and who am I to say he should have pulled himself together, taken a grip and not surrendered to despair? He destroyed everything, Barkasian confirmed, which must include my two paintings. At least I have my "Bridge" drawings. Janet is full of conspiracy theories but I think the simple explanation is that the poor fellow had gone barking mad. Talking of conspiracy theories. I spotted Jan-Carl lunching with Marius Leeping. Two dealers lunching—nothing odd in that. But why do I smell the hand of Marius Leeping in the collector X scam? I telephoned Jan-Carl and told him that I wasn't interested—the Picasso was not for sale. His famous poise became significantly unbalanced. He said that I was a fool, I was already involved and I couldn't back out now, everything was in place, they needed that Picasso. I said I had told him I would think it over, I reminded him, and I have: not interested. Typically

English, he sneered. I said I'd take that as a compliment. *Perfide Albion* lives on. I telegrammed Ben: SWISS HOLIDAY CANCELLED.

MONDAY, 18 JANUARY

I called up Jerry Schubert [Leeping Fils's lawyer] just to check on the Jan-Carl Lang matter, that he could lay no claim to the Picasso. "There's no contract, no bill of sale," Jerry said, "he can't touch you. It was only talk. Everybody talks."

Letter from Lionel saying he may be coming to New York and if so is there any chance of a bed for a few nights? My first reaction was—of course not. But he's your son, you oaf, you moron. Why does his coming disturb you so? Because he's a stranger to me. But maybe it'll be good, you get on, you might actually like him. Maybe . . . It can only be his Mountstuart genes that drew him into the music business.

> [*In the summer of 1960 two young independent film producers called Marcio and Martin Canthaler optioned LMS's novella,* The Villa by the Lake, *for their Hollywood production company, MCMC Pictures. LMS was flown out to Los Angeles for meetings and to explore the idea that he would write the screenplay. As it happened, Peter Scabius was also in town in negotiations over the film rights of his latest novel,* Already Too Late *(a futuristic allegory about the threat to the planet of nuclear war).*]

SUNDAY, 24 JULY

Bel Air Hotel, Los Angeles. Strange feeling of being in some kind of dream. This hotel is a mini Shangri-La. I feel I only start to age when I cross over the little bridge that leads to the parking lot, and when I return time stands still once more. Perfect peace, low buildings sheltered in lush densely planted gardens, a pale blue swimming pool.

I had Peter here to lunch yesterday and I could tell he was a little put out at the hotel's discreet splendour. Who's picking up the bill? he demanded to know. Paramount? Warner Bros? MCMC, I said. Where are you? Beverly Wilshire, he said. Oh, *very* grand, I said, and he was mollified, secure and smug again. He's so easy to handle, Peter, which is one of the reasons I'm so fond of him, I suppose. He's developed a truly superb, magnificent ego over the years, breathtaking in its presumption, and the match of anything you might find in this town. When I think of what a nervous little chap he was at school . . .

The most interesting news is that Gloria has left him for an Italian aristocrat, Count somebody-or-other. He is divorcing her as fast as possible. No problems with the Catholic Church? I asked him. "I lost my faith in Algeria," he said, looking sombre and battle-weary. He's in good shape—better than me—tanned, lean, though his hair is suspiciously dark, not a grey hair, most unusual. Mine is now distinctly pepper and salt, forehead becoming more and more prominent.

MONDAY, 25 JULY

Meeting with Marcio and Martin at their offices in Brentwood. Marcio is thirty-five, Martin thirty-two. Both genial, both slightly overweight, Martin balding, Marcio with a curly, crooner's mop. They have paid me $5,000 for a year's option on *Villa* with the right to renew for a further year.

MARCIO: So, Logan, how was your weekend?
ME: I had lunch with an old friend, Peter Scabius.
MARCIO: Great writer.
MARTIN: Ditto to that.
ME: And I went to a show. At an art gallery.
MARTIN: We love art. Who was on?
ME: Diebenkorn.
MARCIO: We got one of his, I think.
MARTIN: We have two, actually, Marcio.

This is what confuses you out here. You think you are having a fruitless meeting with two affable numskulls and you end up talking about Richard Diebenkorn for half an hour. They want me to write the script, they say, but they don't want to pay me until it's done and they've read

it. But what if you don't like it? I say. You're not going to pay for a
script you don't like. Won't be an issue, Logan, Marcio assures me. We
know we're going to love whatever you do, Martin adds.

Later I telephone Wallace in London and ask his advice. Agree to
nothing, he says, tell them to make all proposals to me. I sense he's a
little annoyed that I'm only consulting him now. I'm your agent,
Logan, he says, this is my job, for Christ's sake.

SATURDAY, 30 JULY

On the plane, Pan Am, back to NYC. Yesterday evening I went down
to Santa Monica and walked by the ocean. I had a couple of drinks in
a bar by the pier as dusk fell and the sky and the sea began to look like
a Rothko colour field. I felt good, lightly tanned, at ease, enjoying the
slow burn of the booze and I suddenly had the fantasy about moving
out here—start a Leeping Fils West . . . As you grow older and your life
becomes more ordered, so too a comfortable, temperate, easy-going
version of the Good Life becomes ever more appealing. I might meet a
nice Californian woman—they seem to have more than their fair share
of beautiful women out here. But I realized, as I explored it further,
that this was and would only be a fantasy: I'd go mad in a month or
two—just as I'd go mad in a cottage in Somerset, or a farm in Tuscany.
My nature is essentially urban and, although Los Angeles is indubitably a city, somehow its mores aren't. Maybe it's the weather that
makes it feel forever suburban and provincial: cities need extremes of
weather, so that you long for escape. I could live in Chicago, I think—
I've enjoyed my trips to Chicago. Also there has to be something brutal
and careless about a true city—the denizen must feel vulnerable—and
Los Angeles doesn't deliver that either, at least not in my short experience. I feel too damn comfortable here, too cocooned. These are not
experiences of the true city: its nature seeps in under the door and
through the windows—you can never be free of it. And the genuine
urban man or woman is always curious—curious about the life outside
on the streets. That just doesn't apply here: you live in Bel Air and you
don't ask yourself what's going on in Pacific Palisades—or am I missing
something?

We resolved the script issue: $10,000 payable in advance; another ten if it's accepted. Wallace did a good job, which made me think: why don't I use him more? When we spoke on the phone I told him about my idea for *Octet* and wondered if we could prise an advance out of Sprymont & Drew. He told me that Sprymont & Drew don't exist anymore. The company was bought and the imprint is defunct. What about Roderick? He's resurfaced at Michael Kazin—at a much reduced salary. He suggested I put the idea down on paper and he said he would see what he could do, but added: "It won't be easy, Logan. I have to warn you—things have changed, and you're not exactly a household name." True. True . . .

THURSDAY, 15 SEPTEMBER

Lionel has been here the last four days. He has untidy long hair that hangs over his ears and a thin patchy beard. I could have bumped into him on the street and not known he was my son. He is still taciturn and diffident and the mood in the apartment since he's arrived is one of self-conscious reserve and scrupulous politeness: "After you with the salt." "You have it, I insist." Lionel seems to know a good few people in the city, what with his contacts in the music business. I asked him about his work and he explained, without my taking much in. His first band, the Greensleeves, changed their name to the Fabulairs and made a successful record—just outside the top-twenty, he said. Lionel was invited over to America by a small independent record company to see if he can effect a similar transformation here. He's very excited, he says: America is the place to be for contemporary music, he claims, just like art. England is filled with pale imitations of American recording stars. I nod, in an interested manner. Lionel played me his Fabulairs hit—pleasant enough melody, jaunty, a catchy chorus. This music does little for me; or put it this way—I enjoy it as much as I would a brass band. *Ganz ordinär*. It's been worthwhile coming to know him better but I'll be pleased to have the place to myself again. He moves into an apartment in the West Village next week.

We've had a few meals out together—we must look an odd couple as we stroll the Upper East Side. He tells me Lottie is well, though I sense he sees little of her. Her two daughters by Leggatt—what are they called?—thrive: one about to finish boarding school, one working on a fashion magazine as a sort of secretary. So life moves on.

We sit in a restaurant and try to chat naturally. Try: I wonder if we can ever know each other well enough so that we no longer have to make an effort, so that our discourse is instinctive and thoughtless. But, I say to myself, why should that ever be? I never experienced such ease with my parents: I didn't expect it and neither did they. Lionel is almost a complete stranger to me as a result of my divorce from Lottie. The fact that he's my son, product of my union with Lottie, seems almost incredible. I have a far closer relationship with Gail. To be honest, I'll be glad to have him out of the apartment—glad, but guilty, of course.

Message from Marcio and Martin—they have significant problems with my first draft. I bet they do—but not as significant as mine. Thankless drudge-work: I sense the Hollywood period of my life has just ended.

1961

SUNDAY, I JANUARY

Saw in the New Year with Janet and Kolokowski. Big, noisy, drunken, depressing party. I popped into Lionel's apartment on Jane Street for a drink beforehand. He thinks he's found his new band—the Cicadas, a folk group, a trio. He wants to rename them the Dead Souls. What, I said, after the Gogol novel? What novel? Gogol's great novel, one of the greatest ever written, *Dead Souls*. You mean there's already a novel called *Dead Souls*? FUCK! He swore and ranted, much to my delight: it was the most animated I'd ever seen him. Look on it as a plus, I said: if you didn't know about it, chances are not many other people will—and those that do will be impressed. I think it's a tremendous name for a pop group, I said. My words elated him and he gave a huge wide smile—and for a poignant instant I saw myself in him, and not Lottie and the Edgefields. I went weak at the knees, feeling a swarming confusion of emotions—relief, then awful guilt, terror and, I suppose, the atavistic stirrings of an almost-love. One of the band members arrived—a sweatered and corduroyed youngster with uncombed hair—and the moment was over. Lionel played me some tape-recordings of the Dead Souls' music and I made the right appreciative noises. He wants to bring me into his world, to share it with me, and I must make every effort to respond. It's the least I can do.

At the party I had a tense argument with Frank [O'Hara]. I must say he's incredibly argumentative these days, quite passionately angry—to the extent that some people are frightened of him. Of course, it was drink-fuelled, like all our disputes. I had said that whenever I was interested in a new artist I always wanted to look at the earliest work of theirs available, even juvenilia. Why's that? Frank said, suspicious. Well, I said, because early talent—precocity, call it what you will—is usually a good guide to later talent. If there's no talent on display in the early work it rather tends to undermine the claims for the later, in my opinion. Bullshit, said Frank, you're so institutionalized. Look at de Kooning, I said: the early work is really impressive. Look at Picasso when he was at art school—astonishing. Even Franz Kline's early stuff is OK—which explains why the later stuff is OK also. Look at Barnett Newman—hopeless. Then look at Pollock—he couldn't draw a cardboard box—which rather explains what happened next, don't you think? Fuck you, Frank railed at me, now Jackson's dead, cunts like you try to cut him down to your size. Nonsense, I said: I expressed the same opinions when Jackson was alive and kicking. He's the redwood tree, Frank said, you're just shrubs and saplings. He gestured at half a dozen startled artists who had gathered round to hear the row.

Met a pretty woman there—Nancy? Janey?—and we exchanged a kiss that promised much at midnight. She gave me her name and phone number but I've lost it. Maybe Janet can track her down. I drank too much and have a sore head and a shivery nervy feel to my body. New Year's resolution: cut down on the booze and the pills.

MONDAY, 27 FEBRUARY

My birthday. No. 55. A card from Lionel and one from Gail. "Happy birthday, dear Logan, and don't tell Mom you got this." I had a vodka and orange juice for breakfast to celebrate, then a couple of slugs of gin mid morning at the office. Liquid lunch at Bemelmans–two Negronis. Opened a bottle of champagne for the staff in the afternoon. Feeling sluggish so took a couple of Dexedrine. Two Martinis before going out to meet Naomi [the woman from the party]. Wine and grappa at Di Santo's. Naomi had a headache so I dropped her at her apartment and didn't stay. So I sit here with a big Scotch and soda, Poulenc on the gramophone, about to take a couple of Nembutal to send me off to the land of nod. Happy birthday, Logan.

MONDAY, 3 JULY

Profoundly shocked by Hemingway's death.* The devastating, sobering, chilling brutality of it. Herman [Keller] said he blew his head off, literally. Both barrels of a shotgun. The room covered in bits of expressed brain, bone and blood. Is that symbolic, or what? All the trouble coming from the brain so disintegrate it. I think of him in Madrid, in '37: his energy and passion, his kindness to me, using his car to find the Mirós. I couldn't read the novels after *For Whom the Bell Tolls*–truly bad work, he had lost his way–but the stories were wonderful and wonderfully inspiring when I first read them. Was that the one moment in his career when he was genuinely blessed? And nothing more after–the Jackson Pollock of American Literature. Herman, who knows someone close to the family, said he was like a little frail grey ghost of a man at the end. Wasted by the shock therapy. Bloody hell: I've been to those dark places myself and know something of the torments that can be suffered. Thank Christ I never had the ECT, though. Of course, Hemingway was a chronic boozer, also–one of those who kept himself topped up all day, just over the edge of inebriation but

*Hemingway committed suicide on 2 July.

not roaring drunk. Look where it landed him. Sixty-one years old—only six years older than me. I feel all insecure and on edge. Called Herman and we agreed to meet. Funnily enough I want to be with another writer at this moment while it all sinks in—another member of the tribe.

[The New York Journal breaks off at this point. LMS made a serious attempt, prompted by Hemingway's death, to cut down on his own intake of alcohol and amphetamines. Always a light sleeper, he continued to use sleeping pills. He stopped drinking liquor and reduced his intake to "under a bottle of wine a day." In the summer of 1961 he took a month's holiday in Europe, spending most of the time with Gloria Scabius, now the Contessa di Cordato, and her elderly husband, Cesare, in their comfortable house near Sienna, La Fucina [the forge], inevitably referred to by Gloria as "La Fuckina." It became something of a home away from home for him: he spent the following Christmas and New Year there and returned again in the summer of '63 for another three weeks.

In the autumn of 1962, Alannah was granted her divorce and she married David Peterman. Gail still sent LMS the occasional card, and contrived to meet whenever she could, but it was made clear by Alannah's lawyer that one of the terms of the divorce was that there was to be no contact between LMS and either of the girls—a stipulation that he always regarded as unnecessarily cruel and spiteful.

The gallery continued to flourish quietly and confidently, LMS building up a substantial but select collection of modern American painters, concentrating on Kline, Elche, Rothko, Chardosian, Baziotes and Motherwell. Martha Heuber remained loyal and Todd Heuber moved from de Nagy's to Leeping Fils in October '62.

LMS's journalism increased also during this period—a reflection of his comparative sobriety, perhaps. He was frequently invited to comment in British newspapers and magazines on American shows that toured Europe. He always rather resented the reputation he acquired as its champion, claiming that his heart always had lain with the classic modernists and the eccentric individualists of the European tradition. Nonetheless, he published important pieces on Larry Rivers, Adolph Gottlieb, Talbot Strand and Helen Frankenthaler in the Observer, Encounter *and the* Sunday Times *colour supplement among others.*

Wallace Douglas secured him a monthly column, "Notes from NYC," in the political-cultural weekly the New Rambler. *The journal resumes in the spring of 1963.]*

1963

FRIDAY, 19 APRIL

To the launch of *revolver*. Ann Ginsberg is funding the whole enterprise by all accounts. Udo [Feuerbach] does it again—though I find it odd that a magazine of the avant-garde arts should take its name from Goering's famous boast.* On second thoughts, perhaps it's rather witty. The old crowd had loyally foregathered—though I think we're all looking a little old and jaded. Frank, puffy-faced and flushed (we promised Ann we wouldn't have an argument), Janet and Kolokowski (what does he do, that man?). One was more aware of the casualty list: Pollock, Tate, Kline. Living this hard in New York takes its toll. As I had promised not to argue with Frank, I argued instead with Herman about the alleged beauty of Mrs. JFK. I said by no stretch of the imagination could she be described as a beautiful woman: a nice woman, yes; a thin woman, granted; a well-dressed woman, indubitably—but beautiful, absolutely not. Herman, who has been in the same room as her, said that being in her presence is like encountering a force field—you're unmanned, stunned. You're just a raving fan, that's all, I said. It's the office that's making you awestruck—the First Lady, and all that—you're not judging, you're feeling. Then I had another argument with Deedee Blaine about Warhol—whom she sees as the Antichrist. At least Warhol can draw, I said: he can do it but he's decided not to—it's quite a different strategy. Naomi broke us up—she thought I was being very provocative.

*"When I hear the word 'Culture' I reach for my revolver."

Ann cornered me later and made me promise to write something. I said I was too old for a magazine as "hip" as *revolver* and she said, "OK, I promise we won't put your age at the bottom of the article." I like Ann—chain-smoking, thin as a stick, voice deeper than mine—and one has to admit she's spread her petrochemical millions around to beneficial effect. She asked me to a French Embassy reception as her escort. I could hardly refuse.

WEDNESDAY, 8 MAY

Lionel calls round full of excitement: the Dead Souls have entered some chart or other at number 68. His beard is no thicker but his hair is over the back of his collar. He has a girlfriend now, he says, a real American girl called Monday.

After he leaves I haul myself into my tuxedo (I'm definitely putting on weight) and wander over to Ann's place on Fifth, whence we limo the few hundred yards to the *soirée*. Ann is greeted like an old friend by the ambassador. I mingle with the other eighty, middle-aged dignitaries sipping champagne under the blazing light of six chandeliers. Very French, such luminosity, I think—like their brasseries: unsparing incandescence. I have a few words with a sweating attaché who seems unnecessarily on edge, continually glancing round to the door. "Ah, les voilà," he says reverentially. I turn round to see the Duke and Duchess of Windsor walk in.

What do I feel? It's nearly twenty years since I was this close to them. The Duke looks old, wizened, very frail—he must be in his seventies.* The Duchess is like a painted figurine under the tremendous lights, her face carved out of chalk, her mouth a livid gash of scarlet lipstick. Neither looks particularly gracious or pleased to be here, but I daresay they can't refuse an official summons from the French—given that the state has let them off paying income tax (a complete scandal, in my opinion).

I circle round and try to find a better position to observe them. The Duke is smoking, asks for a whisky and soda. The Duchess's legs look

*Actually only sixty-nine.

like they'd snap in a frost. She wanders round, greeting people (she seems to know quite a few), the Duke following forlornly in her wake, puffing on his cigarette, nodding and smiling to anyone his gaze lights upon. But his eyes are doleful and rheumy, and his smile is entirely automatic. I stand rigid as they draw near.

It's the Duchess who sees me first and her gash-like mouth freezes in mid-smile. I do nothing. All that stored animosity from 1943 crackles across the room, as potent as ever. She turns to the Duke and whispers to him. When he sees me, the first expression on his face can only be described as fearful, before it shades into a grimace of anger and outrage. They turn their backs on me and talk to the ambassador.

A few moments later the attaché I'd been talking to earlier comes up and requests me to leave the party. I ask why, for God's sake. "Son Altesse" insists on it, he says, otherwise he and the Duchess will leave. Please inform Mrs. Ginsberg I will wait outside, I say.

I spend half an hour pacing up and down Fifth Avenue, smoking. My beat takes me past the door as the Duke and Duchess are leaving. There are a gaggle of photographers and a small crowd of about a dozen people who break into applause as the couple make for their car. I even see some women curtsy.

I can't resist it and shout out: "WHO KILLED SIR HARRY OAKES?" The look of terrified panicked shock on their faces is adequate compensation for me—for everything they did to me, for all time. They can do their worst now. They scramble into their limousine and are swept away. I almost become involved in a fistfight with a portly royalist who calls me scum and a disgrace to America. Warm agreement from the other bystanders. When I explain that I'm English they find it very puzzling. "Traitor," one of them says half-heartedly, as they turn away. "That man conspired to pervert the course of justice," I say to their indifferent backs.

Ann Ginsberg is most amused when I explain what went on. What a funny old life you've led, Logan, she says.

THURSDAY, 11 JULY

La Fucina. A perfect Fucina day. Just the three of us—though we don't
see much of Cesare this year. He's very old and very rigid in his habits,
writing his memoirs in his room all day, only joining us for drinks and
dinner. The house is rambling and airily comfortable with well-placed
sun terraces, set in its own olive and citrus groves at the end of a gentle
valley, facing west, its back to Sienna. I have a room in a separate little
guest annexe and walk across the courtyard for breakfast, at which I am
always the first to arrive. Gloria comes down when she hears me being
served by Cesare's manservant and factotum, Enzo. She wears jeans,
her hair tied back in a scarf, a man's shirt knotted at the waist. She's
more ample now but carries the extra pounds with her usual careless
flair. "I've been up for hours, darling," she says, and I pretend to
believe it. She smokes a cigarette and watches me eat—always poached
eggs on toast, which is as close as Enzo can come to an English breakfast.

Today we went to Sienna for lunch and sat in a café on the Campo
drinking Frascati. Funnily enough the tourists don't bother me—the
square is vast enough for them not to impinge on its beauties. I wandered around and went to the cathedral while Gloria picked up a
gramophone that was being repaired. Then back to La Fucina after a
plate of pasta and a salad. Gloria took her dogs off for a walk—they
have four—and I lay in a hammock and read and dozed. *Très détendu*.

She's still very sexy, Gloria, at least to my old eyes. The other
evening she came down in a cotton sweater and I could see from the
hang and sway of her breasts that she wasn't wearing a bra. After dinner, when Cesare went up to bed and she was standing by the gramophone leafing through her LPs, I went up behind her, encircled her
waist with my arms and nuzzled her neck. "Mmm, lovely," she said.
Then I moved my hands up to her breasts. "No, no, no," she said. "Bad
Logan." "Not even a boff *de nostalgie*?" I said. She put her records down
and kissed me smack on the lips. "Not even that."

The trouble is that when we're alone at the pool she takes her top
off while she sunbathes. Delicious torment for me, eyeing her over my
book. Maybe that's why I've come to love this place—the atmosphere

always spicily redolent of Gloria and our sexual history. I think she likes knowing I'm sitting there, aching with frustration. She had the latest news of Peter. The Cuban Missile Crisis sent *Already Too Late* to the top of bestseller lists around the world. "He does love it when critics describe him as prescient," Gloria said. "He's been to Vietnam twice."

Tonight Cesare joined us for dinner, perfect in blazer and white cotton trousers. He moves very slowly, stiffly, leaning on a cane. Gloria teases him, much to his delight: "Here he is, silly old count."

I'm writing this on the terrace of my little guest house. Moths batter at the bulbs set into the rough stone walls and the geckos eat their fill. Crickets beep, toads croak in the darkness beyond the yellow rim of light. I carried over a big glass filled with ice cubes and whisky. I always sleep well here—no need for my pills.

SATURDAY, 12 OCTOBER

New York. Dinner at Bistro la Buffa with Lionel and Monday. Jack Finar was dining with Philip Guston and Sam M. Goodforth at another table, but I avoided his eye. I won't be popular in the Finar household when he reads my piece in next month's *revolver*. I detest his new stuff. It's always strange when a perfectly competent painter deliberately starts to paint badly. Only the very best can get away with it (Picasso). In Finar's case it looks like a desperate attempt to be fashionable.

Monday turns out to be a dark, strapping girl, of Italian or Hispanic extraction, I would say, with olivey skin, a small, slightly, delightfully, hooked nose (maybe she's Jewish?) and a pointed chin. Lots of thick curly unwashed hair. She looks like she could eat Lionel for breakfast. She used to go out with Dave, the lead singer in the Dead Souls, but has switched her attentions to Leo, the manager. The transfer is an amicable one: indeed the whole group is currently staying at Lionel's apartment, to economize. They haven't managed to repeat the success of their debut single, "American Lion" (number 37 was as high as it climbed in the charts). Lionel and Monday somehow manage to hold hands the entire evening. I ask Monday what her surname is and she says she hasn't got one. What was it before you abandoned it, I insist. Oh, all right then, "Smith." And I'm Logan Brown, I say.

I walked them home and Lionel asked me up to meet the band. Two of them were there, one whom I'd met before, and three girls, all about Monday's age. Half a dozen mattresses with coloured blankets made up most of the furniture. For the first time in my life I felt a sense of ease and relief about Lionel; he'd broken away from the world of Lottie and the Edgefields and he'd found a place where he could be himself. I felt a pang of envy too, as I walked the streets looking for a cab, imagining them all getting ready for bed. No doubt they just fucked when they felt like it—no big deal. Suddenly feeling old.

1964

THURSDAY, 30 JANUARY

One of my rare clandestine meetings with Gail. As she's grown older* her features have sharpened rather, and I can see the Alannah in her more clearly. Her hair is long now like everyone else's, it seems, but her sweet nature is unchanged. She makes all the arrangements for our meetings in a hushed voice over the phone: "Meet me in the diner at the corner of Madison and 79th. I can stay an hour." We sit at the rear (I have my back to the door) and she smokes a cigarette as we drink coffee. She's good at art and she wants to go to art school, but Alannah and Peterman won't hear of it. "It's too bad you and Mom got divorced," she said with almost adult bitterness. "You're a much more interesting kind of stepfather. Even Arlene (she rolls her eyes) thinks so." She lists my virtues: English, works in the art world, knows all the groovy artists, has lived all over the place, has written novels, has been in prison. Even I begin to think what a tremendous fellow I am. I tell

*Gail was seventeen in 1964.

her I can still help her out if she ever needs it. Then I make a little declaration to her that brings a lump to my throat as I say it, taking her hand. We were a family for years, I say. I love you girls and I've watched you grow up. Nothing can change that. The fact that me and your mum couldn't make a go of it has nothing to do with you and me and how we feel about each other. I'm here for you, darling, I say, whenever you want me—always, forever. I can see the tears welling in her eyes and so I change the subject and for some reason ask her where she was when JFK was shot. At school, she says, in a math class. The principal came in and broke the news. Everyone started to cry, even the boys too. Where were you? I'd been on the phone to Ben in Paris. He must have had sight of a television because suddenly he said: "Jesus Christ, somebody's shot your president." I said, "Yeah, yeah, very funny, Ben." Then I heard Helma scream in the gallery and I knew it was real.

THURSDAY, 27 FEBRUARY

Fifty-eight. Good God. I don't think I'll bother making another of these annual assessments—too depressing.

Health: fair. No more teeth out. Haven't had a Dexedrine for months. Drinking more under control. I ration myself to one cocktail at lunch but I probably still drink too much in the evening. Smoking: one pack a day if I don't go out. Somewhat overweight, bit of a belly. Hair receding, greying. Still recognizably the LMS of old, unlike, say, Ben Leeping, now a fat old man, quite bald.

Sex life: adequate. Naomi Mitchell [a curator at the Museum of Modern Art] my current girlfriend. Respectful, tolerant affair—could be more fun. We date once or twice a week when our schedules permit.

Soul: a bit depressed. For some reason I'm worrying more about my future. I can stay on here in New York indefinitely, running Leeping Fils for as long as I want or am able. My salary is good, my apartment comfortable. My journalistic output and influence is gratifyingly high. I move in an interesting, sophisticated crowd; I travel to Europe whenever I wish; I own a small flat in London. So what are you complaining about? I think . . . I never really expected my life to be like this, somehow. What happened to those youthful dreams and ambitions? What happened to those vital, fascinating books I was going to write?

I believe my generation was cursed by the war, that "great adventure" (for those of us who survived unmaimed) right bang slap in the middle of our lives—our prime. It lasted so long and it split our lives in two—irrevocably "Before" or "After." When I think of myself in 1939 and then think of the man I had become in 1946, shattered by my awful tragedy . . . How could I carry on as if nothing had happened? Perhaps, under these circumstances, I haven't done so badly after all. I've kept the LMS show on the road—and there is still time for *Octet*.

[JUNE]

Lionel is dead. There, I can write the words down. A stupid meaningless accident. No one to blame but himself. It happened like this.

Monday called me at about 6:00 one morning, wailing, sobbing, screaming down the phone: Leo's been sick and he won't wake up, he's not moving. I told her to call a doctor and jumped in a cab and raced downtown. The doctor was already there when I arrived and he told me Lionel was dead. He had drowned, in his own vomit.*

Monday and he had had a fight and she'd gone out to see the band play at a club somewhere in Brooklyn. Lionel had taken speed and been drinking before she left and there was an empty bottle of gin and several empty cans of beer in the kitchen. Completely drunk, he had passed out on one of the mattresses on the floor, his head wedged awkwardly—effectively in a booze and amphetamine coma. And when his body rebelled and he had vomited, his unconscious state and the fixed angle of his head had—well he drowned. His lungs filled up with the expelled fluid from his stomach, and he drowned. Poor stupid boy. Poor sad Lionel.

I called Lottie. She screamed. Then she said in a tight grating voice—and I'll never, never, forgive her for this—she said, "You bastard. It's all your fault."

There was a crowd of forty or so at the funeral, nearly all people I

*Lionel Leggatt died on 28 May 1964.

didn't know, and it was touching to see, gathered together, Lionel's small world. Lottie sent a wreath. I gravitated towards Monday and we had a good weep together. She said it was her birthday—she was nineteen—and that was what they had been fighting about. She wanted to go to Lake Tahoe to celebrate—he wanted to go to New Orleans. She said she couldn't stay in the apartment anymore so I said she could use my spare room. She's been here ever since and I think it's helped us both. She takes Lionel's copy of *The Villa by the Lake* everywhere ("He loved that book, Logan") like a talisman.

[JULY]

I've decided not to go back to London and Italy this summer. I'm deliberately engrossing myself in my work: buying wisely, I think—a few Pop Art pieces but mainly picking up a lot of good second-generation Abstract Expressionism as the fashion changes and the patrons and the collectors go racing after Warhol, Dine, Tazzi, Oldenburg and the rest.

Monday has a job in a café in the Village and we both set out for work simultaneously. She has her own keys, comes and goes as she likes. She's home most nights, I have to say. I like her presence in the house—a warm uncomplicated girl. We watch TV, we send out for Chinese or a pizza, we talk about Leo. She's introduced me to the subtle pleasures of marijuana and I've practically abandoned barbiturates and sleeping pills. John Francis Byrne approves. When I go out myself in the evening—to a show opening or a dinner party—Monday waits up for me. I rather wish I'd kept on Mystic House but we're happy enough in the hot city. I receive many invitations for the weekends but I don't think I could really turn up at the Heubers or Ann Ginsberg with Monday in tow—I just tell them I'm busy writing.

[AUGUST]

Problems. I woke at 6:00 this morning and went into the kitchen to make some coffee. Monday was standing by the open fridge, hair tousled, bleary with sleep, naked. She picked out a carton of orange juice and wandered past me back to the room, saying, "Hi, Logan," completely unconcerned.

Unfortunately it's not an unconcern I can pretend to. Maybe living communally as she did, with Lionel and the band and their girlfriends, casual nudity was the order of the day. But as far as I'm concerned it's as if a switch has been thrown and I'm suddenly very aware I'm sharing my apartment with a pretty nineteen-year-old girl. Images of her body fill my head. I find the whole atmosphere in the apartment completely changed—it's charged, now, sexually electric. Sweet suffering Christ, Mountstuart, she could be your granddaughter. Yes, but I'm flesh and blood, blood and flesh. This evening I sat watching her covertly as she moved about the living room, picking up a magazine, sipping at her iced tea. It was hot and she wandered over to the air conditioner to be closer to the flow of cool air. She was talking to me about some obnoxious customer she'd had that day—I wasn't listening, I was looking. As she talked, she gathered her tresses of hair in both hands behind her head, twisted it into a thick hank and spiralled it on to her crown, exposing her moist nape, the better to let the chill reach her. As she collected up her hair I could see her breasts rise beneath her T-shirt. I felt thick-tongued, dry-throated, unbalanced by a desire that was so straightforward and unequivocal it took my breath away. I wanted her, wanted her strong young body beneath me—or on top of me, or next to me.

So at supper this evening I took pre-emptive action. I said I had to go to London and Paris on business and that I'd be away for six weeks or so and that, perhaps, she might find it more congenial to move in with friends while I was away. "What about the apartment?" she said, surprised. "Your things? The plants?" I'll get the agency back in, I said. (I had cancelled my contract with the cleaning agency after Monday moved in. Why?) "No, no," she said. "I'll look after the place for you. I'd like to." She licked a spot of ketchup off her thumb. These natural gestures are intolerably hard to bear now. Fine, I said. Great. As long as you won't feel lonely. As long as you're happy.

FRIDAY, 21 AUGUST

It happened last night. It had to. It was inevitable and wonderful. We'd both drunk a lot. I was standing in the kitchen and she came up behind me, put her arms around me and laid her head on my back. I thought my spine would snap. She put on a "hurt" voice: "I'm gonna miss you, Logan." I turned round. You'd have to have been made of stone. You'd have to have been a eunuch to have restrained yourself in that situation. We kissed. We went into my bedroom and took our clothes off and made love. We smoked some of her pot. We made love again. We woke in the morning, made love, had breakfast. Now she's gone to work and I'm writing this down. She said she's been wanting to do it virtually since she'd arrived. She thought it would make her closer to Leo, in some way. Jesus. But she could see I wasn't interested, and she respected that, happy to be friends. Then everything changed, she said, suddenly she was aware that I wanted her too and that it was only a matter of time. It was that switch-throwing moment in the kitchen. When it's mutual, a man and a woman know, instinctively, wordlessly. They may do nothing about it, but the knowledge of that shared desire is out there in the world—as obvious as neon, saying: I want you, I want you, I want you.

TUESDAY, 25 AUGUST

Crossing Park Avenue, on my way to work, my head full of Monday, I looked to my left and saw the hypodermic syringe of the Chrysler Building flare, hit by the morning sun—a silver art-deco spaceship about to blast off. Is this my favourite view in Manhattan?

THURSDAY, 27 AUGUST

6:30 p.m. I am coming home from work, walking down my street with my briefcase, when I see a man in a seersucker suit, hands on hips, staring up at my building. Can I help you? I ask. He has a saggy, folded face with a heavy blue beard needing a shave. Yeah, he says. Is there a Laura Schmidt in this building? I shake my head and say there's no one of that name here—and I know all my neighbours. Thanks, he says, and wanders away. Now I know Monday's real name. "Monday Smith" is Laura Schmidt. I decide to save the information for later.

SATURDAY, 29 AUGUST

And this is how it has developed. I was a fool to be so unconcerned. Yesterday, Monday and I leave for work together as usual. Seersucker is across the road waiting with another man in a straw hat. Monday sees them and starts to run, like a hare, heading for Lexington Avenue. Straw-hat shouts: "Laura, honey! Wait!" and they take off after her. I intercept, arms spread, hemming them in. Hey! What the hell's going on here? By now Laura/Monday is round the corner, they'll never catch her. Straw-hat yells at me: "You scum! You obscene filth! You pervert! That's my daughter." So what? I say. "She's sixteen years old, that's so what, you disgusting piece of shit." I step back. No no no, I say, she told me she was nineteen. We celebrated her nineteenth birthday. "We're calling the cops," Seersucker hisses at me. "You English loser." LOSER! He shouts once more, and then the two of them walk away.

I go back to the apartment and try to calm down. Jesus fucking Christ. She looks twenty-five, not even nineteen—let alone sixteen. How could I at my age, at my distance, tell if a nineteen-year-old was really sixteen? Even Lionel couldn't tell. These girls, these young women grow up so fast. Look at Gail—I'd say she was in her early twenties. But all this justification and special pleading is after the event. I call Jerry Schubert and explain the situation. He listens. It's not looking good, Logan, he says soberly. The age of consent in New York State is seventeen. Consensual or not, they could get you on third-degree rape. Rape? What should I do, Jerry, I say. I swear to you she told me she was nineteen—she looks older than nineteen. He says nothing. What should I do? You never heard this from me, he says, but if I were you I'd get out of town—fast.

And I do. I'm sitting here in sweltering air conditioner–less London, England, in the front room of my flat in Turpentine Lane.

I hung up the phone. I packed my essential bits and pieces in three suitcases. I threw out all the food in the fridge. I put the plants on the fire escape and called a taxi. I went by the gallery and dropped off my keys, saying I had to make a sudden trip to Europe. I was driven to Idlewild* and bought a ticket to London, TWA. I phoned Monday's café to leave a message. Amazingly, she was there. They'll come looking for you, I said: if they know where you live they'll know where you work. I don't care, she said. I told her what I was doing, gave her my address and telephone number in London and begged her to go back to her family until she was seventeen. Where are you from? I asked. Alameda, she said. Where's that? Little place just outside San Francisco. Go home to Alameda, I said, write to me, tell me when you're really seventeen. She was crying. I love you, Logan, she said. I love you too, I said, the lie slipping oh-so-easily off my tongue.

*Renamed John F. Kennedy Airport on 24 December 1963.

THE AFRICAN JOURNAL

Logan Mountstuart spent the next few months in London trying to sort out, at a distance, the settling of his affairs in New York. Letters were written to friends; Helma packed up his apartment under his instructions, sold his furniture, crated up his possessions and had them shipped to London. Bank accounts were closed; bills paid and so on. No warrant was issued for his arrest, as far as he was aware, and there were no further rumblings of scandal or potential arraignment. Helma did say that, the Monday after he left, two gentlemen called round at the gallery looking for him but were told he had gone to Europe. He met Ben Leeping in Paris and recounted what had transpired. Ben was—typically—understanding, told him not to worry and swiftly set about trying to find a replacement to run the New York gallery. LMS sold Leeping Frères his private collection of paintings and drawings to provide some initial cash flow. He wrote to Naomi Mitchell and said he had suddenly been called back to London and received a reply of civilized regret. LMS's heart was not broken and, clearly, neither was hers. All seemed to be more or less under control. But LMS was not relaxed or fully at ease, constantly expecting the long arm of U.S. law to reach out across the Atlantic and pluck him thither. Thus it was, in the spring of 1965, that he applied for the post of lecturer in the Department of English Literature at the University College of Ikiri in Nigeria. He was interviewed in London and was duly offered the job. His friends thought he was crazy, but he said he needed a change in his life. Apart from Ben Leeping, Jerry Schubert and the Schmidt family no one ever knew the real reason for his precipitate flight from New York. He left for Nigeria on 30 July 1965. The African Journal begins in 1969.

1969

SUNDAY, 20 JULY

David Gascoyne* once told me that the only point of keeping a journal was to concentrate on the personal, the diurnal minutiae, and forget the great and significant events in the world at large. The newspapers cover all that, anyway, he said. We don't want to know that "Hitler invaded Poland"—we're more curious about what you had for breakfast. Unless you happened to be there, of course, when Hitler invaded Poland and your breakfast was interrupted. It's a point, I suppose, but I felt it would be worth picking up this journal again today if only because I've just walked out into my African garden and looked up at the moon. Looked up at the moon to marvel at the fact that there are two young American men walking around on its surface. Even Gascoyne would grant me that.

It was a clear night and we had copious moonshine. The familiar old moon hung up there with a fuzzy corona around it, albescent in the soft black sky. I walked out into the garden away from the ring of light cast by my house and headed for the stand of casuarina pines at the end of the drive where the ground sloped up. A wind blew through the branches and set the huge trees whispering. I stamped my feet, suddenly remembering the risk of snakes and scorpions, and looked up, marvelling.

I had been listening to the news on the BBC World Service, crackly

*David Gascoyne (1916–2001), poet and translator.

with the usual interference, and for the first time in my life wished I had a television set. Perhaps I should have gone next door to Kwaku's.* But in the end I prefer my imagination.

It was strange—vertiginous—staring upwards and thinking about those men on the moon. I felt sad and oddly humbled. Sad, because if there was ever an example, to someone of my age, of life's galloping headlong progress, then this must be it. When I was born the first home-made wood and canvas flying machines had only been taking to the air for four years. And now I was standing in this African garden sixty-seven years after the Wright Brothers, looking up at our moon and wondering what it must be like to be up there looking back. Humbling also to think that we poor, forked creatures could manage such a feat. These observations are banal, I know—but are no less true for that. Still, they probably exemplify Gascoyne's law about journal-keeping. Momentous events do lose something in the telling. Tonight I had a cheese omelette and a bottle of beer for supper.

I came back into the house and locked the door and have written this down sitting at my desk in the main room. Through the mosquito netting in the window I can see the glow of Samson's cigarette in the garage entry [Samson Ike, LMS's nightwatchman]. All's quiet, all's well with the world. Back to London at the end of next week, my first visit home in two and a half years. I suppose all legal worries can safely recede now. The Laura Schmidt affair must be over and done with, finally. I must be safe.

FRIDAY, 25 JULY

Turpentine Lane. A garage has opened at the end of the road since I was last here and music blasts from its forecourt as the young mechanics panel-beat and poke around inside their clapped-out motor cars. I have to keep the front windows closed against the noise even though this is proving to be a hot and irritable summer. A Sikh family has moved in above me—charming and helpful people—but they have

*Dr. Kwaku Okafor, LMS's next-door neighbour.

three young children who appear to do nothing but run to and fro through the rooms above my head. I long for my big African house with its shady veranda and its two-acre garden.

I'm having Turpentine Lane painted and am laying carpet over my rubberized-cork floor tiles. Apart from my Picasso above the fireplace the place still maintains its bare and functional atmosphere. But despite the hazards of city noise and city disturbance I do feel at home here. Was the purchase of this mean little flat the smartest thing I've done in my ramshackle life? At night I read in my armchair and listen to music. Over the weeks of my leave I'll visit the few old friends I have left—Ben, Roderick, Noel, Wallace—settle bits of unfinished business. I'm relatively well off at the moment—I manage to save a fair bit of my U.C. Ikiri salary—but I am conscious, all of a sudden, of my dwindling supply of assets. Wallace has set up a meeting with the editor of a new current affairs/economics weekly called *Polity* (unfortunate name, but sententious enough). They need someone to write about Biafra and the war.*

MONDAY, 4 AUGUST

Wallace tells me he is retiring at the end of the year—he'll be sixty-five. Good God. The agency will continue to bear his name—and he's going to remain loosely attached as some sort of consultant figure—but it's going to be run by a young woman called Sheila Adrar. I met her: she's in her mid-thirties with a slightly fake, busy, bustly manner. And an unnecessarily firm handshake, I thought. Thin, skull-like face. Wallace did his best to booster me—"old, old friend," "part of that great generation" and so on—but it was obvious she hadn't a clue who I was and hardly rated me as an asset to the firm. I related my suspicions about all this to Wallace at lunch and he wriggled and squirmed a bit but had to concede I was right. "It's all changed, Logan," he said. "All they're interested in is sales and advances." In that case nothing's changed, I

---

*The Nigerian Civil War—the Biafran war—had begun in 1967 when the eastern states of Nigeria unilaterally seceded from the republic, taking most of Nigeria's oil reserves with them.

said: it's always been about sales and advances. Ah, said Wallace, but in the past publishers pretended it wasn't. Anyway, Wallace brokered a good deal for me at *Polity:* £250 retainer and £50 per 2,000 word article, rates to be adjusted proportionally.

The editor was a bearded ex-don, a Scot, who looked a bit like D. H. Lawrence, called Napier Forsyth. Somewhat dogmatic and humourless, I thought at first, though he warmed up when I told him he reminded me of DHL and mentioned that we'd met a couple of times. DHL's beard was more gingery, I said, and he couldn't hold his liquor. I think that's what's landed me the job, in fact: Forsyth couldn't believe he was hiring someone who'd actually met Lawrence. For good measure I told him I'd met just about everyone—Joyce, Wells, Bennett, Woolf, Huxley, Hemingway, Waugh. As the names tripped off my tongue I could see his eyes widening and I felt more and more like a museum piece, someone to be pointed out in the *Polity* offices—"See that old fellow over there? He knew . . ." Forsyth had great hopes for the magazine: good backing, good writers, a world in turmoil that needed to be explained sanely and rationally. I applauded his zeal—the zeal of new editors of new magazines the world over. As long as the cheques don't bounce.

THURSDAY, 21 AUGUST

La Fucina. With Cesare and Enzo* gone, one understands the limits of Gloria's housekeeping talents. The garden is overgrown and the dogs have the run of the house. Everything looks battered, scratched and chewed. Gloria suddenly seems old, her face pasty and lined, her body racked by a loose bronchial cough that seems to start at her ankles. I made the mistake of walking into the kitchen and walked right out again. Every surface was smeared with grease and matt with dirt; enamel tins of dog food all over the floor.

Still, to sit in the cool shade of a terrace playing backgammon, drinking Camparis with the Tuscan sun beating down outside, always soothes the spirit. Two lady friends of Gloria are also staying—visitors

*Cesare di Cordato died in 1965, aged seventy-seven.

from the Isle of Lesbos, I would say, but amusing company for all that. Margot Tranmere (fifties) and Sammie (?) Petrie-Jones (sixties). They have a house in Umbria and live comfortably, I would guess, on a handsome Petrie-Jones trust fund. They smoke and drink enough to make me feel abstemious. Sammie claims to have read *The Girl Factory*. ("Disappointing: I was expecting something completely different.")

One evening when they'd gone to bed Gloria said to me: maybe I should turn lesbo, what do you think? I practically dropped my glass in astonishment. You? I said. It's not something you acquire, like a new hat, you have to have a predisposition for it. But I like the idea of a strapping young gel to look after me when I'm old and decrepit, she said. So do I, I concurred, remarking that she—Gloria—was burdened by the fact that she was possibly the most heterosexual person I'd ever met. I was alarmed to see tears shine in her eyes. But I've only managed to marry a swine and then a doddering aristo, she said. Well, look at me, I said, beginning to list my misfortunes. Who gives a shit about you? she said. You'll be fine, you always have been. It's me I'm worried about.

SUNDAY, 14 SEPTEMBER

Ikiri. Term well under way. Gave my third lecture on "The English Novel"—Jane Austen (preceded by Defoe and Sterne). Happy to be back in Africa, happy to be in my home, 3 Danfodio Road. The campus is generous in size and laid out with care, with some thought for grand vistas. There's a main gate, then a wide palm-lined boulevard leading to the group of buildings clustered round a tall clock tower. Here you find the admin. centre, the refectory, the junior common room, the theatre. The style is modern-functional—white walls, red-tiled roofs. Four halls of residence line the main boulevard—three male, one female—and radiating out from this main axis are leafy roads leading to the university department buildings—humanities, law, education, science—and the houses of the senior staff. There is a club house with a bar and a restaurant, three tennis courts and a swimming pool. And on the fringes of the campus lie the villages of the junior staff (for which, read "servants"). It is a well-tended, well-managed, slightly artificial world. If you want something more exotic, more real, more Nigerian, you have to drive three miles into Ikiri, or risk the death-trap road to Ibadan, an hour away, where there are other clubs, casinos, cinemas, department stores and some excellent Lebanese and Syrian restaurants—plus all the *louche* diversions of an African city.

My house is a low, two-bedroom bungalow set in the middle of a mature garden ringed by a six-foot poinsettia hedge. Casuarina pines, cotton trees, avocado pear, guava, frangipani and papaya flourish indecently, like weeds. The house has maroon concrete floors and a long veranda screened against mosquitos. I have a cook—Simeon—a houseboy—Isaac, his brother—a gardener—Godspeed—and a nightwatchman—Samson.

When I arrived back from Lagos Airport I was late. We had been stopped three or four times at military roadblocks on the way and the car had been searched. All four of them were waiting for me, anxiously. "You family welcomes you, sar," Simeon said, as I shook their hands. He was pleased to see me. He was worried that the war might have prevented me from returning.

THURSDAY, 25 SEPTEMBER

Posted off my first piece for *Polity;* an article that tries to analyze and explain why a war that theoretically should have ended in September 1967 with the capture of Enugu, the Biafran capital, is still going ferociously on, two years later. Napier wants something from me every fortnight, he says, which is just about do-able. Cheques are paid to the agency, which banks them in my London account.

To the golf club in Ikiri this afternoon with Dr. Kwaku. We play nine holes and Kwaku wins, three and two. He works the course with more intelligence than I do, firing low skittering iron shots into the "browns" (tar mixed with sand, the truest putting surface in golf). Afterwards we sit on the terrace of the club house and drink Star Beer— big cold green bottles, misty with condensation. Pondering my article, I ask him why he thinks the war is still going on. He says that if you have a rebel army fighting for its life faced with another army that doesn't want to fight—and, moreover, that can only be persuaded to go

through the motions fuelled by free beer and cigarettes—then, by definition, you are going to have very protracted hostilities. He shrugs:
which side has nothing left to lose?

The day is hazy and overcast. The sun, as it sets, is a fuzzy orange
ball above the rain forest. Bats begin to swoop and jink above our
heads. Dr. Kwaku is in his forties with a wide strong face, balding. He's
a Ghanaian, he says, don't ask him to explain Nigerians.

[OCTOBER]

I miss New York more than I would have imagined. I miss those perfect
spring days. Wraiths of steam rising from the manhole vents backlit by
slanting early-morning sun. Cross streets thick with cherry trees in
bloom. The way time seems to slow to a crawl in diners and coffee
shops. There was a coffee shop near the gallery on Madison where I
used to go: I think they had a policy of hiring very old men with hardening arteries to be their waiters. These men moved with a particular
slow, rolling gait and spoke very quietly. All hurry ceased, a curious
calm pervaded this place—time moved at their behest, not vice versa.

All these thoughts of my U.S. years were prompted by a trip to
Ibadan with Polly [McMasters]* to see Shirley MacLaine in *Sweet Charity*. We went to a Syrian restaurant afterwards and ate lamb with raisins
and spices. When I dropped her back at her house she asked me in for
a nightcap and I knew—you always know—that more was on offer. I said
no thanks, gave her a peck on the cheek and went home to Danfodio
Road.

Polly is an overweight, blowzy woman in her forties. Never married,
bright (M. Litt. on Restoration playwrights) and perhaps my closest
friend out here. We are united in our loathing of the Desiccated
Coconut† but I don't want to have an affair with her. However, it
makes me realize that the last time I had sex with anyone was with
Monday in August 1964. The memory is fresh but somehow I'm not

---

*A colleague in the English Literature Department.
†The nickname of the entirely bald Professor of English at Ikiri, Prof. Donald
Camrose.

missing it. Getting old? There is the wife of a man in the French Department whom I covet rather. A tall solemn Moroccan or Tunisian woman whom I see at the club with her young kids. She's a regular on the tennis courts and plays a fierce, concentrated game. She comes into the club afterwards, her shirt soaked with sweat, the material semi-transparent, revealing her brassiere beneath. I've yet to meet her but she's begun to acknowledge my smile with one of her own. You old goat.

Isaac has gone on a two-week holiday back to the east. His parents live in a village near Ikot-Ekpene, an area that has seen a lot of fighting. News came back that the village had been liberated by the Federal Army and he wants to see if the family home is still standing. Most of the damage is done by indiscriminate bombing rather than artillery, and it is the Nigerian Air Force rather than the army that seems to draw the civilians' ire. The air force has a couple of squadrons of Russian MiG-15s piloted by East German and Egyptian mercenaries. I saw a row of them parked at Lagos Airport when I came back; tubby olive-drab planes with a gaping intake at the front like an open mouth. The joke going around is that the pilots have been told that legitimate targets can be identified by the red crosses painted on them. Hospitals were the air force's prime target but now the Biafrans have painted over their red crosses attention has been turned to markets also very easy to identify from the air. Incidentally, all this was the subject of my last *Polity* article. It created something of a stir, according to Napier, and he wants me to go down to Lagos to receive full accreditation from the Ministry of Information.

[NOVEMBER]

Lagos. Press briefing at the Ministry of Information. A smart young captain with an Oxbridge accent blamed this year's exceptionally rainy rainy season for the Nigerian Army's lack of progress. A Polish journalist told me that a Super Constellation flies into Biafra every night packed with weapons and ammunition. They call it the Grey Ghost, and its deliveries are keeping Biafra alive as the heartland slowly shrinks. In fact the Biafran Army has never been better armed and supplied and now there's so little territory left to defend the troops are highly concentrated. When he was asked about starving women and children, the young captain denied there was any malnutrition—all Biafran propaganda, he claimed.

I spend the night at the airport hotel, the Ikeja Arms—I'll fly back to Ibadan tomorrow. I like this old hotel with its big dark bar filled with off duty aircrew and stewardesses. They provide that little hint of raffishness that the transient always brings to watering holes like this. Add to this a tropical night, copious alcohol, a nation involved in a civil war—I almost expect Hemingway to walk in.

FRIDAY, 14 NOVEMBER

A distraught Simeon came to see me and said that he'd received news from home that Isaac had been taken by a Biafran Army recruiting patrol. They are drafting anyone they find into the army—they're not fussy. "Anyone with a penis will do," Simeon said. These men are given a few days' basic training and are then sent to the front. He asked permission for leave to try to find him: I told him he could take my car.

Later. Change of plan. I'm going with him. I was taking the 1100* down to the garage to fill it up with petrol for Simeon when the idea came to me. Here was my chance for a *Polity* scoop. So I filled up and stuffed three extra jerry cans in the boot. Then I went to the bank and drew out 200 Nigerian pounds and returned home to tell Simeon the new plan. I painted PRESS on the windscreen of the car in whitewash and bought a small Nigerian flag that I fitted to the radio aerial. We set off tomorrow, before dawn. We'll drive on back roads to Benin and then head down the Niger River delta to Port Harcourt and then circle round as close to Ikot-Ekpene as we can reach. I calculate it's about a 400-mile drive, all told—about two days on Nigerian roads. In Nigeria time and distance have a different relation to each other than else-

---

*LMS had bought his predecessor's car when he arrived in 1965—an Austin 1100.

where. For example, it's about a hundred miles from Ikiri to Lagos but one allows four hours for the journey: a dry-mouthed, hyper-cautious, nerve-racking drive on the most dangerous highway in the world.

SATURDAY, 15 NOVEMBER

Benin. Hotel Ambassador-Continental. Benin was captured by the Biafrans in 1967 on their blitzkrieg drive west in the early days of the war, the only time they managed to seize great swathes of Nigerian territory. I remember the panic even reached the university: Dr. Kwaku had a slit trench dug in his garden just in case of air raids. The incursion didn't last long but the Biafran Army at one stage was only a hundred miles from Lagos.

In the bar of the hotel I watch news footage on Nigerian TV. Federal forces occupy a Biafran village. Big men with guns—bigger in their uniforms—push around tiny skinny men in tattered vests and shorts.

The drive here was pretty uneventful and we were only stopped at one roadblock. I showed my accreditation papers, my pass and said "Press" to the young soldier leaning through the window. He said, "BBC?" I nodded and we were waved through. Clearly the magic word. I don't think *"Polity"* would have the same ring.

Simeon explained to me that he was against the war because he's not an Ibo. He refers to it as "the Ibo war." He is an Ibibio—they speak a different language from the Ibos. So too do the Efiks and the Ijaws, the Ogoni, Annang and many other tribes all subsumed under "Biafra" by the dominant Ibos. They don't want to be part of Biafra, Simeon said. They don't want to be the wives to the Ibo husband.

Simeon is sleeping in the car and I have a room on the third floor overlooking an empty swimming pool. The hotel is busy, full of different nationalities, and most of them aren't soldiers—Russian engineers, Italian contractors, Lebanese businessmen, British "advisors." I asked a burly-looking Englishman about reaching the front and he said there was no front line, just a series of roads heading for Biafra with soldiers on them. When you could hear gunfire or the soldiers wouldn't let you proceed further you could assume you had reached the front.

I had some chicken and rice in the dining room and returned to the bar for a final beer. There were a few drunk Federal Army officers with their girlfriends. I took a sleeping pill and went to bed.

SUNDAY, 16 NOVEMBER

We came through Warri and skirted Port Harcourt. A lot of military traffic on the road and also the bizarre sight of an ocean-going yacht on board a tank transporter—some brigadier's loot, I suspect, going back to the marina at Lagos. Following Simeon's directions we left the main road at Elele and headed vaguely eastwards. At Benin we had been told that Ikot-Ekpene had been recaptured by the Biafrans and that the front was now on the Aba–Owerri road. Simeon said that if we could reach Aba he would make his own way to the village by bush path. We had one tricky experience at a lonely roadblock where young soldiers, beer heavy on their breath, ordered us out of the car, waving their guns theatrically. I gave them some money and cigarettes, which calmed them down, and they told us that the other journalists were at the Roundabout Hotel near a town called Manjo, just south of Aba. We arrived at the Roundabout Hotel at four in the afternoon. When I stepped out of the car I could hear the distant thud and mumble of artillery somewhere to the north. Simeon slipped off his clothes, down to a pair of shorts, and said he would leave straight away. I gave him some cash and he set off up a bush path jauntily enough, I thought. I think he was pleased to be doing something—and this was home to him, after all. I told him I'd wait for three days, if possible, then I'd have to head back.

I checked into the Roundabout and was provided with a mean, insect-infested room of unpainted concrete. The single bed has grey nylon sheets and the electricity is very erratic. The hotel sits to one side of a half-finished roundabout, hence its evocative name. One metalled road comes into this roundabout and the same one leaves. Other junctions that would have given the roundabout a real function have yet to be created. Not far off is a supply depot for the troops who are either retaking—or consolidating their hold on—Ikot-Ekpene. The bar of the hotel, occupying most of the ground floor, is lit with purple and green fluorescent lights and is populated most hours of the day by a dozen or so bored prostitutes with afro hair and very short skirts. From time to time one of these girls will haul herself to her feet, shuffle over and listlessly proposition you. It's hot in the bar, most of the roof fans don't work, but the beer is slightly chilled.

At about 8 o'clock this evening, a jeep pulled up and deposited the two other journalists. One was the Pole I'd met in Lagos—Zygmunt Skarga—and the other was a lean, twitchy Englishman with long blond hair and mirror glasses. He was obviously put out to see me there and immediately asked if I was working for *The Times*. When I said *Polity*, he seemed to relax—"Good mag," he said. His name is Charles Scully. We drank some beer and talked. Scully has been inside Biafra and seems to have a disciple's reverence for Ojukwu.* Zygmunt was more circumspect. He made the point that it's all very well to secede but if you're going to take 95 per cent of the nation's oil with you there's bound to be a fight. Scully became quite heated at this point—Nigeria was a false nation created by Victorian surveyors drawing arbitrary lines on a map; Biafra had tribal and ethnic integrity that justified its claim for independence. Here I threw in Simeon's point about the other tribes not wanting to be the wives to the Ibo husband. This made Scully considerably more riled and he asked me, quite insultingly, just how long I'd been in Nigeria. When I said four years his belligerent tone modified somewhat—he'd been in the country for six weeks.

MONDAY, 17 NOVEMBER

I went with Zygmunt this morning to interview Colonel "Jack" Okoli, the self-styled "Black Lion" of the Nigerian Army, who was leading the assault up the Aba–Owerri road. He was a handsome, fit-looking man with a thin matinée idol's moustache who never removed his sunglasses. He wore two automatic pistols on his belt and suede knee boots and possessed the massive self-assurance of all military commanders on the brink of victory. I asked him if Ikot-Ekpene was under his control. "My boys are mopping up," he said. He was full of talk about the "chaps," the "fellows," the "guys." Zygmunt told me that

*The Biafran leader, an Ibo.

Okoli had shipped back enough consumer goods to fill a fair-sized department store. Colonel Jack predicted the war would be over by Christmas. I wonder how many military men have made that boast through the ages.

Listless afternoon at the Roundabout Hotel sitting under the ceiling fan that worked, drinking beer and watching army vehicles negotiate the redundant roundabout. I spoke to a young prostitute whose name was Matilda. She suggested we go upstairs to my room. I said it was too hot and I was an old man. She told me she could provide me with a potion that would make me hard like a stick. I gave her a pound and bought her a Fanta. I asked her what would happen when the war was over. "Nothing," she said. "Everything will be as it was before."

Scully told me that inside Biafra "Harold Wilson"* was a curse, a swear word. He had heard a dying child muttering something familiar and had gone over to her to hear what was being said. She was mumbling "Harold Wilson Harold Wilson Harold Wilson" again and again. She died with his name on her lips, Scully said, adding: can you imagine having that on your conscience? He had written personally to Wilson to let him know how hated he was. Not even Hitler achieved the status of being a swear word, Scully said. I was about to say you couldn't equate Harold Wilson with Adolf Hitler but it was too hot for an argument. Scully is violently opposed to the U.K. government's support for Nigeria, so much so that he's writing a book about the war and Britain's role, to be called *Partners in Genocide*. I wished him luck, I said, speaking as a fellow author. He was patently amazed to learn that I was a published novelist. "I even knew Hemingway," I threw in, to see if it would have any effect but he wasn't impressed. That fraud, said Scully. He asked me if I'd ever met Camus. Alas, no, I had to say.

Zygmunt said he was going up to the front with Okoli tomorrow and we were welcome to come, but Scully said he was returning to Lagos. He says he's going to Abidjan in the Ivory Coast and is going to hitch a ride on one of the supply planes that fly into Biafra each night. You should come along, Mountstuart, he said, give you some decent material for your next novel. I begged off, said I was waiting for a friend to arrive.

*Harold Wilson was the then–Prime Minister of Great Britain.

TUESDAY, 18 NOVEMBER

Zygmunt and I rode in Okoli's jeep up the Aba–Owerri road. Colonel Jack was wearing a bush jacket and a beret with a scarlet cockade, and still resolutely sunglassed. We stopped at a battery of guns and watched them firing into the bush. Then we drove on past columns of troops plodding north up the road. We came to a village, which seemed deserted, but Colonel Jack sent his men in to flush out what remained of the population, mainly women and children. They seemed very nervous and ill at ease, standing with heads bowed as Colonel Jack lambasted the black devil Ojukwu and congratulated them on being liberated by the Nigerian Army. He pushed a young girl forward towards me and Zygmunt. She had a baby on her hip, big-bellied and moon-eyed, a dozen flies grazing on the snot that ran freely from its nose. She speaks English, Colonel Jack said. Zygmunt asked her if she was pleased that the Biafran Army had been expelled from her village. "Something must be done," she said, "to keep Nigeria one."

We lunched with Colonel Jack under an awning he had had erected by the side of the road. Folding garden furniture was set out and we ate curried beef and yam, washed down with Johnnie Walker whisky. Colonel Jack had been at Sandhurst and quizzed me about parts of London he had known, casinos and defunct nightclubs he had patronized as a cadet. He asked me if I had ever been in the army and I said, no, the navy, the Royal Navy Volunteer Reserve—in the Second World War. "What rank?" he asked. I told him and he referred to me as "Commander" from then on.

After lunch we motored on up a laterite road until we came upon two Saracen armoured vehicles and about a hundred soldiers sitting on the verges, all with bits of vegetation sticking out of their helmets and intertwined with their webbing. This was the furthest point of the Federal Army's northward advance on the southern front, Colonel Jack said. Then he conferred some way off with a captain, who was accompanied by two machete-wielding civilians, after which he threw a temper tantrum for our benefit, bellowing at his men, calling them bloody damn fools, terrified women, insects who deserved to be doused with pesticide. The Saracens started up, the men rose wearily to their feet and the column moved off up the road towards the rebel heartland once again.

Colonel Jack told us that the civilians had reported that all Biafran resistance in this sector had collapsed because Ojukwu himself had ordered the execution of four local men on the charge of cannibalism. "He accused them of eating Biafran soldiers," Colonel Jack said. "What kind of bloody fool idiot is this man?" The offence to the local tribe was huge, incalculable, and all logistical support in the locality had ceased immediately—no food, no water, no guides for the meandering bush paths. The local tribespeople were now actively helping the Federal Army.

"And so this is how a war is won," Colonel Jack said as we drove back to the Roundabout Hotel. "A question of making a wrong insult at the wrong time. We've advanced twelve miles today." He clapped me on the shoulder: he was very pleased. "I tell you, Commander, I will be Brigadier Jack before Christmas."

Matilda has just knocked on my door; "Hello, sar. Love is calling." I've given her another pound and told her to buy herself another Fanta in the bar. No word from Simeon. I wonder how long I should stay.

WEDNESDAY, 19 NOVEMBER

Spent the morning typing up my piece for *Polity,* called "A Day at the War with Colonel Jack." Quite pleased with it. Zygmunt left for the northern front at Nsukka. He thinks it'll be easier to infiltrate Biafra from there—he wants to meet Ojukwu before the war is over.

I lunched on fried plantain and a genuinely cold bottle of Star Beer—quite delicious.

This afternoon three Nigerian Air Force MiGs came over, very low. Matilda gestured contemptuously at them. "You see," she said, "they no be frighten now."

Later. Simeon came back this afternoon. His parents' house has been looted, cleared out of everything, but is still standing. His family continues to hide in the bush, however, very mistrustful of both armies.

No sign of Isaac, but Simeon seemed unperturbed. The bush was full of deserters from the Biafran Army, he told me, and Isaac would be with them somewhere, safe and well. He was oddly exhilarated, so I suppose we can say the mission is sort of accomplished. We head back to U.C. Ikiri tomorrow. Matilda wants a lift to Benin: she's sick of the meagre returns offered by the Roundabout Hotel.

1970

SATURDAY, 17 JANUARY

Isaac is back from the war. I came out to breakfast on the veranda and there he was, beaming in his khaki shorts and white T-shirt. He was thinner, his head was shaved, but apparently none the worse for his experiences. He had in fact only managed to desert a week before the war ended as he was part of a contingent of troops guarding the airstrip at Uli, where the relief flights came in. As the Federal Army drew ever closer he was deployed on the perimeter, given a hand grenade and five rounds of ammunition (as a guard he was provided with just a single round). Once in the bush he had slipped off his uniform, thrown away his gun and had headed south, homewards.

The war ended so quickly, he said, because a spiritualist leader was executed for "vicarious murder" (Isaac's words). All the Biafran commanders relied totally on advice from spiritualists and so-called prophets—no military order or instruction was issued without the approval of the spiritualists—and when the leader of this sect was executed officers on the southern front simply refused to fight. The exhausted Biafran soldiers, seeing their officers so demoralized, just drifted away, leaving their positions unmanned. The Nigerian Army marched in singing, rifles slung. Another good day for Colonel Jack, no doubt.

FRIDAY, 27 FEBRUARY

Sixty-four. My birthday passed in total and gratifying anonymity. It was marred only by the Desiccated Coconut who, at the departmental meeting, reminded everyone that I would be leaving at the end of the next academic year and that a new lecturer would be needed for the English Novel course. "Dear Logan is retiring, alas. We are losing our Oxford man." There were mutters of commiseration and congratulation. Polly glanced at me, a little shocked: I don't think she had me down as an almost-old-age-pensioner. I don't look too bad, I must say—I suit my sun tan and I only drink beer these days—well, most of the time—which has sleekened me and thickened my waistline.

I played our usual nine holes with Kwaku this afternoon and told him I was obliged to leave next year and wondered vaguely if there was the likelihood of any other job being available to me out here. Candidly, he thought it would be almost impossible—you'd lose your house, he said, you'd get a quarter of your salary. You'd have to go to Ibadan, at least, if not Lagos.

For some reason I don't want to leave Africa—I've come to like my life here—and Britain and Europe seem strangely hostile, now. But I can see that the prospects of employment for a 65-year-old Englishman with a third-class degree from Oxford must be poor. So back to London it shall be, I suppose, back to Turpentine Lane—see what kind of living I can scrape with my pen.

[JULY]

After a swim at the club pool I wandered back to Danfodio Road, feeling the sun hot upon my bare head. I opened a bottle of Star Beer and sat on the veranda, drinking. Then I went out into my garden and wandered around its perimeter touching the trees with the palms of my hand—the casuarinas, the guava, the cotton tree, the avocado, the frangipani—as if this last touch, this fleeting caress, was a way of saying goodbye to them, my trees, my African life. My ears were filled with the metallic static of the cicadas and the faint breeze raised the smell of dust from the bleached grass. I rested my forehead against the trunk of a papaya and closed my eyes. Then I heard Godspeed, my gardener, saying in anxious tones, "Sar—you go be all right?" No, I wanted to say: I go fear I never go be all right never again.

THE SECOND LONDON JOURNAL

Logan Mountstuart returned to London at the end of the summer term in July 1971 and took up residence once again in Turpentine Lane, Pimlico. He only had his old-age pension and his savings to sustain him financially (his few years' contribution to the U.C. Ikiri pension plan was too short-lived to provide anything more than a pittance) so he applied himself to his former profession of freelance writer with diligence if not enthusiasm. Polity, *his main source of income, folded in 1972, and Sheila Adrar at Wallace Douglas Ltd. was unsuccessful (or dilatory) in securing any advance from a publisher for the long-nurtured novel* Octet. *Udo Feuerbach retained him as London correspondent for* revolver *and Ben Leeping, ailing now from prostate cancer, paid him for occasional consultancy work for Leeping Frères. Slowly but surely, over the next few years, LMS became ever more impecunious. The Second London Journal opens in the spring of 1975.*

1975

WEDNESDAY, 23 APRIL

I sacked that bitch Adrar today. I went into the agency to photocopy a few magazine articles I needed for research on *Octet*. First of all, the girl on reception refused to believe I was a client of the firm–then she found my file somewhere. I said that Wallace Douglas himself had given me permission to use the office facilities whenever I pleased. Anyway, there I was, photocopying away, but quite aware of the whispered confusion and semi-panic in the office: who is that old man in the pinstriped suit? What does he think he's doing? Should we call the police? Eventually, Sheila Adrar herself appeared, looking very well coiffed and prosperous in a blue suit with a short skirt. "Logan," she said with the widest and falsest smile, "how wonderful to see you." Then she offered to help, gathering up the loose leaves of paper and checking the counter on the machine. Sixty-two copies, she said, at twopence a copy, that'll be £1.64. Most amusing, Sheila, I said, and took the copies from her and made my way to the door. I'd like the money please, Logan, she said, this is not a charity. Well, I just blew up. How dare you? I said. Have you any idea how much money I've made for this firm? And you have the nerve to charge me for a few copies. Shame on you. You've made nothing for this firm since the Second World War, she said. Right! I shouted, that's it. You're fucking sacked, the whole useless lot of you! I'm taking my business elsewhere–and I strode out.

I went into a pub to calm myself down and found my hands were shaking–with sheer rage, not embarrassment, I hasten to add. I'll call Wallace in the morning and explain what happened. Perhaps he can recommend someone new.

Pleased to have taken up this journal again even if its purpose is more sinister. I fear it will become a documentation of one writer's decline; a commentary on the London literary scene from the point of view of a superannuated scribbler. These final acts in a writer's life usually go unrecorded because the reality is too shaming, too sad, too banal. But, on the contrary, it seems to me to be even more important now, after everything that has gone before, to set down the facts as I experience them. No country house, here; no honour-heaped twilight years, no proper respect from a grateful nation or recompense from a profession I've served for decades. When some insincere bloodsucker like Adrar dares to claim £1.64 off someone like me then I look at it as a genuine watershed—not because of her temerity, but because I actually couldn't afford to pay her. £1.64, judiciously spent, can provide me with food for three days. This is the level to which I have descended.

So here is the reckoning. Assets: I own my basement flat in Turpentine Lane, Pimlico. I own its furnishings. I possess about a thousand books, some increasingly threadbare clothes, a watch, cufflinks, etc. Income: my published books are all out of print, thus income from royalties is nil. I have the standard old-age pension provided by the state with an insignificant addition of almost £3 a week from my U.C. Ikiri pension fund. Freelance work: very erratic.

Expenditure: rates, gas, electricity, water, telephone, food, clothing, transport. I have no car—I travel by bus or tube. I have no television (hire and licence fee too expensive—I listen to the radio and play my gramophone records). My only indulgences, the luxuries in my life, are alcohol and cigarettes and the occasional visit to a cinema or pub. I read newspapers that I find discarded on buses and tube trains.

My head is just kept above water by occasional journalism and consultancy work for Leeping Frères. Last year I earned approximately £650. So far this year I've written a long piece on Rothko (£50), reviewed a book on Bloomsbury (£25) and assessed a private collection of pictures for Ben (£200).

I eat frugal meals of corned beef (the culinary leitmotif in my life), baked beans and potatoes. A tin of condensed soup, well diluted, can be eked out to four or five servings. A tea bag, properly utilized, can make three cups of weakish tea. And so on. Thank God I had a good tailor. My last set of suits from Byrne & Milner will endure many more years with careful maintenance. Underwear, socks and shirts are rare purchases. I wash my clothes by hand and dry them in front of the gas fire in winter or on a rack set out in the basement well in the summer. Foreign travel is out of the question unless wholly subsidized by others. For example, Gloria asked me to La Fucina for "as long as I liked" this summer. I told her I couldn't afford the fare and since she didn't offer to pay I assume she's similarly strapped for cash herself.

I still drink—cider, beer and the cheapest wine—and I have taken to rolling my own cigarettes.

In the day I go to a public library to continue my research on *Octet* or to write my rare articles. I type them up at home in the evening. Then I listen to the radio or gramophone records and read. I might go to my local pub, the Cornwallis, for a half pint of bitter two or three times a week. I have my health, I am independent, I owe no money. I am—just—surviving. This is the life of an elderly man of letters, here in London, in 1975.

[NOTE IN RETROSPECT. 1982. I never noted it at the time but, during these years when I was truly on my uppers, I used occasionally to recall what Mr. Schmidt had screamed at me that morning in New York when Monday/Laura had made her dash for freedom. LOSER! You English loser . . . I suppose he thought it was the most grievous insult he could hurl. But such a curse doesn't really have any effect on an English person—or a European—it seems to me. We know we're all going to lose in the end so it is deprived of any force as a slur. But not in the U.S.A. Perhaps this is the great difference between the two worlds, this concept of Loserdom. In the New World it is the ultimate mark of shame—in the Old it prompts only a wry sympathy. I wonder what Titus Fitch would have to say.]

WEDNESDAY, 7 MAY

To the Travellers' Club for lunch with Peter [Scabius]. I buy a new shirt from a market stall (price 80 pence) and with my dark blue suit and my RNVR tie I think I pass muster. Put some oil on my hair and comb it flat. My shoes still look suspect—a little busted—even after a vigorous polish, but I think I look pretty smart.

Peter has become portly, flushed, with many tedious complaints: his blood pressure, his ghastly children, the unmitigated boredom of life in the Channel Islands. I say: what's the point of having all this money if the money forces you to live somewhere you dislike? He rebukes me: I don't understand—his accountants are immovable. I take the opportunity to eat heartily—three bread rolls with my mulligatawny soup, three veg. with my roast lamb, then apple crumble and cream and a wedge of Wensleydale from the cheese board. Peter is currently banned from drinking (incipient diabetes, he thinks) so I enjoy a half bottle of claret and a large port on my own. He sees me to the door and I notice he's limping. For the first time in our encounter he asks me a question about myself: what're you up to, Logan? Working on a novel, I say. Marvellous, marvellous, he replies vaguely, then asks me if I still read novels. He confesses he can't get on with novels, these days, he only reads newspapers and magazines. I tell him I'm re-reading Smollett, just to make him feel bad, then step out into Pall Mall and flag down a taxi. We shake hands, promise to stay in touch. I climb into the taxi and as soon as it's turned the corner into the Mall I order it to stop and get out. Sixty-five pence for three hundred yards, but worth every penny not to let the side down.

SUNDAY, 8 JUNE

Walked to Battersea Park yesterday and sat in the sun reading a newspaper. I see inflation is running at 25 per cent in Britain, so I shall have to do a quarter more work just to maintain my feeble status quo. Napier Forsyth dropped me a line to say he was now working for the *Economist*. Perhaps there'll be something for me there.

Then I wandered the streets to Melville Road—which was a huge mistake—but I was thinking about Freya and Stella and our walks in the park. Whatever happened to our dog? What was its name?* It shocked me that I couldn't remember its name. Perhaps it was killed in the v-2 blast also. Now I come to think of it, Freya would probably have taken the dog to meet Stella from school.

When I came home I sat for an hour staring at their photographs. Couldn't stop crying. Those were the years when I was truly happy. Knowing that is both a blessing and a curse. It's good to acknowledge that you found true happiness in your life—in that sense your life has

*Tommy.

not been wasted. But to admit that you will never be happy like that again is hard. Stella would be thirty-six by now, married perhaps, with her own children. Grandchildren for me. Or not. Who knows how anyone's life will go? So, fond speculation is fruitless.

I drank a bottle of cider, wanting to be drunk and succeeding. Headache this morning. Mouth rank from my foul roll-ups. Silly old fool.

FRIDAY, I AUGUST

One of those intolerable hot London summer days when the tar under your feet seems to soften and melt. Even I was forced to abandon my usual jacket and tie and found a lurid tie-dye shirt from Ikiri days. I went down to the Cornwallis for a gin and tonic at lunch time, having typed up my review for the *Economist* (Napier's done me proud—I review any type of art book for them: £30 a go). The pub was quiet and clean, every surface freshly wiped, waiting for the lunch-time rush. I sat by the open doorway to catch the breeze, the glass clinking cold in my hand, and heard the following conversation that took place between a middle-aged man and woman sitting on a bench outside.

WOMAN: How are you?
MAN: Not very well.
WOMAN: What's wrong?
MAN: My health. I've got a dodgy heart. And cancer. What you might call both barrels.
WOMAN: Oh, poor you.
MAN: How's John?
WOMAN: He's dead.
MAN: Cancer?
WOMAN: No, he committed suicide.
MAN: Jesus Christ.
WOMAN: Excuse me, it's just too depressing.

She stands up and comes into the pub, goes to sit in a corner on her own.

1976

THURSDAY, 1 JANUARY

Saw in the New Year with a quart of whisky ("Clan McScot") and two tins of Carlsberg Special Brew. I don't think I've been so drunk since university. I feel bad today, my old body trying to cope with the toxins I've poured into it. I face the year ahead in a spirit of—what?—stubborn indifference. It seems to me extraordinary and incredible that, just a short while ago, I had a household of four servants. Simeon sent me a Christmas card wishing me good health, joy and prosperity, and hoped I was writing many fine books. Joy and prosperity seem out of reach so perhaps I should concentrate on maintaining such health as I have, that way I might just finish the one book I have left in me.

I have a piece to write for the *Spectator* on Paul Klee. (To think I used to own a Paul Klee. What life was that?) For some reason the *Spectator*'s rate has dropped to a measly £10.

One of the things I miss most about Africa is my golf on the scrubby Ikiri course with Dr. Kwaku. I miss the golf and our beer on the clubhouse stoop watching the sun sink. What is it I like about golf? It's not strenuous, which is an advantage. I think its great benefit as a sport is that, however much of a hacker you are, it is still possible to play a golf shot that is the equal of the best golfer in the world. I remember one day I had taken a scrappy seven at the par four eighth hole at Ikiri and lined up for the short ninth, a par three, with a six-iron. Feeling hot, sweaty and out of sorts, I swung, struck, the ball soared, bounced once on the brown and dropped in the hole. A hole in one. It was the perfect shot—couldn't be bettered, even by the world's champion golfer. I can't think of any other ball game that allows the amateur duffer a chance at perfection. It made me happy for a year, that shot, every time I recalled it. Makes me happy now.

SUNDAY, 15 FEBRUARY

Strange and plaintive telephone call from Gloria, asking if she can come and stay for a few days. I said, of course—adding the usual warnings: lack of comfort, no TV, dark basement flat in insalubrious area, etc. I said, why do you want to come to London in February? She said, ominously, that she needed to see a doctor.

As far as I know Gloria has a brother who lives in Toronto, a niece in Scarborough and that's it. Well, what are old friends for?

I forgot to say that I woke last Friday with a foreign object in my mouth and spat it out on to the pillow—it was one of my teeth. Possibly one of the most unpleasant waking experiences of my life. At the local dentist, however, the man gave me the all clear. Everything else looks more or less fine, he said, and commented on the impressive crowning and bridgework my mouth boasted. Must have cost a fortune, he said wistfully. Thank you, excellent American dentists of New York. I have an irrational fear of losing my teeth—actually it's not irrational, it's highly rational. But assuming I live long enough it's probably inevitable. Somebody told me (who?) that both Waugh and T. S. Eliot lost the will to live when they had their teeth extracted and were presented with a set of snappers. Is this a writer's problem? A feeling that when we lose our bite we might as well throw in the towel?

FRIDAY, 27 FEBRUARY

Gloria arrived yesterday and I have given her my room—though I have to say I'm too old to sleep comfortably on a sofa. She looks awful: gaunt and yellow, her face shrunken, her hands trembling. I asked her what was wrong and she said she didn't know but was sure it was something major. Her hair is dry and thin, her skin mottled and slack like an ancient lizard's. She thinks it may be a problem with her liver ("Why else would I be this peculiar colour?") but she complains of aches in her spine and hips as well. She's also very short of breath.

None the less, we were pleased to see each other and drank the best part of the bottle of gin she'd brought as a present. I cooked up some spaghetti with sauce out of a can. She hardly touched her food, though, wanting to drink and smoke and talk. I told her about my last encounter with Peter and we laughed and coughed at each other. She has sold La Fucina and is having the funds transferred. "I got nothing for it," she said. "Pennies—after I paid the tax and the debts." I asked her where she was planning to stay and she said, "I was rather planning to stay with you, Logan, darling. Just until the doctor's had a look and we know the prognosis." I'm going to take her to my clinic on Lupus Street.

I am seventy years old today.

TUESDAY, 9 MARCH

Gloria back from hospital. She wouldn't let me come and visit her, or pick her up, for some reason. I heard a taxi dropping her off and ran out to help her in. She'd been shopping and had bought champagne, some foie gras, a plum cake. She wouldn't tell me what had happened at the hospital or what any of her doctors had said.

So tonight we opened the champagne and ate foie gras on toast and she told me she had inoperable lung cancer. "Riddled with it, I suspect," she said. "But they couldn't tell me why my back was aching so— at least not at the moment." She asked if she could stay on with me: she didn't want to end up in a cancer ward or a hospice. I said of course she could but warned her I was very poor, and that what comfort I could offer her would be determined by that fact. She said she had £800 in the bank and I should think of it as mine. "Let's have a high old time of it, Logan," she said with a grin, as if we were schoolchildren planning a midnight feast. I thought that even £800 wouldn't go very far and she must have noticed the look in my eye. She nodded at the double portrait over the mantelpiece. "Perhaps it's time to cash in Pablo's legacy," she said.

WEDNESDAY, 10 MARCH

I called Ben in Paris this morning and asked him how he was. "Ailing but surviving," he said. I welcomed him to the club. Then I told him about the Picasso sketch and he offered me £3,000 there and then, sight unseen.

I took the drawing out of the frame and cut it in two, scissoring off my portrait. On my half it only had my name written, "Logan"—the rest of the dedicatory sentence and the crucial signature being on Gloria's half, which reads "A mon ami et mon amie Gloria. Amitiés, Picasso" and the date. Our respective portions are no bigger than postcards and, without a signature, of course my portrait is worthless, but it's a memento all the same and I'm happy for poor Gloria to be the beneficiary of that lunch in Cannes all those long years ago.

FRIDAY, 19 MARCH

Could be a day in winter. Low slate-grey clouds and a gusty east wind bringing showers of sleet in from the North Sea. Gloria is well established in my bedroom—gramophone, gin, books and magazines. We eat and drink like exiled royalty. A private nurse comes by every day to help Gloria bathe and change (paid for by the Picasso bequest) and the health visitor comes in from time to time to check on her progress and top up her medicaments. Gloria is having no radiation treatment or any of the new "blunderbuss" drug therapies available. She feigns jollity and devil-may-care and says she doesn't give a hoot as long as she feels no pain. "I won't be a bore, darling," she said. "And I won't have you slopping out for me or wiping my bottom and all the rest of it. As long as we can afford the nurses it'll be just like having some cantankerous old friend to stay." So I follow my routine, go out to the library, continue my work and come back in the early evening. Gloria is quite happy to be on her own during the day and can more or less look after herself but she likes company at night, so I sit in with her, read her bits out of the newspaper, listen to music and drink. I am usually fairly drunk by 10 o'clock and Gloria begins to nod and doze. I take the glass from her hand, rearrange the blankets and quilt and tiptoe out of the room.

I sleep badly on the sofa, imagining the cancer cells multiplying next door and trying not to think of the Gloria Ness-Smith I once knew. I wake up early in the mornings and shave and wash immediately so the bathroom's clear. I pray that the nurse will come before she wakes— before I hear her terrified cry of "Logan!" as consciousness returns and she realizes the state she's in. The fear always strikes first thing in the morning, before she's put her mask of hey-ho resignation on.

When the nurse arrives I go out for the day's provisions—often to Harrods Food Hall to find some exotic sweetmeat Gloria fancies ("What about kumquats, today? Candied chestnuts?"). I have an account with an off-licence and they deliver all our booze. A case of gin seems to last a week. If I stay at home we start on the wine before lunch and hit the hard stuff as night falls and the soul buckles at the knees. I asked her if she wanted me to make contact with Peter but she said "no" immediately, so I left it at that.

I don't think back; I don't think forward. I've made no plans for Gloria's death—which is what we're both waiting for—in fact I don't remotely know what the form is in these cases. No doubt I shall learn. In the meantime the here and now is enough to preoccupy me.

SUNDAY, 4 APRIL

Gloria has reached that stage of wastage and emaciation where her features look borrowed: eyes too big for their sockets, teeth too large for their mouth, someone else's enormous nose and ears. Her lips are always wet and shiny and she's now lost her appetite. She can manage half a poached egg or a soft-centred chocolate but her world is hushed and blurry from the morphine cocktail she sips and it's all she can do to focus on me for a minute or two. She makes a huge effort—I sense she doesn't want to feel she's drifting away. I read her the newspaper in the mornings now and she concentrates massively: "Why is Ted Heath such a dog-in-the-manger? What is a 'punk,' exactly?"

We have about £1,200 left from our legacy—enough for another month or so, I calculate—at any rate our drinks bill has plummeted and I am more or less sober again.

A doctor visits regularly from the Lupus Street clinic, a different one each day—there must be dozens of them—and I asked the latest for a prognosis. It could be tomorrow, it could be next year, he said, citing some astonishing examples of people who should have died clinging on instead to this half-life for months. Thank God for opium, I say. The nurses deal with Gloria's bodily functions—I have no idea what transpires.

I sit and read to her, my eyes glancing at the pulsing, cursive vein that bulges on her temple, unconsciously timing my own inhalations and exhalations to its awkward, thready beat. Gloria's clock winding down.

TUESDAY, 6 APRIL

4:35 p.m. Gloria has gone. I went into her room two minutes ago and she was dead. Still lying in exactly the same position she had adopted half an hour previously, her head back, her nostrils flared, lips tightly parted to show her teeth. Her eyes were closed, but, half an hour ago she seemed to squeeze my hand gently when I took hers.

But now her knees were somewhat drawn up, as if the effort of that last search for the last breath had required the whole frail body to do the work. I reached under the sheet and took hold of her ankles and pulled them towards me. Her legs straightened as supply as if she were alive. Why was I so solicitous towards Gloria, I ask myself? Because I liked her; because we had been lovers and had shared part of our lives. Because she was my friend. Also because, having done this for Gloria, I see it as a due gladly paid and I think—wishfully—that therefore someone will be there for me too. Absurd, delusional musings, I know. You can't make these deals with life, there is no *quid pro quo*.

SATURDAY, 10 APRIL

Putney Vale Crematorium on a cold April day must be one of the most lugubrious and depressing places in the country. An absurd Victorian chapel doubles ingeniously as a crematorium set in the middle of a huge, rambling, untidy necropolis. Around the chapel loom dark yew trees, like giant hooded monks, conferring more gloom on an already gloomy scene.

Peter came and a surprising number of strangers also—old colleagues of Gloria, obscure relatives. Peter asked me where she had died. At my flat, I said. *Your* flat? All his old suspicious antagonism reddened his face. Then he collected himself: very good of you, old chap, he said.

He became more voluble and questioning back at his hotel, curious to discover why his ex-wife had died in his oldest friend's basement flat. He asked me if I had really liked Gloria. Of course, I said: she was marvellous company—very funny, very blunt, wonderfully rude.

"You see, I think I never really knew her," he said in a puzzled voice.

"You married her, for God's sake."

"Yes. But I think that was more of a sort of sex-intoxication thing. Never known anyone like Gloria for, you know, getting me going."

We ordered some sandwiches from room service and continued our attack on the whisky bottle. I noticed the waiter called him "Mr. Portman." What's wrong with Scabius, I asked?

"I'm not meant to be here—my accountant would have a heart attack if he knew I was in London."

"Ah, tax. Very good of you to come back. Gloria would have been very touched. No, seriously."

"The very fucking devil, these taxes. I'm thinking about Ireland. Apparently you pay no income tax if you're a writer. But then there's the risk of the IRA."

"I don't think you'd be an IRA target, Peter."

"You're joking. Anyone with a profile like mine's got to be at risk."

"Wonderful houses in Ireland," I said. It wasn't worth it.

"Why don't *you* go?" he said. "How can you live here with these taxes? You work two months for yourself, ten for the taxman."

"I live very simply, Peter. Very simply."

"So do I, dammit. I'm going to regret this whisky. If my doctor saw me drinking this he'd wash his hands of me . . . How's Ben keeping?"

"Cancer. Prostate—but he seems to be winning."

This news depressed him and he started to list his own complaints—hardening arteries, angina, increasing deafness. We're falling apart, Logan, he kept saying, we're pathetic old wrecks.

I let him rant on. I don't *feel* old, although I must confess the signs of ageing are everywhere. My legs have grown thinner as the muscles shrink—and they're practically hairless; my buttocks are disappearing, the seat of my pants loose and empty. One funny thing: my cock and balls seem slacker, lower-slung, hanging freer between my legs. And they look bigger too, as they do when you've just stepped out of a hot bath. Is this normal or is it just me?

I forgot to say in the midst of all this Gloria sadness that I had been left a property in France in the will of a Monsieur Cyprien Dieudonné.* For one mad moment I thought it might have been Cyprien's own chartreuse in Quercy but looking more closely at the address and after consulting my atlas I see the house is in the Lot, a *maison de maître* outside a village called Sainte-Sabine. So I've written back saying, sell it. Gloria too has left me everything she owns, which amounts to £900 in her current account (thank you, Pablo), two suitcases of clothes and the contents of a storage container in a warehouse in Sienna. What am I meant to do with that? What I need is a benefactor of real substance.

[On Monday, 7 June, at 11:30 a.m. as LMS was crossing Lupus Street, SW1, he was hit by a speeding post office van and badly injured. He was rushed by ambulance to St. Thomas's Hospital for emergency surgery. His spleen had ruptured, his skull was fractured and his left leg was completely broken in three places, not to mention serious bruising and abrasions on his body.

After his operation (he had metal pins inserted in his leg) he was moved to St. Botolph's Hospital in Peckham and installed in Ward C. The journal resumes some four weeks after the accident.]

*Cyprien Dieudonné had died in 1974, aged eighty-seven.

MONDAY, 5 JULY

One of the old ladies who comes round the ward with puzzle-books and sewing-kits has procured me a Biro and writing pad and so finally I am able to log my impressions of this infernal place. Swiss roll and lumpy custard for the third time this week. I'm sorry, but Swiss roll is not a pudding; Swiss roll is a cake. Someone in the catering department is raking off money that should be going to provide proper puddings. Completely typical of this place—built in the nineteenth century and still redolent of that century's values and practices. For example Ward C is vast, a huge high-ceilinged room like a village hall or a school chapel, and was purpose-built as a ward with tall thin windows on three sides to let in as much "healing" sunlight as possible. There are thirty beds in here, twice as many as ever intended, and the nursing staff is overstretched, harassed and very short-tempered. I spent two weeks marooned in a middle aisle before Paula—the only nurse I like—managed to have me moved to a corner. So now I only have one neighbour—though the current occupant, an old wino, leaves much to be desired. These warm sunny July days make the ward cook up like a greenhouse. At mid-afternoon we are lying gasping on our beds, running with sweat, those with the energy or power fling back the bed-clothes and fan ourselves with magazines and newspapers. I won't dwell on the noxious marshy odours that rise up from the exposed sheets. It has provided a small glimpse into the physical conditions of the Victorian age: when you come to think of it everyone must have been intolerably hot in summer—clothes were thicker, people wore many more layers of them, it was considered impolite to remove a jacket. The stench of body odour from both men and women must have been overpowering. Then factor in all the horse manure on the street . . . Nineteenth-century London must have stunk like a cesspit.

My left leg is enclosed up to the hip in plaster, rendering me more or less immobile. I piss in a bottle and if I want to shit I have to summon a nurse. I refuse to use a bedpan so they have to wheelchair me to the lavatory. There I park myself on the seat and do my business. There are no doors on the stalls. The nurses hate me for not using a bedpan.

The only vaguely pleasurable consequence of my plastered leg is that I have to have a sponge bath. This is done brusquely and efficiently but for two minutes I return to infancy again—arms are lifted and armpits laved, a cool sponge ducks around my genitals, I lean forward and my back is swabbed. A no-nonsense towelling and a dusting of talcum powder finish off the procedure. If that milkcow Sister Frost heaved out a breast for me to suckle, then the picture would be complete.

The food is disgusting, condemnable—the worst I've eaten since my schooldays at Abbey. We are provided with every institutional horror imaginable—mince with watery mash and tinned veg.; a fish pie with no fish; curried eggs; jammy, doughy dumplings with lumpy custard. You have to eat it—especially me, stuck here in my bed. Once a day someone pushes round a trolley and you can buy biscuits and chocolate bars for extra sustenance. It is a truly terrible diet—everyone complains of constipation.

Paula is the only nurse I like because she calls me Mr. Mountstuart. I thanked her and asked her for her surname. "Premoli," she said. Right, Miss Premoli it shall be, I said, but she asked me to call her Paula in case the other nurses thought it odd. Interesting surname, I observed, and she told me she was from Malta. But you've red hair, I said, unthinkingly. And you've got grey hair, she replied: how funny is that?

[NOTE IN RETROSPECT. My memories of the accident itself were very incomplete and disjointed. I had always noted, since my return to London, that post office vans were invariably driven helter-skelter as if the drivers were in danger of missing some crucial deadline or appointment. The one that hit me must have been doing 60 or 70 mph. But it was entirely my fault: my mind was on something else—I simply didn't look—and I stepped out into the road with as much pre-emptive caution as if I were crossing my kitchen floor. Apparently I was flung some fifteen yards by the impact. I remember nothing of the actual crash itself and experienced no pain. I woke up some two days later in St. Thomas's, wondering where the hell I was and what I was doing. I was very lucky to be alive, I was told. Someone from the post office's cus-

tomer relations department sent me a bunch of wilting gladioli
"wishing me a speedy recovery." Unfortunate choice of adjective, I
remember thinking at the time.]

[AUGUST–SEPTEMBER]

OBSERVATIONS FROM WARD C

Massive bowel evacuation today after what I realize was effectively two
months of constipation. Feel better but become simultaneously conscious of just how much weight I've lost. I'm now a skinny old buzzard
whose hair needs cutting.

This is a geriatric ward though no one will actually admit it. No one
here is younger than sixty. It's a geriatric ward in the same sense as a
cancer ward. We are all old men with old men's problems. Many of us
die. The ward is too big for me to do an accurate count and patients are
always being moved around (to disguise the fatalities?). I would say
around thirty of us have died since I arrived here.

Paula went on her summer holiday yesterday. Where are you going? I
asked. Malta, silly. She wears a gold cross around her neck–good
Catholic girl. Her replacement is a male nurse called Gary–he has
many lurid tattoos.

The man I hate most is four beds along from me. His name is Ned Dar-
win but I refer to him as Mr. No-Fuss. The nurses love him: he never
complains, he always has a bright observation and a cheery smile for
everyone, he seems to relish the food. He has had a stroke but can limp
about fairly well with an arm-crutch. He knows all the nurses' names.
He came up to me on one particularly hot day and tapped my plaster
leg. "Must be itching like crazy under there, I'll warrant." He's the type
of man who uses phrases like "I'll warrant," "yea or nay" and "much
obliged." I told him to fuck off.

* * *

I demanded to see some sort of managerial/administrative figure to protest about the absence of doors in the lavatories (a significant factor in our collective constipation problem, in my opinion). This was rocking the boat in a very unequivocal way and drew darker looks than usual from the nurses. A young, suited man eventually appeared and listened to what I had to tell him. "This measure is in place for your own safety, Logan," he said. I asked him to call me Mr. Mountstuart, which he neglected to do, not employing any name thereafter. Nothing is going to happen: I have merely enhanced my reputation as a troublemaker.

The description of the Pecksniff family's trip to London in *Martin Chuzzlewit* (Chapters 8 and 9) is the greatest passage of comic writing in English Literature. Discuss.

The drain has been removed from the area of my spleen. The ache in my leg seems reduced. No side effects so far from my fractured skull. I must have seen ten doctors since arriving here, each one taking up my case with no evidence of foreknowledge: "So, you were in some kind of a car crash?," "Oh, I see you ruptured your spleen." I don't blame them and I don't blame the nurses. I hate living in this ghastly place—God knows what it must be like working here. The thought remains, however: there must be a better, more humane, more civilized way of looking after our sick and infirm. If the state is going to take the job on, then it has to be done in a wholehearted way: everyone is demeaned by this petty, vindictive, penny-pinching, careless world.

This is the first time in my life that I have been badly injured and seriously unwell; the first time I have had an operation and a general anaesthetic; the first time I have been in hospital. Those of us who have the luck to enjoy good health forget about this vast parallel universe of the unwell—their daily miseries, their banal ordeals. Only when you cross that frontier into the world of ill-health do you recognize its quiet, massive presence, its brooding permanence.

A new sister on the ward: "I hear you won't use a bedpan." You hear correctly, I said. Then she said that if I "needed the toilet" I had to go under my own steam or use a bedpan, nurses would no longer be detailed to wheel me to and fro, it took up too much valuable time. Then you'd better find me some crutches, I said, because I will not be using a bedpan. You're not authorized crutches, she said with a triumphant smile, and a bedpan was brought. So, when I needed a shit I hauled myself out of bed and managed to make my way over to No-Fuss. "Can I borrow your crutch? Thanks." I knew he didn't want to lend it to me because he thought he'd get into trouble. Sod him.

The spleen. My ruptured spleen. I looked the word up in an encyclopedia. "A small purplish red organ that lies under the diaphragm. The spleen acts as a filter against foreign organisms that infect the bloodstream." In the crash my spleen burst. In medieval times the spleen was regarded as the source of melancholy emotions in man. Hence "splenetic"—a tendency to produce melancholy or depression of spirits, having a morose or peevish disposition. I worry that my ruptured spleen has released its special poison into my body. Is this the source of my new bile-filled and rancorous nature?

I worry about my flat—no one's been there for weeks. Paula asked me why I never had any visitors and I said my family all lived abroad—a pathetic lie. I said my daughter was in America. "Still, you'd have thought she'd've come over to see her dad," Paula said.

A Roman Catholic priest came round. "Paula told me you were of our faith." How did Paula know? Do we give ourselves away, somehow? Certain words, expressions, gestures . . . In some way or another our common ground must be revealed. I told him that I was a devout atheist and that I'd lost my faith at the age of eighteen. He asked me if I had never felt God's love in my life. I told him to look around this room with its cargo of human suffering and misery. But God is in this room, he insisted with a smile. I said no plumbline could fathom the depths of my faithlessness—quoting John Francis Byrne, Joyce's friend, at him. He didn't know what to say to that, so I asked him to leave.

The old man next to me died this morning. He lay in his bed as if he had been nailed to it, immobile, an oxygen mask hissing on his face. Only his eyes were expressive and he would roll them alarmingly my way from time to time. Eventually I decided to interpret this as a signal. I swung out of bed and raised his mask.

"You an Englishman?" he whispered.

"Sort of. Yes."

His bulging eyes flicked everywhere like a chameleon's.

"Pull the plugs out, mate. I want to go."

I looked around. For an insane moment I thought I might actually do it but I saw a nurse marching over to us. I put his mask back on. He died about two hours later.

Mr. Singh [LMS's upstairs neighbour] came to visit, bringing with him the accumulated weeks of post. He told me that the telephone and the electricity had been cut off in my flat. He had with him the form from the post office that would allow him to collect my unclaimed pension. Good old Subadar (I should explain; Mr. Singh was briefly in the Indian Army—so I call him Subadar and he calls me Commander). He sat and chatted for a while and told me he had had a vasectomy while I had been in hospital and he had never seen anyone as happy as Mrs. Singh. I sense my status in the ward has changed since his visit—now I am even more a man of mystery. I wrote cheques to cover my various outstanding bills and he took them away to post.

No-Fuss leaves today. The nurses gathered round and applauded him as he limped out of the ward. I can't see this happening when my turn comes around. I have another terminal case beside me—he groans terribly in the night—and I'm beginning to suspect I'm being singled out.

The plaster came off my left leg today—revealing an etiolated, hairy, knobbly thing half the size of its partner. I noticed an odd kink in the shin where the broken bone has not knitted together properly and that had the surgeon frowning. The thigh and calf muscles are almost completely wasted so I am promised two hours of physiotherapy a day to build them up again. I sense an urgency to have done with me, now the physical sign of my incapacity has been removed. The feeling is mutual.

A door has been fitted to one of the lavatory stalls. A small but sweet victory.

WEDNESDAY, 8 SEPTEMBER

I must note this down: something strange has happened to my eyesight. I woke this morning to see half the world—the top half—in my area of vision screened by what I can only describe as a swirling brown fog. It was as if some sort of noxious mist had descended, but as soon as I moved my head I realized the discoloration was a property of my eyesight and not the world beyond.

A doctor was summoned, a young Sinhalese woman. She asked me if I was allergic to certain foodstuffs and booked me in for an ECG test. I told her I had fractured my skull in my accident. What accident, she asked? I've been here so long I'm already ancient history. When I explained she thought I should see a neuro-surgeon: there was no more talk about allergies.

THURSDAY, 9 SEPTEMBER

The mist has cleared. I was shaving this morning and suddenly realized the top half of the mirror was no longer brown. The surgeon, a Mr. Guide, examined me, tested my reflexes and suggested an ophthalmologist. Mr. Guide was civil and seemed concerned. He was an elderly man with thick silvery hair. What do I mean "elderly"? He must be ten years younger than I am.

Paula gave me a St. Christopher's medal on a silver chain. Why, I asked her? It's far too kind of you. To keep you safe on your journey through life, Mr. Mountstuart. Then she said she wouldn't be here when I leave. When I leave? Yes, she said, you're leaving tomorrow morning and I'm on late shift. She kissed my cheek. Look after yourself, take care, watch out for post office vans. My throat thickened and my eyes stung. Dear sweet Paula. At least I'm walking out alive.

FRIDAY, 24 SEPTEMBER

Turpentine Lane. So strange being back, looking at these possessions, these sticks of furniture with a stranger's eyes. This is your home, Mountstuart, these are your chattels. Like boarding the *Marie Celeste*. There was a great drift, two feet deep, of handbills and free newspapers banked behind the door. Much as I hated the place, the hospital was secure, known; now I find the city clamorous and fear-inducing. And I experience my enforced solitude—which I used to relish—as disconcerting, after months of communal ward-life. I sat for half an hour this evening waiting for someone to bring me my supper. There was no food in the house so I limped down to the Cornwallis for a drink (the hospital has loaned me an aluminium walking stick). Here were the same old faces, the same steeped, beery atmosphere. The landlord nodded hello, as if I'd been in yesterday. I'm not one of his favourites—I spend too much time and not enough money in his establishment. I ordered a large Scotch and soda and two pork pies (Subadar had handed over a great wodge of backed-up pension money. I was momentarily flush) and the landlord acknowledged the fact with a rare insincere smile.

I looked at the punters, the drinkers—my species-sharers—and wished them all dead.

1977

When I write my memoirs I will refer to this period of my life as the Dog-Food Years. My prosperity was illusory. I don't quite know how it has come about but since the accident—if it were possible—I have become markedly poorer. Rates have gone up in Pimlico and everything seems more expensive—and it actually cost me money to have my power and telephone restored. I was so outraged I told them to disconnect the phone line again permanently—there's a perfectly good phone box at the end of the road. I do need electricity, unfortunately.

I budget like a miser, endlessly comparing prices in the cheapest supermarkets, my life a checklist of tiny compromises and adjustments. If I washed my hair with soap, I reason, I wouldn't need to buy shampoo; if I shaved with soap I could save on shaving cream; if I bought the cheapest soap in bulk I might have a little extra for food, and so on. I rarely stray beyond a 200-yard radius of my flat—all my requirements are within this small circle. I've given up smoking but refuse to abandon alcohol—and thus my life is pared down to an absolute minimum of needs.

The other day I was studying the contents of what I thought were various tins of stew, looking for one with as many vegetables in it as possible (and thus cut down my vegetable bill), when I was gastrically taken with the rubric on one tin: "plump chunklets of rabbit nestling in a rich dark gravy." I turned the tin around to see that it was branded "Bowser." A tin of dog-food on the wrong shelf. But then I thought that if I bought six tins of Bowser, chopped up a carrot and onion and heated the whole thing in a saucepan, I might have a hearty rabbit stew that would last me a week. I would eat it with my staple diet of rice (Mrs. Singh buys my rice in ten-kilo sacks from some distant cash and carry), my nutritional and culinary requirements would be thoroughly satisfied and I would save considerably. So I did just that, and very tasty Bowser rabbit stew turned out to be, especially with the liberal addition of some tomato ketchup and a good jolt of Worcestershire sauce (these last components, I would say, are essential for all dog-foods, in my experience: there is something fundamentally *gamey* about dog-food, and the risk of a day-long lingering aftertaste—pepper is the best antidote). Now I browse the pet-food shelves, comparing prices and special offers, changing ingredients when one type of meat begins to pall: I tend to avoid beef—liver, chicken and rabbit are my favourites. My economies are substantial.

MONDAY, 28 FEBRUARY

Yesterday was my seventy-first birthday and I decided to change my life. I realized I was turning into a little old man with his ingrained habits, his walking stick, his plastic zip-up purse with 68 pence of change inside, with his favourite seat in the pub and a roll-call of moans and complaints interspersed with moments of a pure, terrifying misanthropy. I was pottering my way to death.

On my way to the Cornwallis to have a celebratory half-pint I passed an old man—a wino, a derelict—who seemed stranded on the pavement's edge, as if the road in front of him were some daunting gulf, an unnavigable ocean. I was about to cross over to help him when I realized he was calmly urinating into the gutter, muttering to himself, unconcerned by the shocked or amused glances of the passers-by (lads guffawing, mothers dragging children away). I stayed where I was, unmanned by a horrible vision of the future. That could be you, Mountstuart, I thought, that death-in-life is not as far away as you think. I had to do something.

I remembered I had seen a poster on the window of a derelict shop: "SPK (Socialist Patients' Kollective). You can help. Make extra money. Join now!" and, beneath the message, a telephone number to call. If I had a little more money, I reasoned, I might have a little more dignity.

I telephoned from a call-box. The conversation went like this:

MAN: Yeah?
ME: I'd like to join the SPK.
MAN: Do you know anything about us?
ME: I saw your poster, that's all. But I do know about being a patient. I've spent months in hospitals. I hated it. I want to do something—

MAN: We have nothing to do with hospitals.

ME: Oh. (Pause) I don't care. I just want to make some extra money. That's what it says on your poster.

MAN: What's your name? Your last name. I don't want to know your Christian name.

ME: Mountstuart.

MAN: Is that double-barrelled?

ME: Absolutely not.

MAN: Are you old?

ME: Well, I'm not young.

There was another pause and then he gave me an address in Stockwell and told me to be there at 5:00 p.m.

The address was Napier Street. Another Napier in my life: the last one had done me some good—so it seemed an acceptable omen. The house was large and semi-detached, in bad repair with crumbling stucco. Sheets and newspapers hanging in the windows acted as curtains. At the last moment before ringing the bell I removed my tie. I was wearing a suit (as I always did—I only had suits to wear). The door was opened by a young woman with a sharp face and a weak chin, with round wire-rimmed spectacles and with her hair in loose, lumpy braids. "Yeah?" she said suspiciously. "I'm Mountstuart—I was told to come here at five o'clock." She almost closed the door. "John?" she shouted into the house, "there's an old bloke here says his name's Mountstuart." "How old?" a man's voice answered. "Really pretty old," she said. "Send him in."

She led me through to a large room on the ground floor. Decorators' trestle tables with Anglepoise lamps on them lined two walls. A quilt was hung at the bow window to block the view to the street and three mattresses were set in a ring around the fireplace. Here and there were rucksacks and carrier bags, piles of magazines and newspapers, opened tins of food, plastic cola bottles. It reminded me somewhat of Lionel's apartment in the Village. On the tables were layout pages for a newspaper and all the attendant paraphernalia—spray-glue, Letraset, Tippex bottles and a couple of electric, golfball typewriters. Apart from the girl who had welcomed me at the door there were three other people present. I was introduced to them. The sharp-faced girl was Brownwell; a pretty girl with dark hair and fringe that fell to her eyelashes was named Roth. There was a man with a poor beard (it looked as if tufts had been pulled out, leaving random bare patches) said his name was Halliday; and, finally, a tall, lean handsome fellow (who looked older than the others, in his thirties, I would say) with long hair to his shoulders parted in the middle said, "And I'm John."

They found a chair and placed it in the middle of the room and asked me to sit down. And then began a form of gentle interrogation. John asked me why I had elected to join the SPK. Thinking this might be what he wanted to hear, I told him that I had been shocked, not to say traumatized, by my lengthy stay in St. Botolph's and that I had wanted to do something about patients' rights. I had imagined that something calling itself the Socialist Patients' Kollective might be exactly the sort of left-of-centre pressure group I was looking for. I wanted to help, I wanted to do anything I could—if they only knew the conditions in today's hospitals, the geriatric wards, the almost totalitarian—

John held up his hand to stop me; I noticed they were all grinning, a little patronizingly. I told you, John said, this is not a movement designed to reform the National Health Service. I said I didn't care, I simply wanted to do something—I wasn't just going to sit around and complain anymore, I wanted to do something active. And, I confessed, a little extra money would help. After a lifetime of hard work and modest success I now found myself scratching a living way below the poverty line. I owed the very roof over my head to the selflessness and generosity of an Icelander, otherwise I'd be homeless. Then I asked the next question: if you're nothing to do with hospitals and patients' rights what are you?

ROTH: We're anti-fascist.
ME: So am I, as it happens.
JOHN: Do the names Debord and Vaneigam mean anything to you?
ME: No.
JOHN: Have you ever heard of the Situationists?
ME: No.
JOHN: Ulrike Meinhof? Nanterre 1968?

ME: I was in Nigeria in 1968, I'm afraid.

JOHN: Anything to do with Biafra?

ME: I went there, right at the end of the war. Trying to get someone out.

HALLIDAY: Good for you, mate.

BROWNWELL: Right on.

There were more questions: had I heard of the Red Army Faction? I
said I had. Brownwell asked me what I thought of "High pigs, judges,
centralism and property." I said I didn't know about all that, I just
wanted to help in some way, just to feel I was not simply taking it all
lying down. My life was drifting by and I didn't want to be a pathetic,
passive old man. After my St. Botolph's experiences I realized I felt
aggrieved and angry at the way people were simply dominated by institutions and authority figures—I wanted to help people stand up for
themselves more. I don't know what it was but these four attentive
young people made me more articulate and passionate—it was the first
chance I'd had to air my feelings and I welcomed it.

Then John explained that the four of them here were part of the
SPK's "Working Circle—Communications." What's a "working circle"?
I asked. A group, a cell, a cadre, I was told. Here in Napier Street they
produced a weekly tabloid newspaper of six to eight pages called *The
Situation*. Sales of this newspaper provided one of the SPK's main
sources of income. They needed people to go out on the streets and
sell it. Ten per cent of all moneys received belonged to the vendor—was
I interested? What do you do with the rest of the money? I asked.

"That's really none of your business," John said. He was a genuinely
handsome man, with dark heavy eyebrows over olive-green eyes. "Let's
put it this way," he said, "what we're interested in is 'intervention.'
When we see a state of affairs we disapprove of, we intervene in some
way—supporting a strike, exposing fascist lies, donating money and aid
to good causes. Intervention can take many forms. We demonstrate,
we protest, we give support to the downtrodden and the put upon.
And all this costs money, the money we earn selling our newspaper."
He had a soft, educated voice and as he spoke these words to me he
gestured for a cigarette and Roth immediately rummaged in her pockets looking for one. John put it in his mouth unlit and I wondered if it

were Brownwell's or Halliday's job to step forward with a match, but he lit it himself after a minute or so.

I said I was interested and they asked me to wait outside.

I stood in the hall and heard footsteps and voices from the upstairs rooms and soon two men came down and passed me at the front door without a glance on their way out. One of them was an Arab. After ten minutes or so I was called back in. Brownwell looked sulky and unfriendly and I suspected she had voted against me.

"Welcome to the SPK," John said and handed me a bundle of a hundred newspapers.

WEDNESDAY, 2 MARCH

This morning's first post has brought the truly shocking news of Ben's death. Sandrine wrote that it had been blessedly sudden, in the end. There is to be a small ceremony at a synagogue in Paris and she very much hopes that I can come. I'll write back pleading ill-health.

Seeing the word "synagogue" gave me pause, reminding me after all these years of indifference that Ben had been a Jew. An English Jew who had contrived to live almost all his adult life out of England. Was Ben the wisest of the three of us?

What can I say? Ben was three months younger than me—my oldest, truest friend, I suppose—though as time went by we saw less and less of each other. After the falling-out with Marius there grew up an awkwardness between us. And Sandrine, naturally, listened to her son's version of events. Ben didn't want to alienate his wife—so the easy solution was to keep Mountstuart at a distance. But Ben came to my rescue after Freya's death and it was Ben who established me in New York. Impossible to imagine my life without that crucial help—but he persistently refused my gratitude. Always remember those paintings you brought back from Spain, he said. They were the key to both our futures. Who knows? The view back is always blessed with 20/20 vision and from that perspective it seems that—bizarrely, absurdly—it was thanks to a Spanish anarchist in Barcelona in 1937 that both Ben Leeping and Logan Mountstuart were able to make their way in the world. Is this the way it works? Is this the truth about the life-game?

SATURDAY, 26 MARCH

I say it with some pride but in a remarkably short period of time I have established myself as the SPK's prize newspaper-seller. Last week I sold 323 copies—£64.60. Ten per cent of this goes to me, in theory, but John was less than candid: the rate is 10 per cent up to a ceiling of £5. So there is no incentive for me to sell more. Perhaps if the entrepreneurial spirit burned brighter in him he'd let me sell as many as I could and take my profit. Not the SPK ethos, however.

At the end of each week the vendors foregather at Napier Street and hand over their takings. Some of us are invited to stay on for a drink at a truly horrible pub in Stockwell called the Prizefighter. There is a far nicer one across the street called the Duke of Cambridge, but John refuses to patronize pubs with royal or aristocratic appellations as a matter of principle. "It's an act of deference on the part of the brewers," he argues, "and why should I be part of that? No drinkers ever choose the name of the pub they frequent and where they spend their money." He has a point, I suppose.

Yesterday was the second Friday that I was invited to the Prizefighter with the SPK Working Circle (Communications). The usual quartet was present: John, Roth, Brownwell and Halliday—but this time we were joined by a German who was introduced as Reinhard. Roth—whose Christian name is Anna—is open and friendly; Brownwell (Tina) is terser and more guarded; Halliday (Ian) keeps his counsel—he has an adulatory reverence for John. As a matter of interest "John" is not a surname, it's John's Christian name. His full name is John Vivian and obviously he doesn't want his co-workers to refer to him as Vivian. I am always Mountstuart—though yesterday Anna asked me my first name. It's all very public-schooly, this use of surnames. I shall work on breaking them down.

[NOTE IN RETROSPECT. The name SPK was taken as direct *hommage* to a radical left-wing group in Germany founded in 1970 at Heidelberg University by Dr. Wolfgang Huber. Huber had aligned the SPK to the Baader–Meinhof terrrorist group in 1971. John Vivian had known Huber and had established the English chapter of the SPK as an act of solidarity when Huber was arrested and imprisoned (the concept of "working circles" was pure Huber). Vivian maintained close links with German radicals—there were often Germans staying at Napier Street—but I was never able to identify them properly.

Vivian had read philosophy at Cambridge in the late sixties and had been arrested by the police at the notorious Garden House Hotel protest in Cambridge in 1968, spending two days in police cells before being released with a caution. The trauma of this episode had driven him to the far revolutionary left (he always claimed close links with the Angry Brigade, Britain's short-lived urban terrorist cell of the early seventies). Vivian had left Cambridge without completing his degree and had travelled first to Paris and thence to Heidelberg, where he came under Huber's messianic sway. He was thirty-one years old when I met him.]

FRIDAY, 8 APRIL

Delivered my takings to Napier Street. The mood was frosty, tense—even by Napier Street standards. Brownwell and John very cold—and I'd sold almost 300 copies. I handed over the money and received not a word of thanks as a five-pound note was thrust at me. I needed to go to the toilet and asked if there was one I could use. Ian Halliday showed me up to the first floor and pointed to a doorway. I entered what was obviously some sort of communal bedroom, one where the walls of the adjacent bathroom had been ripped down to expose the sink, bath and WC. Anna Roth was sitting on the toilet when I went in. "Sorry!" I called and turned about to leave. "Don't worry, Logan," she said. "Just having a crap. Nearly finished." I turned again to see her stand up and wipe her bottom and wheeled round to the window to stare at the waste-land garden below. I heard the lavatory flush. She was keen to talk and wouldn't leave the room so I had to pee with her standing behind me chatting as she rolled a cigarette. I am irreducibly bourgeois, I'm afraid. She said John was in a filthy mood: something that had happened in Karlsruhe, in Germany,* she said. He kept making cryptic phone calls.

For some reason I thought up a title for my autobiography, if I ever write it. It was something I remembered remarking on in New York. I went to the theatre (what did I see?) and I noticed on the ground floor a door with an exit sign above it and, written just below the sign, the words: THIS IS NOT AN EXIT. It all depends on the book cover, I suppose (always a bad sign to be planning the cover before you've written the book), but you could have a photograph of an exit sign and then underneath: "This Is Not an Exit—an Autobiography by Logan Mountstuart." I'm pleased with this idea.

MONDAY, 9 MAY

I picked up my new batch of one hundred newspapers this morning. Anna (we're on first-name terms now) made me a cup of coffee. She whispered to me that John Vivian hadn't left his room for a week. "Very depressed," she said. By what? "By the Stammheim† verdict." Reinhard, the German, wandered into the kitchen. He seems an innocuous fellow, fair-haired, bearded, not much to say for himself.

> [NOTE IN RETROSPECT. I now wonder if "Reinhard" might actually have been Dr. Wolfgang Huber himself. He was released from prison in 1977 and "went underground." Perhaps he'd come to England to check on his SPK foundling. Just a hunch.]

---

*This can only have been the fatal machine-gun attack on the federal prosecutor Siegfried Buback by the Red Army Faction. As well as Buback two others also died.
†On 28 April Andreas Baader, Gudrun Ensslin and Jan-Carl Raspe—all founding members of the Baader-Meinhof terrorist gang—had been found guilty at a special court in Stammheim. Each received a long prison sentence.

While he was making himself some sort of herbal tea, Anna—without a trace of embarrassment—asked me what I had done in the war. Well, I said, since you ask, I was in the Naval Intelligence Division, I said. Does that mean you were a spy? I suppose so, I admitted. She was very impressed and even Reinhard seemed interested. He asked if I'd known Kim Philby.* I said no—and then John Vivian himself appeared, looking grumpy. Guess what, John? Anna said, Logan was a spy in the war. Vivian looked at me keenly and without warmth: well, well, well, he said, who's a dark horse, then?

My newspaper-selling technique is thoroughly tried and tested now. I wear a suit and tie and, unlike my fellow vendors, I never frequent the working-class pubs where they make their modest sales. I go to London University colleges, art schools and polytechnics. Gower Street, around University College and its student union, is my best patch. I try to prowl the cafeterias and refectories at lunchtime. "This is the only newspaper in the country that will tell you the whole truth," is my sales pitch. And in actual fact *The Situation* is not a bad newspaper, of its type. Tina Brownwell writes about 90 per cent of it; John Vivian chooses the headlines and sets the tone of the editorials. The most amusing and interesting section is Tina's analysis of other newspapers' reporting, pointing out the pro-Zionist bias or the crypto-American line as she finds them. There is a long editorial, usually, heavy on political theory (which I find unreadable), with strident headlines of the "Capitalism Must Finance its Own Overthrow" or "Criminal Action is Political Action" variety.

My fiver a week has become something of a welfare lifeline to me and I probably don't need to rely on my dog-food stews for sustenance anymore—though I must say I've developed a real taste for Bowser's rabbit chunklets with—a new refinement—a pinch of curry powder judiciously stirred in.

---

*Philby, the KGB spy, was an iconic figure to the radical left in the sixties and seventies: the ultimate insider—the ultimate betrayer.

TUESDAY, 31 MAY

I've just had lunch with Gail. We ate in the restaurant of her hotel off Oxford Street; her husband did not join us. She had written to me and said she was coming to London and could we meet, giving me her dates and urging me to telephone: "Please, Logan, please."

So I did, and went to meet little Gail, whom I loved so, and found that she has turned into a brisk, unsmiling woman with dyed blond hair and a bad smoking habit. I would say that she was not happy in her marriage—but what do I know, the marriage-expert? Just occasionally the old Gail would flash from her—a rare smile, and once when she pointed her fork at me and said, "You know, Mom was such an asshole." I said I was fine, no really, life was OK, I was coping, writing a new novel, no, fine, fine, really fine. When we parted she held on to me tight and said, "I love you, Logan. Don't let's lose touch." I couldn't stop the tears and neither could she, so she lit a cigarette and I said it looked like rain wasn't far off, and somehow we managed to part.

As I write this I feel that draining, hollowing helplessness that genuine love for another person produces in you. It's at these moments that we know we are going to die. Only with Freya, Stella and Gail. Only three. Better than none.

SATURDAY, 4 JUNE

I was sitting in the Park Café today having a cup of tea and a Penguin biscuit, reading someone's discarded *Guardian,* when I came across the news of Peter Scabius's knighthood for "services to literature." To be candid, I felt a pang of envy before indifference and reality closed in again. It was not so much envy, in fact (I've never envied Peter's success—he's too much of a fraud and an egomaniac to provoke real envy), it was more an impromptu insight into my condition vis-à-vis his. I suddenly saw myself—in this threadbare shiny suit, with my unironed nylon shirt and greasy tie, with my thinning grey hair needing a wash—as a truly pathetic figure. Here I was, well into my seventies, sitting in this undistinguished, overlit caff, sipping my tea and dunking my Penguin biscuit, wondering if I can afford a pint at the Cornwallis this evening. This was not the image of my elderly self that I had conceived when I was younger; this was not the kind of old age I had imagined I would be living. But then I never saw myself as a Peter Scabius–type either: Sir Logan Mountstuart talked to us today from his lovely home in the Cayman Islands . . . That was never for me, never. What was for you, then, Mountstuart? What fond vision of the future warmed your soul?

I haven't worked on *Octet* for months. I've been distracted by the SPK and my paper round. But, in the end, the work—the *oeuvre*—is everything: that's my reply. The books are there in the copyright libraries, if nowhere else. I must press on with *Octet*, I now see—surprise them all.

MONDAY, 6 JUNE

When I went to pick up my hundred *Situation*s today John Vivian asked me to come upstairs—wanted a little chat. Tina was there and Ian Halliday too. We sat in a room with two television sets; the mood was solemn but not unfriendly. "We want to thank you for your work, Mountstuart," Vivian said. "You've been most useful." Then all three of them stepped forward and shook my hand. Not for the first time I wondered where all the cash I made for them went. Anyway, Vivian said that, because of my staunch efforts, he thought the time had come to inaugurate me into "Working Circle–Direct Action" and was I prepared to accept the extra duties (I'd still be flogging newspapers). He explained that in "Working Circle–Direct Action" I would be going on demonstrations, joining picket lines and attending all forms of protest. I would carry an SPK placard mounted on a pole and would hand out SPK flysheets, try to recruit members and sell subscriptions for *The Situation*. There was a bus drivers' strike in Oldham currently going on, Vivian said, and there was a demonstration planned for next week outside the town hall. Was I ready to go? I can't afford to travel to Oldham, I said. "We'll pay for you to be there," Vivian said with a tolerant smile, "all reasonable expenses provided. And if there's a press photographer in sight make sure you get that SPK sign in the frame."

[NOTE IN RETROSPECT. Thus it was that in the summer of 1977 I travelled surprisingly widely (by bus) throughout the British Isles in my capacity as member of the SPK's Working Circle–Direct Action. After Oldham I went to Clydeside, after Clydeside I was on the pavement opposite Downing Street for five days. Striking dye-stampers in Swansea, fishermen in Stonehaven, sweatshops in Brick Lane–I was there. You may even have seen glimpses of me on the television news or in the background of newspaper photographs: the tall elderly man in the dark suit and tie, wielding the SPK plac-ard, being jostled by policemen, shouting abuse at Margaret Thatcher, jeering at scabs in buses. In between times I sold *The Situation* and lived my simple but now committed life, shuttling be-tween Turpentine Lane, the public library, the Cornwallis and the Park Café. I no longer complained about my lot–I felt I was doing something at last.]

THURSDAY, 8 SEPTEMBER

I'm in the Cornwallis this evening enjoying a half pint of Extra Strength lager and a small schooner of Bristol Cream sherry (for any impoverished, committed boozer this combination will work wonders, I guarantee–you don't want to drink another drop of alcohol and you sleep like a baby) when, to my genuine astonishment, John Vivian comes in.

He sits down opposite me, looking dark-eyed and agitated. I have to say the mood of the Napier Street Mob has changed these last few weeks. Ian Halliday has gone away, Tina hardly speaks and Anna seems close to tears all the time. I think Vivian may have started an affair with Anna–anyway, I believe "strung out" is the correct term to describe their demeanour. The last issue of *The Situation* had shrunk to four pages–more of a pamphlet than a newspaper–and half of it was an incoherent editorial by Vivian about "Isolation Torture in West Germany." Most of the rest was a badly translated article written by Ulrike Meinhof in 1969. I made the point that this issue was going to be almost impossible to sell on the streets of London and Tina Brownwell screamed at me, calling me a fifth-columnist and a scab. Luckily for everyone some German industrialist was kidnapped on Monday* and the event managed to raise enough interest for me to sell over a hundred copies.

Now Vivian leans towards me and offers me a cigarette (no thanks) and another drink (no thanks) and asks me if he can have my newspaper money now. It's back at my flat, I say. I was going to bring it along tomorrow as usual. I need it now, he says.

So Vivian comes back to Turpentine Lane with me but won't follow me inside. I fetch the money and hand it over, asking for a receipt. "Still that shopkeeper mentality, eh, Mountstuart?" he says, with a thin smile. But he signs my docket all the same and strides off into the night. It must be drugs: I think they use the newspaper money to buy drugs.

MONDAY, 12 SEPTEMBER

Maybe I'm wrong. Vivian was his usual cool sardonic self when I picked up the new issue today (which was still on the thin side, still largely devoted to the doings of the radical left in West Germany). There was no sign of Anna or Tina. Unusually, Vivian offered me a drink, a whisky, which I decided to accept this time. We had a peculiar conversation.

ME: So—what was your college at Cambridge?
VIVIAN: Gonville and Caius. Why?
ME: I was at Oxford. Jesus College.
VIVIAN: Look at us, Mountstuart, the flower of the nation. You were reading English, no doubt.
ME: History, actually.
VIVIAN: What do you think about what's going on in Germany?
ME: I think it's complete madness. Delusion. Violence isn't going to change a thing.

---

*Dr. Hanns-Martin Schleyer, President of the West German Federation of Industries—kidnapped by the Red Army Faction.

VIVIAN: Wrong. Anyway, it's not violence. It's counter-violence. Big difference.

ME: If you say so.

VIVIAN: You ever been in prison, Mountstuart?

ME: Yes.

VIVIAN: So have I. I spent thirty-six hours locked up in a cell in Cambridge police station. That's violence for you. I was making a legal protest against fascist generals in Greece and the state took my freedom away from me.

ME: I spent two years in solitary confinement in Switzerland, 1944–5. I was fighting for my country.

VIVIAN: Two years? Christ . . .

That shut him up for a while. He topped up our drinks.

VIVIAN: Do you like travelling?

ME: Don't mind a spot of travelling.

VIVIAN: Well, do you fancy a little trip abroad?

Vivian was very circumspect as he outlined the itinerary. Everything would be paid for by the SPK, all I had to do was to take the ferry from Harwich to the Hook of Holland and go to a town near Hamburg, called Waldbach. There I was to book into a small hotel called the Gasthaus Kesselring, where I would be contacted by someone. Then new instructions would be given to me. Every evening I was to call Napier Street at 6 o'clock and report in, but I was to speak only to Vivian himself. Our password would be "Mogadishu." I was to say nothing unless the person to whom I said the word "Mogadishu" repeated it. Only you and I know this password, Vivian said, that way our conversations will be secure.

"Mogadishu in Somalia?" I said. "Why?"

"Has a nice ring to it."

"So we could say I'm on Operation Mogadishu, then?"

"If it makes you happy to think of it that way, Mountstuart, then indeed you are."

We sat and drank some more. I asked Vivian what this was all about. Ask me no questions and I'll tell you no lies, Mountstuart, he said. We were both becoming a little pissed as we neared the bottom of the bottle. What do you believe in, John? I asked him. I believe in fighting fascism in all its forms, he said. That's an evasion, a catch-all, I said, and fundamentally meaningless. Then I told him about Faustino Angel Peredes—my friend the Spanish Anarchist who had died in Barcelona in 1937—and the credo we had evolved between us on the Aragón front that year. I let all these names and dates drop with full self-consciousness, wanting him to weigh up the implicit experience, the lived-life therein. Our credo of two hates and three loves: hatred of injustice, hatred of privilege, love of life, love of humanity, love of beauty. Vivian looked at me, sadly, and poured out the last of the whisky for himself, and said: "You really are an old unreconstructed tosser, aren't you?"

THURSDAY, 6 OCTOBER

I came home this evening to find two envelopes had been pushed through my letter box. The first one contained £100, cash, a train ticket from Waterloo to Waldbach and confirmation that a room had been booked for me at the Gasthaus Kesselring from Saturday onward. The other envelope contained $2,000 in $50 bills and a note to say that my contact in Waldbach would tell me whom to give it to. I am to leave early on Saturday morning—it seems Operation Mogadishu is under way. It may appear strange to make this observation, especially at my age, but I find myself tense with excitement and almost schoolboy anticipation. I could be back at Abbey about to go on a night exercise.

MEMORANDUM ON "OPERATION MOGADISHU"

Waldbach is a small town set on two sides of a slow meandering river (I forget its name). On the southern side of the town is a semi-ruined castle and a few steep-roofed timbered houses clustered around it. North of the river is the new town (largely post-war, dominated by the functional buildings of a large teacher-training college). This was where the Gasthaus Kesselring was situated. I had a room at the rear with a view of a garage and a cinema. I arrived after midnight on Saturday and went straight to bed.

On Sunday I explored the castle and lunched in the small square at its foot. I dined in the Gasthaus restaurant and read my book in the residents' lounge (a biography of John O'Hara—very underrated writer). On Monday, I repeated the process, but instead of reading my book went to the cinema to see a badly dubbed film called *Three Days of the Condor**—which seemed to be excellent, as far as I could understand what was going on.

I made sure to call Napier Street at 6:00 (there had been no reply the previous night).

"Hello?" a man's voice said.

"Mogadishu."

"Hello?"

"Mogadishu."

Someone else picked up. "Is that you, Logan?"

It was Anna. "Yes. Could I speak to John, please?"

"Where are you? Are you all right?"

"Absolutely fine."

Vivian came to the phone.

"Mogadishu."

"Hi, Mountstuart. Everything fine?"

I hung up, then rang back two minutes later.

"What the fuck are you playing at, Mountstuart?"

"Mogadishu."

"All right. Mogadishu, Mogadishu, Mogadishu."

"There's no point in establishing a security procedure if you ignore it."

"Anna was standing beside me. I couldn't start spouting 'Mogadishu' all over the place."

"Shall we change the password?"

"No, no, no. Any news?"

"No sign of the contact."

"That's odd. Well, hang on in there."

On Tuesday I trudged across the bridge that led to the castle, but I

*Starring Robert Redford and Faye Dunaway. Directed by Sydney Pollack.

couldn't stand another tour, and instead settled myself at the café with my book and ordered a beer and sandwich. It was a chilly day so I sat inside—the place was more or less empty.

Then two girls came in and sat down. I sensed they were staring at me and having some sort of whispered discussion. Both of them had badly dyed hair—one blond, one carroty red. Eventually I looked over and smiled—it seemed to make their minds up and they took seats at my table.

"What the fuck are you playing at?" the blonde one whispered harshly at me.

"We've been sitting in that fucking railway station for two days," said Carrot-top.

I explained that my instructions said nothing about meeting anyone at the railway station. I apologized and suggested buying them a drink as a peace offering and they had a couple of beers. They both spoke good English and smoked constantly.

"I'm Mountstuart," I said.

"Why are you so old?" Blonde said. "Can't they find any young people in England?"

"No, no," Carrot said. "It's very clever. Fucking clever, if you think about it. An old guy like him in his suit and overcoat. No one would think anything."

"Yeah . . . ," Blonde said. "I'm, ah, Ingeborg."

"And I'm Birgit—no, Petra," the redhead corrected herself guilelessly. They both tried not to laugh.

"I believe you have instructions for me," I said.

"No," Petra said. "I think you have something for us."

"I'd better make a telephone call."

I went to the telephone-cabin and somehow managed to make a reverse-charge call to Napier Street.

"Will you accept a reverse-charge call from a Mr. Logan Mountstuart?"

"Certainly not," Tina Brownwell said and hung up.

I told Petra and Ingeborg they would have to meet me later that evening after I had made my 6 o'clock call to London and we arranged to rendezvous at a café-bar opposite the station.

I called Vivian at the appointed hour.

"Mogadishu."

"Cut all that crap, Mountstuart, this isn't the Boy Scouts."

"It was your idea."

"Yeah, yeah. What's happening?"

"They've made contact, but they've no instructions."

"Fucking Jesus Christ!" Vivian railed on for a while. "Where is he? Can you put him on?"

"Who?"

"The contact."

"It's a couple of girls, actually. I'm meeting them later."

He said he would make some calls and try to sort matters out. I wandered up to the station and found Petra and Ingeborg sitting in the window of a blazingly bright cafeteria. We ordered some roast chicken and chips and drank beer. The girls smoked. Petra, I suspected from her colouring, was a blond who had gone redhead. She had blue eyes and a sulky, pouting face sprinkled with many small moles. Ingeborg was a dark-haired girl who had turned peroxide blond—thin-lipped, with restless brown eyes and a cleft in her chin.

We ate and chatted as if we were students on an exchange, meeting in the college refectory. They were curious about SPK and John Vivian. I gave them some evasive answers.

"Did you know Ian?" Petra asked.

"Yes, a little."

"Poor Ian," Ingeborg said.

"Why 'Poor Ian'?"

"He was shot by the pigs. They killed him, gunned him down."*

"We must be talking about a different Ian," I said.

Petra looked at me. "Do you have a gun?"

"Of course not."

She opened her handbag and showed me what looked like an automatic pistol.

"I too have one," Ingeborg said. "And here's your instructions." It was the address of a hotel in Zurich: Hôtel Horizont. Back to Switzerland.

---

*She was probably referring to one Iain McLeod, an Englishman who was shot dead by West German police during a raid on his flat in Stuttgart in 1972. It was alleged he was a member of the Red Army Faction—this has never been proved.

*   *   *

I put this down in the interests of candour and what it may reveal about me and the situation I now found myself in. As soon as Petra had shown me her gun and Ingeborg had confessed she had one also I developed a keen sexual interest in these two grubby, neurotic girls. Rather than be alarmed by this turn of events I wanted to invite them back to the Gasthaus Kesselring and have sex with them. Is this the danger of the tawdry glamour of the self-appointed urban guerrilla? That somehow the "game" always tends to obscure the brutal reality? I realized that "Operation Mogadishu" was by now something far more sinister than I had ever envisaged, and yet I couldn't take it seriously, I couldn't believe these inefficient bickering girls with their bad dye-jobs posed any kind of threat. I was intrigued, beguiled, aroused. And then I have also to admit that after a moment's reflection I was shocked at my own stupidity and naivety. What did I think I was doing on this cloak-and-dagger journey across Germany? Organizing some pan-European student demo? Delivering funds for a left-wing charitable organization? John Vivian's bad-boy paranoia and cynicism had seemed nothing more than an attitude, an affectation, a way of appearing "cool"—all with the aim, perhaps, of making it easier to attract pretty young women like Anna and Tina into his Napier Street lair. But I suddenly saw in that overlit *bahnhof* cafeteria the cold and ruthless consequences of this extremism—left or right, they all seemed in their rackety, accident-prone, haphazard way ultimately to involve some degree of violent confrontation and personal injury. The John Vivians of this world painted themselves into a political corner with their radicalism—and the only way out was with a gun or a bomb.

I paid the bill and stood up to leave.

"Nice to have met you," I said.

"Oh no," Petra said, smiling. "We come to Zurich with you, Mountstuart."

Conversation with John Vivian.

"They're *what*?"

"Coming with me."

"Why, for fuck's sake?"

"I don't know. And they've got guns. I want out of this, Vivian."

"They haven't got guns—they're winding you up."

"This isn't anything illegal, is it?"

"You're a seventy-five-year-old man on a European holiday."

"Seventy-one."

"What?"

"A seventy-one-year-old man."

Silence. Then, "Go to Zurich with them and when you make contact there—"

"Who with? With whom?"

"Someone will approach you. 'Mogadishu' is the password. Do your business and dump the girls. And don't worry about this guns nonsense. This isn't dangerous."

"I'm running out of money. These girls say they're broke."

"I'll wire you another hundred at Zurich American Express. Use your credit card."

"I haven't got a credit card."

"Then economize."

Petra, Ingeborg and I travelled very uncomfortably by train—overnight, third class, smoking compartment—from Hamburg to Stuttgart, changed and then journeyed on to Zurich, during which time I managed perhaps two hours of uninterrupted sleep and inhaled the smoke of perhaps two hundred cigarettes. I insisted that we split up for customs and immigration checks—my old NID training awakening in me, I noted with quiet pride. We found the American Express office and I collected another $100, which I changed into a laughably small amount of Swiss francs. Then we checked into the Hôtel Horizont—modern, over-used, anonymous—and were provided with a room containing a double bed and a kind of unfolding metal lounger with a rubber mattress: this was for me. No comment was passed by the hotel staff on the sleeping arrangements: clearly quite demure by the Horizont's standards. The girls immediately went to sleep, curled under the duvet, removing only their shoes and coats—like escapees on the run, the thought came to me. Somehow all my sexual fantasies had dwindled away—now I felt like a put-upon uncle with a couple of disaffected, bolshie nieces.

I telephoned John Vivian at 6:00.

"I need more money."

"I sent you a hundred yesterday, for Christ's sake."

"This is Switzerland and now we are three."

"All right, I'll send more. Have a ball, mate."

"And I've got to get back, remember."

"Yeah, sure."

"And by the way, I resign."

"What from?"

"From the Socialist Patients' Kollective. From Working Circle–Direct Action and Working Circle–Communications. From the Napier Street Mob. Once I get back, that's it. Finito. Kaput."

"You're being over-dramatic, Mountstuart. We'll talk when you're home again. Take care."

That evening I dragged the girls out of bed and we found a pizza parlour on a square somewhere. The girls seemed both sullen and edgy, eating their pizzas without talking. When they finished they asked if they could have some money to buy some "hash"—they said they wanted to get stoned. I said no, and they withdrew into their moody silence again. We wandered around, an odd and uncomfortable trio, looking in shop windows until Ingeborg saw a bar up a side street and suggested a drink. I thought this a better idea and so we ventured in. A cocktail list was proffered but the drinks were shockingly expensive so we settled for marginally less expensive beer. The girls bought cigarettes and I was offered one. I declined.

PETRA: Don't you smoke, Mountstuart?

ME: No. I used to, but not anymore—too expensive.

INGEBORG: Fuck—you've got to have some fun in your life, Mountstuart.

ME: I agree. I love fun. I'm having fun now.

The girls spoke to each other in German.

ME: What did you say?
PETRA: Ingeborg said maybe we shall shoot you and take your money.
INGEBORG: Ha-ha-ha. Don't worry, Mountstuart, we like you.

Once we returned to the hotel the girls became annoyingly coy and insisted I wait in the corridor while they prepared themselves for bed. When they were ready they called me in.

I changed into my pyjamas in the bathroom and on emerging provoked squeals of laughter. Now I felt like a curate in charge of a party of Brownies. "Shut the fuck up," I snarled at them, and eased myself into my creaking cot. I tried to sleep but they insisted on chatting and smoking, ignoring my complaints and curses.

The next day [Thursday, 13 October] I woke early with a sore back. The girls were deeply, profoundly asleep, Petra snoring slightly, Ingeborg with the duvet thrown aside, exposing her small breasts. I dressed and went down to the dining room for breakfast, where I drank coffee, ate boiled eggs, ham and cheese in the company of three verbose Chinese businessmen, talking very loudly. I made up a couple of extra rolls with ham and pickled cucumbers, wrapped them in paper napkins and stuffed them in my pockets: breakfast for the girls or lunch for me.

I picked up another $100 from American Express (thinking I must be draining the SPK's funds alarmingly) and went for a wander, not taking much in, aware only that many church bells seemed to be ringing—a dull, flat, increasingly irritating sound that reminded me of Oxford. After about ten minutes I became aware I was being followed—by a young guy in a buckskin jacket and jeans. He had shiny long hair and a Mexican-style moustache. I turned a corner and stood in a patch of mildly warming sunshine, waiting for him.

"Hi. Mogadishu," he said.

"Mogadishu. I'm Mountstuart."

"Jürgen. What in fuck hell are those girls doing with you?"

"They insisted on coming. I thought it was part of the plan."

"Shit." Jürgen swore some more in German. "Do you have the money?"

"Not on me."

"Bring it to that café there. In one hour."

So I plodded back to the hotel, where I saw the girls sitting in the glassed-in sun porch off the residents' lounge, reading magazines and, it goes without saying, smoking.

"What're we doing today, Mountstuart?" Petra asked.

"It's a free day," I said. "Amuse yourselves."

"In Zurich?" Ingeborg scoffed. "Thank you so very much, Mount-stuart."

"Have fun. Remember?"

In the room I packed my bag and came down the stairs instead of the lift, but there was no need for caution—the girls had gone. I settled the bill and went to meet Jürgen at the appointed café. He arrived ten minutes late, carrying a small suitcase.

"This is for you," he said, handing it over. It was quite heavy. I gave him the envelope with the dollars and for the first time he managed a smile, though he insisted on counting the money, laboriously. When he was satisfied he stuffed it in a pocket and shook my hand.

"Tell John we're ready," he said. "Good luck."

I caught a tram to the railway station and bought a ticket to Grenoble. From there I planned to head north to Paris and cross the Channel back to England via Calais. John Vivian had been insistent that I use a different port of entry for my journey back.

That night in Grenoble I sat in the bar of a hotel near the station watching the evening news. A Lufthansa jet had been hijacked at Palma Airport. The hijackers—four Arabs, two men and two women—demanded the release of all political prisoners held in West German gaols.

I lay in bed that night and wondered what Petra and Ingeborg—my girls—would be doing. I felt a bit of a cheat running out on them that way but I was only following John Vivian's instructions. But in any event, I reasoned, they were too volatile and unpredictable—for all I knew they might have insisted on coming back to London with me. Imagine: life in Turpentine Lane with Petra and Ingeborg . . .*

*"Petra"—Hanna Hauptbeck. Arrested by West German police in Hamburg 1978. Sentenced to seven years' imprisonment for bank robbery and conspir-

The suitcase Jürgen had given me was not only heavy but also securely locked.

The next morning, with the aid of a small screwdriver and a bent piece of wire, I opened Jürgen's case. It was filled with an assortment of second-hand clothes and forty sticks of what I took to be gelignite. Each stick was marked: GOMMEL ASTIGEL DYNAMITE. EXPLOSIF ROCHER, SOCIÉTÉ FRANÇAISE DES EXPLOSIFS. USINE DE CUGNY. I closed the case and thought about what I was going to do. I had about £70 of French francs on me, enough to keep me going for days on my frugal standard of living and allow me to reach home. I obviously couldn't afford to stay in hotels: perhaps if I bought a tent and a sleeping bag campsites would be the answer? Then I remembered where I was—France. I owned property in this country. I picked up the phone and put in a call to Noel Lange's office in London.

Friday evening. I was in Toulouse and stayed at the cheapest hotel I could find. Saturday morning. I caught a bus to Villeneuve-sur-Lot. The newspaper I bought was full of news about the Lufthansa hijacking. The plane was now in Dubai and the demands were more detailed: the release of eleven Baader-Meinhof gang members, two Palestinians gaoled in Turkey and a ransom for the hostages on board of $15.5 million.

I took another bus from Villeneuve along the valley of the Lot to Puy l'Évêque, where I would find the office of the *notaire*, Monsieur Polle, who had the keys to Cyprien's house in Sainte-Sabine. Monsieur Polle, a genial man with stiff cropped grey hair, offered to drive me the forty kilometres or so south to Sainte-Sabine. We travelled through rolling wooded country along minor roads, the sun appearing from time to time through large, rapidly moving clouds, heading eastward on a stiffish breeze.

acy to plant explosives. "Ingeborg"—Renate Müller-Gras. Disappeared in 1978 after a shoot-out with police in Stuttgart. Went underground. There are suggestions that she is dead.

*   *   *

The house, my house, was called Cinq Cyprès and had been on the market since I had learned it was bequeathed to me. I was soon to find out why no one had made an offer. The five cypresses themselves were as old as the house, planted when it was built, I imagined, in the last decade of the last century. They were towering, shaggy mature trees, some forty feet high, and strategically positioned around the house and its sole outbuilding, a stone barn, considerably older. The house was semi-derelict, its unattractive nineteenth-century provincial features more or less hidden by smothering growths of ivy and Virginia creeper. It was set in the middle of a small park with many mature deciduous trees—chestnut, oak, plane—which was reached through rusty old gates, fixed open, only a plastic red and white chain notionally barring passage to the property.

Monsieur Polle opened the front door and led me in, handing me a thickly labelled bunch of keys and muttering, "Félicitations" as I symbolically took possession. Old terracotta tiles clicked underfoot as I looked in on a large ground-floor room containing two leather armchairs, some moth-ravaged curtains and a boarded-up fireplace. I put down my grip and my suitcase filled with dynamite and listened as Monsieur Polle explained that there was no water or electricity connected and he could recommend an excellent hotel in Puy l'Évêque. No, no, I said, I intended to spend the night here before I returned to England. "Comme vous voulez, Monsieur Mountstuart." I liked the way my name sounded in French. Monsieur Polle dropped me in Sainte-Sabine, which was only a kilometre away, and I found a little supermarket there where I bought some bread, a tin of pâté, red wine (screwtop), a bottle of water and some candles. I walked slowly back through the gathering dusk to my new home.

In candlelight I ate my bread and pâté and drank my bottle of wine. I pushed the two leather armchairs together and lay there under my overcoat, watching the light from the candle flame wash over the ceiling and listening to the absolute silence. Absolute until I blew out the candle, when in the impenetrable darkness I began to hear the tiny crepitations of rodents and insects and the strange shiftings and creakings that any old house produces as the temperature drops. I felt very secure.

I spent another two days and nights in Cinq Cyprès pottering around, acquainting myself with the house and its grounds. It was far from beautiful, this *maison de maître,* three storeys high, covered in a grey *crépi* with an out-of-proportion ornamental wrought-iron balcony on the first floor. Built by some prosperous burgher relative of Cyprien who wanted to impress his neighbours, no doubt. Nature had softened its outlines by the overwhelming growth of creeper and ivy—many of the shuttered windows higher up were completely hidden. The ground floor was in reasonable repair—it needed a good clean more than anything else—but as you climbed higher through the house you could see the damage inflicted by damp and mould. There was obviously a bad leak in the roof, and one window had a shutter missing and panes broken that had been letting in the weather for years. The rooms were dark from all the mature trees round about, and it was impossible to tell where the lawns merged with the meadow that surrounded the property. Beyond the meadow, oak woods loomed on three sides and behind the house, slightly offset, was the old stone barn with a small two-roomed labourer's bothy attached.

I found the key to the barn and, poking around inside, discovered some rickety spades and hoes amongst other ancient rust-rotted farm implements. I took a spade and dug a hole in the small overgrown orchard behind the barn and buried my suitcase of gelignite there. I did not mark the spot. Then I walked into Sainte-Sabine for more provisions.

Sainte-Sabine possessed a main street and a small square around which stood a church (badly restored), a post office, a *mairie* and the Superette. In side streets off the square were a couple of bars, a couple of pharmacies, a couple of butchers and a couple of bakers. There was a medical centre with a doctor's consulting rooms and a dentist's surgery; there was a newsagent and a taxi service that doubled as an undertaker's. Just about everything, in fact, that a village of three hundred people might need. The denizens of Sainte-Sabine could feed themselves, run their affairs, be tended when they fell ill, and be disposed of when they died. The main square, Place du 8 Mai, was shaded by ruthlessly pollarded plane trees whose leaves were ankle deep on the ground as I walked through it, heading for the Superette. When I was paying for my goods, the woman at the till said, "Vous êtes le propriétaire de Cinq Cyprès?" I admitted I was and we shook hands. "Je suis Monsieur Mountstuart," I said. "Je suis écrivain." I don't know what made me add that last sentence, but I suppose I thought that if word about me was travelling that fast then I might as well establish my credentials.

On Tuesday morning I shaved in an enamel tin filled with Evian water, locked up the house, and walked into Sainte-Sabine to catch the bus to Penne, where I joined the local stopper to Agen. From Agen I took an express train for Paris and from Paris journeyed on to Calais. It was in Calais that my heart, as they say, almost stopped beating when, in a *maison de la presse,* I saw every newspaper headline shouting one word— "MOGADISHU!" I bought several papers and began to read, slowly beginning to understand something of what I had been involved in.

The Lufthansa Boeing 737 that had been hijacked in Palma on October 13th had made its way from Dubai to Aden. There the captain had been shot dead by the leader of the hijackers (they suspected him of clandestinely passing information to the authorities). The co-pilot had flown the plane from Aden on to Mogadishu in Somalia, always intended to be its final destination. A new deadline was set for the ransom demands. At the last moment a message was received from the control tower saying that the eleven Baader-Meinhof gang members had been released and were now on board a plane bound for Mogadishu. A German air force transport plane landed at Mogadishu Airport in the small hours of Tuesday morning, but there were no Baader-Meinhof members on board. Instead there was a detachment of German commandos from the GSG-9 unit (*Grenzschutz Gruppe Neun*) and two members of the British SAS. Stun grenades were thrown, the Lufthansa jet was stormed, and in the swift and sudden firefight that followed three of the terrorists were killed and one was wounded. The passengers were all released, unharmed.

In Germany, in the gaol in Stammheim where the Baader-Meinhof members were imprisoned, the news quickly broke that the hostages had been rescued. Andreas Baader and Jan-Carl Raspe shot themselves in the head (with guns that had been smuggled into their cells); Gudrun Ensslin, like Ulrike Meinhof,* hanged herself.

The failure of the hijacking had always been considered a possibility and the three original members of the B-M gang had alerted their supporters that, if indeed it failed, they might be killed. Their suicides were meant to look like murders and were to be a last act of revenge against the fascist state. When the news of their deaths broke, there were riots in Rome, Athens, the Hague and Paris. On the next day Dr. Schleyer's body was found in a green Audi in Mulhouse. He had been shot in the head as soon as the news of the rescue at Mogadishu had been broadcast.

So what did John Vivian and the Napier Street Mob have to do with Mogadishu? Why had I been sent across Europe to be a courier for forty sticks of dynamite? My own hunch is that they were intended to be part of the reaction to the potential failure of the hijacking. I suspect they planned to attack specific German targets in England—the embassy, Mercedes-Benz dealerships, perhaps a Goethe Institut or two—to show solidarity and outrage. All that presupposing they could have made the bombs (Ian Halliday's role, I suspect) and that Anna, Tina and John Vivian himself could have planted the devices without blowing themselves up. As I crossed the Channel towards Dover, I was pleased that I had buried those sticks of explosive in my orchard in France. They could decompose quietly there, not cause any harm.

And I wasn't apprehensive about confronting Vivian. I was going to say that Jürgen had sold me a case full of old newspapers. By the time I'd grown suspicious and picked the locks and looked inside he was long gone. What else was I meant to do but come home? I was ready to feign further innocence: what was meant to be in that case, John? Drugs? I was actually curious to see what his reply might be but in the event it never came about: as I stepped off the ferry at Dover I was arrested by two Special Branch officers and taken to the Royal Army

*Ulrike Meinhof had committed suicide in 1976.

Medical Hospital, beside the Tate Gallery, where I was questioned for two hours by a young and pushily aggressive detective called Deakin.

I told Deakin why I had joined the SPK and what I did for them. I said I was returning from a short holiday in Europe, looking at a piece of property I owned there. Did you meet anyone on your travels? Deakin asked. You meet all sorts of people when you travel alone, I said. I mentioned, for good measure, that I had been a commander in the RNVR during the war and a member of the Naval Intelligence Division and I demanded to know what was going on. He didn't believe me. When some underling checked—and reported that it was true—his manner changed dramatically. He said that they had raided Napier Street on the basis of intelligence "received from abroad." My name was discovered on documents seized. Anna Roth and Tina Brownwell had been arrested. Ian Halliday was in Amsterdam. John Vivian had disappeared. I was released at 11:00 that evening. Turpentine Lane was a convenient ten-minutes' walk away. I strolled home through the chilly night. My days with the Socialist Patients' Kollective, and my paper round, were no more, clearly: the dog-food years were about to begin again.

POSTSCRIPT TO THE MEMORANDUM

I saw John Vivian about two weeks after my return. I was in the Cornwallis, sipping my lager with its sweet sherry chaser, when he came in and sidled over. His hair was cut short and dyed grey, he wore a sports jacket with a shirt and tie.

"John," I said. "My God, you look smart."

"I've gone underground," he said. "At least I'm trying to go underground. You can go underground in Germany, no bother, but try doing it in this fucking country."

"The disguise is good, though."

"Thanks. You got the suitcase?"

"I dumped it in France."

His jaw muscles clenched. "Just as well. Listen, you got any of the money left?"

"I gave it all to Jürgen."

"Jürgen?"

"The guy in Zurich. I was going to tell you. After he'd given me the suitcase and gone I got suspicious. Picked the lock—it was full of old newspapers."

John Vivian's face seemed to go into spasm. "Cunt!" he said, several times. Then he sat there for a while massaging his temples.

"What should have been in the suitcase, John?"

"Doesn't matter. Not now. You couldn't lend me ten quid, could you? I'm broke."

"Not as broke as I am. I've got £1.75 that has to last me until Friday. I'm poor, John. Poorer than you."

He looked at me. "Flower of the nation, eh? Jesus College, Oxford."

"Gonville and Caius, Cambridge."

We had to laugh. I gave him a pound and he went away* without a backward glance.

---

*John Vivian was arrested six weeks later after an abortive raid on a sub–post office in Llangyfellach near Swansea. The postmaster, an ex-soldier, recognizing that the gun Vivian was pointing at him was fake, punched him in the face and broke his nose. Vivian was sentenced to seven years in prison for attempted robbery.

THE FRENCH JOURNAL

On 4 May 1979 Logan Mountstuart went to the designated polling station for his Pimlico ward, voted Labour and left the country. By the time Margaret Thatcher was declared the new Prime Minister he was on French soil. When he learned the result of the general election he was even more convinced that his move to Sainte-Sabine had been the wisest and most judicious course of action.

Turpentine Lane was sold to LMS's upstairs neighbour, "Subadar" Singh, for £28,000–cash. Of which approximately £5,000 was designated for the renovation of Cinq Cyprès. Most of the work was to be done on the ground floor–which LMS decided to make his living quarters, not fancying having to negotiate a steep staircase as his age advanced, contenting himself with merely making good the upper floors, staunching leaks, replacing rotten timbers and the like. He created a fairly commodious apartment on the ground floor, consisting of a sitting room with a large fireplace, a study, a large kitchen–dining room and a bedroom with a bathroom next door. His furniture from Turpentine Lane was easily installed, and two walls in his study were lined with bookshelves to accommodate his library and archive. More work was done to the "labourer's bothy" attached to the barn, which was transformed into a small two-bedroom house, somewhat cramped but neat and clean. This he intended to rent out to holiday-makers in the summer to supplement the income he would receive from the remainder of the Singh cash, now safely banked in a high-interest account at the Société Générale in Puy l'Évêque.

LMS calculated he could live relatively comfortably at Cinq Cyprès on £2,000 a year–in any event it would be a better life than anything he could have managed at Turpentine Lane. And, as it turned out, he was able to rent the bothy without difficulty in July and August, tenants returning regularly, year after year.

He acquired a cat (female–to deal with the rodent problem in the house), which he called "Hodge," and a dog, for security and companionship (male, three quarters beagle, one quarter spaniel), which he named, for obvious reasons, "Bowser."

He settled into Cinq Cyprès with little fuss and soon became well known in the commune of Sainte-Sabine. The proximity of the village meant that it was easy for him to walk there, which he often did, maintaining that walking was the best exercise for those of advancing years. On market day, Wednesday, he would ride in on his mobylette and load its saddlebags with provisions for the following week.

He discreetly let it be known that he was embarked on a major work of fiction (Octet), assuming that this would discourage casual visitors and avert questions about what he was up to. His cousin Lucy Sansom would come for a fortnight's holiday each year at the end of May. She always stayed in the bothy and often the day would go by without their seeing each other until they met for an aperitif before supper: both found the situation ideal.

Semi-recluse or not, LMS soon acquired a network of French friends and neighbours who were helpful and accommodating and contributed enormously to the quality of his thrifty life in rural France.

The entries in the French Journal are very random, and undated; sometimes it appears that months had gone by without anything being recorded. The events concerning Mme Dupetit occurred largely between 1986 and 1988.

Of all the wood I burn in my fire the logs from the cherry tree are the hardest. A solid cherry log seems almost as resistant to flame as concrete. Next, in order of difficult combustibility, come cedar, oak and elm. Bringing up the rear is pine–which burns too easily and leaves lots of ash. None of these woods spit, whereas acacia is deadly. Shortly after

I had moved here I made the mistake of laying a fire with acacia logs. As the flames took hold the fire began to sound like downtown Beirut, snapping with sporadic gunshots. Then small hot coals would zip out of the fireplace like spent tracer. I eventually had to douse the whole thing with a bucket of water, thereby filling the room with a damp grey smoke. Never again.

Reading Nabokov's *Ada:* an intermittently brilliant but baffling book– an *idée fixe* on the rampage, leaving friendly readers stunned and exhausted behind. I have to say that as an admirer of style–a loaded word, but actually best thought of as a synonym for individuality– VN's mannered artfulness, his refusal to let a sleeping word lie, becomes in this book more and more like a nervous tic than a natural, individual voice, however fruity and sonorous. The studied opulence, the ornament for the sake of ornament, grows wearing and one longs for a simple, elegant, discursive sentence. This is the key difference: in good prose precision must always triumph over decoration. Wilful elaboration is a sign that the stylist has entered a decadent phase. You cannot live on caviar and foie gras every day: sometimes a plain dish of lentils is all that the palate craves, even if one insists that the lentils come from Puy.

Norbert drove me to VsL [Villeneuve-sur-Lot], where Francine received me with her usual glacial politesse in her bibelot-crammed apartment. We drank a glass of wine and proceeded to the bedroom. Alas, I came within seconds. She washed me off in the bidet–something I've always enjoyed–and then we lay around on the bed for half an hour, seeing if I would grow hard again. No luck, so a swift b.j. before I left. Five hundred francs–worth every brassy centime.

[Norbert was Norbert Coin, Sainte-Sabine's ambulance/taxi driver, LMS's first local friend and ally. For the initial years of his stay LMS, on Norbert's recommendation, visited this discreet forty-year-old housewife-prostitute every two to three months.]

Strange late-afternoon sky—packed with clouds, all creased and gathered like grey linen or damask—and then, as the sun began to set, the light seemed to sluice through the folds, steeping the grey clouds in a fiery gold sunshine.

The simple satisfactions of living in a republic. The plumber calls to fix the broken lavatory in the bothy. We shake hands, address each other as "monsieur" and wish each other good day. He introduces me to his twelve-year-old son. Hands are shaken once more. At the end of the day he calls in to say everything is working. We share a glass of wine, talk about the weather, the prospects of a decent vintage this year, the proliferation of foxes in the neighbourhood. I shake his hand and his son's and wish them good night and a "bon retour."

Lucy left yesterday—Norbert drove her to Toulouse to catch her plane. She asked if she might bring a friend next year and I said, of course. She's heavy and florid but seems in pretty good health—good enough for her to take up smoking in her seventies. She insisted on paying me £200. Her friend is female, she assured me.

General astonishment in the village at the unearthing of an old copy of *Les Cosmopolites* in Moncuq Public Library. Yes, that old geezer in Cinq Cyprès is a writer after all. The book is passed around amongst the people who know me like a holy relic.

Mallowy red in the night sky tonight, just before dark, brilliantly offset by what can only be described as a stripe of pistachio green. I can think of any number of abstract painters who might have longed to re-create such a juxtaposition—it was gone within seconds. All the "shock" effects of a century of abstract art have been quietly replicated somewhere or other in nature since time began. Walked out in the park amongst the trees with my glass of wine. Unusually, Bowser accompanied me, but always at a discreet distance, as if he wanted to keep an eye on me but not interrupt my thoughts.

The depth of shade around the house is so dense and cool that to step into it from the sun on the hottest days is like entering a dark cellar. I remember Monsieur Polle advising me to take half the mature trees down. Thank God there are no conifers (I don't count the cypresses)— conifers remind me of crematoria—grim associations with Putney Vale and Gloria's funeral.

Monsieur and Madame Mazeau's silver wedding anniversary [they ran the Superette]. I was invited to the "cocktail" in the Café de France— something of an honour, I think—perhaps Norbert's doing (Lucette Mazeau is his sister). As we toasted the diffident couple I realized that here amongst their family, relations and neighbours was my new circle of friends—my new *tertulia*. Norbert, of course, and Claudine [his wife]; Jean-Robert [Stefanelli—who helped LMS with his garden]; Henri and Marie-Thérèse [Grossoleil—owners of the Café de France]; Lucien and Pierrette [Gorce—a farmer. LMS's nearest neighbour]. Who else? I suppose Yannick Lefrère-Brunot [the local dentist and Mayor of Sainte-Sabine] and Didier Roisanssac [the doctor] would make up the numbers. I'm humbled by the uncomplicated welcome I've received here and I wonder would an elderly Frenchman be the recipient of sim- ilar friendliness should he decide to retire to Wiltshire or Yorkshire or Morayshire? Perhaps. Perhaps people are kinder everywhere than maps of the world would lead you to believe. We drank whisky and ate little cheese biscuits. Everyone was toasted several times. The success of my novel was devoutly wished and I felt truly happy for the first time in years. Such moments should be logged and noted. I miss nothing of my English life—I can't imagine how I survived there after Nigeria. What was it Larry Durrell called the place? "Pudding Island." I feel no desire to return to Pudding Island ever again. *Quod sit, esse velit, nihilque malit* [Who would be what he is, desiring nothing extra?]. Important to know that, when it happens.

*   *   *

If I were the President of France I would:

(a) Offer tax relief to café owners to replace their plastic chairs with cane or wooden ones.
(b) Ban the piped playing of Anglo-American rock music in the streets during markets or fêtes. There can be nothing more alienating than walking round an ancient French town listening to hit-parade records bellowed out in English banalities.
(c) Restrict each household to only one conifer per garden. Those who cut down a conifer and replace it with a deciduous tree to receive a 1,000 franc bonus.

"My bowels and I never fail to keep our rendezvous." I am I suppose in fairly good health for a man of my age. My leg aches on cold days and from time to time the brown mist fogs my vision. But I still have energy and I sleep well, though less and less each year. My teeth are giving up the struggle and Yannick L-B has made me a snug top plate (free) that replaces all but two ancient worn-down molars. The bottom row seems fine for the moment. My hair appears to have stopped falling out and I'm debating whether to grow a beard—depends how white it is, I don't want to look like Santa Claus. I eat two meals a day, breakfast and lunch, and drink wine and eat potato crisps at night. I feel the lean muscle mass on my body beginning to diminish—everything about my naked body looking slack and swagged. I'm probably as thin now as I was in my thirties. I think about what might carry me off and I have this feeling that something happened to my head in the crash that is lying dormant. The curious foxing of my area of vision is a portent of the way I will go. The overtaxed brain bursting into blood. Fast, though. Sudden darkness and then nothing.

Out in the woods today looking for mushrooms with Lucien. His face is seamed and weather-lashed and his hands are all callous—wholly impervious to extreme heat or cold. He's fifty-six, but he looks older than me, wheezing and coughing as he pokes about the undergrowth.

His family have been here for generations but he says his son has no interest in farming—he lives and works in a garage in Agen. Lucien shrugs: *Les jeunes* . . . A common sigh, hereabouts. But no doubt young Lucien Gorce caused his papa a few anxious moments himself. I calculate how old Lucien would have been during the Occupation (something I unreflectingly do with all elderly French people I meet). Lucien was born in 1928, so he would have been in his early teens during the war. We managed a rich haul of ceps and girolles. I will break my habit and make a mushroom omelette tonight.

I telephoned Lucy from the post office [LMS only had a telephone installed in his house in 1987] to find out her flight details and arrange her collection from the airport. She said, "Wasn't Peter Scabius a friend of yours?" I confessed I was proud to consider Sir Peter as one of my oldest. "Not anymore you're not," she said, "he died last week."

I felt that instant empty feeling, an absence: like a brick removed from an already shaky wall and you wonder if the new weights and stresses on the other bricks will accommodate this sudden hole, if that redistribution will leave it standing or bring it down. The moment passed, but I felt somehow weaker, more ramshackle myself. I sensed that my life, my world, without Peter Scabius in it was a tottering, more jerry-built edifice all of a sudden.

How did he die? I asked. "Pneumonia. He was in the Falklands." Don't tell me, I said, he was researching a new novel. "How did you guess?" Lucy said, incredulous and admiring. Researching a novel: how very Peter to want to write a novel about the Falklands War. So, Ben and Peter *nous ont quittés* as they say here, leaving me alone. Lucy said the newspapers were full of long obituaries and respectful assessments and I asked her to send them on. "Nobody mentions you," she said.

Bowser is an undemonstrative dog, not requiring much affection day to day. However, every week or so, he will come and seek me out and, if I am sitting, he will place his jaw on my knee, or, if I am standing, he will butt me gently on the calves with his head. I know this means he wants some loving and so I scratch his ears, pat his sides and say to him all the silly nonsense that dog owners have regaled their dogs with through the ages: "Who's a good old boy, then?," "What a good dog!," "Who's the best dog in the world?" After about a couple of minutes of this he will shake himself as if he's just swum across a stream and wander off.

The Olafsons are here for their third year running, taking the bothy for a month this time. The sun was hammering down when they arrived, and we sat on the lawn at the back of my house in the shade of the big chestnut and drank cold white wine. They couldn't hide their excitement and pleasure at being here in the warm south, saying there had been a ground frost in Reykjavik the night they'd left. I told them I had visited their home town once (I don't know why I had never mentioned it before, I said). Then they asked me what had taken me to Reykjavik and, as I began to explain, the reason for my reticence became all too obvious. I was telling them about Freya and Gunnarson and the war and how Freya had thought I was dead when the tears started to creep down my cheeks unprompted. I wasn't feeling grief: that hellish chest-crammed agony you feel—but some portion of my brain activated by the memory decided to trigger the tear ducts. They were looking at me, shocked. I said it had all been very sad and tried to change the subject, talking about some new restaurant that had opened in the neighbourhood. But I wept again when they left and I felt the better for it—weakened and purged. I went inside and looked at Freya's and Stella's photographs. Freya and Stella. That was my good luck; those were my lucky years and I can't complain. Some people never have any luck in their lives and during the years I loved Freya and she loved me I was awash in it. And then the bad luck came back.

That's all your life amounts to in the end: the aggregate of all the good luck and the bad luck you experience. Everything is explained by that simple formula. Tot it up—look at the respective piles. There's nothing you can do about it: nobody shares it out, allocates it to this one or that, it just happens. We must quietly suffer the laws of man's condition, as Montaigne says.

*   *   *

Spent half an hour staring mesmerized at the shape of water pouring out of the overflowing pond by the big oak at the meadow's edge. Somehow a large stone had become wedged in the outlet and the water ran over it, smooth and glazed like an inverted bowl or the boss of some great wheel. I dipped a stick in the water and allowed the drops to fall from its end on to this globey running flow, sowing the smooth shoulder of water with seeds of dry quicksilver drops—which instantly disappeared, making no impression on the burnished surface.

Major building work going on at La Sapinière and Sainte-Sabine is abuzz with speculation. The house has been empty—apart from the caretakers—for fifteen years since the last tenants left. La Sapinière is an elegant chartreuse about two miles away from me, hidden behind stone walls higher than a man's head. I hope the new owners aren't British—most of the Brits seem congregated around Montaigu de Quercy way. There's a sculptor on the other side of Sainte-Sabine, an Englishman called Carlyle, who makes sculptures out of old farm machinery—but he's even more of a recluse than me. When our paths cross in the market or the pharmacy we feign convincing ignorance of each other.

Hard frost today, then a slow foggy thaw, the trees in the park spectral, fuzzy constructions—almost artificial looking—as the enveloping fog hid the twigs and finer branches leaving only the massy ones visible to the eye. A child's version of trees.

All day a song has been going round and round my head. An old song, pre-war. Something about the tune makes it naggingly hard to forget.

> *Life is short*
> *Something, something,*
> *We're all getting older*
> *So don't be an also ran,*
> *Something, something,*

Dance little man,
Dance whenever you can

Dance little man. So I shall.

A curdled, mealy sky this afternoon, slowly breaking up as the evening advanced to a brightening blue, but hazy.

The new chatelaine at La Sapinière is one Madame Dupetit—from Paris, no less. Unmarried? Divorced? She is alone, it seems, with no children and a great deal of money. The old caretakers have been let go and a new couple installed from Agen while the renovation work goes on.

May. The first summer-feeling of the year. Verges pricked with primroses. Fat loafy clouds laze idly across the valley. My favourite month, the countryside fresh with the unreal new green of the leaves on the trees. Bees swarm in the roof of Cinq Cyprès and die in their thousands in the upper rooms. I sweep up spadefuls, even though I leave the windows open. Bees appear to be very stupid insects at swarming time, ignoring the open window and battering futilely at the glass panes of the closed ones, until they fall to the ground and die of exhaustion. They seem to regain their senses and calm down once the comb is built and the search for pollen begins.

Tremendous heat today, like August—*caniculaire,* as they describe them here: the dog-days. But there are no dog-days in May, everything is growing with all its might. But in August when the vegetation is on the turn and the nights begin to draw in, ever so slowly, then that heat weakens and depresses you, the sun seems baleful, crushing.

But now even Bowser seeks out a patch of sunshine to sleep in. He lies there sprawled, a leg twitching as he chases dream sheep or butterflies. Hodge steps lightly by and she looks at him with curiosity and a little disdain.

*　　*　　*

I was walking into Sainte-Sabine when a steel-blue Mercedes-Benz estate pulled up beside me. There was a woman driving and she offered me a lift into the village. We introduced ourselves but I knew before she told me her name that she was Madame Dupetit from La Sapinière. She has greyish-blond hair and very pale skin, almost Nordic, and would be an attractive woman if there was not something tight-lipped and reserved about her features, as if determined to deny any sensual or frivolous nature she might have. She was well and expensively dressed, her hair up in a loose chignon, fingers and wrists discreetly but richly jewelled. She was down from Paris to inspect the work, hoping to move in before August–I must come over for an aperitif once she was properly installed. Gladly, I said. She plans to spend only the summers here–perhaps a visit at Easter. She was in the antiques trade, she told me, and had a small shop in the rue Bonaparte. Yes, of course she knew Leeping Frères. I explained my old connection with the firm. By the time I climbed out of her car by the post office we were fairly well informed about each other. I was quizzed pretty thoroughly at the Café de France by Henri and Marie-Thérèse. There is much curiosity about the elegant Madame Dupetit. No one has quite got her number yet.

This year Lucy seems older, more tired. Her friend, Molly, confided her worries to me. She had a bad fall in the spring and knocked herself out for a few minutes. The fall seems to have mysteriously sapped her energy–shaken her up in some fundamental way. One day she was in my study looking through the bookshelves for something to read. She saw the cardboard boxes full of my papers and manuscripts and she asked me what was going to happen to them.

"Happen?"

"When you drop off the perch. You can't just have all this thrown away. There must be fascinating material in there."

"Fascinating to me, that's for sure."

"Why don't I find you some eager young lover of literature to catalogue it all, sort it out?"

"No thank you. I don't want a stranger reading my private papers."

But she inspired me: I have decided to set my house in order.

*   *   *

Rereading my old journals is both a source of revelation and shock. I can see no connection between that schoolboy and the man I am now. What a morose, melancholy, troubled soul I was. That wasn't me, was it?

The idea of a priori moral judgements ("It is morally wrong to inflict gratuitous pain") is completely acceptable to the vast majority of human beings. Only a few philosophers would disagree.

Three bad days of the brown mist so I went to Dr. Roisanssac. He's a good-looking, clean-cut 35-year-old with prematurely grey hair. He checked me out, blood pressure, palpations, blood and urine samples. I told him about my smash-up and he said he could send me to Bordeaux for a brain scan if I wanted. I told him I couldn't possibly afford it. No, no, he said, it's free—Monsieur Coin will drive you there and bring you back. You don't have to pay a penny. It was tempting but I said no: strangely reluctant to have my brain scanned, whatever that may involve. I worry what else they might find.

Drinks at La Sapinière. It's a beautiful house—eighteenth century, with a dusty yellow *crépi* on the walls and steeply angled mansard roofs with fish-scale tiles. Two small wings extend forward to enclose a gravelled forecourt with a fountain. At the back there is a balustraded terrace overlooking a newly planted parterre that will be superb in a couple of years. Inside it is still a little empty-looking, but such pieces as Madame Dupetit has placed here and there are commensurate with the age and style of the building. All very sophisticated but, to my eye, a little soulless, museum-like: Aubusson rugs on glossy old parquet, a pair of precisely angled armchairs, dust-free tables and cabinets. Only the pictures appear commonplace: standard portraits, sub-Watteau *fêtes champêtres*, over-varnished, idealized landscapes. One can't criticize the taste but one misses the absence of life about the house. I wanted a big carnal nude above the fireplace, or a glass and chrome coffee table stacked with books and magazines–something to clash, to jar, to draw the eye–something that says there is a human being living here.

But Madame Dupetit seems more relaxed in her own domain and consequently looked more pretty. Her hair was down, she wore linen slacks and a white blouse. She has a bosom. We drank gin-tonics in my honour and she smoked a cigarette in a careful way that suggested this was a rare, illicit pleasure. When she leaned forward to stub it out, the collar of her blouse briefly parted and I saw the swell and crease of her breasts, held by the embroidered border of her brassiere. I felt that old sensation of weakness bloom at the base of my spine and I was duly grateful. If I had been twenty years younger I might have wished our neighbourly courtesies would lead further.

She was very friendly–perhaps too friendly–laying her hand on my arm, asking if she might call me Logan and that I was to call her Gabrielle. We would be two allies here in Sainte-Sabine, she said, and added that if I ever needed anything I had only to summon her *gardiens*. It was all very civilized, sitting on her rear terrace, watching the sun lengthening the shadows, the swifts dodging and dipping above our heads, talking about Paris. She was born there, she said, after the war. La Sapinière had been an old family property and she had bought it from her brother. I sensed that Monsieur Dupetit, whoever he might have been, had been gone a long time.

Francine has announced that she doesn't want any more visits to her apartment–the neighbours are talking about the men who come and go. She would be very happy to meet me in a hotel, however, and recommended one on the outskirts of town, where she obviously has an understanding with the management. This is unaffordable as far as I am concerned, so the news appears to put an end to my sexual life. I shall miss Francine and her utter lack of curiosity about me. I, by contrast, have always been very curious about her and wonder how this middle-aged housewife embarked on her career as a part-time prostitute. I ask questions but she sidesteps them all.

*   *   *

Consternation at the Superette: frowns, head shaking, dark mutterings. Didier Mazeau asked me if I had seen what had gone up on the wall at La Sapinière. No, I said, what is it? You'd better take a look, Didier advised—me, I'm saying nothing. So I detoured on my mobylette and passed by. And there to the right of the gateposts, set in the wall, was a stone plaque with carved letters that read (in French): "To the memory of Benoit Verdel (1916–1971), known as 'Raoul,' commandant of the Resistance group 'Renard' that liberated Sainte-Sabine from the German yoke on the 6th June 1944." So, more becomes clear: a family property; her father a Resistance fighter, perhaps a local hero. How come no one in Sainte-Sabine knew of the connection and why was Didier Mazeau so frowningly circumspect?

"As sound as a bell of brass." This is a phrase my father used to describe perfectly frozen meat. Can't think why it should suddenly pop up in my head. I haven't thought of him for years and as I bring him to mind, and recall his tolerant sad smile, I feel my tear ducts smart, automatically.

Gabrielle to drinks here. I must say I miss the company of women. Nothing is going to occur between us, but to smell her perfume, to watch her sit back in the armchair and cross her legs, to lean forward and hold a match to her cigarette, to feel the guiding pressure of her fingers on the back of my hand, provide an intense feeling of sensual pleasure. I infuse her presence here in my house with as much suppressed and tender eroticism as I dare without being impolite. I showed her around and she spotted the little Picasso sketch on my study wall. I told her how it had come about and she was, I think, quite amazed to learn that I'd met him. She looked at the piles of books and the boxes of papers and asked me what I was working on, so I told her a little about *Octet*.

    Then I said I had seen the plaque on the wall and she explained its significance to me. Her father had been in the Resistance during the war but she had only learned this after his death. Her mother had told her the few facts that were available: his code name, that he had run a group known as "Renard" in the Lot, and that his orders on the day of the invasion were to liberate Sainte-Sabine and establish strong points on key roads and bridges in the area. From what she had read of histories of the Resistance she knew also that their other tasks were to round up and arrest Nazi sympathizers and collaborators. After the war he had bought La Sapinière but shortly after his business had taken him abroad and the family moved to Paris, where she was born and then her brother, some six years later. "It's entirely possible that I was conceived in La Sapinière," she said with a laugh. "And after my father died, when we discovered we owned the property, the family decided the easiest solution was to rent it out." Then she hinted at her own marital difficulties and, after they were "solved," she decided she needed to make a significant change in her life and thought it would be a fitting gesture to her father's memory to restore the house and celebrate what he had done for Sainte-Sabine. He never spoke about the war, I asked? Never, she said. Even her mother knew very little—she had met her father in 1946 and a year later they were in Paris. You have to understand, she said, that for men of her father's generation the Liberation, however longed for, also provoked enormous trauma: in order to fight the Germans you often had to fight Frenchmen too—and when the war was over there was the matter of justice and retribution. It wasn't easy to live with the knowledge of what he had seen and what, perhaps, he had been obliged to do. *Mieux de se taire.*

Huge storm in the night. Stepping out in the morning to find the ground drenched and sodden but the air seeming fresh, newly rinsed, newly decanted.

Milau-Plage. Hôtel des Dunes. A sudden desire to be by the ocean has brought me here, south of Mimizan on the Atlantic coast. This small hotel backs into the dunes and faces a tidal salt-water inlet-cum-lake, the Étang de Milau. There are six rooms on the first floor and down below there is a restaurant, Chez Yvette, where they push back the sliding doors in summer and place tables on a rectangle of wooden decking beneath a thick and shady vine.

Milau-Plage is a little resort town that is just far enough away from major centres of population to remain essentially unspoilt and unpretentious. On the *étang* side there is the old *quartier des pêcheurs* with its bright wooden fishermen's cabins and around that a couple of streets with shops and bars, the whole town dominated by its lofty red-and-white striped lighthouse. You leave the sheltered streets of the town and climb up through the dunes to find the huge sandy beaches on this west coast of France. Here and there surviving concrete bunkers and gun emplacements of Hitler's Atlantic Wall topple and slide slowly down the eroding dunes to the ocean beyond. Beach life centres around an *école de surf* and a couple of beach shacks selling drinks and sandwiches.

Yannick Lefrère-Brunot recommended Milau-Plage to me when I told him of my urge to be by the sea once more—on the condition that I told nobody else. He also told me to inform Yvette Pelegris, the proprietress of the hotel, that I was a friend of his. It made a marginal difference to her welcome, I think. Yvette is a buxom, hard-faced woman with vivid auburn hair who knows she runs the best restaurant on this section of the coast. Consequently she has hoicked her prices to deter the kids and the trippers, and her clientele is either well-heeled or ageing or both. I have had a good year with my bothy-rentals and I felt I deserved a treat. I booked in here for an initial week but I've already extended it for another. I sleep well and breakfast late on the terrace. Then I wander about the town, buy a newspaper and at lunchtime usually make my way up through the dunes to the beach and have a beer and a sandwich at one or other of the beach shacks. Dinner at 8:00 sharp Chez Yvette: invariably oysters, grilled fish, *tarte du jour* and a bottle of wine. The wine could be better, so I asked Yvette if she would mind if I supplied my own—no problem, she said, as long as I didn't object to paying *un petit supplément*.

So now I sit in an umbrella's circle of shade on the planked deck of a beach shack, a beer in my hand and a book in my lap, and I look at the people as they come and go and listen to the crash and hiss of the breakers as they curve in, flatten and explode on the sand. I must do this every year, while I have the money and the strength—good for the soul, a few days like this.

*   *   *

I had just achieved a neat solution to a complicated time-jump in *Octet*, lunch was approaching and I had just opened a bottle of wine, when Gabrielle telephoned.* She sounded very tense and asked if I would come over straight away. So I jumped on my mobylette and motored over to La Sapinière. Gabrielle was standing on the road by the gates, smoking. We didn't kiss hello—she merely pointed, wordlessly, to the wall.

The plaque had been crudely defaced, as if struck hard by the spike of a pickaxe, five or six big gouges having been torn in the stone, leaving it entirely ruined. Gabrielle was red-eyed with angry tears and quivering with suppressed fury. "What kind of people do this, Logan?" she said in English as if her French was not to be sullied by comment on this sad little outrage. Had she called the gendarmes? Of course. What could they do? Nothing. Kids, vandals—they see something new, they want to destroy it. Then she began to cry—which was very upsetting—and I put my arms around her and walked her back to the house. I stayed for lunch and she slowly composed herself, making plans to replace the stone—perhaps something cast in metal would be better. I applauded the idea.

Here's a dark thought for a dark night: we all want a sudden death but we know we're not all going to be provided with one. So our end will be our ultimate bit of good luck or bad luck—the final addition to the respective piles. But nature does offer some form of consolation, so it strikes me now, as I wonder how I will go. The more drawn out, painful and undignified our dying, the more we long for death—we can't wait for life to end, we're in a hurry, hungry for oblivion. But is that a consolation? When you're comparatively fit and well you want to stay as long as you can and you fear and repudiate death. Is it better to be longing for the end? . . . Now I'm in my eighties—toothless, limping,

*This places the entry in the summer of 1987. LMS had a telephone installed in March.

the brown fog descending from time to time, but otherwise as well as I can expect—I find myself asking the universe for one more piece of good luck. A sudden exit, please. Just switch the lights out.

I suddenly started thinking of Dick Hodge today and I remembered a piece of social advice he gave me if I ever found myself at a dinner party, stuck for conversation. It's incredibly easy, Dick claimed: in order to start chatting, Dick said, just tell lies. Say, to the woman on your right, "I suffer appallingly from insomnia, how do you sleep?" Or confess that your wife's ex-husband has threatened to kill you. Or that you were mugged the week before. It always works, he says. Say you knew someone in a recent air-crash, or that you'd heard that a member of the Royal Family was converting to Islam. Most dinner-party conversations are so boring that you'll have an avid audience for the duration. Never fails, he said.

Interesting to observe that there is comparatively little sympathy in Sainte-Sabine for Gabrielle over the vandalization of her father's memorial. Norbert shrugs—*Les jeunes*. Didier and Lucette observe that these things happen. Only Jean-Robert says that maybe someone has a grudge against her father. Jean-Robert came to Sainte-Sabine in the 1950s, and so knows nothing of the war years, but, by means of a series of eloquent inflections in his voice and little grimaces that he makes, he manages to imply that Sainte-Sabine has many dark secrets to reveal. He's heard a few rumours: "Some people, the older men . . ." He'll go no further.

Thus it is that I find myself, the next market day, looking at the old timers as they stand around and chat. 1940 to 1944—almost anyone in their sixties would be able to tell you something of life under the Occupation in Sainte-Sabine. I know some of these older people well but I'm very reluctant to introduce the subject—I don't want to raise the stone and see what etiolated terrified creatures might be squirming around beneath.

I spoke to Lucien about it. He stuck his hands in his pockets and stared hard at the ground.

"It's a shame," I prompted. "She's an extremely nice woman. She's very upset."

"Of course," Lucien said. "But did she have permission?"

"Permission for what?"

"Permission to put such a memorial up in the first place."

"It's her property, she can do what she likes. She doesn't need permission to honour her father."

Lucien looked fixedly at me. "In my experience, when you're a stranger it's always better to ask permission." Then he smiled, showing me his fine silver teeth, and invited me over for dinner.

The winters here enchant in their own way almost as much as summer. First thing in the morning I come through and build a new fire on the embers of last night's. I lay down a handful of *sarments** and then some sticks of kindling—then a few huffs and puffs of the bellows and we're away. When the flames have taken, I place a couple of split logs against the fire back. Hodge and Bowser like to sit and watch me start the fire and as soon as they see that it is going they wander off, as if the flames are a signal that the day is authorized to begin. We have heavy frosts here that can last for days—the landscape as white and frozen as if it had been snowed upon.

Winter reveals the massive, complex, muscular organization of the ancient oak. Like an old man stripped of his Savile Row, tailored suit—no less impressive in his mature nakedness.

Last week Gabrielle had a new plaque—of embossed metal—set in her wall and this morning it was desecrated again with acid and tar. She was weeping uncontrollably when I went round and I offered to go and see the mayor on her behalf. She was very grateful and I made an appointment with Yannick Lefrère-Brunot for Wednesday.

*Dried shoots from vines that are pruned in the winter and gathered into faggots. Excellent for starting fires and for summer barbecues.

I am aware, though it does not concern me as directly, that I am almost as affronted by these two events as Gabrielle. I know that no community is perfect, but these attacks on Gabrielle's memorial reveal another side of Sainte-Sabine that I find deeply unsettling. Clearly the village shares some dark and shameful secret that Benoit Verdel was involved in exposing—and possibly punishing—in 1944, and, equally clearly, the bitter resentment continues. I feel I am about to turn on friends and family: I don't want to know what went on but it appears I have no choice.

My conversation with Yannick Lefrère-Brunot was not very satisfactory. He offered me a drink and I declined—I wanted this to be formal, official. I asked him if he had any idea who had damaged Madame Dupetit's memorial and he said he had no clue—perhaps vandals? I said I didn't believe him, said I was sure virtually everyone in the village knew who was responsible but they were covering up. I mentioned the word "collaborator" and he shook his head wearily.

> Y L-B: Can I give you some advice, Monsieur Mountstuart?
> LMS: I can't stop you.
> Y L-B: Leave it alone. It doesn't concern you. You are much liked here. Please, don't be any more involved. It will sort itself out.
> LMS: Typical. But you're wrong: you have to take responsibility in life. There's no use turning your back.

He urged me again to leave the matter alone with a quiet vehemence that only increased my suspicions. I reminded him of my profession and suggested—a little vaingloriously, I confess—that this was the kind of story that a writer could easily propagate and embellish. Yannick Lefrère-Brunot seemed genuinely aggrieved and pained at this course our discussion had taken and repeatedly urged me to step back—there was no need to consign anything to print, such a step would be wholly out of proportion. I saw in him all the petty and shameful compromises of political life, no matter how small scale and confined that life might be. Somebody, with some power and influence, is behind all this, and Y L-B is hopelessly stuck in the middle.

Even he doesn't dare risk ventilating the wartime secrets of Sainte-Sabine despite the fact he comes of a generation untainted by the period.

As I left the *mairie* and walked home through the village I felt all eyes were on me, as if I were living in Sicily, dealing with some dark tale of Mafia murders and cover-ups and undying vows of *omertà*. For the first time since I've come here I contemplate moving on.

Brilliant, ravishing sunsets marred by the perfect horizontal contrails of high-altitude jets.

Gabrielle and I formulate our plan. The plaque will be cleaned and restored and will be replaced with as much ostentation as possible. Then at night, after it has gone back on the wall, I will hide up in the small wood opposite the gates and observe the comings and goings. Gabrielle protests—I can see she's thinking: you're far too old for all this—but I'll hear nothing of it. Between midnight and 2:00 a.m. should be sufficient. I'm confident we will catch the culprits—but what then?

This afternoon I found an ideal place behind a thick clump of brambles that gave me a good view of the gates, about thirty yards away across the road. I laid down a plastic groundsheet and hid half a bottle of brandy under a fallen tree. It's dark by 9:30 or 10:00 at this time of the year* and the minimal temperature is forecast to be about 8 or 9 degrees. I'll wrap up well.

The first night—nothing to report. In fact it was rather magical being out in the woods after midnight. It was a cool night but I stayed warm with the help of little burning sips of cognac from time to time. I felt no tiredness: the adrenaline keeping me awake and alert. As a rudi-

*September?

mentary weapon I had an old poker with me from the fire at home—
not that I intended to use it, but it was reassuring, none the less. The
woods were full of movement—crunchings, rustlings—and at one stage
I was convinced there was someone walking around somewhere behind
me. I was aware of a large presence parting the branches, pushing
through the undergrowth, but I realized after a while it must have been
a deer. Between midnight and 2 o'clock I counted seven cars and two
motorbikes and the last half-hour was dead quiet. I could feel my old
heart leap with excitement every time I saw the wash of lights from a
car illuminate the trees. I remembered when I had felt like this before:
my night drop into Switzerland in '44—a few months before Benoit
Verdel liberated Sainte-Sabine.

When I came home both Bowser and Hodge were waiting for me in
the hall—agitated and irritated at my unorthodox behaviour. Hodge
refused to let me stroke her, she was in such a sulk.

I called Gabrielle to report. Again she asked me to forget it: Logan,
please, I don't care what they do—I'll just keep replacing it, they'll get
tired of their game. I said I would carry on for a few more nights. I
think my sense of outrage is exacerbated by the affection I feel for this
place where I've made my home—I can't believe that a little cancer of
spite and vindictiveness can corrupt our community in this way, a
community that is as tolerant, generous and long-suffering as any I've
encountered. I want to know who it is in Sainte-Sabine who is so
ashamed of the past that he (or she?) will attempt this symbolic
besmirching of a good man's name. We shall see.

The second night. Slightly colder with a light wind that set up a constant shushing and shifting in the treetops. Only four cars and a white
van. I finished my cognac. Bowser and Hodge did not deign to welcome me back.

Lunched with Gabrielle. She has a kind of melancholy beauty, with her
long face and her perfectly white skin. I don't know how the subject

arose, but she told me a little more about her marriage. Gilles Dupetit was older than her and had been married twice before but, as she put it, "he was intellectually incapable of fidelity." The marriage had been short and she had resolved, she said, never to put herself in a position where she could be hurt in that way again. That's why she is so upset by this new anguish that Sainte-Sabine has visited upon her. I chided her gently, reminding her that you can't make these unilateral pacts with life. You can't say: that's it, my emotions are securely locked away, now I'm impregnable, safe from the world's cruelties and disappointments. Better to take them on, come what may, I said, see what strength you have within you. Was I mistaken but, when we kissed goodbye, was the pressure of her cheek on mine just a little firmer? Am I falling a little in love with Gabrielle Dupetit? I try to imagine her naked—that pale body, those soft breasts . . . You old fool, Mountstuart, you old fool.

It happened just after 1:00 a.m. I was beginning to feel tired—three late nights in a row was too much for me and I felt my body stiffening up in protest. Suddenly I saw a flare of headlights from a car moving unusually slowly. Then it stopped and I heard the sound of a diesel engine idling for a few seconds and then it cut out and the lights were switched off. Soon I heard a mutter of voices and the sound of footsteps coming along the road towards the gate. It was not a dark night—there was enough moonglow to cast a faint shadow. I saw two men walking along the road, one of them carrying a bulky object in his hand. The first man took up a position of guard in the middle of the road, watching for oncoming lights, while the second approached the plaque. Too late, I realized what he was going to do, but I rose to my feet, poker in hand, and blundered out of the bushes, switching on my torch and shouting, "Right! I've got you! Stop what you're doing! I'm calling the police!" The one on the road began to advance on me threateningly but the man by the plaque said, "Stop. Leave him." I shone my torch in his face—I thought I recognized the voice. It was Lucien Gorce, my friend and neighbour. He had just painted a black swastika on Benoit Verdel's memorial.

MEMORANDUM ON BENOIT VERDEL*

Benoit Verdel deserted from the French Army in October 1939 and joined the criminal underworld in Paris, where, with a certain Valentin M., he was involved in the running of a brothel in the 1er arrondissement. As the German armies approached Paris in the summer of 1940, Verdel joined the tens of thousands of refugees fleeing southwards, where he planned to make for Bordeaux and then the Spanish frontier. In the event he reached no further than Villeneuve-sur-Lot and later took up residence in Sainte-Sabine, where he briefly worked as a farm labourer. With France divided and the Germans secure in the north, there seemed no further need to run and Verdel decided to stay put—and also renew his former profession. He rented a house in Sainte-Sabine and opened it as a *maison de tolérance,* staffing it with four prostitutes recruited from Agen and Toulouse. It was shut down on the orders of the Mayor of Sainte-Sabine, Léon Gorce, with the backing of other local dignitaries—the curé (Monsieur Lasseque) and the doctor (Dr. Belhomme). Verdel was ordered to leave the village and the girls returned to their respective cities.

Nothing more was heard of Verdel until 6 June 1944, when, arriving in the main square of Sainte-Sabine with six other armed men, he declared the village liberated, on the orders of General Charles de Gaulle, and under the command and control of Resistance group "Renard." The Mayor, Monsieur Gorce, the curé, Monsieur Lasseque, and Dr. Belhomme were arrested on suspicion of collaboration with the German occupying powers and were taken to a farm some miles off to be interrogated. On the night of 7 June all three were executed—shot in the head—and were buried in a nearby wood.

In the confusion of the last months of the war Verdel effectively ran Sainte-Sabine and its commune as his personal fiefdom. Evidence of his ruthlessness kept the population both compliant and silent. Verdel used his power and his muscle to grow rich and bought a sizeable property outside the village, La Sapinière, where, in 1946, he installed his new wife.

However, in early 1947 a suit was filed against Verdel for murder by

*Compiled from newspaper reports and the transcript of Benoit Verdel's trial. [LMS's note]

the sisters of Dr. Belhomme and he was arrested and sent to Bordeaux gaol to await trial. Verdel was arraigned before a military tribunal and the trial lasted a full week and was extensively reported in the local press. Details of the exploits of the "Renard" group were vague but Verdel's defence was emphatic: that the three men had been collaborators and that orders issued by de Gaulle before the invasion encouraged *maquisards* to spare no efforts in bringing those who had given aid to the Germans to justice. What he had done in Sainte-Sabine was repeated throughout France—he was simply following orders. Verdel was found guilty and sentenced to eight years in prison, of which he served five before being released on good behaviour.

He never returned to Sainte-Sabine but on his release joined his family in Paris, where, over the next few years, he built up a successful business in the import-export trade. He died in 1971, a wealthy man.

The other man with Lucien Gorce that night was a nephew of Dr. Belhomme. The two of them took me back to my house and explained something of the background to the Verdel story. I went to Bordeaux on Lucien's advice and spent a day in the archives of the *Sud-Ouest* newspaper. I wrote up my account of the trial and gave a copy of it, with huge regret, to Gabrielle. I didn't stay to witness her reaction.

But the next day the plaque had been removed and, shortly after, when I passed the house I saw it had been closed up. The caretakers said they had no idea when Madame Dupetit planned to return. I wrote to Gabrielle in Paris, saying that I was sorry that I had to be the one to tell her the true story about her father's life but that the truth about Benoit Verdel should have no bearing on her relationship with me and vice versa. She hasn't replied, so far.

I also went to see Yannick Lefrère-Brunot and apologized for my presumption and impulsiveness. He was very gracious and said that as far as he was concerned the matter was closed. But as the days have gone by I feel a hot little shame myself—that I didn't trust my instincts and presupposed a malice and venality in these people who had been so cordial and welcoming to me. Christ knows what myths Verdel had spun to his family about his war experience. His wife must have colluded in the mendacity, allowing him to turn his prison sentence into years of fortune-seeking abroad as far as his children were to be concerned. And Gabrielle too thought her father an unassuming hero, self-effacing and traumatized by his experiences. And yet he barely suffered for the murders he committed or for the reign of terror and extortion he instigated in Sainte-Sabine. I can understand the massive affront that Gabrielle's memorial would have given to someone like Lucien Gorce. I apologized to him also. No fool like an old fool, I said. Lucien forgave me and poured me a small glass of *eau-de-vie* that he had made himself—it went down my throat like molten pumice. Then he said: there are things in life we don't understand, and when we meet them, all we can do is let them alone. Sounds reasonable.

Milau-Plage. Hôtel des Dunes. I'm later this year and the place is quieter, the beach virtually empty on weekdays, even when the sun is shining. I spend too much of my time, more often than not, musing on my folly over Gabrielle and her father's memorial. I wrote again and still have received no reply. Reading Montaigne for solace. I think I can forgive myself and I think Gabrielle Dupetit was the last (unrequited) love of my life. I wanted to be the knight errant and expose evil and hypocrisy. At least it sounds like a young man's dementia rather than a senile one's.

Storms looming. Massive anvil clouds to the north: brilliant, gleaming white at their summit shading down through mouse-grey to vein-blue to a dark, bruised grey-purple.

The pleasures of my life here are simple—simple, inexpensive and democratic. A warm hill of Marmande tomatoes on a roadside vendor's stall. A cold beer on a pavement table of the Café de France—Marie Thérèse inside making me a *sandwich au camembert*. Munching the knob off a fresh baguette as I wander back from Sainte-Sabine. The farinaceous smell of the white dust raised by a breeze from the driveway. A cuckoo sounding in the perfectly silent woods beyond the meadow. The huge grey, cerise, pink, orange and washed-out blue of a sunset seen from my rear terrace. The drilling of the cicadas at noon—the soft dialling-tone of the crickets as dusk slowly gathers. A good book, a hammock and a cold, beaded bottle of *blanc sec*. A rough red wine and *steak frites*. The cool, dark, shuttered silence of my bedroom—and, as I go to sleep, the prospect that all this will be available to me again, unchanged, tomorrow.

On Monday I went into the barn to fetch more logs. I should have used the wheelbarrow but instead loaded myself up with a good armful. I was bending down to pick up just one more when I felt a spearing electric pain shaft through my left side, as if my armpit had been run through by a blunt, serrated-edged sword. The pain then ran down my arm, making my hand and fingers fizzle and numb with acute pins and needles. I dropped the logs and reeled back against the wall and I felt my vision darken and I heard a curious sound, a murmuring in my ears like a restless congregation. And then the pain receded and the feeling returned to my fingers.

Dr. Roisanssac said I had had a minor heart attack. He had me off to hospital in Agen for checks and I spent two days there in a room of my own (free) being monitored and examined by a seemingly endless flow of doctors. All appeared more or less back to normal. The doctors said there was nothing more that a man of my age could do other than avoid any undue strain or physical exertion. I didn't smoke anymore, my diet was fine, I wasn't obese but there was no viable operation they could offer—at my age, again—that would ameliorate my state of affairs. Prudence was to be my watchword. And so Norbert drove me back to Sainte-Sabine and my new watchful, softly-softly life began.

As he grew old, all Montaigne asked for was an old age free from dementia—he could cope with pain and suffering and general ill-health. And he did, experiencing terrible agonies in his final years from gallstones. Pain was no problem as long as his mind was lucid. I always thought it would be my brain that would carry me off, some morbid legacy of my encounter with that speeding post office van, but it appears more likely that it will be my heart.

Didier Roisanssac said this to me at my last examination: look at your face in the mirror, he said, it's not the same face you had at eighteen, or twenty-five, or thirty-two. Look at the lines and the creases. Look at the lack of elasticity. Your hair is falling out ("And my teeth," I added). You still recognize that face—it's still you—but it's lived a long time and it's showing the signs of that long life. Think of your old heart like your old face. Your heart doesn't look the same organ as it did when it was eighteen. Imagine that everything that's happened to your face over the years has happened to your heart. So go easy on it.

The springing, young green of the elms. Rooks (and magpies), the most nervily cautious of birds. I open my front door and, half a mile away, they take to the air in agitated fright—the rooks cawing alarm, alarm.

I came through this morning and I knew at once something was wrong. Hodge was sitting on the mantelpiece, immobile. She's never climbed up there before but it was as if she wished to be as far from the ground as possible. Bowser was still sleeping in his basket. "Get up, you lazy old bugger," I said and went to shake him. But he was dead of course— I didn't even need to touch him to know it.

I experienced a form of grief so intense and pure I thought it would kill me. I howled like a baby with my dog in my arms. Then I put him in a wooden wine case and carried him into the garden and buried him under a cherry tree.

He's only an old dog, I tell myself, and he lived a full and happy dog's life. But what makes me unutterably sad is that with him gone— so the love in my life has gone. It may sound stupid, but I loved him and I know he loved me. That meant there was an uncomplicated traffic of mutual love in my life and I find it hard to admit that it's over. Listen to me babble, but it's true—it's true. And, at the same time, I know a part of my sorrow is just disguised self-pity. I needed that exchange and I worry how I'll cope without it and whether I can replace it—if only it were as easy as buying a new dog. I feel very sorry for myself—that is what grief is.

HÔTEL DES DUNES, MILAU-PLAGE

I lunched at the hotel today: half a dozen oysters, turbot, *tarte au citron*. I drank two thirds of a bottle of Sancerre, then I snoozed on my bed for an hour or so before I gathered up my notebook and stick and Panama hat and made my way slowly up the duckboard path through the dunes to the beach.

It is busy—but not high-season busy. I plant myself at my table, order a beer (what's the name of the girl who runs this bar?) and watch the people come and go. Later, when the sun's heat has diminished somewhat, I go for a stroll.

I walk among the holidaymakers and the families noting all the motley types *Homo sapiens* manages to produce. There are as many versions of the basic human body—head, torso, two arms, two legs—as there are versions of the basic human face—two eyes, two ears, nose, mouth. As I pick my way amongst the sunbathers I feel I am moving through a mass of incredibly unconcerned refugees. All the fritter of their individual lives is here—clothes, food, toys, reading matter—and they look, in their state of lounging undress, as if they were deprived in some vague way—that this was all they had in the world—and they were waiting for some refugee commissar or charity organization to tell them where to go next. And yet the mood on the beach contradicted this initial impression—the atmosphere is one of collective idleness rather than fear and unease. The people here participate unreflectingly in the beach's genial democracy and for an hour or so, for a day or so, the fates waiting for them all up ahead are forgotten. The beach is the great human panacea.

Most of the people cluster around the beach shacks and the flags marking the *plage surveillée* as if they are frightened to explore further, as if they need this mass proximity to truly relax. Yet wander a little further and you can have a hundred yards of sand to yourself. This is where the nudists come and as I walk slowly northwards (towards the Channel, towards Pudding Island) a girl rises to her feet from a group of sunbathers and saunters down towards the surf—a long way off now, as the tide is ebbing fast. She is quite naked and as our respective courses intersect she pauses, turns and shouts something (in Dutch) to her friends. She has small pointed breasts and a dense clump of pubic hair. Her tan is complete, opaque brown all over. She continues on without a glance at me, this old man in his cream suit. Two worlds collide at this moment, it seems to me—mine and the future. Who could have imagined that such an encounter would have been possible on a beach in my lifetime? I find it quite exhilarating: the old writer and the naked Dutch girl—perhaps we need a Rembrandt to do it full justice (remember the Hôtel Rembrandt in Paris where I used to stay?). For some reason I find myself wondering what Cyril [Connolly] would have made of such a meeting had it happened to him: delighted incredulity? Or confusion? No, I think serene pleasure—which is what I feel as I plod onward, grateful to this unknown girl with her guileless nakedness. Grateful that the beach should offer me these possibilities, these modest epiphanies.

Back at my beach shack, another beer in front of me, I resume my pose, notebook and pen in hand, but my eyes are flashing around me— there's too much on offer today; the passing parade is profligate. In front of me, seated round a table, are eight French adolescents—four girls, four boys, about sixteen and seventeen, all—to my eye—tanned, slim and attractive. The girls are smoking and it's clear from the group's demeanour that they all know each other well—the talk is about where they should go tonight. The boys and girls are relaxed and at ease with each other in a manner that would have been unthinkable to schoolboys of my generation. Consider this: me, Peter, Ben and Dick—aged seventeen—sitting at a beach bar like this with four girls. I can't—the imagination stalls.

And suddenly I wonder: is it more of my bad luck to have been born when I was, at the beginning of this century and not be able to be young at its end? I look enviously at these kids and think about the lives they are living—and will live—and posit a kind of future for them. And then, almost immediately, I think what a futile regret that is. You must live the life you have been given. In sixty years' time, if these boys and girls are lucky enough, they will be old men and women looking at the new generation of bright boys and girls and wishing that time had not fled by—

One of the girls has just asked me the time (*"cinq heures vingt"*), which has rather jolted me. I think—I feel—I am invisible here. I should be heading home soon.

The girl who asked me the time lights yet another cigarette. I'm sure it's not so much the pleasure of the nicotine that makes these girls smoke so much—they hardly puff at their cigarettes—it's having the thing in their hand to complete the pose. They all smoke with practised ease and naturalism, yet this girl has the gestures off more perfectly than most. How to define it? Some equation of extended fingers and wrist bend, lip-pout and head-tilted exhalation. She smokes with great sexual grace: her body is brown and lean and she's pretty with long milk-chocolate brown hair. And somehow she knows that her perfect manipulation of that perfect white cylinder of packed tobacco sends a subliminal signal to the boys—all their eyes are flicking like lizards'—that she is ready.

And for some reason this makes me contemplate my own life, all my sporadic highs and appalling lows, my brief triumphs and terrible losses and I say, no, no, I don't envy you—you slim, brown, confident boys and girls and whatever futures await you. I will gather up my belongings and wander back to the Hôtel des Dunes and look forward to my supper—the fish of the day and my bottle of wine. I feel, as I sit here—and I should record this as I experience it—looking over the beach and the ocean as the sun begins to drop down in the west, a strange sense of pride: pride in all I've done and lived through, proud to think of the thousands of people I've met and known and the few I've loved. Play on, boys and girls, I say, smoke and flirt, work on your tans, figure out your evening's entertainment. I wonder if any of you will live as well as I have done.

Sultry, fuggy day. No leaf stirs. Butterflies lurch and skitter through the delphiniums I planted around the sundial.

*   *   *

Cinq Cyprès. Sainte-Sabine. Our Indian summer continues here—the leaves are just on the turn but the breeze from the east is warm and the sun shines each day with benign force.

Through a gap in the trees of the park I can see the blond grass of the meadow—turned quite yellow under the sun like the waters of the old River Plate—and the dark green of the oak woods, offset beyond, the trees so densely leafed that they seem to billow out over the sun-bleached yellow grass like smoke or waves. And, closer to, the sharp clarity of the sunlight on the bushes and the creeper around the house is perfect: the perfect balance of leaf-shadow, leaf-shine and leaf-translucence—absolutely correct, as if worked out by mathematical formulae to provide the ideal visual stimulus. Down by the barn a thick patch of thistle is in seed and the wandering breeze snatches the thistle-down and lifts it skyward in small urgent flurries—backlit by the sun so that the down seems to sparkle and gleam like mica or sequins—so much so that it looks like photons of light are taking to the air, flying upwards—rising upwards, blowing away across the meadow—like what?—like glow worms, like lucent moths.

Too nice a day to stay inside. I shall choose an old familiar book and go and read in a deckchair in the cool blue shade of the big chestnut tree. I woke this morning with a transient old man's erection. I was dreaming, I think, of that naked girl who walked by me on the beach. My dreams are so vivid these nights that I wake in the morning blinking, dazed and exhausted from my encounters with my unconscious life, wondering who and where I am. So this morning I took hold of myself, pleased to be so stiff, so virile, if only for half a minute or so. Life in the old dog. Life—still living, pleased to have managed to live in every decade of this long benighted century. What a time I've had—*quel parcours,* as the French say. I think a drink is called for. Yes, absolutely—I will open a chill bottle of white wine and take it out and sit under the big chestnut and drink a toast to Logan Mountstuart. Every decade. All my ups and downs. My personal rollercoaster. Not so much a rollercoaster—a rollercoaster's too smooth—a yo-yo, rather—a jerking, spinning toy in the hands of a maladroit child, more like, trying too hard, too impatiently eager to learn how to operate his new yo-yo

AFTERWORD

Logan Mountstuart died of a heart attack on 5 October 1991—he was eighty-five years old. His heart was not receiving enough oxygen because it was not being allowed its regular flow of blood, as one or more of his coronary arteries had become blocked (they are called "coronary" because these vessels encircle the top of the heart like a crown). Starved of blood, his heart muscle, and its rhythm, broke down and Logan Mountstuart's life ended.

He was discovered towards the end of the day by Jean-Robert Stefanelli, who had come to Cinq Cyprès with the gift of a basket of apples. Receiving no answer at the door, Jean-Robert went around to the rear of the house. There he saw the deckchair under the chestnut tree and beside it a half-drunk bottle of white wine in an ice bucket and an open book, cover-side up (it was the *Collected Plays* of Anton Chekhov). The ice in the ice bucket had melted, and Jean-Robert realized that something was amiss. Wandering around, he soon discovered LMS, dead, face down on the grass beside a corner of the barn where there was a large clump of thistles. He noticed that LMS's cat was not far away, curled up on a stone, watching everything intently.

Logan Mountstuart was buried in the graveyard of the village of Sainte-Sabine. His grave can be found in the north-east corner of the graveyard. He had made provision for a gravestone: a simple black granite rectangle set in the ground, it reads:

LOGAN GONZAGO MOUNTSTUART
1906–1991
ESCRITOR
WRITER
ÉCRIVAIN

In his will he left the house, Cinq Cyprès, to Mrs. Gail Sherwin. She, her husband and their two children spend some weeks there each summer. A search of the property was carried out after his death by his cousin Lucy Sansom (who had been willed LMS's library and manuscripts). No trace of the novel *Octet* was found. Jean-Robert Stefanelli remembers helping LMS build a bonfire a week before he died. "He burnt many papers," Stefanelli recalls. "For an old man he seemed very well, and very happy." There were no obituaries.

Index

ALSO BY WILLIAM BOYD

THE NEW CONFESSIONS

In this extraordinary novel, William Boyd presents the autobiography of John James Todd. From his birth in 1899, Todd was doomed. Emerging from childhood, he rushes into the throes of the new century as a soldier in the Great War. As a prisoner of war, he discovers Rousseau's *Confessions* and dedicates his life to bringing the memoir to the silver screen. Plagued by bad luck, Todd becomes a celebrated London upstart, a Weimar luminary, and finally a disgruntled director and the eleventh member of the Hollywood Ten. Ambitious and entertaining, Boyd has invented an irresistible hero.

Fiction/Literature/0-375-70503-1

AN ICE-CREAM WAR

In 1914, in a hotel room in German East Africa, American farmer Walter Smith dreams of Theodore Roosevelt. As he sleeps, a railway passenger swats at flies, regretting her decision to return to the Dark Continent. On an English riverbank, a jealous Felix Cobb curses his sister-in-law-to-be. And in the background of the world's daily chatter swirl rumors of an Anglo-German conflict, the likes of which no one has ever seen. As the sons of the world match wits and weapons on a continent thousands of miles from home, desperation makes bedfellows of enemies and traitors of friends and family.

Fiction/Literature/0-375-70502-3

ALSO AVAILABLE

Armadillo, 0-375-70216-4
The Blue Afternoon, 0-679-77260-X
The Destiny of Nathalie X, 0-679-76784-3
On the Yankee Station, 0-375-70511-2
Stars and Bars, 0-375-70501-5
A Good Man in Africa, 1-4000-3002-1

VINTAGE INTERNATIONAL
Available at your local bookstore, or call toll-free to order:
1-800-793-2665 (credit cards only).